Books by Carly Alexander

GHOSTS OF BOYFRIENDS PAST

THE EGGNOG CHRONICLES

THE SECRET LIFE OF MRS. CLAUS

Published by Kensington Publishing Corporation

The Secret Life of Mrs. Claus

Carly Alexander

KENSINGTON BOOKS
www.kensingtonbooks.com

KENSINGTON BOOKS are published by

Kensington Publishing Corp.
850 Third Avenue
New York, NY 10022

All Kensington titles, imprints, and distributed lines are available at special quantity discounts for bulk purchases for sales promotion, premiums, fund-raising, and educational, or institutional use.

Special book excerpts or customized printings can also be created to fit specific needs. For details, write or phone the office of the Kensington Special Sales Manager: Attn: Special Sales Department. Kensington Publishing Corp., 850 Third Avenue, New York, NY 10022. Phone: 1-800-221-2647.

Strapless and the Strapless logo are trademarks of Kensington Publishing Corp. Kensington and the K logo Reg. U.S. Pat. & TM Off.

ISBN 0-7582-0925-8

First Kensington Trade Paperback Printing: October 2005
10 9 8 7 6 5 4 3 2 1

Printed in the United States of America

THE NUTCRACKER is for my mother, Susan Noonan—
inspired, inspiring teacher and Baltimorean.
For those who will make the inevitable comparison with Olivia's mother:
charm and wisdom, yes; phobias, no.

CHRISTMAS MOUSE is dedicated to Alex "Nicholas"—
illustrator and master of an endless imagination.

MIRACLE ON THE MAGNIFICENT MILE is for Caroline—
girl of empowerment, fire on the court.
Yes, miracles happen.

CONTENTS

THE NUTCRACKER
11

CHRISTMAS MOUSE
167

MIRACLE ON THE MAGNIFICENT MILE
263

PROLOGUE

Chicago, November 2003

If Santa Claus had flown over the city of Chicago with a Christmas-spirit detection device, the needle would have gone wild as he passed over the block-wide structure that housed Rossman's Department Store on Michigan Avenue. Although November had just blown in with a snappy, windy cold front, Rossman's was fully decorated for the holiday season, outdoor speakers trumpeting a joyous melody in three-part harmony, complete with liquid violins, dancing woodwinds, and bright brass ensemble. A giant red ribbon wrapped the building like a gift package. The overhang of every revolving glass door was topped with a pyramid of holiday trees decked with thick gold ribbons and white lights that glimmered in the wind.

Inside the store, the ribbons from the same gold stock streamed down from garlands of fat, shiny balls in red and gold and green and purple looped around every pillar, linked along every yard of molding and trim. Every floor display was topped by these same ornaments flowing from sleigh-shaped crystal bowls, the red ball at the top capped by a Santa hat.

Nowhere was the spirit more evident than on the ninth floor, the traditional "Santaland" where staffers were putting finishing touches on the multichambered gingerbread house that would allow various Santas, Anglo and African American, Asian and Spanish-speaking, to privately greet their young guests and carry on the long-standing tradition of asking if they'd been naughty or nice, whether they hoped to see a truck or a doll or an electronic robot this Christmas.

"Fabulous, ladies and gents," one designer announced, inspecting the giant sleigh full of toys at the exit of Santa's gingerbread house. "It's really coming together!"

"I hope the rug rats appreciate all this," one store clerk said as he glued a giant Styrofoam peppermint over the window of Santa's house.

His boss took the hot glue gun from his hand and fixed the drooping jaw of a wooden soldier. "You'd better just hope the Rossmans approve," she said. "They're the ones who control Christmas, at least, around here."

Four stories below, Evelyn Rossman stood up from the conference table, smoothed the skirt of her navy Pendleton wool suit, and summoned the others: her husband, brother-in-law Lenny, nephew Daniel, and daughter Meredith. "Let's go up and check on their progress," Ev said, eager for Christmas to begin.

"I don't think they're ready for us on nine, but we can sneak a peek," Karl Rossman said, leading the family down the narrow office corridor of the building the Rossmans had owned for more years than most Chicago residents could remember. The business that started fifty years ago with his mother's knack for fashioning textiles and ribbons into curtains and fine home furnishings had flourished into a full-scale retail business with stores throughout the Chicago and Detroit areas when Evelyn and Karl had married more than three decades ago. Back then, they were the toast of Chicago, Ev and Karl, a celebrated couple, though most of society hadn't suspected the genius that lived beneath his wife's confident smile. With Lenny's help, he and Ev had expanded the business through the rest of the country—two dozen stores throughout the United States, a new one opening next week on the East Coast. He extended an arm over her back and gently ushered her into the elevator. Thank God for Ev, his light, his rock.

She gave her husband a cynical look, then reached down for a handful of tush. No one else noticed, including Meredith, who watched the numbers on the elevator screen blink as if she were monitoring a life-support system. If only their daughter could loosen up, lose some of the sternness and the fierce competitiveness she felt with her cousin. Though Ev had to admit it was never easy being a Rossman. Ev had married into the dynasty with some concern, though she herself had been raised in a moneyed family—"A pickle fortune," as her grandfather used to say—and she'd quickly allied herself with the Rossman family values and work ethic—an ethic her daughter Meredith embraced with ease. Ev wished she could say the same of her nephew Daniel.

"Another big-budget Christmas," he groused. "What's the damage this year?"

"Not so bad," Lenny said, rubbing the furrowed lines in his bare forehead. "We combined some of our inventory decorations, right?"

Meredith checked her clipboard. "Right. The designers are well under budget this year."

The elevator doors groaned shut, and Daniel let out an exasperated sigh. "We ought to fix this thing."

"Why fix what isn't broken? It's perfectly safe, inspected every month," his father, Leonard Rossman, replied.

"I'm talking upgrade. The flooring. The walls. Why don't we have paneling in our elevators?"

"Because we don't waste money on extravagances like fancy freight elevators, thank you very much," Lenny chastised him. "We put our money into the merchandise we sell. Pass it on to the customers. Pass it on."

Daniel slunk back against the rail. "Pass is right. So if we want to cut costs, why don't we take a pass on Christmas?"

"Please, Daniel . . ." Karl waved him down. "You're not scoring any points with that attitude."

Daniel turned to his cousin and mumbled so that only she could hear him, "I'll take a zero."

"Okay." Meredith jotted a fat zero on her clipboard and grinned back at Daniel defiantly. The family inspection of the store's Christmas village was an annual ritual savored by her parents, disparaged by Daniel, and dreaded by Meredith ever since Daniel had been old enough to trade braid pulling and wet willies for cynical put-downs.

Most of the ninth floor had been off-limits to the public for the past week as store employees and window dressers scurried to stage the store's Santaland, a Rossman's tradition for fifty years. Only the café at the back of nine had remained open, cordoned off so that shoppers couldn't see the Christmas kingdom until its unveiling on November 15.

The elevator doors opened on nine, and there was a flurry of activity as the family stepped out. Someone called "They're here!" and two elderly women paused on their way from the public elevators to the café.

"Look, Doreen, it's Evelyn and Karl."

"Evelyn and Karl, how's everything?" one woman asked as her bag dropped from her shoulder to her elbow.

"Everything is fabulous, thank you, Doreen," Karl said, stepping forward to graciously squeeze her hands.

Her friend nudged her. "He called you Doreen. What a charmer."

"Ladies, have you started your Christmas shopping yet?" Ev asked the women. She and her husband never missed a chance to socialize with store customers.

"Please," Doreen rolled her eyes, "let me tell you my dilemma. My husband needs dress shirts but he refuses to go up a size, though he needs it in the neck. A very thick neck he has these days, but will he admit it?"

"Thick neck, thick head," the other woman said.

"I'm going to buy bigger and have different-size labels sewn in. What else can I do?"

Her friend shrugged. "What can she do?"

"That's clever of you," Ev told the woman, then she went on to joke about selling label kits with various sizes just for that purpose.

"Okay, then, we're off for a nice cup of coffee," the friend said. "Be well."

Doreen waved, her charm bracelet jangling. "And merry Christmas."

"That's not PC, Doreen. You're supposed to say 'happy holidays.' "

"They're the Rossmans; they love Christmas."

"Not all of us," Daniel muttered, but no one acknowledged him as the family ducked behind a temporary wall and stepped into the transformed snowy landscape of Santaland.

"A little excessive, isn't it?" Daniel screwed his mouth into an unattractive twist. "All the white, twinkly lights? What's this costing us in electricity? Anyone seen last year's bill?"

"Don't be foolish, Daniel," Karl said gently. "As I always say, it's only money; we'll make more. Besides, you can't cut corners on Christmas."

"I don't know why not," Daniel said, looking away from his uncle. "Macy's got rid of their Santaland. The buzz is that the May Company stores are going to ax them, too. I'm telling you, more and more, the heartland is scaling down."

"You think we should scale down Christmas?" Evelyn asked him.

"I'm just thinking about the customer here. If you listen to what people are saying, they're not so into it anymore. Always complaining how hectic the holidays are. Pressurized. Commercial. Too much food and drink and traffic, long lines at stores, long shopping lists to knock off."

"He's right, he's right. I hear the complaints," Lenny agreed.

"Christmas is our busiest season," Meredith Rossman said, her eyes sharp beneath the lenses of her eyeglasses. "Not to reduce it all to money, but our highest sales months are November and December."

"Yes, yes." Lenny was nodding profusely. "So what's your point, Daniel?"

"Just that we used to wait until after Thanksgiving to start the

Christmas promotions, and it probably saved us in marketing expenses. If people are going to come out for Christmas shopping anyway, why throw money into advertising and marketing?"

"You can never have enough of Christmas," Evelyn Rossman said, her face beaming with pride as she scanned the winter wonderland of snowy white twigs sparkling with silver glitter, crystal pinecones, and white pindots of light. Every beam was hidden, every light filtered by swirls of glittering stars. "First impression is good."

"Very good." Her husband slipped his hands in his pants pockets as he stepped through a trellis made of giant candy canes. "It's like an enchanted lane."

"An enchanted lane . . ." Evelyn nudged Meredith, who trailed with clipboard in hand. "Make a note of that. Great copy for our sales flyers."

Meredith took note as the candy canes gave way to giant sugary gumdrops, then gingerbread figures who raced and tumbled and cajoled as they made their way toward the sparkling gingerbread house of Santaland, where staff were still gluing on giant gumdrops and chocolate chips and peppermints.

"Oh, you're here!" Rahiella, the designer in charge of window displays, clasped her hands together dramatically. "We weren't expecting you till—"

"Not to worry," Evelyn interrupted. "We like what we see."

"You do? You do? Oh, I'm so relieved! Did you see the little cutout chairs for Santa's guests? The craft station where bored little children can decorate a gingerbread cookie or assemble a snowman?"

The Rossmans followed Rahiella through the facility as she explained how the line of children would flow through the snowscape, how the wait would be minimized, how Santa's elves would keep anxious children and their parents amused and distracted. "We're in the process of auditioning elves, and we're calling back the Santas we were so happy with last year. Personnel is on it. Which reminds me, though. While we were trying to salvage items in our inventory of decorations, we came across something that may have special value to you." She summoned an assistant,

who brought over a silver gift box embossed with a swirled *R*—
not the collapsible type used by stores like Rossman's, but an old-
fashioned box constructed of thick cardboard with a lid that
whispered gently over the top third of the box. Rahiella presented
the box with a flourish, and the Rossmans gathered close as
Evelyn lifted the lid.

Evelyn's dark eyes went wide with wonder at the sight of the
crimson velvet trimmed with white fur. "Oh, dear . . . the Mrs.
Claus suit. Where did you find it? I thought it had been given
away years ago." Her hands glowed pink from the warm hue of
the material as she lifted a sleeve from the box.

"Mama made it the first year that Rossman's went national,"
Lenny recalled. "A very lean year, so she thought we'd better
scrape together some extra Christmas spirit from the fabric left
over from the Santa suits."

Karl wagged a finger at Meredith and Daniel. "Back then,
your grandmother sewed all the costumes herself."

"Note how the stitching is so fine—nearly invisible." Rahiella
turned over the fur-trimmed lapel of the jacket to reveal the
smooth seam. "And this beadwork on the jacket. See how the
tiny red beads form a very subtle fleur-de-lis pattern? So subdued, yet it gives a glimmering aura to the entire costume."

"Mama had magical hands." With great care Evelyn lifted the
jacket and held it up to her chin, and everyone seemed to gently
breathe in its sumptuous crimson beauty. The texture and
velvety folds of the coat brought back fond memories for Ev; she
had enjoyed playing Mother Christmas, reassuring nervous children and frazzled parents. She had always considered herself an
ambassador of goodwill, and somehow in the Mrs. Claus suit, she
felt empowered to spread Christmas spirit without shame of
appearing sentimental.

"You were a lovely Mrs. Claus," Karl told his wife. "How many
years did you do it? Six? Seven?"

"Until Meredith was born," Ev said.

"She was in all the papers, written up every year, the only Mrs.
Claus in town," Lenny said, his fingers splayed for dramatic effect. "Let me tell you, it didn't hurt Rossman's great reputation

as a Christmas store. When people shopped Christmas, Rossman's was the place they wanted to be."

"And still is." Evelyn neatly folded the red velvet jacket and let her fingers smooth over the lapel. "You know, it wouldn't be a bad idea to reinvent Mrs. Claus this year."

Rahiella's jaw dropped with a gasp. "Exactly what I was thinking! And wouldn't it be charming if she were played by a Rossman?"

All eyes turned to Meredith, who was scratching a note on her clipboard. "What do you . . . You mean *me*?"

"Do you want to give it a shot?" Evelyn asked, hoping her daughter might muster the desire to play a whimsical, fantasy role just once in her life.

Meredith paled. "Of course not," she sputtered. A year of grad school at University of Chicago and they expected her to play a cartoon character at Christmas? What did she need to do to be taken seriously around here? She didn't see anyone asking Daniel to play Santa.

"Of course not," Ev said, her disappointment apparent.

"*Hello*? Can we just let it go?" Daniel cut in, fed up with the sentimental wave that captivated everyone. "That thing's been sitting in dust for a decade. Time to retire the moth-bitten old rags. Besides, who cares about Mrs. Claus? What power does she have? Kids wouldn't even get near Santa himself if they didn't think he was the conduit of toys."

Evelyn looked at her nephew as if he were speaking an incomprehensible language. "You know, Daniel, marketing is not your forte."

"But who will be Mrs. Claus?" Karl asked.

"It doesn't have to be Mer-Mer." Lenny shrugged. "So we hire an actress."

"I was just thinking we should send it to the new store in Baltimore," Meredith suggested. "They're opening next week and it might be fun to advertise a special visitor in their Santaland." In addition, she suspected it wouldn't hurt to have that suit thousands of miles away—remove it from sight and take away the family pressure to follow so closely in her mother's footsteps.

"Of course! Excellent idea," Lenny agreed, flipping open his cell phone. "I'll notify the store manager. They'll be thrilled, I'm sure."

"I'm sure," Daniel added sardonically.

Evelyn shook out the garment, then refolded it with expert precision."I'm so glad you found it, Rahiella," she said, tucking the lid on gently.

Karl checked his watch. "We need to get this wrapped quickly if we want to overnight it to Baltimore."

"Overnight?" Lenny barked, lowering his cell phone. "That'll cost a fortune. Make sure it goes by two-day express. Such a savings."

Inside the silver cardboard box, the fabric glowed, rich dark red, ready to warm the heart of its next occupant . . .

The Nutcracker

Olivia

Baltimore, November 2003

1

After my involvement with Bobby, I understood why certain species of females devoured the males after the nuptials.

As a kid, I'd found that practice disgusting, barbaric . . . "Gross!" Bonnie and I had said at the same time, our freckled noses scrunched up in horror at the detailed lives of arachnids unfolding on the TV screen. As a teenybopper and dedicated reader of *Tiger Beat* magazine, I couldn't understand why anyone would want to have sex, let alone kill their mate.

But after Bobby, it became clear that the female spider wasn't just killing the male; she was putting an end to the madness, chewing him up before he had a chance to go off and mock her personal foibles with his spider buddies, before he could mate with her friends and suddenly find success and fortune to spend on someone else, before he landed a ten-minute interview on prime-time TV, during which he looked fabulous in the cashmere sweater she'd given him to wear at their engagement party.

Not that spiders wear cashmere or watch television, but the female spider's motivation is now clear to me: eat the sucker before he betrays you big-time.

"I don't know why you're taking this all so personally," my

friend Lanessa had told me one night when she and I narrowly
missed running into Bobby and his crew after they'd just finished taping a segment at the Wharf Rat, a smoky, dark saloon in
Fells Point. "The guy is writing and producing a show. It's what
he does. He was a producer when you were together, right?"

"An *unemployed* producer," I said, gripping the shiny wood lip
of the hundred-year-old bar. Talk of Bobby did that to me—sent
me clenching surfaces with my fingertips or gritting my teeth.
"Always out of work, chasing down deals, sticking me with the
check."

"So be glad that's over and let him do his job. You moved on,
can't he go where opportunity takes him, even if that's Baltimore?"

"I moved back home to Baltimore to save some money and regroup." It seemed like an appropriate distance away from Bobby,
who was into the L.A. scene back then. But I wasn't back three
weeks when I flipped through the trades and read that he was
back in Baltimore, filming a show. "It's bad enough that he came
back at the same time, but he's filming here, right in my own backyard. And by the way, why are you defending him?"

"Man's got a right to earn a wage," Lanessa said, in that judi-
cious inside-the-Capital-Beltway voice. "It's the town he grew up
in, too. And you've got to admit, the idea of another show being
shot in Baltimore is damned exciting. I'm kind of sorry we
missed the shoot here tonight, because you know I'd be right in
their faces, asking them questions. I wonder how they filmed in
here, with this place so dark. I mean, what do you think it looks
like in the light? Scary. And what's the show about? Do you know
the story line? Last time I read about it in the trades, they were
thinking of calling it *The Nutcracker* or *She-Devil*, which leads me
to believe that it's about a demon ballet dancer. Sort of a female
Taz on ice."

"I don't have a clue, and I don't really care." Part of that was a
lie, as I couldn't help but wonder how Bobby had come up with
a concept strong enough to land a production deal—even if it
was to air on the BigTime cable network. When I thought back
over all the "small" concepts he'd nurtured over the years, all the
pitches I'd had to hear over and over again about following the

trail of a penny as it passed from hand to cash register to pocket to sewer grate, about the first Polish man ever to become a cardinal in the Vatican, about the short, sad life of the tallest man in the world (or would that be the long, sad life of the shortest man in the world? I should know; I heard those pitches countless times . . .).

And despite the fact that most of his ideas made my eyes glaze over, instinctively I knew Bobby would make it. With an ego that inflated and the ability to keep a conversation going with just about anyone, Bobby had the tools for success in Hollywood. The killer was, I thought he needed me for that success. I thought we'd be hitting it big together, that I'd be dancing in Broadway shows while he wrote movie scripts or directed television. We were going to be one of those couples you see on *Entertainment Tonight*—the next Brad and Jennifer or J.Lo and Ben, except, of course, Bobby and I would stay together.

When we moved to different cities, there was a plan for our careers to converge in the future, as soon as I established myself as a dancer in New York, as soon as Bobby snagged a deal in Los Angeles.

But Bobby went west and hit a real gold mine, snagging a woman and the chance to shoot a midseason replacement for a cable network. Before I even realized he was auditioning new girls, I was replaced. After six years of paying my dues.

"Six years," I said. "I spent six years with the guy, and wouldn't you know it, the minute we break up, he dreams up a marketable pitch. Where's the justice in this universe?"

Lanessa's amber eyes glimmered over her pint glass. "Kills you, doesn't it?"

"Not that I care or anything."

"Oh, come off it, you big liar. You totally care. And don't think that I'm really defending him, 'cause I'm not. Bobby's a slime mold, but having a show here totally jazzes me."

I took a sip of my beer, a cranberry lambic that suddenly seemed sour. "Does this taste right to you? I should never order these seasonal brews."

"Don't try to change the subject. And admit it, it's cool to have a camera crew in Baltimore."

"The city without pity? Sorry, but Baltimore never did much for me."

"Just because you're biding your time before you can hightail it back to New York, don't be putting my city down, girl. This town is coming around, just as soon as we can undo some of the stereotypes we got saddled with in *Hairspray.*" Lanessa Jones is the most image conscious of all my friends, which probably serves her well in the political arena thirty miles down I-95, where she works as a lobbyist for dairy farmers. "Aren't you happy your ex is bringing new jobs to Baltimore, along with good PR?"

"Please don't call him my ex." Bobby and I had only been engaged when we broke up. "And don't pin the PR of an entire city on me." Feeling shades of the novel *You Can't Go Home Again,* I felt a certain revulsion at having landed in the city of my youth after an injury curtailed my dancing career in New York last March. As far as I was concerned, Baltimore was just a pit stop, a transitional home, a place to hole up while my leg healed and my bank account recovered from a few months of unemployment. Not to mention that I'd thought it best to be close to Mom for a while.

The best laid plans . . .

My leg was healing, the scars from the surgery almost invisible and my gait getting more and more even. Physical therapy had helped, and I'd done my special exercises religiously, two, sometimes three times a day. I figured that right now, my job was to whip this leg back into shape and get back to that March afternoon when my life had abruptly been interrupted. If you could see my life as a timeline, imagine mine dropping off sharply on an icy March day, where you'd see a huge dip, rising again in January when I would get back on track.

My plan was to restart my life in the new year, after the surgeon gave me the green light. In the meantime, I had seen an unusual job listed in the *Sun,* the chance to play a department-store elf, and since the timing worked for me and the role could pump up my résumé a little, I was going to give it a shot.

Heading down the stairs, I was hit by a draft leaking through the hole in the plaster wall. Baltimore Novembers can bring anything from humid tropics to snow, and as I stepped out onto the porch that morning I noticed frost on the leaves of the petunias in Mrs. Scholinsky's planter. The steps were iced with frost and framed by an elaborate network of green and orange electrical cords crisscrossing their way down the marble slab steps.

My landlady had put out her Christmas decorations during the night—a sleigh of toys fashioned out of colored rope lights, an array of cellophane-wrapped lollipops, a skeletal white sparkle-light reindeer with a mechanical nodding head, and a molded plastic Mr. and Mrs. Claus who smiled at each other with knowing grins. A ghoulish ode to Christmas, still glowing in the rising light of morning.

Above me, a window slid open. "Watch your step now, sweetheart. Jack Frost came through last night."

Carefully I maneuvered my way down the stoop, then glanced up to face Mrs. Scholinsky's crooked-tooth grin. Her hair was pinned in tight curls, a scarf covering the top. I suspected she slept that way, an image that brought to mind blunt-needled acupuncture to the head. No wonder she suffered from insomnia.

"Looks like a Christmas elf came through, too," I said, sounding more cheerful than I felt, having to catch a bus on this cold morning. "You're the first one on the block, Mrs. S."

"The sooner the better, I always say. Got me that new reindeer at Costco and I was dying to set it up."

Olivia the New Yorker would have commented crisply on the fact that her landlady had time and money for Christmas decorations while so many house repairs went untended, but that was the old me. Olivia the Baltimorean just picked her way carefully over the cables and cracks in the sidewalk.

"I like my Christmas, Olivia," she went on. "You'll see. One year I left the Clauses out till Memorial Day."

Something to look forward to, I thought as I wobbled slightly on my new shoes. Maybe Dolce & Gabbana heels weren't the best choice when you were auditioning to be an elf, but the shoes were a recent purchase, a gift to myself when the physical therapist deemed my leg healed enough to move beyond my collection of rubber-soled Nikes and Pumas. Although when she made that call, I don't think she was picturing three-inch stiletto heels.

"Where're you off to so early?" Mrs. Scholinsky asked. "Did you get a job?"

"I have an audition," I called proudly, then waved to end our conversation. Although most of the neighbors weren't above shouting down the street at any hour of the day or night, I wasn't quite up to broadcasting all my business to all of Camden Street, a narrow lane among many tiny streets tucked behind the Orioles' stadium in a neighborhood known as Pigtown. How I'd ended up here, in this unfamiliar part of Baltimore, was a comedy of errors, but the rent was cheap, my friend Bonnie owned a row house on the next block, and it was a short ride on the bus or light rail to almost anything worth doing.

"I'd tell you to break a leg," the landlady's voice shrieked down the block, "but don't take it too personal or anything!"

Oh, hardy-har-har. I waved again, not bothering to look back this time. Up ahead I saw two of the neighborhood regulars at the bus stop, a man in a plaid flannel jacket with a watch cap and a young woman with meticulous baby dreads and a warm, puffy down jacket. Once I saw her ID badge from Johns Hopkins and suspected that she worked as a nurse or aide, but then maybe that was wrong of me. What if she was a resident or the head of personnel? Just because she lived in Pigtown didn't mean that she couldn't be the chief of cardiac surgery.

Then again, this was Pigtown.

In historic Baltimore, these streets were home to stockyards and slaughterhouses, Irish and German immigrants. Later, the neighborhood got a big lift when people realized that Babe Ruth was born in a Pigtown home and raised here until he was ten.

These days, the neighborhood's big claim to fame was the stadium built at the old Camden Yards. When the Orioles had a night game, the stadium lights glowed in the sky and vendors set up their plywood sheets of orange and black shirts, caps, megaphones, and foam hands on corners, and traffic streamed into the streets, jamming intersections and parking lots. And the locals loved it, the frenzy surrounding their beloved "O's," pronounced "Ows."

Chalk on a board for me. But at least I was spared embarrassment in the mailing address, which was simply Baltimore, Maryland.

I'd worked hard to lose my accent, and coming back to all this felt like a demotion—bumped from high school to third grade.

This is temporary, I told myself. *Temporary, temporary . . .* my mantra. After the holidays I'd be feeling better, dancing again, taking the train to auditions for Broadway shows in New York instead of the bus to audition for the role of elf at Rossman's new downtown department store.

Cold wind swept down the street, and I pulled my coat closer.

"Got cold last night," the man with the watch cap said.

"Really," I agreed, while the woman in the puffy down coat stared hard down the street, as if willing the bus to come immediately and remove her from this inane conversation.

A strong-willed woman, that one, summoning a bus like that. I blinked in wonder as the frame of the Pratt Street bus lumbered toward us.

The three of us shuffled on the sidewalk, jockeying for position as the bus pulled up to the curb. I teetered carefully in my heels as the side of the bus cruised close, its colorful billboard rolling past.

What was all that red? A cartoon drawing of a wild-eyed redhead, a vixen glowering over the copy:

> *She's got him in a squeeze. Torture or terror?*
> WATCH OLIVIA, THE NUTCRACKER
> Premieres Tuesday at 9 on BigTime Cable

I reeled back, stumbling in my heels. Olivia?
This was Bobby's show?

The impact of seeing a caricature of myself along with my own name on the side of a bus was too much. I went down, my left shoe slipping off as my bottom landed on the cold pavement.

"You okay?" Mr. Watch Cap asked, pausing by the bus door.

I sat there staring at the poster, knowing that I wasn't okay at all. Not with Bobby stealing my name and making me into a caricature soon to be frequenting buses and print ads. "This is not okay," I said sternly as I pressed my shoe to my chest in horror. Not okay for the lying ex to take my name and my red hair and exploit me as some villainous shrew.

"C'mon, hon. You'll be okay." The watch-cap man extended a hand, and I let him help me up, my eyes fixed on the horror.

I wobbled to my feet and staked out the billboard as if it were my opponent in a wrestling match.

Did the boy have a creative bone in his body? Could he at least have taken some creative license and changed a few details of my life?

"Not o-kay." With each syllable, I banged the heel of my shoe against the poster. Surely the stiletto would cut through the poster like a knife, then I could rip it up, shred it off with my fingernails.

"Hey, there. You don't want to be doing that." The man stepped away from me, toward the safety of the bus steps. "You coming?"

With as much dignity as I could muster I put the ad behind me and waddled onto the bus. Click-thomp, click-thomp.

All the grace and finesse of a professional dancer.

With the demeanor of a man accustomed to the shoeless, the toothless, the homeless, the bus driver slanted his eyes at me in annoyance but didn't bother to turn his head. The watch-cap man scrambled into a seat near the driver, giving me a suspicious look as I passed.

"It's my ex-fiancé," I said, trying to explain the unexplainable. "He's the producer of that show, and he's a total asshole."

"That's not what I saw, hon." He spoke like a chastising father. "You can't go pounding on a bus like that."

Passengers' heads lifted, their curiosity piqued at the stylish woman clomping down the aisle like a matinee monster. I wanted to lift my hands and deliver a sermon on the evils of Bobby Tharp, the betrayal of a Judas who sucks your soul, then spins the details of your life into a prime-time TV show.

But they wouldn't get it. Of course they wouldn't.

I sat down alone, pondering the downward spiral. Just when I thought my life had sunk to rock bottom, my marker sent back ten spaces without passing go, Bobby had made it worse by twisting and exploiting it.

He had some nerve, calling me a nutcracker. He was the king of rats, a seven-headed creature deserving a sturdy, well-placed kick.

And I had the perfect pair of pointy-toed shoes . . .

2

Here's the great thing about cell phones: you can reach out to friends when you need them.

Here's the bad thing about cell phones: sometimes, when you're in the heat of a crisis, you call all your friends and no one has time to deal with you, which leaves you feeling small and extraneous, like a royal pain in the ass. That was the case as I rode the bus to Harborplace, having checked in with Lanessa on her cell, crazed with traffic in D.C., with Bonnie's voice mail, with Kate's associate at the aquarium who told me she was "with the dolphins."

Which left me feeling a little jealous that all my friends had lives while I, apparently, needed to wait until Tuesday at nine to see mine on TV.

As we rolled east on Pratt Street, I tried to analyze why Bobby's new show bugged me so much. Was it the betrayal anyone would feel when an ex-lover writes a tell-all? Was it because he'd pulled one of his "in your face!" moves and brought a crew to my backyard in Baltimore? Or was it that, beneath my newly acquired "like I care!" New York facade, I still felt a little pang in the gut when I thought of him, still had the letters he'd written to me, still had a little heart icon next to the "Bobby" files on my computer?

A big dummy-head, I know I am, but I can't help how I feel.

Sometimes I can forget about the feelings for a while when I get distracted. Other times I tamp them down beneath the surface and try to go on, but like dirty underwear that keeps rising to the top of your luggage no matter how many times you bury it under your jeans, those feelings keep popping up now and again.

Over the past few months my friends had bolstered me with all the appropriate responses.

"Don't think he's the last guy you'll ever love," Bonnie had told me. "Not by a long shot. You're so cute and fun and talented. You'll find someone, someone a bazillion times better than Bobby Tharp." That advice was followed by a laugh. "Look at me. I've been married and divorced three times, and do I give up? Ha! I figure the more practice I get, the better I'm getting at this partnership thing."

Kate usually came across more earth mothery, saying things like, "Ooh, I know it hurts!" and "It's okay to go through a grieving period for a relationship," and "Liv, have you tried curling up with a cup of Sleepytime tea?"

And then there were Lanessa's no-nonsense tips, such as "Get a grip, girl." And "Aren't you over him yet?" Lanessa may lose points in the area of sensitivity, but sometimes a stiff, honest kick in the butt is just what a girl needs.

So get a grip, I told myself as the bus pulled up to my stop in front of the building that would soon open as Baltimore's only downtown department store. Rossman's was taking over a building at the edge of the Inner Harbor formerly occupied by the McCormick Spice Factory, and though I vaguely remembered the squarish box of a building, it had cleaned up quite nicely in the renovation. The cumbersome gray stone and ironwork facade of the old factory had been transformed to a pristine finish, and a newly constructed wing rose gracefully from the side like a castle tower, in keeping with the old Gothic style. From the street, the place looked majestic, impressive, a renovation Mom would appreciate if she could just drag herself down here to take a look. My mother is a professor of architecture at University of Baltimore, with a fierce passion for building design and history. I think I was playing with blocks in preschool when she began explaining the differences between Ionic and Doric columns. While other kids were learning their times tables, I was grilled on whether a building was Georgian Revival, Federalist, or Jeffersonian architecture. We spent summer vacations touring the East Coast in pursuit of buildings designed by Benjamin Latrobe, and Mom spent every other weekend conducting tours of his Mulberry Street Cathedral and Mount Vernon Place, along with the Peabody Library and once-infamous Bromo-Seltzer Tower. Much to her dismay, I was always on the verge of flunking history in school. Someone told her that it's a way children rebel against their parents, subconsciously shutting down in areas their parents excelled in. All I know is, I wasn't interested in what a bunch of dead people did, and although I could memorize a dance sequence or repeat a step until I learned it, there was no memorizing explorers, inventors, and dates for me. I barely scraped through high school with Cs and took only the core history requirements in college. Sorry, Mom.

At the moment, Mom was on a self-inflicted sabbatical, but that was another story.

Although the revolving door at the front of the store was locked tight, a guard motioned me in through a side entrance, where I ran into a queue that led to a folding table.

I circled the line, trying to see who or what was at the front.

A heavyset man in black leathers turned and barked at me through his stringy, belly-length beard. "Line forms back that way, hon."

I lifted my hands. "Do you know what it's for? This can't be the right line. I'm here for an audition."

"So's everybody else. Back of the line, Red."

My heels clicked over the marble floor as I stepped back, steaming at the ZZ Top wannabe. And *he* was auditioning to be an elf? Good luck with that.

We were cordoned off in a little side salon, but as the line moved up I got a peek through the doors at the rest of the cavernous space—the main selling floor—which was totally empty except for some elegant crystal chandeliers.

"Well, that doesn't instill much confidence," I muttered. "They're opening next week and there's no merchandise in the store."

Most of the people in the line ignored me, but ZZ turned back and squinted toward the sales floor. "I wouldn't worry."

"They don't have a single piece of furniture. How's it all going to happen in time?" I thought about that. Were we all wasting our time here? "Have you heard anything about them delaying the opening?" I said, lowering my voice conspiratorially.

ZZ leaned close and whispered, "No."

An annoying little man, that biker dude. I folded my arms and tuned him out, tuned out the entire line of elf applicants and imagined myself in a far more desirable line, arm in arm with women my height, our heads turning and legs kicking precisely, in perfect unison.

I'd been a part of that line just last Christmas, dancing at Radio City Music Hall. Back then my life had seemed so rich and full, so organized and smooth, moving from the hectic rehearsals to the challenging pace of the daily matinees and evening shows, the sparkling costumes, the lights, the delighted applause of the audience, the fluttery thrill that never failed me each time the curtain rose . . .

"Would you be available to work overtime? Long hours?"

For last year's Christmas show we'd done between two and four performances a day . . .

"Miss? We're hiring only one person for this role."

I stared blankly at the polite young man from Personnel. "One elf? Santa's downsizing this year?"

"Actually, all the elf positions have been cast at this time."

My heart sank. With my experience in New York, I'd figured this job would be a lock for me.

Wrong again, dummy-head. It was time to find the line for the Christmas hires. Maybe I could spray colognes in the air or wrap gifts.

"I'm sorry," the young man said, his deep voice belying his

wiry frame. He had smooth, chocolate brown skin and a slightly goofy smile that made me want to adopt him as a kid brother. "I thought you were applying for Mrs. C."

"Mrs. C?" I blinked again, wondering what I'd missed.

Mr. Personnel cocked his head to the side, his pat smile hinting that he'd repeated this spiel dozens of times this morning. "As Mrs. Claus, you'd be working in Santaland with the help of a team of elves, managing queuing and diverting groups of children with activities, train rides, and whatnot."

"I can work long hours—I can. I have *mucho* stamina. Did you see my résumé? I'm a dancer." Realizing I hadn't shown him my credentials, I slid a copy out of my portfolio bag. "I've even played Mrs. Claus before onstage." I didn't mention that every woman onstage had been dressed as Mrs. Claus, but really, did he have to know every detail?

His face was stern as he read, but suddenly a smile lit his face. "You were a Rockette? Really?"

I beamed. ZZ was glancing over at me curiously, and I winked at him. "Yup. I mean, yes, I was. I was in the Christmas show last year."

"That's amazing." Mr. Personnel grinned up at me with such admiration, I thought he'd ask me to autograph his necktie. He stood up, stumbling over his chair as he excused himself and went off to show my résumé to his supervisor.

The day took a turn for the better at that point, as the interview turned into a real audition. Behind a sliding curtain, a group of store employees were assessing performers and making final cuts with all the glamour of a tap-dance recital.

A selection committee sat at another makeshift table, eyeing me with all the levity of the Olympic figure skating judges. I smiled, figuring I had an edge here. How many former Rockettes auditioned to be Mrs. Claus at Rossman's Department Store?

The committee wanted to see me try on a Santa cap. They wanted me to sing a few Christmas carols (not my strong point; there was a reason I chose dance, but I can carry a tune). They wanted to see one of the Rockettes' signature eye-high kicks.

I was happy to oblige, relieved that my leg had healed to the point where I could land a few graceful kicks. They seemed to be impressed when I threw in a few anecdotes about sharing a Manhattan apartment with two other Rockettes and winging it when the airline lost my luggage during last year's North American tour.

Within half an hour the audition was over, the verdict still undetermined "though I have a really great feeling they'll choose you," said Charley, the personnel clerk who had first processed my application.

"I hope so," I said, thinking of my dwindling bank account, my rent payment, my copays for physical therapy, my credit-card debt that was going to make Christmas shopping treacherous, all that bobbing and weaving to avoid clanging into the credit limit.

Charley assured me the committee would make its decisions by tomorrow and all Christmas players would be called in the following day to begin training. They would have to, with these ambitious plans for Santaland, including musical productions, skaters, sleigh rides for children. He spoke so fast some of the details flew by me, but it was clear that Rossman's was planning a festive debut in the Christmas shopping arena.

"Can we see the space that will be used for Toyland?" ZZ asked as we were both getting ready to leave at the same time.

"I wish." Charley rolled his eyes. "We can't even get into our offices until tomorrow, something about building inspections, but that'll all be settled by the time you report in."

"Okay, then. Till Wednesday." ZZ stood tall, saluted Charley, then headed out.

I walked a few paces behind him, not really eager to catch up and strike up a conversation. But when he paused at the door to hold it for me, I hurried ahead.

"You seem confident about getting this job," I said.

"If it's not here, it's somewhere else. I've played Santa for the past twelve years, five of those years at Rossman's Miami. 'Tis the season, Red. Or maybe I should call you Rocky, huh? For the next two months, I'm a hot commodity." He looked me up and down as we stepped out into the winter sun. "You ever played Mrs. Claus before?"

"Onstage."

He nodded knowingly.

"Why? Do you think I'll be good at it?"

"Do you like kids?"

I hadn't really thought about that. The truth was, I didn't really know any kids, had no reason to like or dislike them, though when I spotted families with screamers in airport lounges I always crossed my fingers in hopes that I'd be far, far away from them on the plane. The closest I'd come in the past few years was giving autographs to children who waited outside the stage door at Radio City. And I always helped Bobby pick out gifts for his nieces and nephews.

ZZ snorted. "I take that as a no."

"It's not me, it's them," I said. "Kids don't like me for some reason. I don't know why."

"I'd think about that one," he said, heading over to the curb where a shiny, decked-out Harley was parked. ZZ reached over the bike and unclipped a helmet.

"You're kidding me. That's yours?"

"Need a lift?"

I folded my arms across my chest. "Yeah, but I'd like to make it home alive."

"Alive, but not really living." He swung onto the bike and lifted the kickstand. "Think about it, Rocky."

"Would you stop calling me that?" I yelled over the grumble of the engine, but ZZ was already balancing the bike, then roaring off, his beard blowing back over one shoulder as the Harley cruised off toward Fells Point.

Enough with the sage Santa. Like I needed advice from a dude on a Harley. I don't know why I even talked to him, anyway, something about the neighborliness of Baltimoreans. In New York people sat shoulder to shoulder with total strangers for a forty-minute subway ride and never made eye contact, but here, if someone made a comment and you didn't answer, they would keep on you until you acknowledged them. I wasn't sure which social code was preferable.

As the sun had melted the chill in the air and warmed the

brick paving stones underfoot, I stood in front of the new Rossman's building and decided to check my messages. If one of my friends was available for lunch, it wasn't worth the bus trip home right now. The pitfalls of not having a car in Baltimore, a city where most residents owned a car, sometimes two.

There was one message—my mother, telling me she had some library books due this week. Due Friday. Hoped she wasn't inconveniencing me by asking for a favor, but those late fees did add up. In fact, she received a late notice on the Janet Evanovich novel I was supposed to return for her two weeks ago.

With a pang of frustration I turned away from the building and focused on a figure in a dark coat striding purposefully toward the entrance. Something struck a familiar chord. Was it the broad shoulders that seemed so heavy on his small frame, or the way he moved, hesitantly, as if considering each step? This was someone I knew, but as I took in his face, the pinched nose and dark eyes, I couldn't make the connection. Was he a former neighbor, a classmate, a waiter at a favorite restaurant?

He was starting up the tiered marble steps—my chance. "Hey," I called, "how's it going?"

He turned to me and paused, as if nothing were so important as the message passing between us. Then I knew him, my seventh-grade sweetie. That halting look was the tip-off for me.

"Woody? Wood Man Cruise!"

"Livvy . . ." He threw out his arms and I joined in the hug, feeling stiff in my winter coat.

"Great to see you, Woody."

"Actually, I go by Sherwood now."

"Really? Sounds very . . . nerdy."

He sucked in a breath. "You wound me."

"Or artistic . . . That's what I meant."

"Sorry, but I can't let that one go. You haven't changed, have you? Still hurting me after all these years."

"Don't say that," I said, focusing on his eyes, familiar eyes, the brown of brandy. I will never forget the bursts of emotion I have witnessed in those eyes. The first time I'd ever seen the dreamy, tortured facets of romantic love, I was allowing myself a glimpse into his dark eyes before a kiss in a game of spin the bottle. Such a small moment, really, but important in my adolescent mind in that it revealed the consequences and depth of an adult relationship—the simple fact that boys had feelings, too.

There had been other snapshots, too: the competitive shot sent to other boys on the playground during a tackle game of football; the monastic respect he paid the nuns in our school; and the pained, sorrowful disappointment I'd caused him when I'd been suddenly hit by the notion that seventh-grade girls were too mature to date seventh-grade guys.

"So tell me . . ." His eyes softened as if he was relieved to see me. "What the hell are you doing here?"

"Home for a while," I lied. "How about you?"

"I'm crazed today. Chasing down a building inspector who should have signed off weeks ago."

"Really? What are you working on?"

He glanced up the steps, wincing as if a monster crouched over his shoulders. "Another stab through my heart. Tell me you've heard?"

I slid my hands into my coat pocket and shrugged. "Sorry?"

He growled. "Come on! Your mother must have mentioned it."

Let's see . . . In the past two weeks she had mentioned seeing the police poking around the Gilberts' house, she'd reminded me to buy baguettes from Santoni's and Dorchester cheddar from the Broadway Market, to pick up her prescription at Rite Aid, but no . . . not a word about Woody. Or Sherwood.

He rolled his eyes and pointed at Rossman's. "This is my building. My designs were chosen over all the other bidders."

"You're the architect of the renovation?" I glanced at Rossman's, its stone facade twinkling back at me in the afternoon sun. "It's a handsome building."

"Thanks for that, but the truth is, it's got plenty of competition."

He was right. The majestic new Rossman's sat in a neighborhood that had undergone a true renaissance in the past few decades, from the airy Harborplace Pavilions to the towering

World Trade Center and luxury hotels to the zany pyramids and geometric shapes of the National Aquarium. And those buildings were just the first of so many. The old power plant had been renovated to house an ESPN restaurant, a Hard Rock Café, a Barnes and Noble, among others. "The waterfront has its attractions," I said, "but there's always room for more. Brave of you to take on the old spice factory."

"Down here the challenge is to fit into the neighborhood while standing out, to utilize an old structure, and old style, while combining it with something fresh and innovative. But then, you know that, you being the daughter of Baltimore's grand dame of architecture."

Not anymore, I thought, but I suspected Woody didn't know about Mom's meltdown. My sense of pride told me to keep mum on Mom. "I've been wondering, what's in the tower? There are so few windows, and it's such a vertical space."

Woody smiled. "Not a pleasant spot for offices or showrooms, right? So the tower was designed to contain stairwells, just as old castle towers did, and dressing rooms."

"Clever," I said, feeling as if I were channeling my mother. "Appropriate use of space."

"And we're building an enclosed walkway over the street to the parking garage on President Street."

"A place to park in the city? How revolutionary."

He checked his watch, so I pushed on. "It's so great to see you, but I don't want to hold you up. Especially in there." I pointed a thumb at the store. "They're frantic. Can't make a sale without merchandise."

He winced, his screwed-up face reminding me of the twelve-year-old, freckled Woody. "A small detail," he said, taking a step up but not taking his eyes from me. "Let's get together for coffee or lunch or something."

"Sounds great," I called, sending him off with a wave. As he hurried inside I noticed his dark hair, once a full mullet, had been cut short, giving him a sleek, almost intellectual look. Woody was a kind, attractive man, but I hoped to avoid him the rest of my stay here. He was too much a reminder of the old

Livvy, the crazy dancing kid trapped in a city full of people who told her she'd never make it out of this town.

Somehow, running into Woody pointed to the fact that those people might have been right.

"Dancer?" They'd laugh. "Well, maybe if you want to work a club on the block or something. But what would your parents think?"

"You want to be a professional dancer? Do you have any idea of the odds against making it in the entertainment industry?"

"Forget about talent. If you want to succeed in show business, you have to know somebody, and who do you know? Connections, baby."

Those discouraging people, the voices of doom . . . Just when I thought I'd put them behind me, here they were niggling away at my self-confidence. With all the determination of a woman walking away from the quagmire of her past, I picked my way over the brick paving stones and headed toward the bus stop.

3

"Don't worry," I called, pausing in the front vestibule of the Lombard Street house to punch in the security code. Ironic that my mother had gotten an alarm system just recently, after gentrification had chased the junkies and squatters from the neighborhood. "It's only me!"

"My dear, there is no 'only' about you," Mom called from the back of the house. Strains of "Lullaby of Broadway" wafted toward me on a warm puff of savory smells—maybe mushroom and garlic—and I wondered what elegant feast Mom had cooked up today. In the past few months she'd begun preparing theme meals for me—a morning in Paris during which we spoke only French and dipped chunks of baguette into huge cups of café au lait and watched the dance scene from *An American in Paris,* a Caribbean beach party with steel-drum music, lush tropical flowers, and mandatory limbo (not easy when only one person can hold the stick). I enjoyed the meals with her, but I also worried that she was becoming more isolated with each passing week, barricaded inside this house. On the bus ride here I had promised myself that today was the day to broach the delicate issue of my mother's meltdown. A formidable plan, if I could just figure out a way in.

"Something smells delish." I closed the vestibule door and slipped off my coat. This building had been a dilapidated row house when my parents purchased it. They'd stripped the formstone facade down to the original brick and rebuilt three and a half very deep levels, with special attention to restoring the crown molding, the fat newel post, the pocket doors, the tall historic windows, the original brick kitchen hearth in the basement. Mom had furnished the house with Victorian pieces and sweeping velvet drapes, crystal chandeliers, and a marble mantelpiece. Rich Persian rugs adorned the scarred wood floors and colorful blossoms rose up the papered walls along the staircases. The lavish decor hinted at a European palace, and yet, there was something cozy about the arrangement of the furniture, the settee facing the armchairs, the piano at the window presiding over the endless flat-tarred rooftops and smokestacks of southeast Baltimore.

It was home.

"We're doing a matinee today, then a lunch at Sardi's, prix fixe, of course. We'll start with a goat cheese cranberry salad, then on to a homemade mushroom ravioli." My mother appeared, wearing a white tuxedo shirt and black skirt. Her gray hair was swept back in a tight French braid fixed with a rhinestone clip that matched the glimmering buckle on her black pumps. "I know you miss New York, so I thought we'd do our own lullaby of Broadway. I've got the soundtracks to *42nd Street, Ragtime, A Chorus Line,* etc., and sheet music to scores of others. Do you remember *Bye Bye Birdy?* I was just playing the music to that." She dashed to the piano, turned off the CD player with the remote, and launched into the introduction of "Put on a Happy Face."

"Gray skies are gonna clear up . . ." she sang with gusto. I went to the piano and folded my arms, watching her pour herself into the music. The arrangement was sweet, yet full of jazzy chord changes, and I found myself smiling when she sang, "And spread sunshine all over the place . . ."

Hard to believe this was a woman who broke into a panicked sweat at the thought of leaving the house.

"It sounds like agoraphobia," Kate had said emphatically after joining us one afternoon for high tea and the Boston Pops. "A fear of the outside world. I think it's something to do with panic attacks, but I'm not really well versed on the details." A biology major in college, Kate was the most scientific person I knew. Together we did some research on the Web, and our inexpert opinion was that my mother, a woman who had never been afraid of anything in her life, was now experiencing extreme anxiety—panic attacks—when it came time to leave the house on her own. In most cases, she bowed out of outings and opted to stay home. Other times she would go out, but only to familiar places, and only with me at her side.

"Do you think you could get her to see a therapist?" Kate had asked.

"I can't get her to admit she has a problem, but she won't even venture downtown to teach her classes anymore. She's taken a sabbatical to write a paper on the relationship between architecture and socioeconomics, but I'm not sure she's getting any work done. She cooks lavish meals, loves to entertain still, but won't go out, not even to the small Butcher's Hill pubs she used to adore."

"She's so cheerful," Kate said.

"I know, but it's not like my mother to sequester herself inside, to break down like this." This breach of courage and common sense was actually not like my mother at all. Where was the strong-willed, calm woman who had once been the dean of academics in the state university's school of architecture?

It was as if a piece of my mother had broken, and I didn't have a clue how to fix it. So I helped when I could, and I enjoyed her company within the walls of the old Lombard house.

A prison of her own making.

She nodded in time to the music. "You're not singing, Liv. Don't you know this one? Oh, you're way too young."

"No, I remember it. I saw the movie with Dick Van Dyke. Besides, that song is a classic." I didn't tell her that I wasn't in the mood to sing.

"So choose something you like." She motioned me over as she rifled through other books.

I picked an easy song from *Showboat* and sang, "Fish gotta swim, birds gotta fly . . ." It was a song I'd always enjoyed, and Mom was a strong accompanist. Although I'd taken lessons for years, my mother was the real pianist in the family.

After a few more songs we moved into the dining room, where Mom served an elegant meal for two. Sometimes I wondered if she was destined to give up the business of teaching and open her own restaurant, but she thought cooking would become joyless if she had to do it for a living. I mentioned running into Woody at the Inner Harbor, and she told me he was a frequent visitor to the university, eager to "give back" to the institution where he'd received his education.

"Did you know he's the architect on the Rossman's store? It's quite a renovation. I think you'd like it. We should make plans to head down there one afternoon."

"Not necessary," she said. "I've seen photos, and I agree, he's done a fine job melding old style with new function."

"A photo wouldn't do it justice," I said, picking at the last piece of ravioli with some dismay. Not long ago my mother made it her business to be the first to scope out the changing skyline of Baltimore. I can't tell you how many times she was thrown off construction sites. I decided to try another tack. "You know, I think it would mean a lot to Woody if you came down to see the site in person."

"Oh, of course." She stood up and cleared the salad plates, probably to avoid making eye contact. "I'll get there one of these days."

"When, Mom? You haven't left this house for three weeks now."

"Has it been that long? I've been so busy, working on my notes."

"And the last few times you did leave, I was with you the whole time. I worry about the way this whole thing is going, Mom. I'm worried about you."

"Don't," she said, her voice suddenly hard. "Don't go there, Livvy. We've been through it."

"But I want to understand this . . . what you're going through."

"You know I've researched this on-line, in books. The panic is very real. It manifests in physical symptoms that are just crippling. The first time I got dizzy and sweaty while teaching a class, I assumed it was the flu and took a cab home. But the next time and the time after that, standing there with my pulse speeding up to a deafening roar . . ." She pushed herself away from the chair and turned toward the kitchen.

I had heard her describe the attacks once before, months ago, but I thought it would be best to talk about it, get it out there. "It sounds terrible."

"It is."

"But you know it needs to be addressed. You're not alone in this, Mom. Don't run away from me."

"Why can't you leave this alone?"

"Because I'm your daughter." I followed her into the kitchen and faced her across the cooking island. "And I love you."

Her jaw clenched as she glanced down into the sink. "I'm telling you as your mother, this is not a matter for you to negotiate. I'm fine, quite happy with my writing now. Why can't you leave it at that?"

"Because I think you need to be capable of getting out on your own."

"I could leave this house if I wanted to. It's just not . . . not worth the aggravation."

"Mom. What can I do to help you?"

She opened the dishwasher and stacked the plates. "You could try singing Elphaba's part in *Wicked*."

"No jokes. I'm worried about you."

She scraped leftover parsley down the sink and turned on the grinder.

When the obnoxious noise stopped, I continued. "If I brought someone here, would you talk to them?"

She smiled. "Of course I'll talk. I always talk. But you can't expect an outsider to slay the demons I'm fighting. That's something I've got to do on my own." She dried her hands on a dish towel. "Now . . . Come try some homemade pear tart and tell me how your job search is going. This is a new recipe and I need your honest opinion. I think I may have overroasted the almonds in the crust . . ."

I told her about the Mrs. Claus job. "I'll find out tomorrow if I got it, but they seemed fairly impressed by my experience as a Rockette."

"As well they should be," she said, handing me a cup of decaf. "You won yourself a spot on the world's most famous precision dance company. I was so proud of you when I saw you perform in the Christmas show last year."

"God, it seems like eons ago." I took a sip of coffee, wishing I could zap myself through a time warp back to that period of my life. Dancing every day. Living the fast pace of New York, with more money flying into my bank account than I had time to spend.

Leave it to me to end it all with a stupid slip on the ice.

No, not a dramatic dancer's injury that would have put me in line for workers' comp. I had to go and fall in the snow in front of Mario's Pizza, the neighborhood shop where I stopped for a slice a few times a week, the place where Mario himself counseled me on the best subway routes around the city, where Guido was happy to make me a veggie slice any time of day, where Mario's wife insisted I run a tab until I had time to get to an ATM. Mario's family was the closest thing I had to a New York family.

"You could file a suit against the owner of the pizza place," a lawyer had told me on the phone. "It's their responsibility to keep the walkway clear."

But of course, I couldn't do that to Mario. It was my own dumb fault for not paying attention, for wearing high heels on an icy March day.

That had been the turning point of my life, when all the good things just seemed to fizzle into bubbles that popped all around me. The choreographer had been forced to replace me in the lineup, though I was welcome to audition again as soon as my leg healed. I was booted from the Rockettes apartment and had to hobble out before my replacement arrived. And when I called my boyfriend so that he could meet me at the train station in

Baltimore, I got the news—from his mother—that he was out with his new girlfriend. "And I think they're getting serious already," Mrs. Tharp had added with glee.

"What?" I'd gasped. What? How could that happen? How could he get serious with someone else when he hadn't ended our relationship? What about all the promises of "I'll wait for you!" and "We can make it work long-distance" and "I'll move up to New York as soon as you have your own place"? I probably should have put the brakes on then, found some way to stay in New York City while my ankle healed, but at the time I thought I was coming home to hole up in my old bedroom.

Wrong.

And so began my purgatory in Baltimore. I'd expected to stay here with Mom, but when I realized the extent of her breakdown I had to get out. I moved into Mrs. Scholinsky's house in April, just in time for her lawn display of giant ceramic Easter bunnies.

"Livvy?" My mother's voice cut into my thoughts. "I'm sorry if I've reminded you of things you miss. And here I was, trying to cheer you up with a little Broadway revue."

"It was fun, and the food was delicious. Thanks, Mom."

"Oh, dear, look at the time. You'd better get going if you're going to make it to the library before it closes. You're going to have to take the bus."

"Please, no!" I gave an exaggerated gasp. "Not another bus with my picture on the side."

"What's that?"

I told her about the morning encounter with my name and likeness on the bus billboard, which had been compounded when I'd spotted a similar ad on the way here. "It looks like Bobby is trying to suck my soul dry."

"Booby!" Mom winced, using her old nickname for him. "I always did worry about you when you were with him. Morally depraved, that boy. So needy and conniving."

The same qualities had seemed so attractive when we were together, when he was going to write a show that proved his worth to those big bad network boys. Bobby had always been just on the verge of a big break, so close, and yet in need of much coddling and encouragement every time a rejection damaged his delicate ego.

"So when is this show on? Shall I watch it?" My mother had never been a fan of television but occasionally tuned in to PBS specials.

"It's only on cable, Mom." My parents were never avid television watchers. Dad used to insist that it rotted the brain. "Besides, I don't think he paints the Olivia character in a positive light."

"Not on normal TV?" She waved it off. "I wouldn't worry about it then."

I hoped she was right.

"Let me get you today's list." She removed a pushpin from the bulletin board over the kitchen phone. "Not too extensive. You can swing by Reggie's on your way back from the library. The Sinays are coming for dinner tomorrow, and I need some heavy cream to make the lobster bisque."

I accepted the list with my usual air of confusion, wanting to help but worried about being an enabler. The few times I'd suggested that Mom go down the block and shop for herself, she had countered with small excuses like, "It's just a few items. Nothing out of your way." Or "I know Reggie's is close, but you don't mind, do you?" Or "Can't you do your mother a small favor this one time?" Even though the "one time" had been spun into a hundred times over the past few months.

And of course, I always caved. My parents had raised me in an atmosphere of mutual respect, a calm haven in which voices were not raised and issues were discussed with the ease and finesse of debate-team captains. My parents had taught me well, though my education was lacking in one area: at the age of twenty-four I had not learned how to say no to my mother.

"Okay, Mom," I said as she started the soundtrack to *Promises, Promises!* "I'll be back shortly."

Behind me a young Jerry Orbach sang, "Things that I promised myself fell apart . . ."

Ain't that the truth.

4

It was almost noon on Wednesday and I was trying to work up the enthusiasm to do my physical-therapy exercises, although I was still feeling a little sleepy. My landlady suffered from insomnia, a condition I didn't think was contagious until I moved into the apartment underneath hers. Every night, just after midnight, the noise begins. First, pacing footsteps, then falling tools or rolling doorknobs, banging hammer, whirring power drill. Mrs. Scholinsky thinks she's handy, and someone told her that when you have trouble sleeping you should tire yourself with work. For her, that means a home fix-it project. For me, that means late nights of buzzing, banging noises punctuated by the occasional old-lady curse.

Last night I think she dropped a whole can of screws around three A.M. I can't be sure, but there was the distinct sound of a thousand dervishes twirling on the wood floor, followed by cursing, then fifteen minutes of high-pitched vacuum suction. "Clang! Kink! Klink!"

This was my illustrious life of late: physical therapy for the ankle twice a week, exercises daily, sometimes twice a day because I am so fanatical, and bussing it over to Mom's to pick up shiitake mushrooms or a book she's reserved at the library.

So . . . It wasn't just slacker tendencies that had me under the covers until noon. When you're in a construction zone till three in the morning, you gotta pull the swing shift. I was working my way to a workout, having plunked the videotape the physical therapist gave me on top of the television and set my weights onto the floor when my cell phone began to chime its reggae tune. It was Charley from Rossman's, telling me I was hired. Swinging into a victory dance in the kitchen, I suddenly noticed how enormous my butt looked reflected in the toaster. I stopped dancing and heard him say that I needed to report for training the next day, but could I stop in this morning to fill out some forms?

I looked down at my flannel pajama bottoms, sweatshirt, and fluffy slippers. "I'm afraid I'm unavailable this morning," I said in my most corporate voice, "but how about this afternoon?"

Most Wednesday nights were an abbreviated girls' night out for us. Since Lanessa and Bonnie had to work in the morning, we kept it short—usually just a dinner. Since I had spent the afternoon doing paperwork at Rossman's, I was the last to arrive at Bertha's, a Fells Point restaurant famous for their delicious mussels and hence the bumper stickers that read, EAT BERTHA'S MUSSELS. Fells Point resembles a colonial seaport village set in the middle of a city, its cobbled streets and brick houses much coveted since it was saved from demolition in the 1970s. It's also a hub of activity, with dozens of antique stores, novelty shops, restaurants, and popular bars.

"Drinks are on me!" I announced as I unwrapped my scarf and took a seat. "As of tomorrow, I'll be earning a paycheck, at least for a while!"

Bonnie and Kate applauded, but Lanessa lowered her menu and cocked one eye. "Oh, Liv, I know you're cutesy-wutesy, but don't tell me you're playing a Christmas elf?"

"Even weirder," I said. "I'm going to be Mrs. Claus at the new Rossman's." I filled them in on my new job, the posh new look of

Rossman's, the ZZ Santa, the skating rink. "They're hoping to put together a show on ice, though it doesn't sound like they're very organized. Either way, the pay is good, and I've got a job, ladies! I'm coming out of the slump. Once my bank account is solid and my ankle healed, I'll be on my way again."

"Going back to New York already?" Bonnie stuck her lower lip out. "You just got here, honey."

"I am already so done with Baltimore," I said, thinking of the mantra that had sustained me: *This is temporary. This is temporary.* "After Christmas, I'm out of here."

"Mrs. Claus—how cute is that?" Kate said. "And it will keep you too busy to worry about your mother and Bobby and the show."

I sipped some chardonnay and nodded. "Bobby *who*?"

We exchanged news in rapid-fire delivery. Lanessa had begun pining for another lawyer she'd been working with lately, someone who worked in the office of a senator from Wisconsin.

"Dairy lobby meets state of Wisconsin," Bonnie mused. "Sounds like a match made in heaven."

"We'll see," Lanessa said. "Right now I can't tell if he's frightened or awed by me. Everything's still so new."

"Has he seen you chew up a brief and spit it out?" Kate asked.

"Sure. Just not *his* briefs."

We all laughed, but Bonnie couldn't seem to stop. I turned to her as she put down her wine and dug into her purse for a tissue. She was crying.

"Bonnie . . ." I touched her arm. "You okay?"

She nodded. "Fine. I just . . ." Her words were swallowed by a sob, then a hiccup.

"It's Jonah, isn't it?" Kate said, and as Bonnie nodded quickly I was once again amazed at Kate's uncanny sensitivity, as if she sensed and could monitor a living pulse that the rest of us weren't aware of. No wonder Kate was so good with animals.

"I just . . ." Bonnie sobbed again, and Lanessa pulled two clean tissues from her bag and thrust them across the table.

Kate pressed her fingertips over the back of Bonnie's hand. "You miss him?"

Bonnie nodded.

"You wish it weren't over?"

Bonnie shrugged.

"You know, it doesn't have to be," I said. "That's the beauty of a separation. You're not divorced yet."

Bonnie shook her head. "He served me with the papers today. He wants the divorce now."

"Oh, Bonnie . . ." Kate continued to massage her hand.

"You don't have to sign anything right now," I said, glancing back at Lanessa. "You were a lawyer once. She has time, right?"

Lanessa's dark eyes softened. "Plenty of time. Don't let the man rush you, honey. You take your time, and chances are, everything will fall into place. You just think of how you want it to work out and it'll happen for you."

Bonnie took a deep breath and blew her nose into the tissue. "Thanks, guys. I'm going to be okay. Just going through a bad patch now."

"Take your time with it," I said. "Don't close the door on him if you still care."

Lanessa shot me a lethal look, but I had to be true to myself, knowing that if Bobby walked through Bertha's door right now and showed the slightest interest, I would forgive all his transgressions and welcome him back into my life.

Bonnie sniffed. "I feel so stupid."

"Intelligence and reason have no place in certain matters of the heart; sometimes you fit another person into your life, trimming this and curtailing that to make it a good fit, and the adjustments you make become so second nature that you don't know how to undo the changes when they're gone. Suddenly, the guy is gone and so is your self-instinct, your strong sense of choice and direction." I knew it was true for me, and I thought Bonnie should have the space to take her ex-husband back if that was what she really wanted.

"Hold everything." Lanessa's hands splayed over the table. "Instead of pulling the man back as a quick fix, wouldn't it make sense to rediscover your sense of self so you're not reliant on someone else?"

Bonnie and I looked at her, then back at each other. "No!" we answered.

"Didn't I just say that it doesn't always make sense?" I said.

While Bonnie dashed to the ladies' room to wash up, Kate brought us up to speed. "Turtle and I had a huge fight." Kate twirled her wineglass, not meeting our eyes.

I bit my lip, waiting for Kate to tell her side of the story. Turtle worked for the same institution as Kate—the National Aquarium, where he was a turtle specialist—and he and Kate had been dating since college, sharing an apartment for almost a year now. Maybe it was because Turtle had more longevity than any of the other boyfriends, but I felt very comfortable around him and was always glad to run into him with Kate or see him at a party. There's something very turtlelike about his appearance—his helmet of straight hair and pale eyes that seem to recede beneath his glasses—but he's also a wealth of information and a fun conversationalist. The guy can talk about the stock market or the latest Hollywood scandal just as easily as he discusses captivity of the Indian star tortoise in Singapore or the Aboriginal harvest of long-necked turtles in Australia.

"Maybe I'm making a big deal out of nothing," Kate said. "Tell me if I'm wrong, but he freaked me out, making a move without discussing it first. He's applying to an aquarium in San Diego. Can you believe it?"

Lanessa shrugged. "So is he planning to move?"

"That's what I said. I feel like he's making plans without me. Pulling away."

"And what does he say about that?" I asked.

"He says no. If he gets an interview, he wants us to fly out together. They're always looking for marine biologists, and I could probably find a job."

"Could be good," I said.

"You're right." Kate sighed. "I just hate it when we fight."

Bonnie returned. "So what did I miss?" She squinted at Kate. "Not you and Turtle?"

"Sounds like he's packed his bags for sunny So-Cal," Lanessa said.

We ordered mussels (and a burger for Bonnie, who can't stand to eat anything that resembles a diaphragm) and tried to assess whether Turtle had emotionally checked out of the relationship. Somehow the talk spun back to Lanessa's new hottie. Nessa was going through various scenarios for getting the man alone in the conference room when two servers delivered our food.

As they lifted the domes from the steaming clams, I sensed the servers staring at me, studying me. "There you go."

The woman, a petite thing with hair streaked in various shades of butter, unfurled the napkin and placed it in my lap.

"Here are some extra hand towels for when you're done." The waiter placed a fat wad of them in front of my place. I sensed heads turning toward me in Bertha's dining room.

Did they think I was a celebrity? Or was I just looking particularly hot tonight?

"Enjoy your food," the waiter said. "And let us know if you need anything else, Olivia."

I thanked the quickly disappearing staff.

"Well, that was weird," Lanessa said.

Kate stole a fry from Bonnie's plate. "Do you know them?"

"No, but they seem to know me," I whispered, feeling flattered.

"Maybe it's your picture in the ladies' room," Bonnie said.

"What?" the rest of us chimed.

"There's an ad for the TV show. A tiny little billboard in each stall, and you're right, Liv. That chick in the illustration is a dead ringer for you. I'll bet Bobby gave the graphic artist one of your photos to work from."

The thought of it, my screaming shrew head blaring at every Baltimore girl taking a pee, gave me a sinking feeling. "I knew my life was in the toilet, but this gives it all a whole new meaning."

"So when does the show air?" Lanessa plunged a mussel into garlic butter and waited till the sauce stopped dripping. "It's so exciting—our own Liv on television. We should all watch the first episode together. When's it on?"

"It premieres Tuesday," I said sullenly.

"Tuesday's bad for me," Kate said. "The aquarium is open late."

Bonnie added ketchup to her burger. "I have yoga."

"I'd miss yoga to see Olivia on television," Lanessa prodded her.

"It's *not* me. That's what people just aren't getting. I had absolutely nothing to do with the show, except that my former boyfriend seems to have modeled it after my former life. I thought you guys would understand the betrayal in this."

"I totally get it, Liv." Kate broke off a piece of bread and passed me the basket. "What Bobby is doing is a violation of your privacy. To portray his main character in your likeness and use your name? It's not fair to you."

"Thank you, Kate." I took the basket gratefully. "At least someone sees my point."

"I get it," Lanessa said, "but I think the whole TV angle is just too juicy to resist. If my ex were launching Lanessa the Ball-Breaker, honey, I would arrive on the red carpet in a Versace gown."

"TV shows don't do red-carpet premieres," Bonnie pointed out.

But Lanessa just shook her head. "My point is, suck up the glamour and attention while it lasts. Instead of denying your connection, let it work for you, Liv."

"I wish I could. I'm just not like you, Lanessa."

"And maybe Olivia doesn't want to be connected to Bobby's creative vision, whatever that is," Kate went on. "So far, we're just talking about the way the star of the show looks. We don't even know if he's used personal anecdotes from your life. Like the time you two sneaked onto the golf course at night and got buzzed by that helicopter. Or your driving test. Remember that shirt you loved with the loose buttons in front? And the way the man from the DMV stared at you after the test, after the seat belt had worked your shirt open?"

I squeezed my eyes shut at the memory. "Ugh. Tell me he's not going to get that personal."

Lanessa and Bonnie were laughing.

"Oh, God, I forgot about that," Bonnie said.

"And did you pass the test? Did you get your driver's license? Of course, you did," Lanessa said smugly. "And you girls think it's wrong to use sex appeal to swing things your way? I rest my case."

"Come on, guys. That open blouse has always been a source of embarrassment for me." Bad enough that my friends found so much humor in it. Kate's suggestion slammed me with a frightening epiphany, making me realize the extent of the damage Bobby could do with this show. "Would Bobby really show something like that on television?"

"He could," Bonnie said. "There's no copyright on your personal life events."

"Oh, God." The horrid possibilities hit me with a dull thud. Or maybe that was the sound of a black shell dropping into the reject bowl. "What if he *does* use my life? What if he uses my most embarrassing moments? My secrets? Our sex life . . ."

"You have secrets?" Lanessa licked her lips. "Do tell all."

"Nessa . . ." Bonnie shot her a warning look. "It's all fun and games for you, I know, but Olivia is in a real dilemma here."

I was. And since, for once, it was a dilemma I did not create for myself, I was clueless as to how to get myself out of it. "Oh, God." I tore open a moist towelette. "This is bad. I may have to change my name. Dye my hair. Move somewhere else." Perhaps I'd be heading back to New York sooner than I'd planned.

"Where can you escape to?" Bonnie asked. "It's a national show. It'll play in Peoria."

"For those Peorians who have cable," Lanessa added.

Kate pressed a napkin to her mouth, her eyes huge with worry. "Don't panic. You don't know what the show is going to include. Most likely it has nothing to do with you."

"But what if it does? What if he mocks me on national TV?"

No one had an answer. I looked from one face to another, Bonnie's nervous blink of sympathy, Kate's fawning look of compassion, Lanessa's cool, what-the-hell flip of a mussel shell.

"Listen up, Olivia . . ." Lanessa dipped a mussel in spicy red sauce and popped it into her mouth. "I know it seems like this man has got you by the short and curlies right now, but there's something you need to remember. He might be a backstabbing, low-life bottom feeder, but you, girl, have your dignity. You got your pride, and nobody can take that away from you."

Kate was nodding, her eyes burning with staunch support.

"And you have us," Bonnie said. "We'll do whatever we can to help."

"Starting with watching that show next week." Lanessa wiped her hands on a napkin, then pointed one manicured finger in the air, instructing all of us. "Ladies, clear your calendars for Tuesday night. We are going to watch the premiere episode of the *Nutcrapper* together."

5

"Your turn, Rocky," ZZ said in a gravelly voice that resembled rocks churning in a mixer.

Just my luck. He'd been hired not only as a Santa, but head Santa, the big cheese of all five male Clauses and Mrs. Claus, too. My immediate boss. I didn't catch his name, so I still thought of him as ZZ Top, although this morning he'd revealed a softer side, leading the group gently through introductions. At the moment, the odd assortment of Santas and elves was waiting for me to cough up my name and a few touchy-feely details to be lapped up by our "caring, sharing circle," as ZZ called it.

I thought of Mrs. Atwater, the manager of the Rockettes, who resembled a Barbie doll and seemed to have been with the dance troupe since its 1932 debut. Mrs. Atwater would not approve of head Santa, nor would she spare the time for flowery employee orientations. In fact, I think she would enjoy frosting over some of these lost elves with her ice queen glare, especially when they crooned of their "Luv fer the little woons," and their desire to make Christmas special in every heart.

"God bless us, every one," I said caustically, checking for signs of intelligent life in the eyes of this motley crew. The gawky former exchange student from Australia seemed to catch my drift, as did a well-dressed African American woman who kept her enviable purple leather Coach bag close to her body.

"Care to introduce yourself, Rocky?" ZZ prodded.

I gave him a sour look. Not to be the problem child of the group, but when they said *orientation* I didn't envision hours spent singing "Getting to Know You."

Well, at least I was getting paid for this.

"Sorry." ZZ grinned. "I call her Rocky because she was a Rockette at Radio City. Danced in the Christmas show last year. She'll be our Mrs. Claus." He folded his arms over his belly. Today he'd traded the leathers in for jeans with red felt suspenders, and with his beard looking a little better groomed, white and fluffy, he did resemble St. Nick. "Want to fill in the blanks, Olivia?"

"You want the standard setup? I'm a single white female. I like Broadway musicals and moonlit walks on the beach. My favorite color is blue and I'm a Taurus, so don't get in my way, okay?" I shrugged. "Next?"

"Thanks, Olivia. Let's move right along . . ."

Personally, I wanted to move right out of this windowless conference room in the Rossman's building and scope out the activity in the rest of the store, where scores of employees were scrambling faster than these elves, mounting shelves, lighting up glass display counters, wheeling in racks of merchandise. As I'd peeked in over the two-story main sales floor, I was amazed at how much of a department store is portable; it's all in the merchandise. I wanted to be a part of the action out there, not cooped up in here discussing the dreams and goals of strangers.

Besides, as seasonal employees, we got a 10 percent discount, and I was dying to be the first to rifle through a pile of cashmere sweaters. Ka-ching!

"I'd like to seed one more activity before we break for lunch." ZZ clasped his hands together and pressed his fingertips to his lips. "When we head over to our 'space' this afternoon, you'll see that there's a large gas fireplace with a mantelpiece perfect for hanging stockings. Each of you will hang one stocking this afternoon, and inside you will place your ultimate Christmas wish written on a piece of paper."

"Right, Poppy." Carlos, the youngest Santa, a short, dark-haired Latino man stretched out his legs, his untied construction boots dangling. "And you're going to make our wish come true? I can save you some time if you just deliver a Porsche to me now."

"Ah ah ah! Don't speak too soon." ZZ held up a finger. "You ask for a car, but after the initial thrill, will a car make you happy? Will it change your daily life for the better? Would a Porsche help you attain personal fulfillment?"

The elf shrugged. "I could handle it."

"Well, think bigger, Carlos. I'm not saying that you shouldn't wish for a Porsche. But don't rule out other wishes that might surpass a hot car. Maybe you want to be the top elf. Maybe you'd like to get a long-term job offer from Rossman's after Christmas. Maybe you'd like to buy a dream home or create a patent that brings in millions of dollars before the end of the year."

Carlos laughed. "Yeah, sure, I'll take one of each."

"Ah, but you only get to put one wish in the stocking, so don't limit yourself. There are no limits."

Except to my patience.

"Are we done yet?" I checked my watch, not wanting to keep Kate waiting. We were meeting for lunch at Phillips and I had a feeling that ZZ was one of those long talkers who ran all over everyone else's time. "Woo, look at the time."

"Yes, you can go, but think about your wish!" he admonished us.

I flew out of there faster than Santa's sleigh, my hair flying wildly in the wind. Clicking into my New York pace, I rushed over a quaint walking bridge and paving stones, around ambling groups of tourists, to the Harbor Pavilions. Kate had already snagged a table, and we decided to do cafeteria style, two crab-cake sandwiches and Diet Cokes. I launched into complaints over the morning training session, tossing in a few jokes about ZZ and comparing the selection of elves to escapees from Munchkinland, but Kate wasn't laughing.

"Something wrong?" I asked.

She blinked. "What? Oh . . . Sorry. Turtle and I had another argument this morning. That makes three in three days. Three more than we've ever had." She balled up her sandwich wrapper. "At first I thought that there was something messed up between us, that he was looking for an out, but that's not it. Yesterday he told me he also tossed in an application for a job at the Seattle Aquarium. It's not just about moving to San Diego; he doesn't seem to care where he lands. He's just determined to leave here."

"I can understand that. Right now, Baltimore is just a stop along the road for me. Once my ankle checks out, I'm on the next Metroliner to New York."

"Because you want to dance, and New York is a cultural center for performing arts. But Turtle can be a biologist in lots of places."

"And you can't?" I prodded. "Why aren't you sending out applications, too? Go on-line and check out some different cities, see if anything strikes your sense of adventure. You've always lived here, Kate. Don't you want to explore other options?"

"Why would I? My family and friends are here. I've got a job I love, with a strong sense of commitment to the dolphins, especially the new calves. I've got a great apartment, peace with my neighbors, and I know all the best places to eat and shop and walk the dogs. Baltimore is my home; why would I want to leave?"

"To try something different. Your dogs could run wild on an island in Seattle and you could take a ferry to work every day and sip lattes by the water. Or San Diego. With that weather, the dogs could be outside every day. Think of dolphin presentations in the sun, you swimming side by side in a sparkling lagoon. I'm kind of with Turtle on this one. Your life could be so much better—"

"Different isn't always better," she interrupted. "Why don't you get that? You and Turtle . . . As if everything I've always loved suddenly isn't good enough anymore. You know, the grass *isn't* always greener in another city."

"Maybe it isn't, but you won't know what's out there until you take a look. And you know me, I spent most of high school just waiting to get out of Crab Town."

"That nickname . . ." She shook her head. "It nearly killed Sister Mary Agnes." Our freshman year at Spaulding, Lanessa had stuck a bumper sticker onto her binder that read, "I got crabs at CRAB TOWN," and the nun who taught us science freaked out. Lanessa kept explaining that Crab Town was a restaurant, but Sister Mary Agnes made her write an essay on the dangers of double entendres.

Kate's eyes went wide. "Don't look now, but somebody you don't want to see is here."

"Sister Mary Agnes?"

Her head shook faster, like a broken bobblehead. "No. Worse. Duck under the table."

"But everyone will see me." I was dying to turn around. "That'll attract too much attention. Who is it?"

"Go hide behind the relish and pickles—quick!" she whispered, motioning me aside frantically.

I wasn't going to slink behind the ketchup and tartar sauce, and I couldn't stand the suspense; I had to turn around.

Three feet behind our table, Bobby Tharp balanced a tray of salad as he scanned our area for a free table. He didn't seem to find one, but he did catch sight of me.

I turned back to Kate and mouthed, "Oh, no!"

Kate folded her arms in sanguine resignation. "Should have gone for the condiment table when you had the chance," she said as his tray slid onto the table between us.

"Livvy . . ." His low growl reminded me of intimate moments, playing under the covers, kissing on the beach at Ocean City, snuggling at the movies. "And Kate! Wow, what a blast from the past. Mind if I join you two?"

My blood thrummed in my ears as I held my breath and reluctantly let myself soak up Bobby—all six feet of him—looking taller and leaner, as if he'd lost the freshman ten. His hair seemed golder—maybe touched up?—and he had the angular, loose demeanor of an athlete.

No, maybe that was the red and white University of Maryland letter jacket. A letter jacket—as if he'd ever jogged a mile, let alone achieved varsity status in a sport. *It's all part of the image, part of the fake Bobby he wants everyone to buy into,* I told myself. If only I could convince myself that he was a fraud, make my pulse slow down, squelch the urge to jump up, straddle him, and press my face into his chest like a koala.

With Bobby so close, it was resoundingly clear that I was still buying into the whole package. And if I could just get my heartbeat to slow and my palms to stop sweating, I would have the good grace to feel embarrassed at my own vulnerability.

Kate stood up. "I've got to get back to work. I'm on for the two o'clock dolphin show."

"I've got work, too," I blathered, knowing I needed to get back but not so sure I wanted Bobby to know about my new job. Let's see, hotshot TV producer or department-store Mrs. Claus—which was the more marketable career?

"I keep hearing that you're back in Baltimore. I figured if it was true, we'd run into each other." Bobby set his food on the table and handed his tray to Kate. "Just shoot that over there, will you?"

"Oh, sure." She moved behind him and lifted the tray as if to slam him in the head with it.

"I'll call you later, Kate," I said, resigned to my sorry fate, a few minutes spent opposite the man-boy of my once and future dreams.

"Ciao, Kate!" he called, saluting her.

"I kept meaning to call you, but with the show and everything . . ." He shoved a tomato wedge in his mouth as I considered how I would have reacted hearing his voice on the other end of the phone.

I wish you'd called. No, I don't. But I'm glad you were thinking of me.

"You can imagine. Not a minute to myself. Thank God for hiatus."

I wish you didn't look so good now. I wish you ate salads when we were together. How did you get your skin to clear up? How is it that you look so damned good when I know you're so damned bad?

"So, go on, Livvy. Let me have it. Rip me a new one. I know you're pissed."

How could I ever be angry with you when I'm still crazy about you?

His eyes flickered with amusement, eyes darker and greener than I'd remembered. "Oh, I get it. The silent treatment."

"Are those colored contacts?" I blurted out.

He rolled his eyes. "She speaks."

"I probably shouldn't," I said. "I should just have my lawyer call you after the first episode airs."

"Ouch. You don't have to draw blood."

"You started it. Did you think I wouldn't notice that you were using my name? An actress who looks like me? Filming in the city I grew up in? Thought you'd just slide that one past me, huh?"

He sighed. "Of course not, but you'd moved on. You were dancing in New York, on to another life. I didn't think you'd recognize yourself, certainly didn't expect you to land back here."

"What you did was wrong, Bobby."

"Probably. But I did change the name in the script. A dozen times. Global replacement. But every time I looked up and saw 'Kelly' or 'Alicia' or 'Jennifer' on the page, it just didn't feel right. You were the inspiration for my stories, Liv. Without you, they don't sing."

"Oh, whoop-dee-doo." I stood up and turned away so he couldn't see the conflicted emotions on my face, the war between flattery and betrayal. He had invaded my privacy by using me as a basis for his character, and yet, somehow, I was a little tickled that I'd left such an impression.

"I mean that, Liv. You are the pulse of this show."

I pulled my coat on. "Great. I'm looking forward to getting my cut."

He leaned back slightly, cautious, shocked at my bitchiness.

How could I be such a bitch? That sort of behavior would never make him love me.

But then, deep down I knew it was too late for all that, with Bobby married now. Funny that her name hadn't come up in the conversation, but Bobby probably figured it would piss me off

that much more. I decided to take "Destiny" into my own hands.
"So where is your wife? I've read that you two are inseparable."

"She's running a few errands. Manicure, hair appointment.
Girl stuff."

"Really? And here I thought she was a busy working girl."

"The two of us are crazy busy when the show is filming.
Destiny is my coproducer."

That would be my job, I thought. *And that would be my man, if only
a few things had played out differently.* That queasy feeling rose inside me, another session of making myself sick over my mistakes.
I wasn't up for it. "I've got to get back to work," I said.

"Yeah, what's that about? Did you really give up the Rockettes
thing?"

"I sort of had to take a *hiatus* when I broke my ankle. The
Rockettes look down upon dancers who can't walk. Sort of ruins
the lineup."

"I knew about the accident," he said, waving a hand. "By the
way, did you sue? Hope you got a bundle out of them. Immigrants, right? Probably illegal."

My jaw dropped in revulsion. "Mario? Don't you remember
the pizza place we loved?"

He shrugged. "Anyway, your ankle looks fine. What about the
Rockettes thing?"

Since the day of my audition at Radio City Music Hall, the
"Rockettes thing" had been a problem for Bobby. Although he'd
never been too concerned that I was the one paying our bills
when we lived together in Baltimore, the fact that I'd pulled
ahead to pursue a high-visibility showbiz job in New York was too
much for his delicate ego to balance. He had helped me move
into the apartment with the other two dancers, had spent a
weekend at a nearby motel, had even stayed for my first performance and brought me a bouquet of flowers backstage, but inside I think he was beginning to disconnect. Despite the pledge
to make this long-distance thing work with Metroliner trips and
daily phone calls, Bobby was working up a Plan B, which involved jetting out to L.A. to pursue a separate career and audition stand-ins.

"Are you done with New York?" he added.

"I'm on hiatus," I said, flinging back his insider lingo. "I'm going back to New York after Christmas." That much was true. He didn't have to know I'd need to audition for the Rockettes all over again. "So . . . I'll let you know how much I really hate you after I see the first episode. Of *my* show."

Such a bitch!

"You're kidding . . . I know you are. Listen, we're all getting together at Club 13 to watch the series debut—the cast and crew, lots of media people. Got to make a splash in Baltimore, of course, and it's such a great angle, that homegrown thing. You know, they'll probably want to talk with you, the inspiration for the show. Why don't you come?"

"I don't think so."

"Come on," he growled in that jovial way. "I mean it. The media people are going to want interviews with the real Olivia."

"I have plans," I said firmly, though an invitation to the premiere party was enticing. When you're in show business, you develop this instinct to go toward the cameras, grab the attention of reporters and media people whenever you have the chance. Still, there was no way I could watch at such a public place, not knowing what to expect from Bobby's show. Talk about blindsided.

"Let me know if plans change." He saluted me with two fingers. "Ciao."

I was tempted to respond with a one-finger salute but restrained myself. After all, I was Mrs. Claus.

6

To my surprise, ZZ didn't glower or grouse when I crept back into orientation ten minutes late. He was passing out stockings and lecturing once again on the importance of setting goals, on the amazing impact this Christmas wish could have on our lives.

Blah blah, blah blah, blah blah.

I tuned him out immediately and refocused on Bobby and the debut of the show and the fact that this city would continue to close in around me, shrinking my life down to a claustrophobic sack once the tales of wicked Olivia aired on television. I'd once complained that I'd never felt embraced by this city, but now I was feeling its grip quite well, a firm grasp tightening to a stranglehold.

"Don't check out on me," ZZ said softly, leaning close to my ear. He handed me a red stocking with "Mrs. Claus" embroidered over the fuzzy white cuff.

"To be honest, I'm already gone." My heart was back in New York, dancing on the line, having brunch with friends and not having to worry about eating waffles or pancakes or bacon because in three performances a day you burn it all off, rushing from my apartment to fit in Christmas shopping before the early performance . . .

"Emotionally, that may be true," he said. "But since your body is still with us for the next few weeks, it would be nice if the spirit could join in."

I gave him a curious look.

"Metaphysically speaking." He straightened, addressing the group once again. "You'll find a small card inside your stocking. Take it out now and fill in your Christmas wish . . ."

Maybe I'd misjudged ZZ. After all, he could have spent this entire day making us read the corporate policy on sexual harassment and chronic tardiness. I took the white card from my stocking and mulled over my secret desires. Not that I am superstitious or even a believer in quiet goal setting. I'm the sort of person who strikes out after what she wants, working through obstacles with single-minded determination. The approach usually worked for me—had landed me a position on the Rockettes. But lately, I was stuck waiting—for my ankle to heal, for my mother to swing back to normal, for Christmas to come and go so I could head back to New York.

What to wish for? That my ankle was all healed and I was back in Manhattan, back in the Rockettes?

That would have been my primary desire a few weeks ago but now, somehow, it was not enough. My future seemed tainted by Bobby's impending show, a commercial franchise with the potential to exploit and malign my image and my name. And then there was Bobby. Blissfully self-absorbed Bobby. Despite his tendencies toward the asshole brigade, despite the fact that he was married now, I still felt that flush of warmth around him, the undying attraction that would have me tossing rose petals onto his grave when I was ninety. Fatalistic, I know, but if his bad behavior hadn't killed the attraction by now, I had to resolve myself to living with it.

I wanted it all—the love of my life, my anonymity, my dancing career.

"Remember, you can only write down one wish," ZZ said as he paced the room. "You need to focus, people."

Fine, I thought. I would wipe the slate clean.

I wrote: *I wish for a do-over.* Thinking like a lawyer. I figured that left a lot of things open, but then a lot of things in my life needed fixing.

That afternoon ZZ handed out our costumes and sent us off to the store dressing rooms to try them on. "Report back to Santaland as soon as you're in costume," he ordered. "We have a tailor coming this afternoon to mark alterations, and I want to get started with the Santaland protocol."

While the others received costumes sealed in plastic bags, mine came in a big, wide gift box made of silver cardboard. "I understand this costume is a Rossman's family heirloom." ZZ held the silver box before me, and I couldn't help but run my hand over the large embossed *R*.

"Why would the Rossmans send a family heirloom to the Baltimore store?"

He shrugged. "The grand opening. Charley said they wanted to send us luck. Rumor has it that Evelyn Rossman wore this suit years ago when the chain was just starting up in Chicago."

I slid off the lid, and rich red jewel tones winked up at me, scarlet beads, burgundy shadings on ruby velvet. It was a fine garment, reminding me of the spectacular costumes I'd worn onstage at Radio City. "Wow."

"Gorgeous, isn't it?" ZZ's eyes twinkled over his white beard as he grinned, reminding me of a real Santa Claus. "Go ahead, try it on."

Up in the spacious new dressing room I placed the box on a bench and worried about the vast alterations that would probably rob this costume of its shape. Department store maven Evelyn Rossman was a tall woman, broad shouldered and solid, while I was short for a dancer—having just made the Rockettes' five-foot six-inch minimum. I dropped my black sweater onto an upholstered chair and worried about the color clash. With my orangey red hair, I avoided wearing the color red, which often made my skin look jaundiced, my hair shriek with flames.

I slipped on the jacket and it buttoned closed with a soft,

soothing sigh. The tucks and darts were perfect, accentuating my small bustline while giving me stately shoulders and a classic cinched waist. The dark tones of the burgundy complemented my hair and skin, giving my cheeks a rosy glow, my hair the look of burnished copper. The velveteen pencil skirt fell just at my ankles, where a kick pleat in the back revealed the black Jimmy Choo boots that I'd handpicked from Rossman's newly stocked shoe department that morning.

"Ooh . . ." A quiet thrill passed through me at the prospect of wearing this lovely costume every day. I might have to deal with more than my share of squabbling rug rats, but I would be the picture of tolerance in my smokin' costume.

Pulling on the matching cap and staring in the mirror, I had to smile at myself. My orange curls spilled out under the white trim of the cap, framing my face, which looked sprightly and fresh. Not your traditional notion of an elderly Mrs. Claus, but also not Olivia Todd, dancer and single white female.

"You look quite different," one of the elves told me, the punker from Australia, whose gem-pierced right ear looked elfin under his floppy striped cap. His name was Regis, and we'd caught each other's eyes often enough during the training to realize that we were on the same wavelength. "A little touch-up on your make-up and you'll have all the Mr. Clauses inviting you into their sleighs."

I shot him a grin. "Hardly my holiday goal, but thanks."

"What's wrong, fear of flying?" he teased, nodding toward the line of Santas waiting for tailoring. "What tidy elf wouldn't be honored to fly off to the North Pole with any of those fine specimens of Claus-hood? Watch it." He pulled me out of the way as one of the Santas tripped over his bootlaces, falling into line.

"Damned trousers," the Santa grumbled, clutching his pants up to his undershirt. Skinny Stu. He would definitely need some padding, as would Chet, a ruddy-faced man with a barrel chest and feisty, strong chin. Chet reminded me of my grandfather, and I suspected he shared Grandad's hearing disability as he was a little slow to respond, but generally cheerful.

He fell into line behind Archie, a dark-skinned, ample man

with a natural Santa physique and a rich, contagious laugh that could rock the room. Everyone liked Archie.

Then there was Carlos, beautifully fluent in Spanish but a little on the young side when it came to playing a centuries-old icon. "We'll get you a nice, authentic-looking beard," ZZ said, patting Carlos's shoulder.

Carlos let his head loll back as he gave ZZ a tired look. "Don't worry about it, man. A week or so of working with you old guys and my hair's gonna be snow-white anyway."

"Nonsense! The fun is just beginning, dude." ZZ patted Carlos's shoulder, then slipped his thumbs under his red suspenders to survey the motley Santas. "By gosh, by jingle, it's time for carols and Kris Kringle!"

Somewhere in the back of Santaland, someone was shaking jingle bells. The overhead lights cut out, sending a gasp through the group that rose into an awed sigh as tiny white lights sprang to life along pillars and snowpiles and silver trees.

It was all as corny as an old-fashioned Christmas card, and I smiled in spite of my usual cynicism. Something about the line of bedraggled Santas and the elves, struggling to walk in their curl-toed shoes and dopey green-striped caps, and the Santaland touched me with a feeling I hadn't felt for years.

Christmas spirit? Joy? Hard to say. Some feelings are impossible to label, but for that moment, I let go of my plans for the future and soaked up the here and now, my Christmas in Baltimore, my holiday as Mrs. Claus.

7

Tuesday, the night of the infamous *Olivia, the Nutcracker* premiere, we planned to watch the show at Bonnie's, dulling the pain with tacos and margaritas. Easy for me, since I was just a block away, and I headed over early to help Bonnie.

Bonnie's face was tense when she met me at the door. "He's here," she said, her jaw strained as she nodded to the next level up.

I couldn't see him, but I knew she was talking about Jonah, her current husband, who'd recently moved out.

"Want me to come back later?"

"No, you're fine. Come on up." She leaned forward to close the door behind me and whispered, "Just wanted to warn you. He's in a vulnerable place."

I nodded, wondering how to deal with that, as I'd always felt uncomfortable dealing with the austere Jonah even when he was coming from a secure place. Jonah works as an underwriter and apparently he's an amazing number cruncher, but his passion is art photography, and I don't think Bonnie or anyone in our circle of friends has a clue about what Jonah sees in a photo. Once, when I was pulling together my portfolio for auditions, I asked if he would take some head shots for me—apparently the ultimate insult to an artist. I don't think he's ever really forgiven me for that.

"I was just about to start chopping things for the tacos," Bonnie said as she led me up the half flight of stairs to the front parlor where a dozen or so of Jonah's framed prints were propped on the floor, leaning against the black leather love seat and chair.

"Hi, Jonah." I jumped in. "How's it going?"

He nodded, meeting my eyes with that dark intensity that Bonnie kept falling in love with. "Olivia."

"Jonah is trying to choose a photograph for a contest," Bonnie offered.

"A competition," he corrected, kneeling down in front of three shots of the Baltimore skyline. "A cityscape. It's always difficult."

Bonnie stuck her pinky to her chin. "It's always hard to decide."

"I like making choices," I admitted, bending down beside him. I sensed Bonnie tensing, but Jonah seemed interested in watching me examine his work, intrigued or amused, I wasn't sure.

I moved down the line, soaking in each piece, but I kept coming back to one I'd seen before. "I can't help it, this is one of my favorites." It was a shot of a small memorial in Fells Point, rows of concrete steps rising out of the cobbled square. The background was a blur of putty-colored concrete, but two subjects were in sharp focus in the foreground: a man in an overcoat slumped on the steps in the foreground, his expression distracted, distant. A few feet away from him on the same stair sat a pigeon, its profiled head looking flat and smug, confident, as if it had a right to be there.

"There's something about this one, the conflict between man and nature, between belonging and displacement..." There, I'd said it, a dash of honesty for the vulnerable but austere Jonah. "I'm no expert, but I think it's a strong example of your work."

"And the textures are vivid," Bonnie joined in. "The chiseled cobblestones, the pockmarks on the concrete." She looked over at Jonah. "I think this is the one."

He nodded, staring at the photograph as if he was seeing new layers and dimensions. "Do you think? I don't know." His dark eyes found me, and I sensed that he was seeing me for the first time, too.

"It gets my vote," I said, deciding to back off and let him make a choice. I went up to the kitchen to root around in the fridge to give him and Bonnie a chance to be alone, to finish their conversation as he put away the photos.

Bonnie and Jonah had remodeled two years ago, gutting the house and rebuilding with glass brick and spiral staircases and split-level floors covered in shiny pine and edged in dark cherry. The decor was black and white, with a white sectional couch and museum-mounted photos Jonah had taken over the years. It's not the sort of design I would choose, but it comes together so intricately that every time I visit Bonnie, I feel a little more grown-up just knowing someone with such a cool home.

I was drying a head of lettuce and two peppers when he called a good-bye up to me.

"Well, that was interesting." Bonnie appeared, bearing a gallon of tequila tucked in one arm. "He was a little more open to you tonight, wasn't he?" This was a game we played, with Bonnie always trying to see ways that Jonah was warming up to her friends while we gently pointed out the truth.

"He's still a long way from warm and fuzzy."

"Jonah will never be warm and fuzzy. Why do I always pick men who have all these issues swirling under the surface?"

"Your curse." I didn't know exactly why Bonnie was attracted to Jonah—none of us did—but Lanessa once pointed out that if Jonah made love with the same intensity that colored his daily activities, well . . . hot damn.

"Did you have a chance to talk to him about things?" I asked. "About your relationship?"

"We had couples therapy tonight, our first time together."

"Really? That's great, right? I mean, you want to try and save the relationship."

"Yes, I do. Definitely, but Jonah chose the therapist, a man, and the old guy always rattles my cage. He acts as if I forced Jonah to marry me. Like I pushed him into every aspect of our relationship." She dumped ice into the blender and shoved on the lid. "If it were up to Dr. Kleban, Jonah wouldn't have fucked me if I hadn't pulled down his zipper and yanked it out."

"Ooh, I'm sensing a little anger here."

"I'm angry all right." Her face puckered in fury, she pressed the blender on. When it whirred off, she took a deep, cleansing breath. "Aah, that's better."

"Isn't that displacement? Or transference? I mean, aren't you really angry with Jonah but pretending it's all about Dr. Strange-love?"

"What the hell do I know? I majored in technology and marketing." She pressed the blender on again, then poured the frothy mix into two glasses. "Let's just say that, sitting in Dr. Kleban's office, I felt very sure that Jonah and I are very sane and reasonable. We're capable of making things work. If Kleban doesn't fuck it up for us."

"Two swear words in one night." I made two tally marks in the air. "Looks like our little Bonnie is growing up."

"Liv, if the TV critics are correct, *you'll* be swearing before the night is over." She handed me a glass with a salted rim. "And you'll want a few dozen of these, too. Don't worry, I have plenty of tequila, and you don't have to drive."

"Oh, I could drive, but that might pose a problem . . . for the car I don't own. You know, I never realized how long it takes to bus it around Baltimore. You really need a car here. And now that I'm riding the bus, I get to see all the nasty *Olivia* billboards up close and personal." I took a deep sip of my drink, then put down the glass to chop scallions on the granite board. "Mmm, that's yummy. Can we talk about something more positive? How's work?"

"Don't go there . . . rumors of downsizing." She took the shiny silver grater down from a rack. "How's the Mrs. Claus gig working for you?"

"It's actually going okay. I'm going to get more hours than anyone else, since there's only one Mrs. Claus, so I'll be raking in the cash. And I'm in love with the costume I get to wear."

"You are kidding. Does it come with fanny padding?"

"Nope. I get to be my hottie self. And it's styled like an Oscar. I'm telling you, Sarah Jessica Parker would wear this dress at a Christmas party."

Bonnie put the slab of cheddar on the cutting board, her eyes narrowed. "I gotta see that. I'll have to stop by sometime."

"We open Thursday," I said brightly, carried away with my own enthusiasm. "The store's grand opening will be this weekend, but we're going to be ready to have kids visit Santa by Thursday at noon."

"Christmas already? It's barely November." She flaked the cheese into a bowl. "Remember the days when no one used to put up decorations until after Thanksgiving?"

"Those rules are out the window." I peered over the kitchen island to the wide windows at the front of Bonnie's house. "You know, you should put up some lights this year. Maybe simple white lights in the front windows? It'll give you a lift."

"Jonah wouldn't approve. He's always felt that Christmas lights are white-trash tacky," she said, and I glared at her. "But then, he isn't living here at the moment, is he?"

"Hey, how about red?" I suggested. "A few strings of those chili pepper lights?"

"I love those!" The doorbell rang and she wiped her hands on a towel and ran down to open the door.

Lanessa appeared, bearing a small cheesecake. "Pure evil," she said, hoisting it onto the counter with a smile.

Five minutes later Kate arrived, and we all grabbed drinks and made a mess of Bonnie's cooking island, tossing cheese and chopped veggies onto our toasted shells. As we took seats at the bar we laughed over the varied taco approaches. Kate was the most aggressive. With her hair tucked back in a French braid she was free to dive in and let the stuffing fall where it may, even if that meant bouncing off her sweatsuit. Lanessa carefully tucked a napkin over her silk suit, an unusual ginger color that complemented her dark skin.

I felt oddly aware of my own nervousness but also happy to be here with my friends, laughing and joking, back to the best parts of my life in Baltimore. I had fallen hard for the excitement and fast pace of New York, but this was something I'd missed, hanging with my real friends, the easy good time.

I was on my second taco when Bonnie clapped her hands. "Let's step it up, girls. Show starts in two minutes. We'll do dessert afterward."

With a groan I sank onto Bonnie's sectional sofa and buried my face in my hands. "I can't watch!"

"Oh, go on!" Lanessa smoothed her skirt over her knees. "You've got to be excited. Bobby's making you a star, honey."

"I'd rather have a root canal," I said as the camera opened on a freckle-faced actress with exotic red hair.

"She's beautiful!" Kate slapped my knee. "You're gorgeous. At least Bobby did something right."

"It's not me," I insisted.

The premise of the show was fairly simple: Olivia, a ballet dancer who has found her fame in New York City, now returns to Baltimore to direct the city's dance company. But during her run in New York she developed champagne-and-caviar tastes, and now nothing in Baltimore meets with her approval.

"Get those little monsters out of my studio!" she shrieks, chasing after local schoolchildren clad in pink tutus with a stick. "I work with professionals!

"I asked for New York bagels! I want them FedExed!" she protests, slamming a bagel onto her assistant's desk.

"Who called for the yellow cab? I ride in limos. Black. I do not ride in yellow cars!"

There was a romantic subplot in which TV Olivia abused her boyfriend until he broke off their relationship. "You leave me no choice," the actor said dramatically, pulling his hand out of hers.

"Oh, please! That's so simplistic. I'm surprised Bobby didn't play the role himself."

"And he makes the boyfriend look so noble," Bonnie said. "Not the way it happened. When he broke up with you, you'd just broken your ankle."

"And he didn't even have the grace to tell you he was breaking up," Kate said. "This part is way off."

"It's not supposed to be my life," I reminded them. "It's not me." But no one seemed to be getting that as the TV Olivia merrily bulldozed over everyone in her path, unconcerned about the destruction left in her wake. In one scene she jaywalked and snarled traffic all the way to Interstate 95. In another scene, after a bus sprayed her with a puddle, she filled the seats with shaving cream, which the audience seemed to find hilarious.

Through it all, TV Olivia criticized life in Baltimore at every turn, complaining about the slow pace of business and the smallness of events, about the stoop sitters and the crab pickers, the downtown traffic and the hicks of Highlandtown. She mocked the Baltimore accent and called the commercialized Harborplace a tourist trap.

I think that was the most disconcerting element—the way this character disparaged the entire city, all its customs, people and landmarks.

"She's nothing like me," I said when the TV Olivia dressed down a traffic cop, telling him he needed remedial traffic school. "You call this a city? You shouldn't be on the same coast as New York, palsy."

"See?" I defended myself. "I would never call a police officer pal-zee."

As if in unison, the girls turned to me with accusing eyes.

I licked salt crystals from the rim of my glass. "What?"

Lanessa cocked her head to one side, the cool stance of a lawyer launching into cross-examination. "Oh, I think this is one part of the character that matches you. Not that it's anything to be ashamed of, but you've said it yourself. You're so done with Baltimore. What do you call it? The city without pity?"

Bonnie scraped at the crumbs in the pretzel bowl. "You've always planned to head back to New York when you put your life back together."

"Baltimore is just a stop on the road, right?" Kate added.

"Well, maybe in *my* life, but I didn't mean to imply that it's a bad place to live." I shook my head, as if that could toss off the accusations. How could my own friends twist my words that way? "You guys aren't being fair. I just had my life raked over the coals and broadcast on television. On prime time!"

Lanessa cocked an eyebrow. "I thought it wasn't you?"

I flung out my arms, exasperated. "Hello? Do you really think that show was about me? Nessa, come on. I thought you knew me better than that."

"Hold on, girls." Bonnie popped up and moved a metallic sculpture from the coffee table. "Just need to protect the valuables in case you two decide to arm wrestle or something."

"To be fair, let's not forget that Olivia has suffered a violation of her privacy here," Kate said evenly. "And a betrayal from someone she really cared about. That's a major transgression."

Lanessa cocked her head. "Meaning?"

"Meaning you need to be nice to me right now," I said petulantly. "Defend me. Tell me how stupid the show was. Ply me with cheesecake."

"Actually, I thought the show wasn't too bad," Bonnie said. "But I'll get right on the cheesecake."

"We're on your side." Kate patted my arm. "Even if you don't love Baltimore, we can deal with that. You found a new home in New York, a career you love . . . Don't let Bobby's craziness derail you." She shot Lanessa a look. "Say something nice to Olivia."

Lanessa rolled her eyes. "Let's not go all Ricki Lake here. Of course we support you, Livvy girl. But come on, if we can't fun with you, who can?"

I picked up a black and white patterned throw pillow. "I am so glad my mother doesn't have cable."

"A lot of people don't have it," Kate said. "I'm sure a lot of people missed that show."

"We'll know in the morning." Lanessa kicked off her pumps and tucked her legs under her on the sofa. "A lot of the trades list the overnights on-line."

Kate and I exchanged a look of surprise. "Nessa, how do you

know these things? You work for the dairy lobby, not a TV producer."

"Are you kidding? I spend half my morning reading on-line magazines. *People, In Style, Variety, Time* . . . not to mention the *Times* and the *Wall Street Journal.* A big part of my job is staying in touch with the social climate."

"I don't think those papers will even pay attention to *The Nutcracker,*" Bonnie said as she handed Lanessa a plate of cake. "It had its moments, but new shows take a while to build a following. And it's not a reality show. Who's going to care?"

Kate nodded, licking cheesecake from a fork. "It's just a cable access show. How popular could it be?"

8

"Twenty million viewers." Lanessa sounded excited, as if she'd discovered a hidden treasure in one of her file cabinets.

"No!" It was as much a protest as a gasp of disbelief and shock at the cold since I'd just opened the front door. "Hold on a sec." I momentarily moved the phone away from my ear so that I could wrap my scarf around my head. A brutal winter morning, unusually cold for a November in the city without pity.

I was navigating around Mrs. Scholinsky's Christmas figurines when the window behind me creaked open. "Don't forget what I told you last night, Olivia," she barked at me. She'd seen the show and refused to believe that I was not the ruthless title character. "Show some compassion."

I raised one gloved hand to her. "Merry Christmas, Mrs. S."

Lanessa was still going on about ratings and time slots. "Twenty million for the first episode. That's exposure for you. If my bosses could get that kind of free airtime, they'd be in cow heaven."

"But I don't need exposure, especially not bad press."

"It's not about you, remember?" Lanessa reminded me. "I

doubt that anyone else will make the connection. So you have the same name as a character on a show. No one is going to put that all together."

No one but Mr. Watch Cap, my bus-stop buddy.

As I moved to the back of the queue for the bus, he turned back to grumble something in my direction. Maybe I was being paranoid, but I thought he said, "Saw you on TV last night." Or maybe it was "So yon be a sight." Shakespearean? From the scruff of beard under his watch cap, I thought not.

"Nessa, I gotta go. I'm just getting on the bus, and I'm sensing hostility."

"Later, honey!" she sang.

I flipped my phone closed and shuffled up with the line. When I lifted my boot to board, the door of the bus slammed shut, nearly snatching my foot in its fold.

"Hey!" I banged on the Plexiglas. "Hold on!"

The door whooshed open, the driver staring down at me with a deadpan expression. "Back off, Olivia. I can't let you board if you're armed with shaving cream." He glanced back at two passengers sitting near the door, and they shared a hearty chuckle.

"That show is not about me," I protested, mounting the stairs.

"What's that?" The driver folded his arms. "You telling me you're not Olivia?"

"I am. Just not that Olivia. Not the *Nutcracker*."

"Uh-huh." The driver smiled at me in his rearview mirror. "And I'm not really driving a metro bus in the city without pity."

That brought another round of laughs at my expense, which I tried to ignore as I found a seat in the rear of the bus, a quiet spot to begin plotting my revenge against Bobby Tharp.

Without my morning caffeine my plans were lackluster, consisting of slapping Bobby and the BigTime Channel with a lawsuit or dipping Bobby into the shark tank at the aquarium. Leaning toward shark bait, I stopped into the coffee shop across from Rossman's and asked for my usual—coffee with milk and a toasted bagel.

The man behind the counter hung his head to the side. "'Fraid we can't make you a bagel, hon."

I squinted at him, not getting it. Was their toaster broken?

He leered at me. "We didn't get 'em FedExed in from New York City."

Very funny, I thought, handing over two bills. He took out money for the coffee and slid the cup toward me. "I ain't kiddin'. Don't want to be having any arguments here over fancy bagels and whatnot."

Grrr!

I considered throwing a tantrum, raising my voice and pounding on the counter, but that would only fulfill Bobby's vision and satisfy expectations of every curious observer in the coffee shop.

Apparently the citizens of Baltimore were not only tuned into BigTime Network last night; they must have gone to bed seething about Olivia's antics and woken up plotting vengeance on the evil diva.

I couldn't stand it. I went to the back of the coffee shop and flipped my phone open to call Bobby, then realized I didn't have his number. Damn! The counter man reluctantly let me borrow a yellow pages, and I paged through the Hotels section until I felt confident I had a hit.

The Harbor Court, a first-class hotel right at the Inner Harbor, a place we had stayed one Valentine's weekend, the most romantic interlude of my life, except for the fact that I'd been stuck with the bill. Part of that whole starving-artist role Bobby used to play. The hotel clerk answered, and I gave his name. "One moment, I'll put you through."

I closed the phone book, my mouth gaping open as I stared out of the coffee shop, devising new forms of vengeance.

"Hello?" His voice was sleepy, that sexy morning rumble.

"It's me, calling to ask you what the hell you were thinking when you showed that script around at the networks."

"Who is this?"

"Olivia," I said through gritted teeth.

"The real one? I mean, not from the show?" He maintained the smooth deejay tone but his panic came through; he was discombobulated. "Olivia Todd?" When I didn't respond, he added, "How did you find me?"

"Oh, please! I just flipped through my copy of *City Smart Baltimore* and found the hotel with the most dollar signs and an on-site racquetball court. How could you stay at the Harbor Court after—" I stopped myself, not wanting to let on how much it hurt, not wanting to obsess on the small fires when the entire forest was in danger of burning. "Do you have any idea of the damage you've done in my life?"

"Hey, Olivia," the counter clerk called. "I'm going to need my phone book back."

Phone to my ear, I lugged it back over to him and realized most people in the shop were watching me. A woman with a little kid in a high chair kept handing him tidbits of bagel—the bagel that could have been mine—but she kept her eyes on me the whole time, as if I were her favorite daytime soap opera.

"Where are the cameras?" an elderly woman asked. "Are we being filmed? I've got a hair appointment this afternoon."

After a vacant silence Bobby went on. "We've been all through this, haven't we? People break up, hon, and—"

"I am not talking about our breakup, Bobby. I am talking about the way you twisted the details of our lives and put them out there for everyone to see. What *were* you thinking?"

"It's called fiction, Liv. Everyone knows the character in the show isn't really you."

"Oh, really? Well, you should tell that to the driver of my bus. And to my landlady, who pounced on me as I was getting home last night and gave me some advice on treating people with kindness. Oh, and the people in this coffee shop. Would you mind taking a moment to head down to the Double T Coffeeshop? The counter clerk would like to talk bagels, and there's a lady here who wants to be on your show."

"I got to get my hair done first, hon!"

"Just as soon as she gets her hair done."

"Liv . . ." He sighed, a long, dramatic whisper of breath. "I don't know what you want from me."

"An apology would be nice, for starters." From there, what did I really want? I knew the show was like a snowballing avalanche;

not even Bobby was capable of pulling the plug on a successful television show. Twenty million viewers . . . just my luck.

"I'm sorry, Liv. The show wasn't created to hurt you, and you know . . ." I squeezed my eyes shut as he launched into his "I never meant to hurt you" speech. I was so sick of that speech, the monologue that implies that Bobby owns control, that he has all the power, and that I am just a poor, pitiful victim of his choices.

What was wrong with me? I was a proactive girl, not the victim of other people's whims!

Feeling a twinge in my ankle, I shifted from one foot to the other. Just the cold? Should I move my doctor's appointment up? I wasn't scheduled to check in with the orthopedic surgeon until the new year.

I sat back on a vinyl chair. Here I was, a disabled dancer, displaced from my home and now the laughingstock of an entire city, maybe even the country. I was a joke for twenty million viewers.

"So I don't know, really, Liv," Bobby was saying in that affected tone. "I feel for you, I really do, but you shouldn't be calling me to cry on my shoulder anymore. I mean, I'm married and everything. Happily married."

"Is that what you think? That I'm crying on your shoulder?" I wanted to cry with frustration.

"Don't get snarky, hon. Word to the wise: figure out what it is you want, and go for it. Isn't that what got you to Radio City? You inspired me, dropping everything and moving up there. And I followed your awesome example. I picked a goal and I went for it and the rest . . . well, the result is twenty million viewers."

"All because of me? You really do owe me, Bobby."

"I wish you the best, Liv," he answered quickly. "Pick that goal. Aim high. Gotta go."

As the phone clicked in my ear, I tried to visualize what my next goal might be. Full recovery of my ankle. Back with the Rockettes. Living in New York City again.

Somehow, it was a tired, dusty dream.

Staring out at the majestic Rossman's building across the

street, I thought of the wish I'd placed in the stocking. A do-over—a chance to go way back and start again. This time I'd do it right, hold on to Bobby . . .

Or would I?

Realizing I had to get to work, I grabbed my coffee cup and headed toward the door.

"When is Bobby coming with the cameras?" the woman asked.

"I wouldn't count on it," I answered, noticing an elderly man sitting at a table behind the door. As I yanked the glass door open, he turned and I saw his face for the first time.

ZZ.

Oh, great. The small part of my life that hadn't been exploited on television last night was now going to be locker-room scuttlebutt at work.

Disheartened, I dragged myself into the employee entrance of Rossman's and joined the group moving through turnstiles that scanned ID cards. During the past week, more and more employees had been reporting to work to prepare the store for the grand opening. Every day the level of activity heightened exponentially, with designers and buyers and carpenters and electricians scurrying around counters, setting up tables and shelves, filling display cases, and wrapping the entire store in ropes of garland lined with fat Christmas balls, sparkling crystal snowflakes, and wispy white lights. The empty space was quickly filling, and I'd begun to feel proprietary about "our" store. The air was loaded with cheer and everyone shared high hopes that Baltimoreans would turn out in large numbers to try "the Rossman's experience," as commercials touted.

The employee lounge was well hidden behind a camouflaged door in the back of the men's section, and I quickly changed into my Mrs. Claus costume, smoothed down the fake white fur, and shut my locker.

As I crossed the main sales floor, I noticed a thick, cabbage-flower carpet runner—a new addition today. It cut a swath over the shiny marble, pointing the way to the escalator with a flourish. I let my boots sink into the rug that was still covered with plastic wrap and imagined I was a young heiress—Evelyn Rossman in her heyday—presiding over my kingdom as the escalator wound around the crystal chandelier and emerged into the cool blue light of the snow scene on the second floor.

If the first floor was festive and welcoming, the second floor was a tranquil haven for shoppers. Aah . . . I felt a calm pass over me as I entered the doorway of an "ice" house illuminated with tiny blue and white lights. "A Swedish spa," Regis called it. "Don't you feel the Nordic calm? It's like visiting one of those ice hotels in the Arctic Circle." The ice house had various chambers, one that resembled Santa's workshop, where three wrappers dressed like elves received packages from anxious shoppers and covered them with Rossman's complimentary silver foil paper with red ribbons. Shoppers would be able to view "Santa's workshop" through one of the glass walls, then the path led them on to a Christmas shop containing ornaments, stockings, holiday dishware, and elf pajamas.

The Santaland was on the next floor up, a candy-covered gingerbread house with a toy train that children could ride through the Christmas landscape. Every time I passed under the candy-cane arches I felt transported to a faraway time and place, a place apart from my own pressures and stresses. I realized that might change when the children gained admittance to Santaland on Thursday.

Besides, the balance was likely to change today, since a few of my coworkers were bound to be among the twenty million who had come to know and hate Olivia last night. Quietly I took my place in front of Santa's hearth and proceeded with caution in our morning "sharing circle." By the time the Santa cap made it halfway through the group, I figured I was safe, and then Carlos burst out, "Hey, what was the deal with that Olivia show last night? Dat girl, she looks a lot like you, you know? And she was a dancer in New York."

That did it.

I told them the whole story. Well, the abridged version, but I made it clear that Bobby had done the show without my knowledge or permission, and that only some of the details of my life were accurate.

"Wow. That dude did you some dirt," Carlos commented.

The others agreed, wholeheartedly.

Skinny Stu looked at the others, taking silent consensus. "We feel for you, Olivia."

"I'll tell you one thing," Archie assured me, mopping his brow with a handkerchief, "that Billy Boy's gonna get coal in his stocking this year."

"And no one in here will blame you for the actions of the Olivia on television," ZZ said. "I'm glad you brought this to our attention and shared this with us. Thank you."

The others nodded, and I felt my spirits lift a little. Let me tell you, this eclectic assortment of Santas included some of the sanest, most decent people I have ever met. I was proud to be working with them.

As the meeting broke up and everyone headed off to their next exercise, ZZ approached me. "I just wanted to let you know, if you ever need to talk . . ." He bowed his head slightly.

"I don't think talking is going to accomplish anything at this point," I said, thinking that it was time for me to act, do something. Though I wasn't sure what to do.

"You'd be surprised at what you can accomplish through therapy," he said seriously.

Therapy? Me? I'd never needed professional help before. "I'm not crazy," I said.

"I shouldn't even validate a statement like that with a response. However, let me point out that it wouldn't hurt to work through some of that bitterness."

"Bitter? Me?"

His eyes were steady, reassuring. "I'm a licensed therapist. I recognize bitterness. Used to think I owned it."

"You're a shrink?"

"A Jungian therapist. Not a medical doctor."

"But, you?" I blinked. "Did you ever practice?"

"Eight years in Miami, five in Aspen. Had to drop out, tune

out, scale down for a while, but I still maintain phone sessions for a handful of clients."

I couldn't imagine myself stretched out on a couch and discussing my problems with anyone beyond Lanessa, Kate, or Bonnie. But ZZ did get me thinking. "Do you make house calls?" I asked. When he cocked his head, hesitant, I added, "Not for me. For my mother."

"Oh, sure." He smiled. "Denial. Oldest trick in the book."

"No, really, it's my mother! She needs to talk with someone. She wants to see a therapist."

"She needs to take the first step, take initiative."

"But she can't bring herself to leave the house. Think about it. How does the agoraphobic get therapy if the therapist won't make house calls?"

He stroked his beard. "I see your point."

"She used to leave the house with me, but even that is changing. She's getting worse. It's been weeks since she left the house, and though she's on a sabbatical from her teaching post right now, that won't last forever. She could lose her job."

He nodded sagely. "Okay, let's see what we can work out."

I clasped the fur trim on my Mrs. Claus bodice. "That is the best news I've heard all day."

9

"It's all about the children," ZZ kept telling us during Santa Squad training. "Don't worry about language barriers or irate parents or crying babies. Just focus on the kids, their meeting with Santa. It's up to us to make this a warm, welcoming experience."

That first day I learned that it's easy to be warm and welcoming when toddlers fall in your arms, when preschoolers skip together toward the train, when their parents thank you profusely for guiding their children through Santa's gingerbread house.

Unfortunately, ZZ's philosophy wasn't completely effective on the parents from hell.

"Max, no! Would you stop that? You wanted to wait in line, so stand up properly and wait your turn." Max's mom stamped her foot on the floor as if she were ready to throw a tantrum.

The boy straightened, then doubled over so that his fingertips swept the floor.

"Stop that!" Max's mother hissed. "I said don't touch the floor!"

"He can come over here and color this name tag," I suggested, waving the child over to a craft station.

Max leaned up slightly, propping his elbows on his thighs.

"Aren't you nice and limber," I teased. "How would you like to sit down for a while and make some decorations?"

"That's okay," the mother responded. "We don't want to lose our place in line."

I stepped toward her so that I could discreetly lower my voice. "He won't lose his spot. We have a system designed to pull children out of line and let them pass the time with an activity. At this stage it's name tags. Or he could design a Christmas card." I bent down toward Max. "Does that sound like fun?"

Max puckered his chubby cheeks, stealthily reached out, and grabbed a handful of hair at my ear.

"Max! Don't you . . . Stop that!" she gasped, yanking his arm back.

"It's okay," I insisted. Actually, it didn't hurt at all until the woman started tugging. "How old are you, Max?" I asked, trying to engage him again.

"The terrible twos," his mother answered.

Still a baby, I thought as his mother pulled his hand out of my hair and demanded that he apologize.

"Go on, Max. Tell Mrs. Claus you're sorry."

"Ah sorry."

She let out a frustrated breath. "I wish he would say it like he meant it."

Max turned away from us and did a little pirouette, landing on the floor near a Styrofoam gumdrop. "Wanna go home."

"No, Max, we are not going home. You said you wanted to see Santa and that's what we're doing."

He frowned. "Wanna go home." His voice cracked and I knew tears were on their way.

One of the elves glanced down the line at me, and I shrugged. Short of yelling, "Cleanup on aisle five!" I wasn't sure how to handle Max's mother.

"Don't start that," the mom said. "Come on, Max. Don't be a baby!"

"But he is a baby," I said gently. The words floated in front of me like a lily pad on the water, and for a moment it seemed as if someone else had said them.

Max's mother reared her head back and she fixed her eyes on me like a bobcat about to strike.

"He's really an adorable baby," I went on. "Curious and full of energy. Did you know that a learning specialist designed these craft stations for toddlers his age because it's normal for them to get bored while waiting for a prolonged period?"

"But I want him to learn manners." Max's mother kept trying to lift him to his feet, but he curled himself up into a ball. "I want him to follow through in his life."

I felt Olivia the bitch struggling to get out and shriek, *Back off, Ubermom! Can't you see he's just a baby? And he'll remember more about manners if you quit complaining about his every move and give the kid some positive reinforcement!* Olivia the bitch would have chopped this woman into mincemeat and made a holiday pie out of her.

But Mrs. Claus was patient. Maybe it was all that pop-psychology training from ZZ, but I listened as Max's mother itemized her unrealistic goals for her two-year-old son.

The response that finally flew out of my mouth could have been scripted by ZZ. "It's admirable that you've set goals for your son. We all need to have challenges to meet. However, do you think Max would have the same goal as, say, our elf Regis here?"

I slung an arm around Regis's shoulder, hooking him into our conversation. He forced a grin for the woman. "Hi."

"Of course not," the woman said. "That would be inappropriate."

"That's just what I was thinking. And I see you're moving up in the line quickly. In the next station, Max has a chance to ride on Santa's train, full of toys. Would that be all right with you?"

She crossed her arms and looked down at the balled-up boy on the floor. "Would you like to ride on a train, sweetie?"

He nodded.

I extended a hand toward Max. "If you like, I'll show you the way to Santa's train station." He stood at attention and took my hand, suddenly on his best behavior. "Your mom will meet you at the end of the ride," I said, leading Max to the small train.

"Look, sweetpea, there's Mrs. Claus," someone called out, and a little girl with tiny dreadlocks clasped in pink barrettes waved at me.

I bent down to squeeze her hand, then kept moving down the line.

"I'd love to conduct a psychological study on how many of these brats actually make it off Mummy's couch," Regis said through gritted teeth as we backed away from the moving train. "And how many spend their lives on a psychiatrist's couch."

"The kids aren't the problem," I said, smiling at a handful of kids who tumbled over the puffy marshmallow cushions in the gumdrop garden. "It's their psycho parents."

"That and the fact that you're working a double shift. I can't believe they hired only one Mrs. Claus. What were they thinking?"

"Something about the fact that they had only one costume . . ." And with that I was summoned to the giant chair in front of Santa's hearth to have photos taken with some of the children. As the end of the night neared, I realized that our Santa Squad had worked well together. The elves and I had kept the lines moving, kept kids from melting down with boredom and acting out anxieties over meeting the big man from the North Pole.

Playing Mrs. Claus was worlds apart from my role of last year, dancing in the precision line with the Rockettes, and yet the hours spent among gingerbread walls, giant gumdrops, brightly wrapped gift boxes, and twinkling lights were cheerful, as if I'd been assigned to work in a Christmas spa.

As I smiled for the camera, I realized I didn't mind working the overtime. The extra money would come in handy, and already I was starting to feel comfortable in the Mrs. Claus suit, graceful in the role, and relieved that no one seemed to recognize the young Mrs. Claus as the evil "Olivia," ball-breaking Nutcracker of Baltimore.

That night, as we were getting ready to finish up, a woman waved frantically from the entrance,

"I know it's late, but I promised her she could see Santa . . ."

the woman said, wincing. "We got held up in housewares, and then she fell and hurt her knee, and store security wanted to take a report . . ."

"Lexie wants to see Santa," the little girl sobbed, strands of her pale yellow hair sticking to her wet cheeks.

Regis and I exchanged a concerned look. "I'm not sure that Santa is still here," I said cautiously. Most of the guys had punched out, and the last time I saw ZZ he was heading toward the elevator.

"I'll go find him," Regis said, jumping over one of the ginger-bread barricades.

"I am so sorry," the woman said.

"Not to worry," I lied, "I'm just hoping my elf can find Santa before he heads back to the North Pole for the night."

"Want to see Santa!" the little girl pleaded.

"Just follow Mrs. Claus," her mother said.

I led them to Santa's gingerbread house through the winter landscape that seemed almost magical in the dark, quiet store. The track of Christmas music was still running, with a bell choir version of "The First Noel" ringing softly. Although normally the visitors waited outside, I decided to take the woman and her daughter into ZZ's room. Lexie took one look inside at the empty chair and a new wave of tears hit her. "Where's Santa?" she sobbed.

"Santa should be back in a minute," I said, as Lexie's mom rubbed her shoulders consolingly.

Trying to think of a distraction, I searched the room, its small tree lit with colored lights, its gold garland swirling down onto the gifts spread in a circle under the tree. Beside the tree was a small table where stuffed bears sat, having a tea party. I asked Lexie if she wanted to play with the bears, maybe have a tea party with them, but she shook her head and pointed to a small book-shelf.

"Lexie wants to read."

I doubted that she could read a book, but I let her pick one out. She brought it over and held it out to me. "You read, Mrs. Claus."

I glanced at her mother, who nodded pleadingly. Feeling unsure, I sat down in Santa's chair, and Lexie put her patent-leather shoe beside my knee and hoisted herself up into my lap. The little girl felt more solid than she looked and smelled like vanilla wafers and baby shampoo.

"See my bandages?" she said, showing me her knee, where three fluorescent pink bandages adhered lengthwise. "Lexie fell down and made a miscrape."

"A miscrape?" I asked.

Lexie's mother smiled. "I said you scraped your knee, hon."

The little girl explained, "My knee hurt very, very much. I cried and cried and got scared, but Mommy said it's just a miscrape."

"I see." It sounded like she'd had a hectic evening, and I worried that it would get worse when she learned there'd be no Santa tonight. "You must be a very brave girl."

She nodded, sighing. "Yes, I am."

Taking a deep breath of little girl, I fumbled the book open and began to read. The book seemed too long and meandering for a kid Lexie's age, a version of the Gingerbread Man, and as I read Lexie seemed to sink into my arms like a stone. I was three-quarters of the way through when Regis appeared at the door, shaking his head.

"Sorry. Santa seems to be gone for the night."

"It's okay," Lexie's mother said. "She's sound asleep."

From behind the little girl I could see the easy rise and fall of the velvet buttons on her coat. "She must have been tired. Can I carry her downstairs for you?"

I don't know what possessed me to offer, but Lexie's mother nodded, thanking me with a tired look. We talked quietly about the best deals at Rossman's on the way down in the elevator, and when I turned to her at the door, her eyes glistened with tears.

"Thank you so much," she said, her voice cracking. "I'm sorry, sorry to keep you late. I always seem to be running late these days, and . . ." She let out a quavering breath. "That single-parent thing. But I appreciate you taking the extra time. Lexie loves it when people read to her."

Seeing her stress, her anxious emotion, made me choke up, too. "It's my pleasure, really," I said. "Your daughter is a little delight." I transferred the little girl into the woman's arms, somewhat awkwardly, and Lexie sniffed slightly but didn't wake up. "I hope her miscrapes get better soon."

As I watched her go, I wondered if I was complaining a little too much over my life when other people had untold things going on. I headed toward the bus stop with my hair tucked into my coat and a beret pulled low over my forehead to cover my "Olivia-ness."

Olivia's life was riddled with mis-crapes, but Mrs. Claus . . . Here was a woman who had chosen wisely through her life, a woman who instinctively knew how to help other people.

For now, I was happy to be Mother Christmas.

10

On Saturday, Rossman's held its grand opening, complete with a ribbon-cutting ceremony, free Christmas cookies, a free concert on the ice from the Baltimore Symphony Orchestra, and fireworks over the harbor in the late afternoon. Of course, no one on the Santa Squad was able to see the concert or fireworks since the line of children waiting to see Santa never let up, but I didn't mind at all. This was the opening I'd hoped for—crowded, festive, busy. With a reception like this, Rossman's stood a chance of surviving in downtown Baltimore.

The ribbon-cutting ceremony in front of the store was attended by the architect, my old pal Woody, or rather, Sherwood Cruise, a few Orioles and Ravens players, and the mayor himself, whose jazz band was slated to perform later in the store restaurant. I tinkled my fingers at Woody across the plaza in front of the store while the mayor spoke to the crowd, hundreds of people thrumming along the marble stairs and cobblestone square. I think Woody nodded back, but then maybe he was just ducking his head against the wind that had begun blowing in off the water that morning, lifting skirts and swirling debris in grand city fashion. The whole scene reminded me of a political rally, complete with applause and cheers and music booming from high-amped speakers. The big difference here was that these people were motivated not by free speech but by a free cookie and a chance to get a jump on their Christmas shopping.

A little thrill had rippled through the Santa Squad that morning when we learned that Evelyn and Karl Rossman, of the department store dynasty, had flown in from Chicago to take part in the store's opening ceremony.

"Do you think we'll get to meet them?" Skinny Stu wondered. "I've always been a fan."

"Like royalty!" Chet beamed. "My wife won't believe this."

"But she'll see it on the news," ZZ said. "I understand all the major networks in Baltimore have their satellite trucks parked in front of the store."

Although the Rossmans were aging royalty now, Evelyn seemed quite gracious, with ivory skin like porcelain, and Karl seemed so earnest when he explained to the crowd that ribbon cuttings were becoming a lost art.

"Nowadays, they take a giant pair of ceremonial scissors and smack the ribbon down. Not here at Rossman's! We guarantee, no lip-synching, no fake scissors. Today we'll be cutting the ribbon with a pair of scissors we sell in the store, which you can use for anything from butterflying a chicken to trimming poster-board for school projects. They come apart for easy cleaning in the dishwasher." He demonstrated. "Voilà!"

Evelyn nudged closer to the microphone. "Karl, I thought you retired from that sales position."

"Can't take the sales out of the boy," he joked, turning the microphone over to the mayor.

"Do you believe in Baltimore?" the mayor asked, smiling as the crowd roared its response. He talked about the continuing pledge of Baltimoreans working together for safer streets, new opportunities, and the hope of a better future for the children of Baltimore.

As he spoke, I flashed back to the time when my parents had purchased the house on Lombard, when every third house was boarded up and occupied by vagrants or drug users. I'd been sent to Catholic school because the local schools were in turmoil, the reading and math scores substandard. And as I walked two blocks to the bus stop, I had to pass an overgrown alley littered with shattered glass and trash, sometimes crawling with rats.

So much had changed.

Now my mother's Butchers Hill neighborhood was a showcase, its annual fall house tour a magnet for decorators and historians. With gentrification, the vacant homes in her neighborhood had been renovated and were now occupied by residents who cared about their communities. Debris was cleared from alleyways by neighbors who took pride in their homes. Real estate prices had risen steadily, as had test scores for first and second graders. One brick at a time, one child at a time, my old hometown was improving.

The mayor summed up his comments, saying that the battle for Baltimore was a continuing effort—a long-term commitment. He celebrated Rossman's share in that commitment and pointed to this department store as further evidence that Baltimore was the place to be.

As people applauded, I glanced across at the Rossmans and the mayor and Woody and felt my eyes sting with tears. I quickly rubbed them away, embarrassed at misting up over my feelings for a city, especially a city I didn't claim as my home anymore. But I couldn't help but feel for the schoolkids and the people who took charge of their neighborhoods, picking up trash and joining citizens on patrol.

Okay, maybe I wanted to take Manhattan, but for now, in this moment, Baltimore was a good place to be, and I was proud to be a part of it, even if my contribution was to play Mrs. Claus and perk up a few little kids.

After that there were a few carols from a children's choir, and finally, drums rolled as the Rossmans stepped forward and cleanly snipped through the red and gold ribbon with that pair of shiny kitchen scissors. "Eighteen ninety-nine in our housewares department!" Karl said proudly as he held up the scissors.

After the noontime ceremonies, Santaland was flooded with

children, the lines extending to the gingerbread maze for the first time. My training kicked in, and I moved through the line, teasing the children and asking them questions, sending sections off to craft stations where they could kill time making name tags, sending other sections off to pass the time riding Santa's toy train. For the most part the compartmentalized queues worked efficiently, and I was amazed to see that little children could endure a solid hour of waiting as long as they were distracted.

Time passed quickly for me, too, and before I knew it the crowds were thinning. Most families were home for dinner hour.

One of the elves stepped in front of me, blocking entry to the toy train terminal. "You've been at it since noon, Olivia. Go take a break."

"You know, Shayna, I think that's a good idea. We don't want the little ones to have visions of Mrs. Claus fainting in their heads."

She laughed. "Whoo, no. That would not be one for the Rossman's memory book."

In the employee lounge I exchanged my Mrs. Claus top for a black button-down fleece and headed up to the store restaurant for a quick bite. The mayor's jazz band was just packing up its gear, and there was a cluster of activity near the sound equipment as customers vied for a few words with the popular man. I ducked into the self-serve line for a Caesar salad with chicken, emerging into the quieter section of the dining room lined with poinsettias and white holiday lights. As I moved past a table of business suits, someone called my name.

"Olivia?"

Bracing myself for a barrage of insults based on the show, I turned and realized it was Woody. Sherwood Cruise, architect of the month.

"Oh, I didn't notice you. I mean, I didn't notice you were dining with friends."

"We were just having coffee, waiting for the mayor." He gestured toward the empty chair. "Have a seat. It's good to see you."

I moved to the empty chair, trying not to gape at the beautiful people flanking my seventh-grade sweetie. The man on his left looked like he might have just stepped out of *GQ,* and the woman on Woody's right could have been Business Suit Barbie. Short blond hair in a fashionable cut, chiseled cheekbones, the dignified look that I envied. At the moment she was laughing over some exchange between the mayor and a young boy in a baseball cap.

Funny how you run into an old boyfriend and immediately sense that the thrill is gone . . . until you see them with someone else.

"Are you finished for the day?" Woody asked me.

"Just on break." I nodded toward the others, but he didn't seem to get it. Giving up, I extended my hand. "Hi, I'm Woody's friend Olivia Todd."

The woman shook my hand, her eyes opening wide. "Oh, don't let us interrupt." She gave a quick shake, then smoothly rose from the table.

The man in the suit also got up. "You have a good evening," he said warmly as he started across the dining room and paused a few feet behind the mayor.

"They're the mayor's security team," Woody explained. "Bodyguards. I was waiting for the mayor to finish up so that we could go over a few projects."

"Oh." The sound came out more like the native "Oow . . ." but I didn't want to think about it too much. "Aren't you the entrepreneur. But taking a meeting on a Saturday night?"

He shrugged. "Nine to five is boring. You know me, I never did well inside the box."

"None of us did well inside the box, but most adolescents grow out of that."

"What happened to us? Why didn't we grow up and begin conforming? Neither of us got real jobs."

"Woody, I may be pursuing the life of the tap-dance kid, but look at you. Architecture school, which has got to be more math than most people can tolerate in one lifetime. And now dinner with the mayor? Hardly the work of a rebel."

He twirled the pepper shaker on the table. "So, you've been on the job here a few days now. By the way, I'm digging the Mrs. Claus suit."

I crunched on a mouthful of lettuce, nodding happily.

"So what do you think of my work? I mean, how is the whole Santaland thing working out with the design of the third floor?"

"It's a great space. The maze for the waiting area works well, and the train is a real crowd pleaser."

He grinned. "Great, glad to hear it. I wrote a proposal to keep the train running after the holidays. That whole area was designed for baby-sitting while parents are shopping, but Rossman's is still looking into it. Liability issues, I think."

We talked about possible design changes, the need for more bathrooms on that floor, the need to move the dressing rooms for the Santa Squad a little closer to Santaland. "Can't have a little kid running into five Santas on the escalator," I explained.

He nodded, his dark eyes squinting as he took it all in. I imagined he might have the same look as he shared this information with the Rossmans and pitched some minor design changes. I didn't know what Woody's contract with Rossman's entailed, but it seemed to me he was sticking on the project longer than most architects, with care toward function more than structure. This was a man who cared about the building and his vision for the people who used it.

I wanted to fall back in love with him right there and then, but a very rude woman was suddenly leaning between us, in my face.

"If you like New York so much, *Olivia,*" she said, "how 'bout a slice of New York cheesecake?"

I turned and only got half a glimpse of her when a plate of cheesecake filled my line of vision and wonked my face with its sweet, cheesy, moist mass.

There were cries and gasps of "Oh my gosh!" "Did you see that?"

I dug two wads of cheese paste from my eyes and blinked at my attacker, a woman with a blond beehive do and too much blue eye shadow. "Do I know you?" I asked her.

"You know my type," she said. "Don't you remember what you called us in the show? Balti-morons."

The show. Of course. The wicked Olivia.

I was about to defend myself, to recuse myself from Bobby's skewering spoof of this city, but suddenly it seemed like such a lost cause that I just scraped off some cheesecake with my fingertips and took a taste.

"Are you okay, Liv?" Woody asked.

"I could be worse," I said. "I could've moved to Boston. Then I'd be wearing Boston cream pie, and brown is not my color."

In the aftermath of the attack I came to think of as the Cheesecake Toss, a dozen things happened at once. A few people called the police on their cells, while the mayor's plainclothes security guards moved in and handcuffed the tosser.

The mayor was whisked out of sight, off to a secure location, lest there be a second deranged doughnut flinger or pie pelter lurking in the kitchen.

The attacker's friends sat down beside me and tried to rationalize their girl Doris's behavior, explaining she was "pretty darned serious about her TV shows," how she'd been having a bad run with her husband getting transferred up to Mount Carmel, Pennsylvania, "And him 'specting her to leave her family and all and move up to that godforsaken backwoods and all."

Many of the diners pushed in to surround our table, some curious, some sympathetic. The guy bussing tables eyed me with suspicion, as if I were a ketchup graffiti artist, but Woody sent him for a few hot towels, which he brought promptly. Through it all, Woody remained beside me, the calm voice of reason in a sea of hysterical, shrill voices.

By the time the police arrived I didn't want to press charges, and I convinced them to release Doris, who promptly burst into tears and told me I wasn't at all like my character on the show. "You're a real decent human being," she sobbed.

We hugged and everyone applauded.

"And that's what this is all about?" Woody said aloud. "Bobby's show?"

I had forgotten that Woody knew Bobby. They had both gone to Mt. St. Joe's, and even though Bobby was two years older, Woody would have witnessed the bohemian artist period, the leather-jacketed bad boy of Baltimore phase, the quick cleanup and tutorials to land a college scholarship at the end of junior year. What a relief! Woody was totally wise to Bobby's act.

"I don't understand that at all," Woody went on, looking Doris in the eye. "If you don't like the show, why don't you speak to the man who created it?"

"We don't care about a bunch of writers," one of Doris's friends said. "Everybody knows that the bad girl herself is here in town. Why waste your time on a bunch of writerly types when you can have the Nutcracker herself?"

"Still . . ." Woody shook his head, letting out a long breath. "When I saw the show, I never thought it was you, Olivia. Not for a minute."

"I love this man!" I said, throwing myself against his chest for a big hug. He smelled surprisingly sweet, sort of like baby powder. No lingering traces of the seventh-grade grass-stain-and-sweat smells.

Well, of course not, I thought, stepping back to smile up at him and wipe a smudge of cheesecake from the lapel of his suit. Why did I keep trying to plunk this man back in the seventh grade?

As most of the people moved off and Doris and her friends began to speculate where the show might go in the second episode, I realized I had to get back to work.

"Time to hit the showers," I told Woody, glad that he'd had the foresight to install a few showers in the employee locker rooms. "It may take some deep cleansing to remove the cheesecake masque."

"Thanks for sharing your dessert with me," he teased, looking down at his suit. "A ribbon cutting and a flying cheesecake all in the same day. Way too much excitement for a nerdy architect."

"Nerdy? You're going to be on the front page of the *Baltimore Sun* tomorrow. Me? I may go down in infamy as the craziest woman in city history."

He frowned. "Actually, you don't compare with Sewer Sadie."

I rubbed my chin with one of the soggy towels. "I'm afraid to ask."

"In 1909, when the city was just completing a brand spanking-new sewer system, a photojournalist named Sadie Miller decided to check it out firsthand. She climbed into an old jalopy with her husband and some friends, and they cruised through miles of sewer pipe. When they hit the end of the line, they realized their car was too wide to turn around."

My jaw dropped. "Yuck! What happened to them?"

"They had to back out—six miles of curving pipe. Plus a flat tire."

I could imagine the choice words that passed between Sadie and her husband that day. "So you're saying I should be reassured that I'm not stuck in a poop chute like Sewer Sadie?"

"It's all relative."

I headed off, then pivoted and stepped back to him. "Why don't you stop by and see how Santaland is working firsthand?" I thought of his suggestion of coffee the other day, how I'd brushed him off so quickly. Nice move, dummy-head.

"I hear it's pretty busy down there."

"I've got an in with the big guy. I could get your name on the 'Nice' list."

"You'd do that for me?" He laughed. "Why don't we meet outside the store, away from our mutual clients. But wait, aren't you working, like, ninety-hour days right now?"

"I don't start till noon. How about breakfast?" Maybe I sounded way too eager, but when you've been pied in the face in front of a guy, it breaks down certain barriers of etiquette in my book.

"That might work." He plunked my cell number into his cell and promised to call me and set it up.

"Don't forget," I said, lifting a stiff lock of hair away from my face. "You wouldn't want to cheese off Mrs. Claus."

"Been there, seen that."

I smiled as I headed toward the elevator. The Wood Man and I still had something. Definitely something.

11

After opening week, the number of children visiting Santaland tapered off. Gone were the overwhelming crowds, though there were enough children in line to keep me on my toes.

"It will be slow now through Thanksgiving," ZZ predicted. "Then, soon as December starts . . ." He clapped his hands together. "Whammo!"

True to his word, he had joined me last week on a trip to my mother's house, where he had swirled cabernet and discussed the hidden mythology of the film *The Wizard of Oz*, which had been Mom's theme that night. ZZ had stayed well into the evening, then asked my mother if she wouldn't mind another visit, next time in the morning, before Santaland opened for the day. Mom seemed to enjoy his company, and I decided this was one situation I could back away from for the time being.

Back at Rossman's I used the lull to refine my "Mrs. Claus" style with the younger kids, the ones who ducked behind Daddy's legs or clung to Mom's coat. Not having much experience with children, I initially fell into the habit of raising my voice to a giddy, baby-talk mode and leaning in toward the little cuties.

Not a particularly effective approach.

The goo-goo face usually sent them burrowing for cover. Sometimes it provoked tears.

I called Kate at the aquarium and asked if I could borrow her nieces and nephews for a workshop. When I explained my predicament, she told me I was focusing too much on the age difference, not enough on methods of communication.

"Many animals are intimidated by direct confrontation. That in-your-face thing is the approach used by the alpha male in the wild. It's the challenge to do battle, and with you being so much bigger than the kids, you can imagine how intimidated they feel."

Hmm. "Okay, so what can I do? Always keep back fifteen feet like I'm following a fire truck?"

"It might help to get down on their level. The dolphins seem to relate best when we're in the water with them. Try to get down on their level, not hover over them. And don't try to talk them out of feeling shy or intimidated. There's nothing worse than having an adult tell you not to feel something you're feeling. Instead, let them know their feeling is valid and okay. You could say, 'I know how it feels to be scared,' or 'Sometimes I still feel shy.'"

"How is it that we went to the same college and you are a freakin' wealth of information and I'm a big boob?"

"Too much television, Liv. It rots the brain. Hey, have you heard from the Wood Man yet?"

"He called. Right now we're still playing phone tag." I tried to appear casual, though I'd been wondering why Woody didn't just drop by Santaland. He knew where to find me. "How's Turtle? What's the latest?"

"I can't talk about it now."

"Uh-oh. Are you okay?"

"Not great, but I'll fill you in when I see you tomorrow. We're still going out, right? Boycotting the next episode of *The Nutcracker*. Isn't that the plan?"

"Absolutely. I could use a night out, and I refuse to contribute to the viewership of that show. Do you know that the guy in the coffee shop next door still refuses to sell me a bagel? And people pick me out as the Nutcracker every day."

"You're a celebrity!"

"Then why do they treat me as if I'm from *America's Most Wanted?*" I sighed. "At least customers don't recognize me when I'm in the Mrs. Claus costume."

"You're a Christmas Jekyll and Hyde."

"Kate, if you don't stop being so perky I'll have to kill you."

"Sorry. I'm overcompensating for my bad mood. Let me go jump in with the dolphins before I start spout off Hallmark phrases."

Thanksgiving came and went with typically heightened family stresses all around. Kate regretted agreeing to spend the day with Turtle's family. They didn't serve turkey, the men sat in the den watching games while the women scoured pots in the kitchen, and for dessert—frozen pies. Lanessa felt pressure from her married sisters to "spawn wildlife," as she puts it, and before she left her mother's house there was an argument because Nessa's sister let the nieces play with their dolls in the back of her BMW and consequently they spilled their juice boxes on the leather upholstery. Bonnie enjoyed spending the day with Jonah but felt guilty about neglecting her family.

With the long hours I was putting in at Rossman's, Thanksgiving Day had sprung itself on me with surprising swiftness. The night before I had called my mother with some degree of panic since I hadn't done any grocery shopping at all, but she'd assured me not to worry, that she and "Hank" had it under control.

Hank. It was still hard for me to think of ZZ that way, but apparently that was the name he went by outside Rossman's, where he would always be "Head Santa."

Thursday afternoon I got off the bus on Lombard Street expecting a quiet dinner, but a dressed-up couple was ahead of me, passing through Mom's double doors. From the front vestibule I could see that the leaves had been added to the dining-room table, which was set for more than a dozen with the good china. Classical music and laughter spilled out from the parlor, where I recognized friends, neighbors, and Mom's colleagues from the university. A couple from the university squeezed into the vestibule, admiring one of Mom's statues, and the two men from Mom's bridge club in Patterson Park wanted to know where to put the cranberry relish. In the kitchen, the head of the Butchers Hill Neighborhood Association was cracking walnuts with her grown son, and she winked at me, wryly asking, "I suspect you've had it with nut cracking, eh, Olivia?" One of the profs was handing out mimosas in tall crystal glasses, and I gratefully took a sip, using the moment to regain my composure and balance.

Of course Mom had a houseful of guests! Just because she couldn't cope with venturing out didn't mean she wanted to be cut off from the world. Subconsciously I had thought that Mom was so bad off, trapped in this house; I had forgotten that she possessed the charm to transform it into an intellectual haven.

"I can't bear to think of anyone alone on Thanksgiving," she was saying to one of the neighbors, Carol Sawiki. "When my husband was alive we began the custom of inviting strays and loners, our own lonely hearts club, and over the years it's extended to neighbors and friends."

"It's a great tradition," ZZ said as he set a plate of crudités on the kitchen counter. "Sometimes the most cohesive families are the ones who come together by choice."

That night, after the guests left and I was sipping wine with my mother and ZZ, I couldn't help but ask Mom about Darcy, her new therapist. To my surprise, she was willing to talk about it.

"There's actually an interesting therapy being used. In theory, they break the huge panic monster into a bunch of small but pesky dwarves. The notion being that the panic is too overwhelming to fight, but each smaller component of it is somewhat manageable."

ZZ was nodding as if it was familiar ground.

"Dwarves and a monster?" I tucked my legs under me. "Sounds like a Grimm's fairy tale."

"Darcy is taking me though a cognitive-behavior therapy called MAP." Mom's pale gray eyes held a glimmer of fear, something I was not used to seeing. "That stands for Mastery of Your Anxiety and Panic. The therapy teaches you to slow down the panic response, to break it into different elements so that they can be addressed one at a time. As opposed to the huge, overwhelming panic monster that no one can fight."

"I'm so glad you're doing this," I said quietly.

"Darcy was a find." She turned to ZZ. "Thanks to you, Hank."

"I'm glad she's working out for you, Claire." Stroking his beard thoughtfully, he seemed so different from the first day I'd met him. Civilized and even intellectual. *Note to self: try not to make snap judgments.* "Darcy and I did our clinical work together in Miami. We're friends from way back. Like family."

"Do you have any family, Hank?" Mom asked.

"Blood relatives, no. But I have family all over the country. The ever-extended family of friends."

His observation resonated for me over the next few days as I continued to fight off the Olivia haters each morning, then settled into my large, magnanimous role as Mrs. Claus, the nurturing goddess to parents and children. The first days after Thanksgiving are some of the busiest for retailers, and as I wove through crowds of children, sending them to craft stations or helping them board the train, I thought of how family had been redefined for me over the last few years. In the years since my father had died we'd lost touch with his family, two brothers, lobstermen in Maine. My mother occasionally talked to her sister in Ohio, but I hadn't seen my cousins for years, and if I had to summon someone in a crisis, I knew it would be one of my three friends, the three phone numbers I knew by heart.

I felt fortunate to have my urban family here. Even when the rest of Baltimore's population had turned against me, my friends were there for me.

Would I miss them when I headed back to New York?

Although I hadn't mentioned it, I had moved up my appointment with the orthopedic surgeon to the week before Christmas.

Once he gave me his blessing I would go back to full-scale work-outs to get ready for the New York stage again. And one morning before work I gathered my nerve and called the Rockettes director, Mrs. Atwater, on the phone. I'd been doing my physical-therapy exercises in my apartment, and I looked down at the leg warmers, thinking of the old days when I'd worn them in the New York rehearsal studios. Mrs. Atwater seemed happy to hear from me and hinted that my audition would be a cinch.

A cinch.

A mixture of excitement and dread swept through me as I hung up the phone. This was what I'd been waiting for, what I'd been working for, and somehow the prospect of going back to New York made me feel a little queasy.

My parents used to call it Olivia's lament—this devastating in-decisiveness that started to peak when I was in junior high. I would struggle with a decision, make my choice, and then began the tears and lamentations and regrets over the choice I had made. It happened with clothes and prom dates, trips and classes. Spring ski trip or Ocean City? Whatever I decided, I spent a day or two crying over the fact that the beach was so pretty in spring. Or that this would be my last chance to ski this year, how did I blow that?

Olivia's lament.

One year, when Bonnie and Lanessa and I were caught up in Easter dresses—and does that tell you we did not have a lot going on?—my mother took me shopping and I narrowed the field down to two dresses, one lace-covered loose shift in my fa-vorite shade of lavender, the other a pink, pinstriped cream puff of a dress with a drop waist and puffy sleeves. I must have tried those two dresses on six times in the Hecht's dressing room. With my mother's patience wearing thin, I finally chose the lavender shift, sure that it was the dress for me because it was my favorite color. But even as I walked to the parking lot with the bag clutched in my hand, misgivings attacked. The dress was so formless, so unshaped, it took away the few subtle curves I'd de-veloped. It made me look like an elephant; it made me look like a baby.

My mother endured two hours of my sobbing that night, determined not to buckle to "Olivia's lament." The next day, we went back to Hecht's and exchanged the dress.

And now, at least ten years later, I felt that same sense of indecisiveness over the future. Not that there was any question about going back to New York, but I did have a growing sense of the things I would miss once I left Baltimore.

Then again, I could walk the streets of New York without being sprayed by shaving cream. If I'd ever had a choice, Bobby had made it for me when he named that character after me.

Just point me north . . .

12

"If you don't like Jimmy's Grill, just don't say anything," Woody said as we walked down Broadway, the wide main street of Fells Point, one December morning. "I love this place. It's open all night, and I come here when I'm stuck on a project. Helen, the woman who runs the place, doesn't care if I sit for hours over a cup."

"I'm sure it's fine," I said, noticing the way the sun cast pasty light over the cobblestone lane as we headed toward the water. "Besides, I'm not picky."

"Not what I've heard."

"You must be talking about that show, which I have no affiliation with."

"Actually, I was thinking of something your mother told me—how you can never make up your mind."

Olivia's lament!

"That's so not true."

"Come on, Liv, you never could. Remember when you could only try out for one team—basketball or softball? How you kept changing your mind? You drove Sister Catherine Charles crazy. Right here." He reached for a weathered screen door with a

Plexiglas plate tucked in, and I realized he'd been talking about this downtrodden coffee shop on the corner. All this time, I never knew it had a name.

"Ach! *This* Jimmy's? It's the worst."

His eyebrows shot up as he held the door open for me.

"Kidding. I've never been in here."

"Well, be nice and we might be able to avoid another cheese-cake facial." There was an old luncheonette counter on the left; the rest of the spare room was filled with plastic-covered tables and wooden chairs. The most upscale item in the entire diner, with its scarred wood floor and dark three-quarter paneling, was probably the old Coca-Cola clock on one wall. He leaned close to the counter to call something to the waitress reaching into the refrigerated pie case, then waved me on toward the back of the room. "Let me show you my favorite table."

The place was more than half empty, so we could have had our choice, but Woody put his worn leather softsider on a table in the corner and took a seat under a clock made from a kitchen plate and fork. "I make it a point not to look at the clock. It just pressurizes things when I'm trying to think. Some of the other patrons, in the middle of the night, they've got to get back to Johns Hopkins or on the city desk at the *Sun*. They need the clock."

"This is fun." I sat down opposite him, better off watching the clock since I had to be at work by noon. "I like seeing you in your niche, with your Woody idiosyncracies."

"Oh, do I amuse you?" he said archly, a poor mafioso imitation. "I don't come here in the morning so often, but I know the former mayor and his cronies used to favor that round table in the corner." He handed me a menu. "And I'm a sucker for bacon and eggs, but the oatmeal is pretty good, too."

"When did you become such a creature of habit?"

"Honestly? After my divorce." I must have looked shocked, because he added, "You didn't know about that, huh? Yep, I guess a lot's happened since seventh grade."

The waitress, Joanne, came over and took our orders without writing anything down, then moved off casually.

"So what's been keeping you so busy these past few weeks?" I asked him.

"Besides Rossman's? The city has a project in Sandtown—a community center—and I've been trying to get a better feel for that area so I can draft a design sample. I'm working on a few renovations for private homes, but no one wants to talk about ripping their house apart until after the holidays. And there's a property for sale here in Fells Point, over near the old wharf. I thought we might want to walk over and take a look after we eat."

"Sure. I'm still exploring the waterfront here. Some of my favorite shops and pubs closed down when the hurricane flooded these streets."

"So you were the smart one," Woody said, balancing a spoon between his fingers. "You and Bobby never got married."

"Stuck on the serious stuff? No, thank God, we didn't. How long were you married?"

"Three years. Liz and I were still finishing college while she planned the wedding."

"Wow." I curled the corner of the plastic menu. "Was it rough? Did you stay friends?"

"The relationship stuff . . ." He shrugged. "You get over it. But the heartbreak of it is that I rarely get to see my daughter. Chloe is four now. She lives with her mother in Rhode Island."

"You're a daddy? Woody, I didn't know . . ." I pretended to look at the menu so that he wouldn't read the jealousy in my eyes. Married and a parent? If you were keeping score, Woody would be way ahead in the life-experience category. Of course, he'd probably lose points for being divorced, but I couldn't get over how he'd lived so much while I was perfecting my eye-high kicks.

We talked about Chloe for a while—her interests, her fears, her two-week visit the previous summer. I thought of the kids I'd been working with at Rossman's, Lexie, whose mother was feeling the strain of single parenting, of a little girl who'd told me that her daddy moved out and maybe someday he would decide to come home again. It was heartrending, that tug and shift of relationships, a difficult dance in which no one was sure of all the right steps. Watching the light in his eyes as he talked about Chloe, I sensed Woody's care for his daughter, along with his loss of control.

"But you struggle with the guilt?" I asked.

"Long-distance parenting . . ." He shrugged. "It sucks. And I still have a lot of anger toward her mother. Liz grew up in Rhode Island, and once she got pregnant she wouldn't hear of living anywhere else. She wanted me to leave Baltimore, but . . ."

"You stayed."

"This city is so wrapped up in my identity, my whole life is here."

"But—and I'm playing devil's advocate here—did you consider moving? Trying someplace different? It could be better."

"I moved to Providence for six months, but it didn't work for me."

I loved his honesty, the fact that he'd learned this painful fact about himself, though it struck me as odd that I wasn't repulsed. This was a man who was stuck in Baltimore—a most unappealing quality in my mind, but Woody wore it well.

He squinted at me, as if framing my face in his mind. "Olivia Todd. I can't unglue myself from this place and you couldn't wait to tear off. What the hell are you doing here, anyway?"

"It's temporary. I'm heading back after the holidays, but I needed a place to hole up and recuperate. I broke my ankle on the ice last spring."

He winced. "And you had to give up dancing?"

"Temporarily. But the physical therapy's been going well. I thought it would be easiest to come back, stay with Mom. But Mom has her own issues, and the day I moved back I found out that Bobby and his wife are here from L.A. filming all over the city. And suddenly, my life is a sitcom and I'm the starring villainess. Thank God for my friends, and for Rossman's. The Mrs. Claus gig saved my sanity."

He bit into a crispy strip of bacon. "It's a wonderful life."

"And changing every day," I said, thinking of my upcoming doctor's appointment, of the green light I was waiting for. My happiness hinged on it.

"At least your ankle is healing, right? You'll dance again?"

"Definitely. But look at you, Woody, big-shot architect. The nuns at St. Rose of Lima would be proud."

"Nah. Just eking out a mouselike existence, mostly work. I'll probably end up like Godefroy, a shunned municipal architect, up to my knees in mud laying sewer pipe."

"Godefroy? Refresh my memory."

"After Latrobe, Maximilian Godefroy was Baltimore's most prolific architect in the nineteenth century. He sought exile here from France after opposing Napoleon. He and Latrobe were good friends until they argued over whose designs would be used for the Merchants' Exchange. He designed quite a few churches here, the Washington Monument, the Battle Monument. But his differences with Benjamin Latrobe seemed to define his downfall. Embittered and vindictive, he blamed Latrobe for his inability to find more work in America. He packed up his family and sailed back to Europe, but his daughter died of yellow fever on the journey, and when he arrived in England he was treated like a criminal, his drawings seized by customs officials. It's not clear how he died, but he ended up working in the trenches, a municipal architect in France." Woody shook his head. "It's a wonderful life, huh?"

"You architects do lead glamourous lives," I teased. Through my mother's passion for Benjamin Latrobe, often considered to be America's Leonardo, a botanist and designer and artist, I had learned that he also felt undervalued and underpaid for much of his life. He'd commented that both the working class and the wealthy shunned him.

"Sometimes I think about Godefroy, how the breach with Latrobe defined his life, how one event can define a person's life."

"Yes, but it could have been different, the outcome would have changed if Godefroy let it go," I said. "If he *refused* to let it define his life . . ."

"Exactly! We can't control the events in our lives, but we can control our response to them, whether we learn from them, whether we let them set us back, change the course of our lives."

I sat back in the wooden chair as the underlying truth hit me. "You're right. I get it." And I could see it in my own life, in Bobby's show, in the negative attention and nasty attacks that rattled me . . . because *I* let them unnerve me.

"This was very good oatmeal," I said, resting my spoon on the table. "They should add a little slogan on the menu: Enlightenment in every bowl."

13

For days after that breakfast with Woody I was walking on air. Something about the unconventional meeting—breakfast and a walking tour—had intrigued me after more than a handful of noisy club dates in New York, during which the ritualistic process of drinks, light conversation, and noncommittal sex were supposed to play out. And there was something else about Woody—the substance, the spirituality. I couldn't quite put my finger on it, but the depth of our conversation had left me feeling liberated as I walked down the street in my own skin and able to relax as I played Mrs. Claus, nursing scraped knees, soothing lost children, entertaining the bored.

When I met my friends that Tuesday night at Peter's, a funky neighborhood bar/restaurant in Fells Point, I couldn't help but bubble over with talk of Woody. "We left Jimmy's and we walked to this property he wanted to check out, and all along the way he pointed out architectural features unique to early Baltimore." We were waiting for a table at the bar, an aged wooden slab with stools that resembled seats pulled right off old Harleys. "Like Shakespeare Street, with its local red brick and marble slab porches. The mansard roofs and the different types of brickwork, Flemish and Dutch cross bond. I used to ignore it all when Mom was lecturing, but somehow, now it interests me."

"Because Woody was talking," Bonnie said dreamily.

Lanessa rolled her eyes. "Two people find each other through architecture? Very touching, hon, but when I'm on a date you won't catch me talking gargoyles and mansard roofs."

"Are you seeing him again?" Bonnie asked.

I nodded. "Sure. Though it's sort of hard to find a time. A lot of his evenings are committed to community meetings. He's making a bid on a building for the city, and he feels obliged to engage the people it will involve."

"This boy may have political aspirations," Lanessa said.

"Why don't you meet in the morning again?" Bonnie suggested.

"I thought of that." I shrugged. "We could do it. But . . ." I lowered my voice. "It's not the most romantic lead-in. Sort of awkward."

"Oh, please." Lanessa lifted the olive skewer from her martini. "No need to act so coy. Just tell him to meet at your place. You make the coffee, he can bring bagels and a box of condoms."

We laughed. "Sure. Mrs. Scholinsky would love that."

"She'll never hear you over the racket she makes," Bonnie added.

I turned to Kate. "You're awfully quiet today. Everything okay?"

Her lips pressed into a fine line, she nodded. "I've got news, sort of a bomb, and I don't know how to say it."

The three of us stared at her. "Well?" I prodded.

"I might be moving to San Diego with Turtle," she said. "They've offered him a job, and I've applied to work with their marine mammals. I'm flying out for an interview in January, but Turtle's new boss seems to think I've got the job." She shrugged. "I guess I'm moving to the West Coast."

We shrieked and cheered and hugged wildly. Behind the bar, the tattooed waiter folded his arms and grinned in amusement. "Chick love," he muttered to some guy at the bar.

As we moved to a table, we prodded Kate for details, details. "I'm excited about the possibilities. Nervous and worried. Feeling a little guilty about being excited and about leaving you guys. Worried about living so far from my family. And since it's still not definite, I can barely talk about it."

"I'll bet Turtle is thrilled," Bonnie said.

She nodded. "He sees this as an adventure, while I see all the things that could go wrong. I guess he's just more of a risk taker."

"You'll be fine," I told her. "Look at me. I made the leap and I never wanted to come back."

"Oh, no. Don't start chanting the 'Baltimore sucks' mantra again," Lanessa told me.

"I'm not complaining," I said. "Just want Kate to know that there are so many exciting adventures ahead for her, and we'll all come visit."

We were comparing notes on San Diego when one of the patrons at the bar came over to our table and stood staring at me. I took a deep breath, having enough experience to anticipate his comment.

"I heard you talking about Baltimore. You're that Olivia from TV, aren't you?"

I folded my arms. "You wouldn't happen to have a cheesecake behind your back, would you?" When he seemed confused, I went on, "Cocktail fork? Olive skewers? Any sharp objects at all?"

He lifted his hands innocently. "You know, you're downright nasty on that show. You treat people like dirt."

"Am I? First, let me tell you that it's not my show, and it's fiction. And I didn't see last week's episode, but I read the synopsis in *TV Guide* and I heard some people discuss it."

Apparently, in last week's *Nutcracker* Olivia had fired one of her dancers after he'd missed a rehearsal to attend his father's funeral. She had told a little ballerina that she'd never have a career and suggested that the kid try some other venue, like cooking or nursing or cleaning hotel rooms. Olivia had stormed into the mayor's office—with a cameo from Hizzoner, the mayor—and complained that the mayor should not have a personal parking spot right outside her studio, telling him that his car ruined her view of the Charles Center.

"And you know what I decided? Although the TV Olivia and I

don't have a lot in common, I'm beginning to find her amusing.
Hurray for a woman who stands up to a man. Three cheers for
someone who tells people what she's really thinking. I find that
shocking but refreshing, don't you agree?"

Beside me, Lanessa made a growling sound. "From the ashes,
a Phoenix rising."

The man shoved his hands in his pants pockets. "I guess." As
he moved back to the bar to brag to his friends of how he'd
braved the wrath of Olivia, I felt myself grinning.

Bonnie nudged my shoulder. "You really turned that one
around."

"How'd that happen?" Kate asked.

I thought of my conversation with Woody, about letting events
shape our lives. "Something I learned over a bowl of oatmeal," I
said. "That show isn't going to get to me anymore. From now on,
I own it."

Once the month of December began, time seemed suspended, as if I were a tiny Mrs. Claus figurine inside a snow
globe hanging on the tree. Although I worked long hours—
sometimes ten to ten, seven days a week in Santaland—those
hours were a whirlwind of giggles and carols and wide, waiflike
eyes. Not that we didn't have our share of nervous tears and
whining children flinging themselves down to pound the floor,
but somehow we managed to dry the tears and circumvent the
tantrums and keep the children moving on to their meeting
with Santa.

Every morning when I slipped on the deep red velvet jacket of
the Mrs. Claus costume, a feeling of contentment fell over me . . .
one big smile. Although I was getting more and more accustomed to the role of Mrs. Claus, my enthusiasm wasn't fading
with time. Silly, I know, but I'd gotten more attached to this role
than any part I'd ever danced with the Rockettes.

Through portraying Mrs. Claus, I had found some surprising
qualities within myself. I could be nurturing, soothing, whimsical, or lovingly firm. Not that I'd been thinking of having kids
any time soon, but if I decided to go there, at least now I could

hold my own with the little rug rats I'd once found so mysterious.

A few times Woody popped into the store and I managed to have a quick bite with him at the restaurant in Rossman's. I sensed that he wasn't ready for more than that, which bugged me a little. What did it all mean—that he wanted to be with me, but only for brief spurts, in public places? Sometimes, at night in bed in the minute before I fell asleep, I wondered if he was holding back for some strange reason . . . like, he was secretly married or engaged. Or maybe his one bad marriage had pushed him over to the other side. Or maybe he just felt sorry for me because my ex had dumped me with a broken ankle and launched a show that pinned a scarlet letter *O* to my chest—and we are not talking about the Baltimore O's.

I would have been overcome with self-doubt, but I was so crazy busy that the only time I had to worry about Woody was in that last second before I fell asleep.

One rainy night when Santaland was fairly quiet, Woody appeared around dinnertime. ZZ graciously told me to take a long break, and Woody and I made the short walk to Little Italy, where the scent of garlic hung heavy in the wet air, making me long for the whole night off, time to take off my damp boots and slip on warm, fuzzy socks. Time to stretch out on a blanket beside Woody and really talk, along with a few more horizontal activities. We settled at a small table near the window in Caesar's Den, where a small cistern candle drew us both toward the center of the table. Woody joked that I was a cheap date when I ordered spaghetti marinara, but I tried to stay focused, not wanting to get derailed from my question.

I waited until we were sipping red wine, breaking apart crusts of garlic bread. "I have to ask, are you avoiding me?"

"What do you mean? We see each other a few times a week. I'm always dropping in on Santaland."

"But it's always on your terms, always brief conversations in very public places." I leaned closer to the flickering flame. "Are you embarrassed to be with me?"

"Of course not. How could I be?"

"I was thinking maybe the red suit and suggestion that I'm married to a man with flying reindeer who sends toys sailing down the chimneys of anonymous homes."

He grinned, and tiny laugh lines emerged beside his eyes. "Actually, Mrs. C., that's one of the things I find strangely attractive about you. I dig the costume, and you wear it well."

Okay, I could strike "team defection" from the list. "So what is the problem, then?"

"I'm moving too slow for you?"

I glanced away thoughtfully, then faced him. "Well, yeah."

"And you have no sense of what's been going through my mind."

I shrugged. "I have a million theories, most of them ludicrous."

"It's because I can't afford to get trounced again. You might have forgotten the details, but you split with me before, and I spent a year serenading you on the phone, trying to win you back."

"When we were in seventh grade. We weren't really dating, Woody. We were like, twelve, and all ecstatic that someone had invented cookie-dough ice cream. The vice president was freaking out over Murphy Brown's baby. What the hell did we know?"

"It mattered to me. It was an important part of my life."

I covered his hand with mine. "I don't mean to minimize it, really. But I was totally dumb back then. Indecisive and insecure. I had no idea what I wanted, which is obvious from the fact that I followed Bobby Tharp around for ten years."

"So here we are, all these years later, and honestly? It's not the kind of thing you rush."

"A pacing thing, Woody. You're running into the tide in slow motion. Which is actually more difficult than just leaping in."

"So what are you saying?" He glanced down at his plate. "That you want more involvement? More time together? A deeper involvement?"

"Two from column A. Twenty zillion from column B."

He laughed. "Aw, Liv. You're going to make me blush."

I slurped long noodles in and wiped my mouth not too seductively. "That is exactly what I had in mind."

14

Just as it seems to go with every new television show I loathe, *Nutcracker* found its humongous audience immediately. Bobby's luck, my curse.

So in our own unique form of boycott, Bonnie, Lanessa, Kate, and I made Tuesday night our girls' night out. While the rest of the world was watching *The Nutcracker*, my friends and I had our run of Baltimore city, and we took advantage of every freebie we could find. Lanessa got us passes to a party at the Museum of Industry, where she pointed out her great-grandaddy in a photo of the Platt Oyster Cannery. We attended Bonnie's company Christmas party at the Walters Art Gallery, where we ended up on our backs in a small room that was part of the illuminated manuscript exhibit. When a docent showed us the illuminated ceiling panels, each one depicting a different fable, Bonnie insisted we all play the game. We lay there with our heads together like girls at a slumber party, calling out as we identified scenes: "A bird in the hand beats two in the bush!" "The grass is greener on the other side!"

One Tuesday when the later Christmas hours had kicked in, I

finagled some late-night ice time at the new Rossman's rink, and afterward we did a quick sweep through the store, searching for presents to buy with my employee discount.

Lanessa found a fabulous dress with a short plaid jacket with fake fur lapels—perfect for her family Christmas celebration. The Jones sisters had a tradition of dressing up for the holidays, trying to best each other and scolding anyone who dared show up with chipped nail polish or reinforced-toe stockings in open-toed shoes.

"Do you think this makes my ass look fat?" Lanessa asked us, backing toward the mirror. "Daria just lost ten pounds and she's a twig. Making us all look like elephants."

"Your ass fits with the rest of your body," Bonnie said.

Lanessa's brows shot up. "What's that supposed to mean?"

"We love the dress," Kate insisted, "and we love you in it. Just buy it, will ya? I have six nieces and nephews to shop for, and the store closes at midnight."

Down in the toy department I helped Kate find some awesome kits—chemistry experiments and rocket building, robot assembly and stained-glass baking. "Very cool," Kate said, stacking them on the counter. "Can I blame you when my sister-in-law's eyes bug out?"

"They encourage creativity!"

"Creativity comes with a price. Like the carpet cleaner's bill." Kate winced, but she managed to hand over her credit card and buy the inventor's kits.

Next stop, the main sales floor, where a group of carolers dressed in turn-of-the-century clothing got us into the spirit. I found two possible gifts for my mother—a Hermès scarf and a white cashmere sweater set.

"Ooh!" Lanessa touched a finger to one cheek. "A little pricey, aren't they?"

"There's my employee discount," I said. "Besides, I'd like to do something special for Mom this year."

"Admit it," Lanessa prodded, "you just don't want to make a decision. Olivia's lament."

Bonnie sampled the texture of the cashmere. "Nice. I'm sure

it's been a relief for Claire to have you here, with everything she's been going through."

"Thank God you were here and able to get her into therapy," Kate said.

"And do I sense a little romance brewing between your mother and that biker Santa?" Lanessa asked.

"I'm not sure," I said, "but they're definitely friends. From the start he backed away from being her therapist. I guess that means something." ZZ had removed himself from Claire Todd's "case" the first time he met her, explaining that he thought another therapist would serve her better. "Besides," he'd told me, "it's really not ethical for me to treat her if I'm a friend." Which made sense to me. I folded the scarf and took it to the counter, adding, "ZZ has become a good friend to Mom, and to me. But the other thing I've realized is that she still has lots of friends. Oh, she may call me to pick up shiitake mushrooms or crabmeat from Lexington Market, but that's just because she's accustomed to asking. She's got at least a dozen neighborhood friends who would be happy to do her favors and run errands. Besides that, it's not as if her social life has ended, it's simply moved inside her house."

"So, basically, you're off the hook?" Kate cocked her head to the side, that special way she lets you know she's listening. "After your ankle checks out and you pack your bags for New York, will you feel guilty leaving her stuck in that house?"

I shook my head. "She doesn't expect me to stay and take care of her. My mother has never been one to be dependent, and this new therapist has been coming to the house. She doesn't need me."

"Oh, Livvy!" Bonnie blinked rapidly, her eyes shiny with tears. "I can't believe you're leaving again. Just when we were all getting into such a great groove again." She puckered her mouth, trying to keep from crying.

"I'm not out of here yet. There's still a few weeks. I'm committed to work through Christmas Eve."

Bonnie hugged me close. "I know, but it's coming, sooner than later."

"Jesus H." Lanessa rolled her eyes. "Can we save the tears for the bon voyage party?"

Bonnie shook her head. "It's just that this Christmas reminds me so much of that last year of college, the last year that we were really together." She turned to Kate. "And don't even get me started on you, because if I really believed you were going to hightail it across the damned country, I'd be bawling like a baby."

Kate shrugged and glanced away, as if trying to avoid her own future. "I'll know for sure in January."

"You'd just better not leave us like this New York girl!" Bonnie pointed an accusing finger at Kate. "No pressure, though."

"Oh, please." Lanessa pressed her fingers to her temples. "Can we skip the blood oath and go straight to a round of beers at the Cat's Eye before I blow it and start shouting out secrets of the divine yahoo sisterhood?"

15

"Got some exciting news, everyone," Charley said. He opened his hands to the group assembled at his feet, reminding me of a preacher blessing the Rossman's congregation.

He'd asked us to assemble in front of the big stone fireplace, its flames dancing warmly on this frosty morning less than two weeks before Christmas, and although Charley's request pushed us to be in costume and out on the sales floor ten minutes earlier than usual, a cheerful mood prevailed. Skinny Stu had brought in a cinnamon coffee cake baked by his wife that very morning to be shared by all and had made charming glitter pinecone ornaments for Santa Squad members to take home. Although we were quickly moving toward the week before Christmas, our yuletide workforce had pulled together, a sprightly, festive family.

"Rossman's is going to have a special visitor on Wednesday," Charley went on. "A television show is set to film here next week, and they want to set their cameras right here in Santaland."

"I love it!" cried Debbie, one of the elves on winter break from University of Maryland. She waved her hand in the air, as if waiting to be called on. "Is it *AM Baltimore?* Or someone from the *Today Show?*"

"No, no, it's not interviews." Charley pointed his pen in the air, ready to burst the rumor bubble before it spread. "No, we're going to be part of a dramatic comedy on BigTime Cable. It's called *Nutcracker . . .*"

I nearly snorted a cinnamon crumb out my nose. Had he said . . . ? No, I had to be dreaming. A feverish nightmare.

"The *Nutcracker* production team handpicked us for a location shot," Charley went on. "They want to pretend their characters are actually shopping here, going to Santaland, all that great stuff. Of course, the Rossmans are thrilled."

"Oh. My. God." I backed up and felt something probing my ass—a branch from the artificial tree. I moved right to catch my balance and stepped on the edge of a foil package. ZZ and Regis reached out and held me up from either side before I went down, taking the tree display with me.

"Easy there, Red," ZZ muttered.

I gaped at him. "Tell me they're bringing in the Nutcracker ballet company."

He winced, his eyes small slits in his crinkled, weathered skin. "Nnnno. That would be wrong."

"You're telling me it's Bobby?" I asked. "He's really coming here with a camera crew?"

"And his wife and all the producers' kids and the entire cast of the show."

"Fu—" In that millisecond I caught four pairs of Santa eyes slant my way. I was one consonant away from having my name slashed from the "Nice" list.

"—dge. Fudge!" I finished. "Can't eat it," I told Carlos and Archie. "I'm totally allergic."

The Santas lost interest in my outburst and turned back to conversation of TV appearances, big breaks, and looking chubby on camera.

"Sorry, Olivia," Regis said, his lyrical Australian accent such a delight to hear. "People seem to have forgotten what an ass the bloody producer is. Shall I fill Charley in on it all?"

"No." I sank down a few inches, bone weary. Charley had a job to do, just like the rest of us. Even if he cared enough to try, he would be powerless to stop this freight train from roaring through another aspect of my life.

ZZ clapped a reassuring hand on my left shoulder. "Tough break, kid."

"Give me the day off." I turned away from Charley and the others, zeroing in on ZZ as if my eyes held hypnotic powers. "I can't be here when Bobby and his wife and his crew come blazing through. I need next Wednesday off."

"No can do. You heard Charley. They want the whole Christmas enchilada—Santaland, Mrs. Claus, elves and all."

"Mr. Claus . . ." I looked ZZ right in the eye. "Do you have any idea how uncomfortable this is going to be for me?"

He patted my shoulder again. "What can I say? Adversity builds character."

"Oh, please, if that were true we'd all be superheroes."

ZZ crossed his arms over his belly, his feet planted wide apart in a bounding stance. "And who says we're not?"

16

As Christmas week began, the pieces of my life were coming together quite neatly. On Monday I was early for my ten o'clock appointment with Dr. Riddle, the orthopedic surgeon, who examined my ankle and my X-rays and uttered those words I had been longing for: "Looks like you're good to go."

"You really mean it?" Why did I sound like a contender on *American Idol?* I knew doctors were not in practice to give a false prognosis.

Dr. Riddle scratched the thin hair on his forehead. "You must have gone wild with physical therapy. There's no sign of muscle atrophy at all."

I gasped. "I can dance . . . on Broadway?"

He frowned and flipped through my file. "That I can't say. I'm a surgeon, not a producer."

I squinted at him, and he cracked a grin. "Kidding! If you've got the talent, you've now got a healthy ankle to go with it."

Before I'd even given Dr. Riddle's receptionist my copay, I was on the phone with Mrs. Atwater, making an appointment for January 2, figuring I'd need next week to work out with my dance coach to hit my mark again.

"This might develop into a situation mutually convenient for us both," she said sternly, and I could imagine her penciling me in on her ever-present clipboard. "I've had three girls down with the flu all week, and you know how that goes. You can dance with a cold, but when it hits the lower G.I. tract, no good."

"I'd love to be a stand-in," I said emphatically.

"We'll see, dear. We'll see."

When I returned to my apartment, I saw the place with new eyes. Suddenly the hole in the wall exposing insulation didn't bother me, nor did the clanging pipes that indicated heat was pumping into the already hot space. None of it mattered now; it was all temporary.

It's all temporary. . . . Hadn't I told myself that a thousand times?

Now that I believed it, I realized the work ahead of me. I needed to pack, ship some clothes up to my friend's apartment, cart the rest of my stuff off to Mom's basement to store until I knew where I'd be living. If I was taking the train on the twenty-sixth and working through Christmas Eve, I would have to move most of my things on Christmas Day.

Crazy, but doable, especially with the fires of motivation burning my ass. I changed into sweats, collected some boxes from behind the Wawa on the corner, and started sorting sweaters and books, lingerie and CDs. I had taped off two full boxes when someone rapped on the door.

"It's me!" squealed Mrs. Scholinsky.

I opened the door, surprised to see her hair unfettered by curlers. It was artfully combed out, the gray covered with an attractive shade of gold that might have been called caramel corn.

"This letter came while you were gone, special delivery." She held the envelope level under her chin. "I had to sign for it, but I told the postman I don't mind. I'm your landlady, for godsakes, I can sign."

"Thanks," I said, wondering who'd want to track me down. "You look nice today."

"I've got a boyfriend," she said proudly. "A Belair man. Alan down at the Stop and Shop introduced us. He works the deli counter."

The information passed over me; I was focused on the return address—New York City.

Mrs. Scholinsky noticed the boxes. "You're packing? So you're really going to be out by the first of the month?"

"That's my plan."

"Heading back to New York, hon?"

I nodded. "I'm trying to hook up with the Rockettes again." If that didn't pan out for me, I had saved enough money to last a month in Manhattan, maybe two. With costs so high in that city, my share of the rent had been more than one thousand dollars. I had spent the afternoon working on budgets, a little more leery of the adventure this time around, now that I knew what it cost to live in New York. All afternoon my excitement was twisting inside me, a ball in my chest that was surprisingly similar to stress. The pain spiked whenever I thought of the logistics and the expense of moving back to New York. It was not a thrifty move, but a dancer needed to be in New York.

Not Pigtown.

Mrs. Scholinsky mentioned something about bringing in a construction crew to finish all the renovations—just my luck, fix up the place as soon as I leave!—but I only half heard, eager to close the door and open this odd letter.

Inside, one page was handwritten on notebook paper, as if torn from a school binder.

Miss Olivia, I hope you don't mind that I track you down through your friends the dancers. Everyone here, my Gia and my brothers, we worry about you and your career since that day you fall on our steps.

We are sorry to hear you had to move from New York, but we wish you good luck and good health there.

Miss Olivia, we feel your accident is our fault. Thank God you are a good person and do not sue me and close down my business. Please accept this check, as some compensation for the loss you endured. My lawyer calls it a bad idea, but I tell him he don't know

*you. You are a good person, Miss Olivia. God bless you, and come
see us next time you visit New York. My Gia will make you that eggplant you like.*

Very truly,
Mario D'ellessandro

Inside the envelope was a cashier's check, payable to me in
the amount of twenty thousand dollars.

Within fourteen minutes all my friends knew my fabulous two-
part good news.

Virtuous Kate focused more on healing than the cash. "That's
so wonderful about your ankle," Kate said. "I knew this injury
wouldn't derail you for long. See? It was just a temporary setback."

When I called Lanessa, the lawyer emerged. "The twenty
grand was a very smart move on their part. Saves everyone court
expenses and spreads goodwill all around."

"But I wasn't going to sue Mario," I said for the bazillionth
time.

"Whatever. Take the money and run, hon."

Bonnie was more pragmatic. "I can't believe the pizza man
sent you all that money," she said. "What are you going to do
with it? You need an investment strategy. Let me get you my ad-
visor's number. And most important, did you really see Mrs.
Scholinsky without her pinwheels and scarf?" My landlady was a
Dippity-do legend in Pigtown.

"There is hair under those rollers," I said. "And an even bigger scoop, she's got a boyfriend in Belair. She's considering
shacking up with him, leaving Pigtown for good."

Bonnie gasped. "No!"

"Uhm-hmm." Maybe it was true; maybe our lives didn't have
to be defined by outside events. If Mrs. Scholinsky could get the
hairpins out and meet a beau, there was hope for the rest of us.

17

"Oh, would you quit being so maniacally happy," Lanessa said as she stabbed a cube of pineapple with a toothpick. We'd all been invited to the aquarium Christmas party as guests of Kate and Turtle, and to everyone's surprise Bonnie had walked in arm in arm with Jonah, her soon-to-be ex-husband. So far Jonah had kept a quiet distance, studying blown-up photos mounted in the "Marsh Life" exhibit.

"I'm not as blissful as I look," I said, backing into a couple in a three-quarters snuggle near the recessed glass of a Chesapeake marine life tank. "Really, I'm a bundle of contradictions. Not that you could tell in this light."

The National Aquarium had always struck me as being a surprisingly dark, shadowy place, a welcome break during the hot summer, but this time of year I often came upon couples in bulky sweaters and jeans taking advantage of the pockets of shadow. Stolen moments. I'm not sure what bothered me more, seeing these people breathing heavy and entwined while I had no one, or the fact that it had never occurred to Bobby or me to head over here when we were teenagers in search of make-out locations.

"Where are the clown fish?" I asked Kate. "And the blue one that looks like Dory?"

"Aren't you a little old to be finding Nemo?" Bonnie teased as Kate motioned our group toward the display of tropical fish.

"It's her lucky day," Lanessa said. "She could probably find Waldo in that display of brain coral. Can you imagine, hitting the mother lode and finding out your ankle is whole all in one day? It worries me to think what you might do tomorrow. Cure cancer and win over Simon and Paula?"

"Nessa, first of all, my good luck was accidental, not something I earned or achieved. And you make it sound like I've actually got a career. Remember, I haven't danced in months. I still have some trepidation over returning to New York, auditioning all over again." If I did make the cut, I would be dancing three shows a day, two when we went on tour in the spring. It would be great to have the work, but I would have to dance, dance, dance my little butt off.

"You don't look scared," Turtle said. "Besides, you've done this before, so you pretty much know the deal. Kate and I are looking at moving to an unknown place. Imagine not knowing where to buy milk. Or maybe you're heading home from work and you don't even know how to get there. You can't find your apartment. That would be wild."

"Don't remind me," Kate said. Her hair was pulled back into a tight French braid, and she was still wearing a wet suit from the final performance of the dolphin show, in which we'd all watched Kobee the dolphin propel her through the giant pool. Of course, I'd seen the show a half dozen times before, but who else could see their best friend play fetch with two dolphins?

"So what have you heard from San Diego?" Bonnie asked. "Are you guys going to be leaving us, too?"

"They've made me an offer, and they really want Kate, too. She's just got to go through the formality of an interview after Christmas." Turtle rubbed his chin, his eyes sparkling. "Let me tell you, I am psyched."

"And Kate?" Lanessa prodded.

"I'm psyched . . ." Kate pulled her braid in front and fiddled with the end. "And very nervous. A move across the country . . . It sort of feels like jumping off a cliff . . . backward . . . without a bungee cord."

"We'll come visit you," Bonnie said.

"We're definitely getting a place with a guest room, so you all have to come," Turtle said, and I realized this was the most I'd heard him talk without bringing up reducing traffic mortalities of turtles or combating the Asian turtle crisis.

"Two of Turtle's friends from college live in San Diego," Kate said.

"And they love it," Turtle went on. "One of them specializes in the preservation of Indian star tortoises. He's a very cool guy, trying to set up a symposium in Singapore and . . ."

And so ended Turtle's nontortoise streak.

Jonah rejoined us, carrying two glasses of red wine. Without a word he handed one to Bonnie, and she nodded, thanking him in that unspoken language lovers have.

Lanessa was into a story about a convention she'd attended in San Diego, and I turned to Jonah. "Hey, whatever happened with that photo contest you were entering?" I asked him.

"I haven't heard anything yet," he said quietly. "But actually, I used the photo you chose."

"Oh, good." I nodded. "That way, you can blame me if it doesn't win."

Bonnie's jaw dropped in horror. But Jonah let out a nervous laugh. "True. It'll be all your fault, Olivia."

"No problem." I pointed a thumb to my chest. "I can take it."

In one of her usual social feats that demonstrates her lobbyist prowess, Lanessa convinced the two guys to go off to the sea horse exhibit so that we could dish for a few minutes. Kate hurried us along the shadowy spiral walkway that displayed coral reef fish, then various types of sharks, their prickly overbites cruising by the glass just above our heads. As we hustled along, Bonnie did her usual survey of Jonah's response to us.

"I think he's really warming up to you guys, especially you, Liv."

"I admit, I've seen a flicker of emotion there the last times I saw him. Warm may be an overexaggeration. More like a warming trend. A thaw—"

"Can I ask you what the hell he's doing here?" Lanessa cut in. "Aren't you guys doing the divorce thing?"

"We were separated, but actually, that changed, just this week. Jonah moved back. I asked him to, and he said that's what he wants, too."

Kate let out a little squeal. "Bonnie, that's so great! I mean, it's what you want, right?"

"Are you kidding? I was looking at my third divorce."

"Hardly motivation for a reunion," Lanessa said.

I linked my arm through Bonnie's. "We really want you to be happy, Bonnie. But Nessa's right. Don't patch things up with him just to avoid the divorce stigma."

"I'm not afraid of getting divorced," Bonnie said, "but I am afraid when I think of living the rest of my life without Jonah. Not that I wouldn't survive, but I would feel unbalanced, unfulfilled. We complement each other when we're together—"

"And you're both oddballs on your own," Lanessa cut in. "You get so darned sentimental and he's such a cold fish. Honey, you two need each other."

Bonnie scowled at Lanessa. "Thanks . . . I guess."

"I mean it in the nicest way." Lanessa rose on her toes, kissed Bonnie's cheek, and gave her a hug. "Good luck to you."

"You've got to come back this spring and we'll all go to a game," Bonnie said. "The O's are trading like crazy. Scuttlebutt says we might be getting Sammy Sosa."

Bonnie lifted her wineglass to me. "Woody is a big Orioles fan, isn't he?"

"Woody who?" I took a deep sip of wine. "I'm telling you, I scared him away. In baseballese, I invited him to third and he decided to forfeit."

"Liv . . ." Bonnie's eyes opened wide, as if her face were about to pop. "Before you completely embarrass yourself—and don't turn around—Woody is here, standing right—"

I was already twisting and peering around one bubble cylinder to find him.

"I said don't turn around!" Bonnie hissed. "Nice, Liv. Very subtle."

"I don't see him, and what's he doing here, anyway?"

"Bonnie invited me," he said, joining our group from the ambient darkness. With his hands in the pockets of his leather jacket, his tie loosened in that studious disheveled look, he was cute in that rebel-nerd way.

"Oh, hi." My voice sounded sprite and chipper, as if I were going out for the pep squad at Spaulding.

"Livvy . . . How've you been?" His brown eyes locked on me, so intense and edgy, as if my bullshit answer to the bullshit question really mattered.

"Busy. You know how it is, the Christmas rush."

He nodded.

"And how about you?" I moved closer, so that everyone in the aquarium wouldn't have to hear us. "To cut through the crap, I was a little surprised not to hear from you the past few weeks. I mean, if you're not interested you could have called with some made-up story. Like you have to go get hair implants or your dog needs surgery."

"I don't have a dog," he said.

I pointed from my eyes to his. "Honesty, remember?"

He drew in a deep breath. "I'm sorry, Liv. Honestly, you scared me. You sound so cavalier, but really, for the two of us to get involved, it's a really big deal for me."

"Really? So, are you telling me you don't sleep around?"

"I didn't say that. But you and I can't be friends with benefits. It wouldn't be just sex with you."

I swallowed hard at the sudden image of the two of us naked, in each other's arms. A smoky image that made my knees go weak. I tried to look away casually, but he caught my arm, did the eye-to-eye thing right back at me, forcing me to connect.

"We've got to be careful, Liv. I've got this really dangerous pattern of falling in love with people I can't have."

I nodded, still heated at the thought of how his skin would feel, what we could do to each other, with each other . . .

18

When he asked me if I wanted to go with him to check out a property nearby, I didn't hesitate. I would have preferred a trip straight to his apartment, but I was beginning to see that for Woody the route from point A to point B zigzagged to various landmarks around Baltimore.

Tonight's project was in Canton, a harborfront community east of Fells Point and walking distance from my mother's neighborhood, so I knew a little bit about it. Canton had undergone a more recent renaissance, so its prices were still affordable, but perhaps not for long. Much of Canton had been canning factories and small row houses built to house the workers. Now the refurbished American Can Company held bookshops and restaurants, cafés and small boutiques.

Woody's project was a smaller warehouse, only two stories, a brick structure with very few windows, though the glasswork that remained was set in brick arches.

"I never noticed this building before," I said.

"It was run down, almost torn down till the developer and I convinced the city we could do a historic renovation that wouldn't compromise the neighborhood. The first floor is currently a pottery shop, doing well so far."

"Not surprising," I said as we passed the windows decorated with bright green glassware and curling gold ribbons. The shop was bright and cheerful, one of those places you enter in search of a gift and exit with three heavy shopping bags for your kitchen.

"Upstairs isn't completely finished yet, but I use it as a makeshift office."

He opened the door to a wide, deep room of low-gloss wood floor and craggy brick walls. "Kind of bare, I know. I just wanted to grab two files." He went to the corner where a sofa faced a coffee table overwhelmed with newspapers and files that toppled onto the floor.

"Love the filing system," I called to him as I tested the open space. Only one wall held windows, but the rest of the space felt safe and very familiar to me.

Music wafted up from downstairs, classical Christmas music, and as I listened closely I realized it was the Sugar Plum Fairy's dance. I laughed out loud, hugging my waist.

"What is it?"

"Downstairs in the shop they're playing *The Nutcracker*." I lunged into a hamstring stretch. "This would make a great dance studio." I gathered spine tall, shoulders down, arms aloft, and pirouetted gracefully.

"Very nice," he said admiringly.

He watched as I did a few steps, a short sequence. Balanchine's choreography is difficult, but every dancer knows at least a part of *The Nutcracker*. For a minute or so I lost myself in the music, transported, moving without thinking about the parts of the dance.

Woody's silence brought me back to earth. Pausing, I pressed a hand to my chest. "It's been a long time. Phew! What a relief. I can still do it."

"Sure you can."

"You should have seen me on the StairMaster last summer,

barely walking. But really, what a great space. Has anyone thought of a studio?"

"Mmm, we can't zone it for housing because of the lack of windows, but actually I was thinking more of a radio or television studio."

"That might work. But you know, there isn't much rehearsal space in Baltimore, and you could really use another dance studio here."

He scratched his head. "Could I?"

"First of all, there's no great academy here, no jumping-off point for the talented dancers growing up in this city and its suburbs. I can tell you that because I lived it. My parents spent pots of money sending me off to dance camps in New England each summer. And B, Baltimore needs a dance school for little kids that isn't just a cheesy showcase for a tap recital once a year."

"Sounds like every little girl's dream."

"My parents didn't listen when I bugged them to let me pursue dance. And it's funny, but watching the parents with their kids at Rossman's? I see that hasn't changed much. Some parents don't seem to hear anything their kids say. It's like they're deaf."

"I've noticed that, too. I have some friends who have picked out colleges and careers for their infant children. So you've enjoyed your Mrs. Claus gig at Rossman's? I thought that by this point you might be happy to see it end."

There was that damned knot again. If this kept up, I'd have to get screened for an ulcer. "Rossman's has been great to me," I said, turning away, looking for a distraction. I went to one of the high windows and opened the small hatch, letting in a burst of cool air that tossed my bangs back.

Footsteps behind me. "Do you see the lights on the other side of the water? That's Fort McHenry. On a clear day you can see the flag from here."

I was always rotten at history. "So much history in our hometown. Yes, I see it. Now, wasn't that the battle when 'The Star-Spangled Banner' was written? On a boat in the harbor?"

"Right. 1814. Francis Scott Key."

"Refresh my memory. Who was the enemy?"

"The British, once again. The cannons of Fort McHenry saved us all from liver pudding and Liverpudlian accents."

The rooftops tiering down to the water reminded me of the roofs where the chimney sweeps dance in *Mary Poppins*, their flat tar squares, black steps against the gray sky. Some of the houses were jumbled so close, so on top of each other that I felt sure I could do the dance, leaping from one roof to another as if they were stepping stones to the horizon. A few rooftops were framed by strings of red or white Christmas lights, others cut a swath of black contrasting to the gray sky. White smoke billowed from a few smokestacks, a counterpoint to the bold white cloud that clung to the sky over the dark waterfront punctuated by dots of light. "It's really quite beautiful." And beauty was something I rarely noticed or expected in Baltimore, unless of course I was viewing a Latrobe design or a painting in a museum.

"It is."

I turned around, saw his eyes fixed on the view through the small window. Such sincere eyes. How did this man survive with such sweet, intense eyes?

"I don't know how you get any work done here. I would just stand at this window and drink in the view all day."

His hands moved to my shoulders and I wanted to melt against him. "Who says I get any work done here?"

I thought of the sofa over in the corner. The bare floors would be hard, but that sofa might work. Not that it really mattered.

Right now I would make love to him anywhere.

I turned to face him, and the motion made one of his out-stretched hands sweep my shoulders and breasts. He held his hands up, surrendering. "Sorry."

"Don't be." I took his right hand and pressed it to one breast, holding it there as he let out a breath.

His eyes held a certain light, a tentativeness I found so appealing as he caressed me through the fabric, then leaned toward me and brushed his lips against mine. It felt good, the tease, and I lifted my hands to his face, capturing the slightly bristled skin along his jawline.

With a breath, I sank my fingers into his hair and we both moaned in pleasure as the kissing went on, a moist, hot connection that made our intentions very clear.

He sucked in a breath, then pulled my body against his, pressing his hips to mine as if seeking a niche. I could feel his erection, my own body's response, the tingling nerve endings responding to his hands on my lower back, curving over my bottom.

"Livvy . . ." he whispered, "we fit together so well."

He was right . . . Our bodies did seem well matched, a perfect alignment, something dance partners cherish.

I closed my eyes and kissed him, opening my lips to his, opening myself to the rising heat. How I wanted to tear away the clothes that separated us, the coats and jeans. We would tumble onto the floor and enter each other's worlds in intimate ways, probing and teasing and stroking until we writhed to a climax together.

He pulled his lips away and pulled my body closer against his, kneading my ass. "I can't believe we're doing this," he whispered. "Can't tell you how long I've dreamed of this . . . wanting you . . ."

His voice was gentle, reminding me of the kid Woody, the one I had spent hours on the phone with in seventh grade, the boy I'd tried to ease away from by sending him the lyrics to Carole King's "It's Too Late." His friends told me I broke his heart, but our phone calls continued, hours of sharing old songs, reading poetic lyrics we'd found. Each night he'd sing me Sly Stone's "Everybody Is a Star," and I'd enjoy his company, my friend Woody.

"Oh, no." I froze in his arms, pulling my hands to my face.

His body went still. "What is it?"

My pulse was still pounding in my ears. "I want you so much, I do, but I can't do this. We can't, Woody. I'm out of here at the end of the week and . . . Don't you think this would just tear at both of us?"

His arms fell away from me and he stepped back, his face pinched with betrayal. "What? What are you saying?"

"I'm sorry, I just . . ." Just what? Couldn't bear to break his heart again? Couldn't seem to move past the Bobby years?

"Just go." He turned away.

I stepped back reluctantly. "I'll call you, okay? We'll talk this out. Get square with each other."

"Just go on, Liv."

My heart was heavy with guilt as I turned and ran down the stairs.

19

After that night with Woody, after I'd looked into his eyes and seen the pain I'd caused, I wanted to take the next train out of Baltimore. I fantasized about arriving in New York a week early, taking a small hotel room, visiting galleries, spending afternoons reading novels in coffee shops, and generally escaping into some other woman's cosmopolitan life. I came this close to leaving, but in the end, I couldn't give up on Mrs. Claus that way.

"Are you crazy?" Lanessa told me over the phone. "First of all, you and the Wood Man are both consenting adults, so really, I'm not busting a gut crying over that one. I mean, got a sensitive nose, then don't go sniffing around. That's what I say."

"You have never said that. And I feel really bad about it. I can't help how I feel."

"Yeah, yeah, whatever. But that's one thing. You staying in Baltimore for some two-bit department-store Santa job, that really rattles my cage. I mean, what do you get, minimum wage? To baby-sit snot-nosed droolers while their mommies go off and spend pots of money that all goes to Rossman's?"

"I'm the only Mrs. Claus they have. The kids need me."

"The kids need a sitter. You need a life."

"It's only one more week," I said. "After that I'll have a life again, but for now, I don't know, it just makes me feel good to do something special for other people every day. Isn't that what Christmas is all about?"

"For me? Christmas is about finding a suit that doesn't make my ass look too fat beside my skinny-butt sister who won't come off Atkins. But if the Mommy Claus thing makes you feel good, more power to you, honey."

Having spent months rehearsing in dance studios to escape my feelings for Bobby, I considered myself a master of sublimation—an acquired skill, which I would need to rely on over the next few days. It helped that I worked in such a busy, cheerful place—a department store at Christmas—and I soaked up that Christmas spirit, admiring the dedication of my coworkers and the service of all the retail clerks in the store. In its own way, Rossman's was pulling off a Christmas production that rivaled all the bells and whistles of the show I'd danced in last year, and I saw rave reviews every day in the wonder that lit the faces of children who believed they were about to meet their greatest hero of all time. Every time the carolers sang "tidings of comfort and joy" or "deck the halls," every time the toy train pulled around the gingerbread house full of expectant children, each time I squatted down to meet a child on his or her level, I felt very much a part of Christmas.

I tried not to lose that connection when the dreaded day of *The Nutcracker* filming arrived. It was unsettling to see the production crew treading on our Santaland displays when I reported in that morning, but we all tried to be patient.

"It's overlit!" someone yelled so loud that the child I was leading to ZZ's cozy Santa home winced. "I need gels on this tree over here."

"Okay, Virgil," I said to the boy, pointing to three cables snaking across our path. "Do you think you can jump over these the way Santa's reindeer hop over a house?"

"Sure." He hopped merrily in his mini–Air Jordans, then glanced up at me for approval.

"Good job," I assured him, weaving around the new tier of employees who were adding to the noise. So far there'd been no sign of Bobby or Destiny, but one of the carpenters told me that the talent and producers were the last to arrive on set.

"And who is this?" ZZ asked, smiling at the shy boy holding my hand.

"This is Virgil, Santa." I began to lead him over to the large velvet chair, but Virgil pushed ahead and lifted his hands so that ZZ would pull him into his lap. The boy's aunt took a seat on the sofa.

"Thank you, Mrs. Claus," ZZ told me. "And would you be so kind as to ask those young people to quiet down a bit? Virgil and I need to talk."

I nodded, feeling weary already. "I'll do my best."

Out in the gingerbread maze waiting area, no one on the crew wanted to hear my "Quiet, please!" message.

"It's a bit surreal," Regis told me as we watched a man on the crew struggle with a scaffold, cursing all the way. "They want us here for background, and yet they really want us to be invisible. Now I understand why those Hollywood types call the people in the background 'atmosphere.'"

As the day wore on, I began to feel more and more invisible. The cast began arriving, and they imposed more than the crew, asking us for coffee runs and telling two of the elves to leave because their costumes clashed with the show designer's scene. ZZ seemed determined to keep the peace, though even he drew the line at dismissing our elves, who were sent to the front door of the store to hand out coupons.

At one point, while sitting on a gumdrop chair, trying to console a lost child, I looked up to find the TV Olivia standing over me, her hair swept back with a fat headband, her blouse covered with a white paper bib, most likely to contain the crimson gloss on her lips and the heavy pancake make-up covering her skin.

That chin . . . That tiny nose! Up close, she looked more like the anti-Olivia.

I squinted at her, wondering why her features didn't come together as an organic whole in my mind. Most likely because she was not me, not at all. And there was also the possibility that the individual pieces had been doctored beyond natural proportion—but that was a matter between the actress and her plastic surgeon.

She looked up from her script and met my eyes with keen recognition, and I braced myself. *Here it comes, the moment of connection when this actress realizes how Bobby exploited me.*

When she pointed at me, my heartbeat thundered in my ears, and my nerves were on edge. "I need to sit," she said simply.

I looked down, realizing that I occupied the only adult-sized gumdrop seat in the candy garden. She wanted my seat. The woman was building a career on my ass, and she wanted me to give up my seat.

Stung by adrenaline, I rose, ready to lunge at her, send her pretty fake red hair flying in a catfight . . . but I was caught by a slight hiccup beside me from the girl who'd lost her mother. And it occurred to me that a mud-wrestling Mrs. Claus was not the best image to impress upon a worried child.

Oh, hell, the obtuse actress could have my gumdrop chair.

"Come on, sweetie," I said, taking the child's hand. "Let's look for your mommy near the Santaland entrance."

As we made our way through the maze, the set now swarming with taut production people talking into headsets, I tried to take a deep, calming breath. No matter what happened today, I had to remember my role, my image, my elegant red suit. Mrs. Claus would not engage in catfights. Mrs. Claus would not kick her ex-boyfriend in the nuts and curse out his wife . . .

No matter how tempting the opportunity.

It was another two hours before Bobby and Destiny arrived and started adding their varied opinions as to the setup of the scene to be filmed. By that time my anxiety had begun to fade, but it all came rushing back when I locked eyes with Bobby.

Oh, shit.

I squeezed my eyes shut to break the connection, relieved that I hadn't cursed out loud. Not that the twin toddlers I was escorting would notice, but their dad was right on my heels. I helped the boys off the train, trying to map out a way around Bobby and Destiny without having to climb the fake mountain of snow. Unless these toddlers learned to master fiberglass-mountain pickaxing really fast, that was not gonna happen.

"Let's go see if Santa is ready now," I said, taking their little hands and walking with my head down.

As I passed the crew, Destiny was engrossed in a critique of a sweater she'd seen downstairs on the sales floor, but Bobby caught me.

"Hey, there," he said, nodding. "What are you doing here?"

"Just doing my job." I forced a smile, hustling the boys along.

"No, wait," Bobby said, tapping one of the elves on the arm. "Hey, mac, help us out and take the kids?"

The elf, an out-of-work welder named Alton, eyed Bobby with sleepy eyes, but welcomed the boys. "Follow me, guys."

"This is Olivia, honey," Bobby said, sounding forlorn.

I thrust my hand at Destiny, the blond Hollywood daughter of tabloids. "Hello, I'm Olivia Honey."

No one noticed my joke as Bobby reminded his wife, "Remember I told you she was here in Baltimore?"

"Now, wait! Is this the *other* Olivia?" Destiny eyed me hungrily, and I had a feeling that any blemish, any perceived flaw would be devoured with relish in a later conversation. "Ow, how cute! Did our casting director hire you to be Mrs. Claus?"

I shook my head. "Actually, I work for Rossman's."

"Ow, how funny. Isn't it funny? And what, you gave up the Rockettes for this?" She gestured around our beautiful Santaland as if it were a washroom at Penn Station.

"I like it here," I said slowly. "And I love Baltimore. Unlike your Olivia."

Her smile didn't reach her eyes. "Yeah, well, that's all very nice, but Bobby, did you see the way they have Olivia and Frank entering through that maze? It's a problem." And with that, Bobby and the crew were pulled over to the other side of Santaland to deal with the many "problems" that disturbed Destiny's delicate sensibilities. She didn't like the snow background or the giant gumdrops. "What are they, stalagmites?" she snapped. "And these elves look like escapees from a North Pole prison. I think we need all new casting on the elves."

I couldn't hear her response when Bobby explained that the elves were free atmosphere, compliments of Rossman's. I didn't care how they decided to shoot around our winter wonderland or if they decided to edit out our gumdrop haven.

At that point, I felt such a strong sense of relief that I wanted to laugh out loud.

"That woman is a holy terror," Regis confided.

"Isn't she?" I smiled.

"The whining. The complaints. Every other word out of her mouth is 'problem.' How can anyone stand to work with her?"

"Ha!" I slapped my fingers. "It's so perfect. I totally get it now." When he shook his head in confusion, I explained, "Since that show premiered I've been wondering how Bobby dreamed up the Olivia character, so bugged that he could have seen all those negative qualities in me. But now I get it. I see who really inspired the villainous Olivia."

He gasped. "Of course! His own wife."

I nodded so vigorously the tassel on my Santa cap shook. Suddenly one of the worst days of my life was transforming into something else, a day of liberation.

The Nutcracker was not me.

Destiny could take all the credit for inspiring Bobby to create the bitch of Baltimore. And somehow, when awards were being handed out, I was sure Destiny would be there, her iron jaws ready to smash and devour his nuts, the academy's nuts, the network's nuts . . .

20

Santaland got even crazier when Bobby's nieces and nephews arrived. Ranging in ages from two to nine, they appeared with shrieking police cars and gurgling stuffed toys and musical instruments since Bobby's sister, chaperone of the day, had made the unfortunate decision to stop in the toy department first.

"Look who I found in the toy department." Charley, the shining star from Personnel, led them over, apparently in an attempt to reduce losses in the toy division.

The oldest boy swayed in, swinging a portable electric piano playing a programmed version of the Beatles's "Let it Be." Three others zigzagged around him in a game of Monkey in the Middle that had one of the little girls sobbing, demanding her stuffed toy back. A younger boy marched behind him banging on a boxed drum slung around his neck.

"Uncle Bobby! Listen to this . . ." the oldest boy shouted over the music. "Gunnar and I are starting a band. Can you film us? You can do our music video." Gunnar launched into a drum roll, while the stuffed animal flew into the line of waiting toddlers and one of the nephews dived in after it.

"Bobby . . ." Destiny pressed a hand to one temple. "They're giving me a migraine. Make it stop."

"Please, Uncle Bobby," chimed in his sister, whom I remembered as Chelsea, "make it stop. I've been stuck with them since Christmas break began."

Bobby raised his hands. "Hey! Trevor? We've got a show to do here. Ugh . . . guys? Boys and girls . . ."

A tug-of-war was going on over the stuffed animal, while Gunnar began to tap out a beat on one of the camera cases.

"Cut!" Bobby shouted. "We need quiet. Trevor? Turn that off!"

Trevor gave him a thumbs-up, then switched to a canned version of a Ricky Martin song, while two of the other kids were now rolling on the floor, wrestling over a toy.

Two of the Santas peeked out from their doorways, while Charley from Personnel shouted something to Bobby. Destiny was complaining to Chelsea, who sank down on a gumdrop and buried her head in her hands.

Enough was enough.

I went over to Trevor and flipped the black switch to Off, killing the music. "We'll return this for you," I said, slipping the strap off his shoulder. "Why don't you go say hello to your uncle."

He squinted up at me. "Hey, I remember you. You've been at our house."

"You must be mistaken," I told him. "I'm Mrs. Claus."

Next I closed my hands over the drumsticks and told the banging boy that he'd better get in line if he wanted to see Santa. The stuffed animal was returned to the youngest one, while the other toys were quickly collected and the nieces and nephews joined the line.

Handing the drum over to Charley, I was relieved to hear strains of "Joy to the World!" once again. These kids had always been a workout; why did Bobby think they belonged here while he was trying to shoot a show?

Within a few minutes, order was restored. The nieces and nephews had moved on to see various Santas, Destiny had returned to the hotel to nurse her migraine, and the crew was sent off for a lunch break.

I tucked a toddler onto the train and stepped back with a sigh. "At last," I told Regis, "peace returns to the North Pole."

"Not for long," Bobby called from one of the trees where extra lights were being strung. "My guys will be back in an hour, and then we'll finally start shooting."

"Finally is right." I joined him, feeling less stressed now that Destiny wasn't here to dissect me. "Your crew takes forever."

"We're perfectionists."

"Good luck with that. Just try to stay out of the way of our youngest customers. Santaland is a special experience for them, and swearing cameramen shouldn't be a part of it."

He laughed. "You know, we could use someone like you to keep the crew whipped in shape. A tough production manager is hard to find, and I like the way you took control of the situation back there. I think Trevor is still stunned."

"Hey, Mrs. Claus does not mess around. You can spend days futzing around on one shot, but Christmas comes only once a year. The Claus trade is a seasonal business."

Bobby released the strand of lights and turned to face me. "I miss your sense of humor, Livvy. Your quick wit."

"You think I'm being funny?"

"You always did make me laugh. Picked me up when I was at my lowest." He glanced over at the cameras set like three aliens across the maze. "I'm sorry you weren't a part of this, Liv. It should be your success, too."

"As I told you, any time you want to send me a check, I'm easy to find. Mom's still got the house on Lombard. You do remember it, don't you?" I wanted to add that we'd both lost our virginity under that roof, but somehow it didn't seem an image befitting Mrs. Claus.

He picked up a strand of my hair and studied the curl at the end as if it were a precious gem. "I'll never forget that house. I can't forget you, Liv."

"Well, considering the fact that you're married to someone

else and I am not the type of girl to mess with a marriage, I think you'd better start forgetting fast. Amnesia, if possible."

"I made a mistake. Destiny doesn't make me happy."

"So find a therapist. And really, Bobby, why do men think the world owes them happiness?"

"I keep comparing her to you. To the way you made me feel." He dropped the strands of hair and let his fingertips slide down the side of my neck. "We were good together. Don't you ever think about me, about us?"

"Think about us?" I wanted to ask him where he was when I broke my ankle and needed a ride to physical therapy. Where was he when I had to hobble up icy stairs on my ass? When I had to close up my apartment and pay an arm and a leg to have things shipped? I'd been thinking about him a lot at that point, lots of toxic thoughts. Like why was he seeing Destiny behind my back, laughing in the warm California sun while I was dancing my butt off in the Christmas show? Where was his freakin' brain when he should have at least called me and let me know he'd had a change of heart?

I wanted to make him regret his actions. And most of all, I wanted him to regret breaking up with me.

See what sanity you could have had if you'd stayed faithful to me? See how happy we'd be if you hadn't slept with a producer's daughter and pawned me off as the best TV pitch of your life?

"The thing is, Destiny and I have been on the rocks lately. We've discussed divorce. I know it's a big *if,* but if things worked out that way, would you give us a chance, Liv?"

My pulse grew loud in my ear as his words took impact. This was my chance—my do-over! Bobby wanted me back. We could have our life together . . . an entertainment couple, our photo in *People* magazine, our mailbox full of invitations to red-carpet premieres and awards ceremonies . . .

We could have it all back, including our crappy, dysfunctional relationship in which I exhausted all my energies to nurse his delicate ego.

"I know, this is really sudden, and I don't mean to overwhelm you."

I blinked, suddenly realizing how weak his chin was without the beard and the way his upper lip curled into a constant half smile; once I'd found that smirk attractive, rebellious, and bold. Now, it just struck me as the smirk of a weenie.

"To be honest," he lowered his voice to that dream tone, "I've been asking around to see if you'd hooked up with anyone. When I heard you were still on your own, I figured we might have a chance."

"Really?" I smoothed the white fur jacket hem over my hips, wondering what sort of married man sniffed out the dating status of other chicks. How could Bobby have sunk so low? He'd become such a disappointment as a husband, even if he wasn't *my* husband.

With a deep breath, I let him have it. "The truth is, we would never last together."

Bobby cocked his head. "What?"

That sinking-heart feeling came over me as I realized the time and effort I had sunk into foolish dreaming. "You're married, Bobby."

"But maybe not for too long. And you're not involved with anyone. We could hook up again, Liv. Just like old times."

"It's not going to happen," I said, trying to bow out gracefully.

"And why the hell not?" His eyes flashed with anger, and I could see that once again it was about boosting Bobby's ego, another exercise in face saving.

"Because she's with me." The scratchy voice came from behind me, and I turned as ZZ stepped forward and slid an arm over my shoulders. "Liv and I try to be discreet, but we hooked up a few weeks ago."

Bobby cupped a hand over one eye, then lifted his forehead, as if peering through a scope at this new worldview. Or maybe he was getting a migraine, too. "Really?"

I flattened my palm against ZZ's back, glad for the support.

"We've got some plans," he said, stroking his beard. "Looking forward to the end of this gig. We figure we'll head south, tour the Florida Keys on my hog."

"Love the hog," I said, turning to ZZ, "but, honey, it's not very practical here in Baltimore."

"That's why we're out of here, Red."

Squinting at me, Bobby shook his head. "You should've told me before I . . . Never mind. Okay, guys, I'd better get back to work now."

As Bobby disappeared behind the hill of snow, ZZ still held on tight for effect. "No wonder your mother calls him Booby."

"He's an asshole, I know. Thing is, he used to be the asshole I loved." I wasn't sure how I felt. Disappointed at Bobby's lack of morality? Pleased that he'd wanted me back? Relieved to be free of him?

ZZ shrugged. "Consider yourself liberated."

"Or something like that."

21

"Love and joy come to you, and to you your wassail, too, and God bless you and send you a happy new year . . ."

Christmas Eve, the strolling carolers swung through our Christmas Village a few extra times, probably because the rest of the store was so crowded with shoppers they welcomed the comfortable space of Santaland.

It had been a quiet day for the Santa Squad, the lines short and our clientele mostly older kids who came shopping with their parents and decided to do the Santa thing for fun.

"It's ending, Regis," I said as the train swept past us. The knot of stress inside me had grown thorny and large, now hitting the walls of my chest. "It's over for us."

"Chipper up, Mrs. Claus. We're not goin' down with the *Titanic*, are we? It's just the end of a holiday job."

"I know, but I'm going to miss this job." More than I wanted to admit. Although Lanessa called the job glorified baby-sitting, I had enjoyed connecting with the little kids, hopping around to keep them distracted, and the staff had become like an extended family. ZZ was spending Christmas with Mom and me, and Regis and I had made plans to hook up after the holidays.

The line fizzled down, the carolers swept by again, and Charley came around to give us our personnel debriefing.

"What, you going to remove the Christmas spirit microchip from behind our ears?" Regis teased him.

I'm not sure that Charley got the joke, but he motioned us into the tiny little break room behind Santaland, where people were singing along with the carols on the loudspeakers. Archie mopped his brow under his Santa cap and bet Chet that we would get a Christmas bonus. Shayna slipped off her curly elf shoes and rubbed her feet. Carlos lifted up his pant leg to show us the socks his girlfriend had bought him, patterned with flying Santas in biplanes. I slid off one boot and showed them the socks I'd found, with martini olives capped by Santa hats. "No way!" Carlos grinned.

Familiar exchanges, though it struck me that this was the last time I'd be part of this easy banter.

With entertaining pomp and circumstance, ZZ distributed our final paychecks, along with bonus gift certificates for Rossman's, which were met with oohs and aahs. Declaring himself unofficial Santa mouthpiece, Archie stood up and tipped his hat to ZZ, thanking him for making the Santaland experience "a true holiday blessing."

ZZ's eyes twinkled as he surveyed the group, paused, then swiped at his eyes with the back of one hand. "It's been real, ladies and gents, and I thank you for sharing the best part of yourself with these children. Now, if you'll follow me to the hearth, there's one more thing for each of you—a stocking hung over the fireplace for you to keep. And don't forget to look inside."

Two collegiate elves raced to the fireplace and pretended to madly tear at the stockings. Instead, they took them down one by one and distributed them.

Although no one but ZZ knew what each person had wished for, the gifts hinted at their desires. Carlos received a free driver's training class, Maisie a corked glass bottle filled with glitter and labeled Christmas Magic. Skinny Stu received a voucher for a free pound of fudge in the gourmet department, and Archie received two CDs of blues music.

Regis, who told me he'd asked for a "slice of home," received two free dinners at the Outback Steakhouse. "Blooming perfect! My folks are arriving from Australia this evening, and they'll get a real charge out of this."

I was slow to open mine, knowing it was a final gesture that would close this period of my life. Inside the Mrs. Claus stocking, in place of the wish I had tucked in six weeks ago, was a small silver Rossman's box. The lid opened to a bed of velvet where a tiny gold charm nestled—a dancing shoe. "Sweet." I touched the shoe and noticed engraving on the bottom that read, Do Over.

"Very clever." I smiled up at ZZ, who had joined us with a proprietary look, and reached under the fur neckline of my Mrs. Claus suit, fishing for my gold chain. "I think these would work well together." I handed Regis the gift box while I reached back to undo the clasp.

"It's for a charm bracelet," Regis insisted. "It would be totally vamp to wear it around your neck. A *Cosmo* don't!"

"Oh, don't be so in-the-box." ZZ threaded the chain through the charm's loop, then laced it around my neck like a bridesmaid. "Perfect." My fingers pressed against the charm, and I liked the security of having it hang near my heart. "Thank you," I told ZZ.

Regis conceded, "Actually, it looks okay."

"You know . . ." ZZ folded his arms, assessing. "When people ask for do-overs, they usually envision going back to a certain place in time to fix one thing. A very limited vision, one of my pet peeves as a therapist. If you want a do-over, then I say rewrite a part of your history that will really make a difference. Don't just win back an old boyfriend or buy a different car. Take yourself way back. Fix your life at the first fork where you went wrong, the first bad turn, which ended up blossoming into a series of wrong turns."

I nodded, pretending to hear his advice, but mostly trying not to look back at all, not to worry about the things I was leaving behind but to look ahead to that audition with Mrs. Atwater. If I could just get back with the Rockettes, back on the line, back in my apartment, back on tour with the girls . . .

Closing my eyes, I tried to imagine being back onstage again, the glare of the lights, the sizzling excitement that filled the auditorium of Radio City as the curtain rose. I was happy on that stage once, though it was hard to recapture that feeling in my mind, that period of my life.

I could go back there, couldn't I? I could fix my life, right?

All around me people were talking about their plans for Christmas, their last-minute stress over getting Christmas shopping done, picking up the roast from the butcher, baking cookies, or preparing that favorite family dish. They shared the anticipation of seeing family and having their children or grandchildren visit. I had planned a quiet Christmas with Mom, though she couldn't resist inviting neighborhood stragglers over for dinner. Not that it mattered. With the momentum of my life lately, tomorrow was just the stepping stone between now and the day I would leave.

Tonight, at Mom's request, ZZ and I were going with her to midnight Mass at St. Stannie's. I thought it was a good thing that Mom wanted to get out of the house. ZZ agreed but he reminded me not to push, to let Mom move at her own pace, in her own comfort zone.

"Ladies and gents, please fold your costumes neatly so they can ride unwrinkled to the cleaners to be stored for next year's staff," ZZ was saying as he circulated, shaking hands and exchanging a few personal good-byes. "We'll be turning them over to Personnel outside the employee locker rooms, so I suggest we get downstairs and change so we can all get home to celebrate Christmas with our families."

We gathered our things and streamed through the emptying store, an odd assortment of men and women in red velvet suits, in green-striped lederhosen with curled-toe gold booties.

Inside the locker room, taking off the Mrs. Claus suit for the very last time, I became so overwhelmed with emotion that it took all my willpower to keep from moving at all. In slow motion

I ran a hand down the white fur trim for the last time, slipped out of the graceful skirt, and folded it neatly into the silver box. The jacket, its beadwork beaming as brilliantly as it had weeks ago, seemed to wink a good-bye as I folded it squarely and let it rest on top of the skirt. How many years ago had this suit been made? It had to be at least fifty years old, and yet it had held up, its color unfaded, its fabric plush and shiny.

Maisie called out a good-bye, then ducked out the door, the last woman to go. I waved back, sitting there in my black camisole and cotton boxers.

And then I couldn't help myself. Tears stung my eyes and quickly spilled over, running down my cheeks. It was so silly, so sentimental, but I didn't want to let this time go, wasn't sure how to move from the era of Mrs. Claus to the next phase of my life. The thought of taking that train to New York the day after Christmas made me feel cold inside, but I hadn't left myself another choice. No clear Plan B. Olivia's lament, without a second choice.

As I leaned over to touch the velveteen fabric one last time, a teardrop slipped from my eye and splashed on the suit.

"You big dummy-head . . ."

I quickly rubbed it dry with my fingertips, then leaned back against the locker and tried to calm myself. It was just a costume. Just a role I'd played. Temporary.

Well, maybe for me, but someone else would probably use this costume next year. I fished a pen and tiny notepad out of my purse, deciding to leave the next Mrs. Claus a message. After some thought, I wrote:

This suit brings luck. Go with it.
—Mrs. C.

Maybe it was corny, but if I found a note like this, I'd get a kick out of it. Like finding a poignant prediction in a fortune cookie. And at least writing the note gave me enough of a boost to pull on my jeans and sweater and get the hell out of there before they closed the store around me.

When I finally swung out of the locker room, my coat flying behind my heels, only ZZ and Charley remained.

"There she is!" Charley beamed his ever-present smile.

"Before I forget—" ZZ pointed a finger at me, "Regis said to tell you he had to run, something about picking up his parents at the airport. But he's going to call you on your cell after the holidays."

"Okay." I lifted the silver box and pressed my lips together tightly as I handed it over to Charley. "Merry Christmas, Charley."

"Thank you, Mrs. Claus," he said. "And best of luck to you back in New York with the Rockettes. Or should I say, break a leg?"

I thought about telling him that a broken leg was just the first crack in the huge tectonic-plate shift of my life, but then it was such a long story that I just smiled and wished him happy holidays.

22

Dinner at Mom's was lovely, with the lights dimmed, candles lit throughout the main floor, an orchestra playing Handel's *Messiah*, and the strong scent of pine in the front parlor.

"We just picked up the tree this morning," Mom said, recalling how she and ZZ had bartered with the tree man at the market. As I studied the ancient ornaments from my childhood, Mom rushed off to open the door for one of our neighbors, Fritz, who'd brought a very smooth oyster chowder he'd made from a recipe on the cooking channel. Mom tried to keep things simple with a main course of shrimp scampi, but other friends contributed cheese blintzes and mandarin almond salad, pumpkin pie and mince tarts.

Although I helped Mom serve and clean up, changed CDs of Christmas music, and pulled door duty, I kept returning to the tree, the ornaments that had taken me through my childhood. A plain red ball with my name in glitter, decorated when I was in Girl Scouts. My replica of the Bromo-Seltzer Tower, an architectural atrocity that I'd never seen but adored. A sparkling red dancing shoe given to me by Bobby during our last year of college, a time when so many good things seemed possible, just

down the road for us. It struck me that I wasn't always unhappy
here; the Baltimore of my childhood had been a wonderful
place to dream and plan and fall in love for the first time.

Tucking my legs under me on the sofa, I gave my old Christmas snow globe a shake and relaxed with the crowd, part of the
ebb and flow of the party. So easy to lose myself in my mother's
house, in her circle of friends and music and cultural projects
and committees. How easy it had been to become a Rockette. To
portray Mrs. Claus. To play the role of Claire Todd's daughter.
Had I become a talented assimilator, a sponge ready to suck up
alternate worlds?

Any world but my own.

Soon after dessert people began to head out, and while ZZ
rinsed more plates in the kitchen, Mom pulled a chair closer to
the sofa and handed me a rectangular box wrapped in burnished gold foil. "Merry Christmas, sweetie."

"Mom . . ." I sat up straighter. "Your gifts are upstairs. I wasn't
planning to exchange until tomorrow."

"That's fine. I just wanted you to open this tonight." She
tapped her lips as if trying to hold back a grin. "I think I nailed it
this year. One of the best gifts I've ever given you."

I pulled off the foil wrap and found a manuscript bound in a
red ribbon. "*The Moron's Guide to Baltimore Architecture?*" I read
the title.

"Dedicated to you, my dear. I started writing it as a simple
guide for you, then . . . The project sort of took off."

"You were writing for me?" I shook my head. "But I know my
way around town."

"When Carol showed me a tape of that *Nutcracker* show, it
forced me to think about my own daughter and her attitude toward the city I love."

"Mom, that character is not me—"

She held up a hand to cut my objection. "I'm not saying that it
is, Livvy. But you must admit, history and architecture have always been your most hated subjects. Perhaps I forced too much
on you when you were little. Those Latrobe tours and such. I accepted your rebellion, your choice to pursue a different area of

the arts, but I also think you have come to the age where you'll begin to appreciate history and art."

"Uh-oh." I bent down one corner of the manuscript, trying to steal a peek at some of the text. "I guess this is chock full of lessons to be learned from history. All that stuff I learned then forgot in high school?"

"There comes a time in your life when you realize the relevance of history. It's more than learning from the mistakes of others. Fine architecture demonstrates the marriage between function and beauty. It is only after we appreciate the past incarnation of a city that we can become a useful part of its daily function, eventually melding into its history."

I had untied the ribbon and was looking at the contents page. "Ghosts in These Walls?" It was the title of an early chapter.

She nodded. "I like to think of the people who used this house before us, and the people who will live here in a hundred years. We can be a part of that timeline, Livvy, and not just in this house, but in the library, our church, Fells Point, Mount Vernon Place . . ."

My fingers moved through the manuscript hungrily. So she really had been working during her seclusion. "And this is going to be published?"

"Not with a scholarly press, but with a trade house." She smiled. "It's really going to be a Moron's Guide. Sounds ridiculous, I know, but when I learned of the number of people this market reaches, it seems far more effective than pouring my efforts into a rarified textbook that a few hundred students will be forced to buy and will never crack the spine on."

"I'm shocked, and surprised. Very surprised. But thanks, Mom." I stood up to give her a hug and suddenly ZZ appeared with our coats.

"We'd better get going if we're going to make midnight Mass."

As they bundled into gloves and hats, I turned down the house lights and headed out. One of the grand double doors pushed open into a shower of fuzzy snow.

"How beautiful!" Mom clapped her gloved hands together as she emerged from the house. It struck me that this was the first time I'd seen her outside for weeks, with a new calm about her, even a festive air. She descended the stairs, her face lifted to the night sky. "There is something magical about a having snow on Christmas."

"Olivia, you'd better be careful on these steps," ZZ said, reaching back to give me a hand.

"I'm fine," I insisted, though I leaned on him till I reached bottom. Healed, yes, but I could be cautious too.

As the three of us walked down the hill at Chester Street, the city was quickly beginning to resemble my snow globe ornament on the mantel, its streets and stoops and cars blanketed with a new-fallen snow and a hush that hinted of peace—the sort of calm that can only inhabit the pure of heart.

Not for me tonight.

Twisted and tortured, I followed my mother and friend through the snow, wishing desperately that this were my city, my place in time to enjoy as Mom had said. She'd written a whole manuscript to help me understand this city, and somehow I couldn't find a place in the elaborate, historic timeline for myself. Electric orange candles lit every other window, some of them half caked with snow, and one illuminated tree seemed to quiver slightly, its lights peeking through the white powder. We passed other delighted walkers, a handful of older kids out to scoop up what they could, an occasional stoop sitter in cap and coat gathering white stuff like a lawn ornament.

Such a festive moment, a magical Christmas, except for me, Olivia the Nutcracker, able to wreck the perfect holiday with untold anxiety.

In a daze I followed into St. Stannie's, genuflected, took my seat, and stared ahead at the ornate carvings over the altar. Although more than half of the masses here were in Polish, my mother always chose St. Stannie's for its classical architecture— the rose window, towering nave arcade, flying buttresses. A mini-Gothic cathedral in the neighborhood. When my father died five years ago of a sudden heart attack, his funeral was held here in St. Stannie's, the first and only time I had sat in the front row, an uncomfortable spot for the lapsed Catholic in me. For a while I had thought that the funeral would make me feel a sadness each time I passed this church, but the opposite had happened; St. Stannie's was a peaceful connection with my dad, the scene of our final good-bye.

The church organist was playing "O, Little Town of Bethlehem," and the end of every other row was decked with a sprig of pine tied off in a red bow. We were sitting at the end of an aisle, right beside the panels of stained-glass windows that were oddly illuminated from the whiteness of the snow outside. St. Stannie's was known for its stained glass, stacks of square windows in jewel tones with sacred images like doves and chalices, mangers and crowns, and embedded words like *gloria, ave Maria, INRI* and *pax.* I craned my neck to take in the windows on the other side, such pleasing, reassuring designs, the symbols universal. The window nearest me honored the Assumption, though I couldn't decipher the symbols in gold at its center—sort of a twisted *SR.* The letters were surrounded by a ring of stars and a simple mosaic patchwork of glass in various hues of blue, from Caribbean turquoise to a deep indigo. It gave me a sense of timelessness, of the Christmases that had been celebrated in this church, of the baptisms and the funerals that had passed here and those that would transpire in the next hundred years. I shivered, oddly connected to the mystical beauty of these windows.

As the Mass began in Polish and I heard my mother reciting, "Glory be to the Father . . ." in English beside me, I realized what an achievement this was for her to be outside the house in a very crowded public place. She was making real progress, and all along she hadn't been wasting her time at home. To think that my mother would be publishing a *Moron's Guide to Architecture.* And I was her inspiration . . . scary. So Mom's hermitage had been fruitful, and now she had a therapist and ZZ and a good prospect of returning to teaching next fall.

Whatever Mom's relationship with ZZ, she didn't need me here. She was capable, and my ankle was healed, and Mrs. Atwater wanted me back, and I had a twenty-thousand-dollar check handy, good for a year's rent in New York, two if I got in with a roommate.

I was one lucky girl. Lucky, yet still in turmoil.

My fingers closed over the dance-shoe charm in the crook of my neck, and I wanted to cry. My do-over, my wish come true. How could I be so ungrateful?

Suddenly the air inside the church felt hot and stuffy and I needed out. Quickly, I squeezed out of the pew, hating the sound of my heels tapping down the aisle to the back of the church.

The vestibule was much cooler than the crowded church, with winter air seeping in through the ornate double doors, beautifully crafted but not well insulated. I touched my fingers to the cold stained glass and breathed deep. Behind me, the priest's voice carried on, patient yet firm, in the rhythmic language that had once enveloped this community, wafting through its markets and bakeries, rising over dining-room tables, punctuating the air as neighbors passed each other on streets lined with marble slab porches. I was not Polish but there was something comforting about this language of my neighborhood, the solidarity of this culture, now living side by side with Chinese shop owners and African American families and Johns Hopkins residents from Chile and India and Canada and France.

This was the neighborhood I had fled for the sophistication and excitement of New York, where I lived in a tall glass building surrounded by neighbors I didn't know. I'd been convinced that I was trading up, leaving Baltimore for the thrill of Manhattan. Now I wasn't so sure.

The door creaked back a few inches and a woman squeezed in, her narrow, slumped shoulders fitting easily through the small space. She said something in Polish, blinking as she untied the scarf at her chin. "They have started!" she whispered.

I nodded, then moved to open the inner door for her. As she passed inside with a distant smile, my eyes met ZZ's. He'd been standing by the door.

"I came to check on you. Everything okay?"

"Not really. And I don't know how to fix it, but I realize now that I asked for the wrong thing when I put that wish in the stocking. I thought I wanted a do-over with Bobby, a chance to go back and make our relationship work, but I was so wrong. Being with him was toxic for me; I see that now." I raked a bunch of damp curls off my forehead. "Anyway, you asked and I'm giving you the sound-byte version. Not your average church chatter, but that's it. I'm kicking myself for making that stupid wish."

"There's nothing wrong with examining our pasts, Olivia. We can savor the moments when we felt happy and try to get there again."

I shook my head. "I don't think so. I won't ever be so blindly happy again."

"You're right." ZZ took one of my hands between his and held it tight. "Next time, you'll be an informed, wiser person. No more dumb luck for you, Olivia. From now on, you're going to make your choices instead of following the path of least resistance."

As he said it, I saw it so clearly—how my relationship with Bobby had been about following him, basking in his confidence and talent. Although I had been the one paying the rent and buying groceries, I had deferred to Bobby on life choices, on artistic decisions. He was the one who pushed me to audition for the Rockettes, the one who'd told me about the dance troupe at Towson State, who'd made sure that I kept up with ballet, jazz, and tap lessons. Bobby was my stage mother, and now that I had really and truly separated my life from his, I wasn't sure who owned my career goals. Who really wanted Olivia to be a dancer?

Was that a part of my life that needed a do-over, too? "I've botched up so many things."

"Have you really?" ZZ folded his arms over his belly. "Were the last few months a mistake? Dancing in New York? Do you regret the people you met in the last six weeks?"

"No, of course not," I answered quickly. "They're not the problem. It's my own choices, that's what I regret. Bad choices."

"Honey, it's all grist for the mill. Haven't you ever heard the old pearl about learning from mistakes?"

"Maybe that's my problem. All these mistakes and I still don't have a clear path. I just wish I had a chance to start over."

"Well, then, this is your lucky day." He reached out and touched the heavy door, pointing to the street. "Olivia, on the other side of the door waits a new start. A chance to begin again."

I frowned at the door.

"Every day is a do-over, Red. Every new morning holds infinite possibilities. Whether you choose to take a train to New York or join a circus in Kalamazoo, you are in control. You are seizing the moment. We only go through once, Red, far as anyone can guarantee, and already you've accomplished some pretty cool things. Keep at it, but don't think you have to follow any certain track."

The old church door loomed before me, beckoning, intimidating.

"Go on," he said. "Go for it."

Did he think I was going out there in the cold, right now? "You mean out in the snow?"

"A little snow never hurt anyone." He stepped back from the doorway, giving me full access. "Don't worry, I'll see that Claire gets home."

"Okay, then . . ." I put my hands against the door and shoved, and a hundred tiny crystal flakes skittered around me. Feeling a little silly, I stepped out, let the door close behind me, and descended the church steps, the first steps in my symbolic do-over.

One car passed by, then another. A man walked his dog down the side street, moving slowly, the dog trying to sniff footprints in the snow.

I wondered what it would be like to live here again, to stake my future in this city, set down roots and start a business. The money I'd gotten from Mario's wouldn't go too far in New York, but here it could be a down payment for a house or condo, seed money for a business.

What had ZZ said? Infinite possibilities.

I took a few steps away from the church, glancing at the Christmas trees in the windows of homes I passed. Heading west, toward the hub of Fells Point as if I actually had somewhere to go this dark Christmas morning.

I turned down Wolfe, passing the house Woody had pointed out, 927 Wolfe, which was once occupied by an ice company. In old Baltimore the company sent crews to the Susquehanna River each winter to cut ice and haul it into storage. It was shipped to Baltimore by boat each spring, used in iceboxes to preserve food.

I had always been surrounded by this city's history, but somehow, I'd never felt as if I were a part of it until Bobby's show had pushed my name into infamy. Here was my chance to reverse that, my chance to make my own mark, do something positive, make some waves instead of just dodging the ones that came my way.

And suddenly I was running down the street, my boots skidding slightly in the slush, snowflakes battering my eyes. I ignored it all, forging ahead as if I were running straight into the frame of a Frank Capra film. A right on Thames Street, past the water, another right on East Broadway.

The storm door of Jimmy's rattled slightly as I tugged it open and burst inside, my nose frozen and my eyelashes wet with snow. The waitress looked up from the counter, unfazed as I swiped at my eyes and looked in the corner . . . And there he was, at his table under the clock, reading glasses balanced on his nose as he sketched in a notebook. His shoes were kicked off under the table, his gray-socked feet rubbing against each other for warmth.

I pressed my eyes shut against the rush of emotion I felt at the sight of him—Woody, alone on Christmas Eve, drawing up plans. It was a beautiful sight, mostly because I could see my reflection in the glass of the clock over his head. In the reshaping of my life, this was a frame I could fit into.

Of course, there were dozens of other factors to take into consideration, so many things that would have to weave together, but I wasn't going to sweat the details now.

Instead, I shook the snow from my coat, wove between the tables, and met Woody's look of surprise head-on. "Merry Christmas," I said.

He swiped off his glasses, a slow grin dawning. "Liv . . . You found me in my mouse hole."

Impulsively I grabbed his coat from the chair and tossed it at him. "Come outside. The snow is beautiful."

"It's after midnight."

"Christmas morning. Come out to the square." I turned and fled out the door, knowing he would follow. Everything was covered in white, a quick-falling powder, hard to pack into a snowball, which I discovered when I bent down in the square and tried to bunch it together.

Behind me, Woody whistled through his teeth. "It is gorgeous. Notice how it puts a hush over everything? Footsteps, street traffic."

I straightened and lobbed my snowball at him.

"Hey!" He shifted at the last minute, dodging it. Then he dropped to the ground and pressed a handful of snow together. "What's that about?"

"I'm not leaving. I'm staying in Baltimore. I want to take a do-over, Woody."

He tossed it at me, hitting me softly on the shoulder. "Well, it's not as easy as that, not like buying a vowel on *Wheel of Fortune.*"

"So it's not easy. The thing to remember is that it's possible. Remember what you said? About letting events shape our lives? Well, I'm not going to live someone else's life so I can escape Bobby and the madness he's created. Besides, who ever said that anything worthwhile is easy?"

Brushing his hands together, he moved toward me, close enough that I could see his breath in the air. "Are you sure about this? You're not going to wake up in a sweat and jump on the next train to New York?"

"No regrets. I'm done with Olivia's lament. Right here, at this moment, I know this is exactly what I want to do. This is where I want to be." I reached up and placed one hand on the sleeve of his leather jacket. "I guess my question is, would you like to help a prodigal daughter see her hometown in a brand-new way? Sort of a visionary do-over?"

He laughed. "I think I'd like that." Clumps of snow gathered on his dark hair, making him look a little silly but festive.

Stepping back, I spun around in the still, cold air, snowflakes flying as the hem of my coat lifted. I felt a sense of history, a sense of timelessness here on this canvas of snow by the harbor. Like a black-and-white Latrobe etching in one of Mom's architecture books, we were two dark figures in the center of the square, two people surrounded by the white that was quickly blanketing Fells Point in the dark hours before Christmas morning.

Christmas Mouse

Cassie

San Francisco, 2004

1

"You know this is a special treat. It's almost bedtime." I pulled the lopsided fleece hat down so that it covered both of his rosebud ears.

My son tipped his chin up to me and pushed the cap back again. "Okay, then. Let's go."

With a deep breath I straightened and clasped his hand, and we rounded the back corner of Rossman's and entered Union Square, where one rival store had hung giant red balls from their awnings last week, a display some locals called "Eclipse of Mars." Rossman's other big competitor had unfurled the giant blue bow that wrapped the four-story building from roof to ground, and at the moment "Jingle Bell Rock" rolled from the store's speakers.

Coming up on the main facade of Rossman's, its garland-draped entrance flanked by ten square luminescent shapes aglow against the darkness, I looked down at Tyler, who marched by my side like a dutiful soldier. "Christmas is really coming, T." I launched into the jazz tune from my beloved *Merry Christmas, Charlie Brown*: "Christmastime is here . . ."

Tyler's hat tipped up, revealing a scowl that ended my singing.

"But not for a long time. Thirty-eight days." He'd been counting the days, x-ing off the squares on the Shrek calendar taped to our fridge.

"It'll be here before you know it."

We could have gone out the front entrance and just stepped right over, but I had wanted to take in the whole effect, to come upon them slowly like casual shoppers from another era instead of just sucking them up in a passing glance. Maybe I'm just a window designer who talks like an artist, but this was my first real design job out of art school, my key opportunity to make a name for myself as a Bay Area designer. This was the big one—the Christmas display at Rossman's Department Store at Union Square—and I'd been squeezing my friends dry, sucking up all the moral support they could spare, dragging Tyler here after day care so that I could feverishly work toward this deadline while he read in Santa's sled or built Legos on the carpet or napped in his sleeping bag a few feet from his frantically crafting mother. Although this was among my dream jobs, I'd had no idea the budget would be so low, the deadline so tight. I had envisioned leisurely trips to fabric stores where I would twirl swathes of gold and blue ribbon, sample bolts of purple and red velvet, inspect glittering bell and star ornaments, all to be patterned and cut and sewn into the trappings of Christmas by a capable team of seamstresses.

The reality was a team of one—*moi*—scrounging through the storeroom in an attempt to salvage old decorations and transform them into something clever and fresh and full of Christmas spirit. Apparently, this branch of Rossman's had been underperforming, and the punishment for low profits was a very low operating budget.

As the windows came into view I squeezed my son's hand tighter. "Ooh, I'm so excited. My first Christmas windows."

He squeezed back, but I sensed that he was indulging me, my five-year-old son who probably should have been in bed an hour ago. Maybe I was expecting too much, expecting him to care about something so far off in the adult world. Hard to sell department-store windows in the cold when the cool excitement of a Japanese cartoon and the comfort of a warm bed waited at home, but this was the unofficial debut. I had just removed the panels from the windows thirty minutes ago, unveiling the Christmas displays, and although the store's bigwigs would swagger by to see them in the morning, I wanted the preview to be the advent of Tyler's Christmas. Maybe this would become a new tradition for us? Maybe next year his dad would join us.

This year was the first time Tyler comprehended the rituals of Christmas—the coming of Santa, the birth of a Savior, the exchange of gifts—and I felt responsible for creating traditions that would define his Christmases for the rest of his life.

No pressure.

"Hark the herald angels sing, glory to the newborn king . . ." My breath formed puffs in the cool night air as I swung his hand merrily.

"Stop it, Mom," he said firmly. Just like his father, he resisted when I overplayed the cheer card. "Can we just see the windows?"

"Sure." As we moved closer, the tiny white lights of the garland framing the square window danced before my eyes. The garland was a new purchase I'd acquired from a discount wholesaler, as the greenery in storage was pressed flat and shedding. But I'd enjoyed working with the fake pine boughs, twining clear lights through it and shaping a few yards into spiral topiaries.

The first window was a scene from Santa's workshop, with Santa checking a long scroll of a list, elves hammering and sizing toys, Mrs. Claus delivering a plate of cookies. The figures were somewhat abstract, made from Styrofoam forms that had been used for Christmas trees, which suited the flared skirts of Mrs. Claus and the female elves well. The others I'd had to carve off and shape, then cover with felt.

"What do you think?" I asked.

"Cool." Tyler pressed his fingers to the glass, measuring, calculating.

"Do you get it? Can you tell what it's supposed to be?"

"Sure, I do. It's Santa's toyshop. Where'd you get those hammers?"

"I made the top half out of clay. The bottom part is an ice-cream stick."

"My clay? Did you use mine?"

"No, sweetie," I said, moving him to the next window, where merry elves strung lights and ribbons through a grove of topiaries. Next three elves perfected a fat red bow on a gift, their tiny wrap room strewn with scraps of glimmering holiday paper. Tyler began calling out each scene, then running on to the next window.

"Elves loading Santa's sleigh," he gasped, racing on. "Mrs. Claus sewing Santa's red suit. Elves painting stripes on candy canes. Santa trimming his beard. Where did you get all that white hair?"

"It's actually pasta. Long rice noodles."

"Can we eat them after Christmas?"

I laughed. "I think the glue might stick in our teeth."

I followed him at a slower pace, pleased that he'd warmed to this late-night activity.

In the last window, my favorite, a dozen Mrs. Clauses performed extraordinary tasks, checking reindeer tonsils, repairing a runner on the sleigh, trimming the topiaries, sweeping a chimney, and decking the Golden Gate Bridge with lights. I'd loved the notion that Mrs. Claus could do it all, and my friend Jaimie, a longtime employee of Rossman's, thought the window would play here in San Francisco.

Tyler scratched his forehead under the cap, knocking it off. "How come you made all those Mrs. Clauses? Everybody knows there's only one."

"Artistic license." He frowned, so I added, "I was just having some fun with it." I cupped my fingers over one eye, forming a scope. "If you focus on one, you can imagine that it's one person doing all these jobs at different times."

He made his own curled-finger scope. "Oh. Can we go home now?"

Home is the third-floor studio apartment in the turret of a Victorian apartment house in Noe Valley, a quiet neighborhood near the Mission District, just eight blocks' walk from the streetcar or BART station. I was saving up for a car, but that was part of the long-term plan, so for the time being Tyler and I covered San Francisco by mass transit.

"Let's go inside and get our stuff. Did you like the windows?"

"Sure. Can we make one of those hammers for me?"

"Ha! You liked the hammers?" Leave it to my son to find the one tool in the panorama of Santa Claus lore. I tugged open a door of the main entrance. "We'll see."

2

"**O**h, thank God you're still here." Jaimie Mayhews reached toward us as if she were extending a lifeline to save us from drowning in the employee locker room.

"We're on our way out." I was zipping up Tyler's bag of Legos and books and emergency snacks, and Tyler was swaying against the painted concrete wall by the door, dusting it with the back of his coat as he munched cheese crackers.

"No, you can't go!" Jaimie tucked the thick, wavy tendrils of her hair behind both ears. We're both brunettes, but her hair springs forth in lush Victorian curls while mine is the straight-as-a-flat-ribbon variety. Jaimie is petite and sweet looking, but that wiry frame is solid and strong as a bull, which fits Taurus, her birth sign. We've been friends since junior high when she felt sorry for me sitting alone in the lunchroom with my plantain chips and carrot juice. She offered me a seat at her table and half of her Hostess Ding Dong; we've been friends ever since.

"There's a meeting in the buyer's conference room and you have to be there," she said urgently. "Chicago has sent us a new manager, a hatchet man, I think, and he came here straight from the airport and I think he's going to fire anyone who didn't work a full shift tonight."

"That's ridiculous," I said. "Probably illegal, too."

"He's the kind of guy who'll fire first, worry about lawsuits after the smoke clears."

Tyler's chin lifted. "Does he have a gun?"

"No, honey, it's a figure of speech." Jaimie kneeled beside him. "But your mom needs to talk with him. Do you want to come up to my office?" Jaimie is a buyer at Rossman's, which is a godlike position that requires a phone and an office—an oasis of calm. When she was pregnant with Scout we all worried that she'd be kicked out the door through some loophole, but in fact Rossman's wanted her back, even on her terms: job sharing with another experienced mother of three. "We can set up your sleeping bag, and you can watch my portable TV," she told Tyler. "How about that?"

"We need to get home," I said. "And I'm an hourly employee. I don't have to work full shift."

"Just come." Jaimie took the bag in one hand, Tyler's hand in the other. "If you're good, you can read the new Captain Underpants book that someone gave Scout."

"Scout is three months old," I called after her. "Who'd give a book like that to a baby?" Ever since Jaimie and her husband Matt had their first child, she'd been showered with gifts from coworkers and family, many items, like batting helmets and footballs, a tad inappropriate for a teething blob o' baby.

"Just come on," Jaimie insisted.

It was an exercise in euphemism to call the cold tiled room with vinyl chairs and a Formica table a conference room; the drab, windowless space was a sad indicator of the run-down inner workings of this branch of Rossman's, but tonight the room was brimming with employees churning with suspicion and discontent. The seats were filling up fast, so Jaimie and I squeezed into two chairs between a heavyset man with thick black eyeglasses and a young woman with exotic dark eyes and an impressive row of gemmed piercings along her right ear.

"This is ridiculous. I don't have time for this. Will we be paid for attending this meeting?" The young woman cocked her head, catlike, as she spoke.

"Lucy, I honestly don't know," Sherry Hayden answered from the head of the table. The chief of personnel tried to restore calm with her quick smile and her amazing retention of every single employee name, probably because she'd hired all of us. Sherry had one of those ageless faces, smooth chocolate skin and barely a crease. In the two months that I'd worked here Jaimie and I had played a guessing game about Sherry's age. If this new manager was truly going to downsize, I figured Sherry's job was safe; she had seniority over all of us. "You can save your questions for Mr. Buchman, who should be here momentarily."

One of the men I recognized from the security team asked what the meeting was about.

"Right now, I don't have any more information than you have yourself, Tadashi," Sherry was telling him as the air seemed to thin.

"Good evening," came a brisk voice with a British accent.

I looked up. Chicago had sent us a Brit? It was so unlike the Rossmans to outsource, but apparently the character of the company had begun to shift with the tragic death of the famous Rossman couple last December. As he entered he worked the room, making contact with all of us briefly. I liked those eyes, round and blue, like the eyes of a waif pasted on the face of a prince in a rumpled suit. "Thank you all for staying. I would be the dreaded, sure-to-be-maligned Samuel Buchman. But please, feel free to call me Mr. Buchman."

A few people snickered.

"I'm afraid I'm serious. Well, then, Ms. Hayden, thank you for holding the rank and file for me. Given the lateness of the hour, let's dispense with formality and get to the point. If you are in this room tonight, you are designated to be trained and deployed as overtime staff during this holiday season. Of course, you will be paid double rate for the overtime hours you work. This measure is designed to A, maximize our use of personnel, since all of you will have the training to serve in more than one department, and B, eliminate the excessive expense of hiring an additional Christmas crew who will need training, training, and more training, then will leave us in January." He loosened his necktie. "Well, then, that's all for now."

"Hold on a second," Fred chimed in. "Fred Chalmers from the maintenance crew. Correct me if I'm wrong, but are you telling me you expect me to work in another department, too?"

Mr. Buchman pointed at him. "Precisely, sir. If you know maintenance, we will teach you how to operate a terminal on the sales floor or how to size a foot in the shoe department."

Everyone started talking at once, voices of dissension.

Fred shook his head. "That is crazy."

"It's also textbook management theory," Jaimie muttered under her breath as she sized up Buchman. "This one's a climber."

"This has got to be a bad joke," I said, rubbing the back of my neck.

Buchman swung around to face me, clapping his hands like a magician.

The room fell silent as he scowled at me. "Your name, please?"

"Cassie . . . Cassandra Derringer."

"No, Ms. Derringer, it most certainly is not a joke. If you haven't heard the advance rumblings, I am your worst nightmare—the no-man from headquarters here to trim off excesses, fire the slackers, consolidate departments, push the staff until they give 150 percent, and if all that fails, ultimately, I am the one who will recommend closing this branch of Rossman's. Yes, the stakes are high. Your store is in jeopardy of being wiped from the streets of San Francisco, Ms. Derringer. Do you think that's a joking matter?"

"Well . . ." I wanted to reply that it wasn't my store, that I was an hourly employee hired just two months ago, but two dozen employees with vested pension plans in this store were staring at me, and I had a strong feeling Mr. Buchman's question was rhetorical, anyway. "As you can see, Mr. Buchman, I'm not laughing."

He nodded and turned, as if to dismiss me.

"But I'm also not completely on board with your plan."

He turned. He glared.

"And your department is . . ."

"Design. Window displays, floor displays. Christmas decorations."

"Design?" He pressed two knuckles to his chin, right under a cleft that would have been attractive if he weren't so obnoxious. "I look forward to reviewing the necessity of your department, Ms. Derringer."

Translation? *You and your silly jingle bells are history.*

Lucy the earring girl shot me a frown that said, *You are busted.* And though I didn't cower under Mr. Buchman's glare, I had a feeling she was right.

Although I felt possessed by an overwhelming desire to jump up and shout "Fire me now!" I managed to restrain myself until the meeting wound down. Mr. Buchman assigned Sherry Hayden the task of handing out our dual assignments in the morning, which had to mean she was going to be up all night trying to make appropriate matches, but sleep deprivation seemed to be a minor factor in Mr. Buchman's diabolical plan to ruin Christmas for all of us.

As soon as the meeting ended, Jaimie and I moved quickly to her office.

"I don't even want to talk about it now," she said, glancing over her shoulder as we passed down the dark hallway to her office. "If I lose my job sharing . . ." She shook her head.

We both knew that a full-time position was out of the question for her right now, not with Matt working on an expansion in Tokyo, Scout crying for hours at night, and Jaimie trying to strike that delicate balance between having a life of her own and devoting her life to this precious new bundle of needs.

"Tomorrow," I said, quietly rubbing her back between the shoulder blades. "We'll straighten it out with Sherry."

Jaimie's office was quiet, a soft pool of light sweeping under her desk lamp. "I'm not even going to check my e-mails," she said, clicking the mouse. "I haven't worked this late since before Scout was born. Let's get the hell out of here."

A momentary panic hit me as I wondered where Tyler had gone. Then I saw him facedown in his sleeping bag, his little body curled up like a worm in the rain. I touched his forehead lightly, raking back the damp hair there. "He's out."

Jaime peeked over her monitor, her lower lip jutting out. "Oh, look at the lovey . . . I am definitely driving you home."

Normally I would have insisted that we could make it on our own, not wanting to take Jaimie out of her way, but I couldn't do that to Tyler, couldn't bear to disrupt the downy rhythm of his sleep. "Okay." I shrugged on my coat, scooped him up into my arms, and pressed my lips to his forehead. "But just this once."

3

Have you ever noticed how so much of our life is framed in rectangular vision with three-to-five ratio? The three-by-five photograph, the computer monitor. Postcards. Business cards. The rent check. Placemats. Windshields, windows, the ATM screen. And the box, the boob tube, the television screen that had paid my way in the world for more years than I'd like to remember.

Recently I realized that whenever I thought of my ex, I pictured him on the television monitor, usually at the top of the show delivering his monologue in front of that cheesy replica of the Golden Gate Bridge, one hand in his pocket, the other jabbing at air, fingers splayed as if trying to grasp a ball of sanity in an insane world. That was part of the charm of TJ Blizzard, the Snowman, the Blitzer, the frat boy who never got past the food fights and farting contests. Although TJ often seemed capable of reaching out of the box and grabbing the most laconic viewer in Peoria or Kalamazoo, in reality he was stuck behind that screen, and I liked picturing him that way, static and flat, ineffectual. My way of pantsing the powerhouse quarterback.

Gripping my coffee mug as the sun began to sneak through

the slats of the wooden blinds of the turret windows around Tyler's bed, I realized my ex had appeared in a vague dream last night: TJ on the three-by-five monitor, his lips curling in that goofy smirk.

The meaning of the dream was clear: time to circle back to him for the one thing that mattered right now, a father for my son. Although TJ sent money occasionally, the one thing I wanted and needed from him was to be a dad to Tyler. I rubbed my eyes, trying to think through the day, the morning at Rossman's, lunch with Jaimie and Bree, and the afternoon off. I had hoped to take Tyler out of day care early, but instead I would have to squeeze in a visit to the studio.

When we moved here from TJ's Pacific Heights house, the turret was Tyler's space. We had painted the walls cloud blue and cut a thick foam pad to fit the floor, his place to laze and roll, invent and sleep at night. I kneeled down next to him, pulling the comforter back and pushing aside Lemon Bear to kiss his smooth cheek. "Good morning, sunshine."

"I'm still tired." He stretched, gazing at me through eyes closed to a sliver. "Come back later. Good night, moon."

That morning I arrived before the Rossman's big shots and went right to the front facade, checking the windows for balance of composition and making sure none of the figures had fallen out of place. Would my displays come close to competing with our Union Square rivals, Nordstrom, Gump's, Neiman Marcus, and Macy's? As I walked along the facade, jazz piano played in my head—the song Schroeder plays in *A Charlie Brown Christmas* while the kids are supposed to be rehearsing but instead just dance merrily. Sometimes I wake up with those Vince Guaraldi riffs in my head. The windows did bring a smile to my face, each scene silly and bright, like an animated feature, and I felt sorely tempted to spring into a Snoopy dance right in Union Square.

Warm sunshine broke through the clouds overhead, and I turned toward the square, the wide expanse across Geary Street dotted with palm trees and framed with trim green landscaping. The Christmas tree was surrounded by scaffolding, where workers were hanging electric lights. This time next week the square would be thick with shoppers, even before the tree lighting on the day after Thanksgiving.

Someone nudged me, a woman passing too closely, and she turned toward me with a sweep of her ivory cashmere coat and blinked. Just blinked. No apology. No begging pardon.

I drew back into my coat and watched her walking off, this woman from a club I'd grown familiar with—the Rossman's shopper. On my first day at Rossman's when I'd climbed into the dusty window display in my jeans and sweatshirt, I had noticed these creatures moving through the store in their shopping trances, gazing at merchandise through highlighted, feathered bangs, the women in winter white, so coiffed and calm.

I never felt like an ugly duckling until I started working at Rossman's Department Store. Which doesn't really make sense when you consider that I'd just come from six years of working as a scenic designer on a late-night show where celebrities arrived in their limos every afternoon and breezed past me down the hall in their designer garb, carrying garment bags packed with more designer wear. And yet, in that jocular, hurry-up-and-wait milieu, I never worried about the fact that Elle had a set of legs I'd never compete with or that Renee Zellweger had knocked off her Bridget Jones weight in record time while I was still fighting off the mommy pounds.

But something about the ladies in white was different. I have to admit, I was jealous the first time one of the ladies glided past me, her eyes fixed on some luminescent bottles or squat jars of miracle make-up in a distant display case.

There goes a beautiful woman with a perfect life, I thought, impressed by her confidence and easy grace. Shopping in those shoes? How did she manage to keep her balance, not to mention negotiate the hazardous hills of San Francisco? But silly me, the winter-white women did not chase after streetcars. How I envied them their perfect lives.

My life was like a relief map of mountains and valleys, bumpy foothills and yawning craters. I'd made my fair share of mistakes.

Blame it on too many late nights playing quarters in college. Or the days when trays of cocaine were passed around like Cheez Whiz at parties. Jaimie and I joke that the late eighties, when we hit our twenties, are still a blur. Or maybe it's wrong to blame the era; maybe the problem is my compulsive nature. Running away from home at sixteen and returning with a gorgeous golf pro, whom my mother promptly stole from me. Bumming my way across Europe in the summer after my freshman year of college. I'd been irresponsible and reckless, and it was a wonder I'd survived my own bad behavior.

But now that I was a parent, a mom, priorities had fallen into place for me. Right now, I needed to live right for Tyler. My life had been patched up and pulled together in the last few years.

A life on the mend, but still worlds apart from the ladies in white.

"I'm not sure that these windows have the sparkle we need to compete with Macy's, Neiman Marcus, Gump's," Daniel Rossman told the management group that gathered in front of the store a few minutes later. The department-store heir apparent had flown in from Chicago with Mr. Buchman last night but skipped the meeting and went straight to the hotel. "It's a shame they couldn't be mechanized."

"Mechanized?" Sherry Hayden squinted. "I'm not following you, sir."

"Like the windows at Lord & Taylor in New York," Daniel Rossman said impatiently. He was an attractive man until he opened his mouth to criticize my work. "Like the little dancing dolls in Small World at Disney World. Moving around and dancing. Real entertainment."

"Wouldn't that be expensive?" Sherry asked. "We've been given a slim budget for new decorations this Christmas, not just the windows, but everything inside the store."

"Ah, yes, how amusing that would be," Mr. Buchman cut in. "However, as we are retailers and not in the entertainment industry, I think we can dispense with dancing Barbies and stick with the charming scenes Ms. Derringer has created here." He glanced down at his Palm Pilot. "Did you stay on budget, Ms. Derringer?"

"I did." I stepped forward, surprised and relieved the wicked Mr. Buchman seemed to be saving me from Daniel. "The forms for the elves and Santas were actually old Styrofoam Christmas trees and I—"

"On budget, that's all we need to know," Mr. Buchman cut me off. "That's it for our window displays. Let's move inside and examine one of our register terminals. I have noted that the software was last updated three years ago, and customers have complained ever since . . ." He disappeared inside the door, followed by the others.

Sherry Hayden fell out of line to touch my arm. "Nice job, Cassie. Don't let Rossman's comment derail you. I understand he's the financial liability of the family."

"A major liability. When is he going back?"

"Tonight, I think. But we're stuck with Mr. Buchman till the new year at least." Frowning, she glanced inside. "I'd better get in there before the men do something we'll all regret. Stop by my office in an hour or so. I came up with a cute second job for you."

"But I don't want one."

"Just stop by."

"Mrs. Claus?"

Poor Sherry fished through papers on her desk, clearly rattled by this extra work. "Cassie, I know it's an inconvenience at this time; however, Mr. Buchman is inflexible on this."

"Sherry, I'm a single parent with a five-year-old son. I can't take on another job."

She looked up at me over her reading glasses. "Not when it pays time and a half?"

Quick calculations in my head floated by like visions of sugarplums. Insurance money. A down payment on a car. Christmas presents. "The money would be great, but I've got Tyler."

"Bring him to the store."

I thought of his interest in the elves' hammers. "What if he dressed up as an elf? I think he'd like that, and he could stick close by me."

"Horrors." She rolled her eyes. "Child labor laws."

"You won't be paying him. He'll just be playing dress-up with me."

She winced. "I should probably say no, but if you want to try and sneak that one past Mr. Buchman, I have an elf costume that's too small for anyone on staff."

"Okay, then, I guess we have a deal. But does Mrs. Claus matter? I thought Buchman was trying to pare things down to essential personnel."

"The Mrs. Claus costume has sentimental value for the Rossmans. Evelyn used to play Mrs. Claus when she was alive, and, well, the family has been known to fly out and check on the costume, make sure it's being used."

I rolled my eyes. "Sorry, Sherry, but Mrs. Claus?"

"I know, I know." She put her hand over mine. "How'd you like to be a security guard hearing that you've got to start fetching designer shoes for women and making sure they wear their footies?"

I took a deep breath. "I see your point."

"And you know what? Before you say one more thing, let me just show you this Mrs. Claus suit . . ."

4

"I'm telling you, that suit seems magical," I told my friends as we broke into the bread basket at Kuleto's, an Italian restaurant near Union Square where we usually shared a bottle of wine and a bunch of appetizers. "Wait till you see it . . . maroon velvet that's exquisitely tailored. The skirt drapes so softly. It's like it was made for me, with two fleur-de-lis patterns sewn on the bodice in dark red bead. Beadwork! Like a vintage gown. Rumor has it that the original Mrs. Rossman sewed it herself. Can you imagine?"

"Whoa, there, chattermuffin." Bree broke a small jalapeno corn muffin in half and popped a piece in her mouth. She's probably a full head taller than Jaimie and me, even sitting down, but with her crisp-cut blond hair, high cheekbones, and sky blue eyes, Bree could be a model. Whenever the three of us walk into a party together, Bree is the guy magnet. "Have you thought about how this might hamper your Christmas holiday? I mean, working up until Christmas Eve."

"But it's a great way to demonstrate Christmas spirit for Tyler, don't you think? With his mom playing Mrs. Claus?"

Jaimie shrugged. "I think Freud would have a few choice words to say about that."

"But I didn't tell you the best part. When Sherry wasn't looking, I found a note in the pocket. It said that the suit is lucky, and it was signed by Mrs. Claus! Doesn't that make you melt inside?"

"Sweet." Bree nodded. "Do you think the personnel lady baited you?"

"No! She wouldn't do that, and I like the idea of involving Tyler in Rossman's Christmas campaign. The thing is, I love Christmas so much and I want Tyler to have that, too."

"But you weren't raised with holiday traditions, and you turned out okay," Jaimie pointed out. "You've got the spirit. You don't suffer bouts of depression at holiday time. You drink your share of eggnog lattes and partake in the obligatory kiss under the mistletoe. Somehow, you learned all that stuff, which makes Christmas a learned behavior."

"You didn't celebrate Christmas?" Bree's eyes narrowed. "How did Agate pull that one off?"

"She was boycotting America's most commercial holiday."

"You didn't have Christmas at all? No toys or cookies? No fruitcake?"

"Oh, we strung cranberries and moon pies on a tree in the yard for winter solstice. The birds liked that. But Agate refused to savagely end the life of a living thing just to have a Christmas tree. And she didn't believe in wasting natural resources to burn Christmas lights. And while other kids were baking chocolate mint brownies and gluing candies to gingerbread houses with vanilla frosting, Agate reminded me how destructive processed sugars could be and handed me a scoop of carob chips, raisins, and walnuts."

"Oh, God, I remember those carob chips." Jaimie tucked her thick dark hair behind both ears. "It's a wonder those things didn't kill us."

Bree's gaze switched back and forth, following along. "Okay, help me keep score. Are you saying that you're going to take this Mrs. Claus gig?"

"The outfit is gorgeous, and I could use the extra money, and it's double time, and they'll let me bring Tyler at night. So, yes, I'm going to do it."

"You're crazy," she said, turning to Jaimie. "She's nuts. How about you?"

"I'm not that crazy." She took a sip of chardonnay. "They were pushing me into a second job, but then Stephanie whipped out our contract, the one her lawyer pushed when we decided to do the job sharing. It's right there in black and white: we can't be forced to do overtime. Sherry Hayden says that Mr. Buchman will honor it."

"He has no choice. It's a freakin' contract."

"The law doesn't seem to mean much to Mr. Buchman," I said. "He's probably got a string of lawsuits following him around from store to store. But at least he's got some balls."

Bree lifted her wineglass in a toast. "Here's to men with balls."

We toasted, then I told them about how Buchman had fended off Daniel Rossman's attack on my windows.

"Daniel Rossman? The rich guy?" Bree pressed a hand to her cheek, playing coy. "So, is he cute? Would you do him?"

Thoughtfully swallowing a piece of rye roll, I lifted my wineglass. "Daniel Rossman is a dick."

"But heir to the Rossman fortune?" Bree blinked merrily. "The man must have some redeeming qualities."

"No," Jaimie said, snitching an olive from the antipasto. "I've watched him operate on the fringes the past few years, and I can say with confidence that Cassie is right. He's a dick."

"And not just because he criticized my windows," I defended. "Sherry calls him a financial liability."

Bree put a hand on my wrist. "By the way, I passed by the store on my way here, and your window displays really look great. Love the little pixie figurines. Reminds me of Claymation."

"I'm so glad they've passed. With the budget Rossman's gave me, I wasn't sure what to do, and I've still got a slew of decorations to mount inside the store." I told them how I'd been working on a garland with the pixie figures riding on jingle bells.

"Well, here's to you, honey." Bree toasted me again. "May you jingle all the way."

"Aren't you light and loose with the toasts today," Jaimie told her.

"Reason to drink," I said.

"Ladies, I have news, too." Bree put her glass down in a dignified gesture. "I just came from an interview with KTSF. Do you know their morning show? They're looking for a writer."

"A job? Bree, that's fabulous."

"And in time for Christmas." Jaimie rubbed her hands together. "Guess I'd better pull my list together. Remember that Fendi bag we saw? And the scarf in the window of the Pendleton store . . ."

"Oh, you bad girl." Bree took another muffin. "If I get you anything, it'll be for that cutesy-wutesy Scout."

"He's got tons of stuff," Jaimie objected, pointing to herself. "Diaper Genies out the ying-yang. When is Santa Claus coming to Mama?"

"I think you'd better talk to Matt about that," I teased.

We laughed as the waiter brought more appetizers, then Bree told us the details of her interview for *AM San Francisco*, a morning show with floundering ratings, where the producers hoped to spice things up by hiring a former comedy writer from TJ's show.

"The job is a breeze, some brainstorming and a few one-liners here and there. The staff seems to have a lot of fun together, a real family atmosphere, the way TJ's show used to be. The only downside is getting up at four-thirty in the morning." Bree held her hands up like scales. "Get up early, or eat beans from a can. Which would you choose?"

"I hope you get it, Bree. Let me know if we can do anything to help." I pulled a grape from the fruit plate. "I'd ask TJ to make a call for you, but that might backfire." Although TJ's talent for mockery played well on television, in business people found him annoying at times.

She nodded. "I already thought of that. I'm using network people and one of the executive producers as references."

We discussed plans for Thanksgiving next week, and I shared my plan to nail TJ down to a regular visitation schedule when I saw him at the studio today.

"Good luck on that," Bree said. We had worked together on TJ's show and she was well aware of the quirks of his personality. "I hear that they've now fired the second set designer. TJ's people have been lost since you left the show. Did you see the replica of the Coit Tower they stuck in the background behind the interview chairs? Gives new meaning to the word 'dickhead.'"

I squeezed my eyes shut. "Ooh, there are some things I really miss about working on *TJ's Night*. I may despise him but I love the other people on the show." The gaffers and assistant directors and producers and PAs and interns and writers all became my work-world family, my colleagues through thick and thin, laugh tracks, and sweeps week.

"You were miserable there at the end," Jaimie pointed out.

"But TJ and I had some good times together. That's what I want for Tyler . . . a healthy relationship with his father."

"Hello?" Bree pretended to knock on my head. "You're talking about a man who puts the 'fun' in dysfunctional. Try anything regular, normal, or healthy and he's not going to get it."

"But he's Tyler's father, and Tyler needs him." I'd been over this territory a thousand times before. "It's so frustrating. When is TJ going to figure out that he has a son, ready and willing to love him? I've heard the excuses before, but how could any man in his right mind refuse a five-year-old boy something he needs?"

"We're not defending him, Cassie," Jaimie said softly, "but just be prepared for rejection. Think back on TJ's response to Tyler, his lack of responsibility. I mean, the last time he took Tyler was when? Months ago? And they went to Cliff House, right? It's like taking a preschooler for drinks."

"They watched the seals on the rocks," I said. "TJ would never hurt Tyler."

"Of course not," Bree said, "but we all know he's not father material. And really, honey, you're doing so well, just you and Tyler. Why do you want to screw things up with TJ back in the mix?"

"He's Tyler's father, and a boy needs his father," I said firmly.

"I agree that every kid needs a father figure," Jaimie said. "But it doesn't always work out that way. You know that, Cassie. More than most."

I knew it all right, having spent a lifetime without even knowing my father's name. My mother, who goes by her Wiccan name Agate, prides herself on being a free and independent spirit. So independent that she didn't need my father in her life. Apparently she never acknowledged him, never even informed him that I'd been born. And she would not tell me his name. "At least I've figured out a way to vent that issue," I said through a strained smile. "I just blame Agate."

"What she did was wrong, I know," Bree said. "But didn't she ever give you a hint who he was? Maybe some letters left in a drawer, or old photos?"

I shook my head no. "And knowing Agate, my father could have been anyone. The president at the time . . . or the man who sold us yogurt-covered raisins at the organic grains store."

"Oh my God, who was president in 1969?" Jaimie pushed her thick hair behind both ears. "Reagan? No, Nixon!"

"Now that you mention it," Bree said, assessing me carefully, "I think you have his nose."

"That's right," I said quietly, "laugh at the orphan."

Bree kept smiling, but Jaimie's face grew serious. "Oh, come on, Cassie, you've joked about that yourself. Besides, you're not really an orphan. Agate is still just over in Marin County, right?"

"As far as I know." The last time I saw her was six years ago, and I remembered the scene at her house, a mud stucco cottage in Marin County, vividly. Dressed in a loose white gown, Agate was distracted, trying to collect the right herbs and gems for her ritual in the woods with her Wiccan friends. I had just learned that I was pregnant, although I didn't tell Agate that, but I had come for information about my father, medical information to help the genetic counselor guide me regarding my baby's health.

"I need his name, Agate," I'd told her, waving the medical form in front of her to help plead my case. "My father's name and some medical history."

"I can't talk now, my darling. We've got a healing ritual to perform for Marakesh's daughter." Bent over a low cupboard, she slid an old paper egg carton out of a cubby and waggled her fingers over the compartments. "A pinch of marjoram, holly for balance. Lilac and rose petals." As she muttered, she shoved dried leaves into a small velvet pouch. "And amaranth, of course. Most important, amaranth restores a broken heart."

"Don't put me off, *Mother*. You've done it all my life and now I really need to know. Who was my father?"

"That's where you're wrong, Cassandra. You do not need to know. You've prospered and thrived without that information."

"I need to know!" I slammed my hand on the counter, making her egg carton shiver with the impact. "I deserve to know."

Her gray eyes flashed with intelligence beyond the black eyeliner, eyes so clear I could see tiny lines of red at the edges. "You're going to need some anger management, my dear."

"Give me his name or I swear, I will never speak to you again. I will not visit or take your calls. I will wipe you from my life."

She clasped the small velvet pouch to her breast, letting out a deep breath. "I'm sorry, Cassie, but I cannot speak his name."

I glared at her, wishing I could tear it from her mind, thinking how incredibly unfair life was to plunk me into Agate's life while other children had two stable parents, reliable cars that drove them to soccer games, dinner on store-bought china instead of in rough kiln bowls.

Other kids had parents who guided them on the standard path . . .

While I had a witch mother who cast a wisdom spell on the teacher who was picking on me in class.

In a fit of rage and disappointment, I tore out of Agate's mud hut, slamming the door behind me.

I never spoke to her again, had never answered her calls in all this time, though she stopped calling after the first two years. A month or so after that last encounter, I received a blue velvet pouch in the mail with a note that said, *For love and healing—Agate*.

Late that night while TJ was working on the next day's show

with the writers, I pushed open the window of TJ's Pacific Heights house and turned the pouch upside down, watching with dark satisfaction as Agate's herbs floated off in the wind.

Now, six years later, I can still see those flakes of brown and green disappearing into the night. And I remember thinking that I didn't need Agate's love and healing as much as I needed her to be a mother. But no, she had signed the card "Agate." She was her own separate self named for a soothing stone.

And so I said good-bye to the woman who kept my father from me, the woman who refused to be my mother. And oddly, with the coming of my own child, I gave up caring for the people who gave me life and prepared my heart for my new family.

5

In this world of disposable, replaceable, new and improved up-grades, I am one of those people who cling to the old original. I still have all my high-school and college yearbooks, my third-grade Peanuts lunch box with Lucy holding the football, a piece of Juicy Fruit from the pack that Craig Keyser bought for me on my first "date" to the movies, and the first book report I ever wrote about a bunny who had vampire tendencies.

I am a saver. I love keepers.

Which is as close as I can get to explaining the lingering relationship I have with my ex. Although the romantic, physical aspects of our relationship dwindled soon after our son was born five years ago, I have tried to hold on to TJ as a partner, as a friend, as a father for our child.

"You will always be his father," I have told TJ countless times. When Tyler was an infant he would respond with things like "That's true," and jokes like "So you say," and "Then why does he look like the cable guy?" which only mildly perturbed me since I was used to TJ's sarcasm and goofy humor. Back then his re-sponse didn't really matter since we shared so much, spending our days together in the downtown studio, our nights in his

Victorian in Pacific Heights. In that first year, that copacetic interlude of bottles of sticky formula and sweet-smelling Onesies and padded tushy, I could not imagine a time when TJ would not be in our lives every day.

"You will always be his father," I assured him when Tyler and I were moving to the apartment in search of some independence, cheaper rents, and residential quiet compared to the hub that the Heights had become. I had never felt completely at ease in TJ's Victorian mansion, admittedly; neither had he, and I assumed that eventually he would follow us south to the less tony, more residential Noe Valley.

"Don't be so dramatic. I'll always see you guys around," TJ had responded with that wry grin. "It's not like you're leaving town, Cassie, and with you working on the show, I think I can make my way from my dressing room to the art department."

"You will always be his father," I told him my last day on the set, after I'd given my four weeks' notice and gotten my acceptance to the design institute.

"Ah, but I don't have to be." Hands thrust in his pockets, shoulders up by his ears. How many times had I massaged that tension away? It had seemed so easy once. How had it come to this, face-to-face with a stranger who wrings himself inside out because he has to talk with me about our son? "If there's someone special in your life, you know I'll step aside and let him raise the kid."

"I can't believe you're saying that." I picked up my box, loaded with shoes and tampons, green tea bags and desk toys and thingamabobs Tyler had made in preschool. "I am not hearing this." I turned and walked down the shadowy corridor of the television studio, suddenly wishing the soles of my shoes had metallic studs capable of tearing off the glossy surface of the floor.

"If it's about money, I'll pay," he called after me.

"It's not," I shouted without turning back.

If my friends hadn't pushed me, I wouldn't have taken TJ's money at all, but Jaimie kept reminding me about Tyler's future, and Bree kept pointing out that two thousand a month wouldn't be missed with TJ's income. So I accepted it, my 17 percent child support. Most of it went into Tyler's college fund, though I had used some for art school with the logic that my education would lead to a better job and a more secure future for the two of us.

Throughout my relationship with TJ, I didn't want to hurt him for not loving Tyler as I'd expected. I assumed that special relationship would develop in time, realizing that not all men are so enamored of the baby stages, the diaper changes and crawling feats, toddling through neighbors' gardens and scattering finger foods on the kitchen floor. Tyler was beyond those stages now, an intelligent, creative little boy, and I knew it was time to invite TJ back into our lives, time to nurture a father-son relationship for these two.

As I stepped in through the double glass door of the studio, the security guard jumped up from the reception desk and pulled me into a hug. "It's you!" Darlene squealed. "How are you, honey? I haven't seen you for months."

"I'm doing great! I finished design school. Got a job doing windows at Rossman's Union Square."

Another squeal, more subdued. She leaned back to take a good look at me. "That is so great. I want to get back to school, soon as the kids are in school full-time."

"You should do it, Darlene. Not that you don't get all the stimulation you need here on set."

She waved a hand. "Please, if I have to run backstage and open one more limo door because some star wants hotshot treatment, I promise, you'll hear me screaming down at Union Square."

I laughed as I leaned over her desk, signed in, peeled off a badge. "Well, much as I love my new job, I miss you guys."

She waved at me. "Nothing's changed around here, except the set. Have you seen it? That Coit Tower that looks like a horn growing out of TJ's shoulder?"

"I've heard about it." We talked a little about Tyler and Darlene's sons as we walked toward the studio door. The red studio "taping" light was on, but Darlene let me in. "They're taping the last segment," she said. "TJ should be done in a few minutes."

Moving quietly, I hugged Sally from make-up, then swept past the cluster of writers, mostly new faces now. The AD pointed a cross finger at me. Concepcion had always been a tad bossy, which helped move people along onstage. I braced myself for a scolding, but she gave me a hard time for being so scarce. "Did you completely forget about us?" she cooed. "And have you noticed, we're badly in need of a set designer." We both glanced over at the dinky miniature of Telegraph Hill and laughed till someone shushed us from the wings.

I ducked backstage and tiptoed past my old work space, a warehouselike section large enough to store flats and furniture. I felt a sudden pang for the life I'd once had, the creativity and security, the late hours and the daily bubble of excitement over whether TJ would follow the monologue, run off set, offend a guest . . . He was full of surprises, full of energy, the hyper kid on the block.

The sudden shift of noise and footsteps made me realize that the show was ending. Concepcion led a very tall man to a dressing room—a pro basketball player, I suspected—then slipped off her headpiece and called out a good-bye. Cameras were being rolled off set, crew calling out instructions, and there was TJ, hands shoved in his pockets as he meandered down the hall.

TJ possessed an underdog quality that always garnered sympathy: that dog-ate-my-homework, too-many-cowlicks, hands-in-the-pockets everyman quality of Charlie Brown from Schulz's comic strips. I had always had a weakness for Charlie Brown, the downtrodden average kid who was always seeing the football swiped away just as he was about to kick it, and hence, all those years ago, I fell in love with TJ, a man who could string an hour-long comedy show out of his rich neuroses.

"Hey! You *are* here! I thought I picked up a whiff of you backstage. Were you actually laughing at my jokes?"

I grinned. "Do you think?"

He grabbed my hand and yanked me toward his dressing

room. "I've been meaning to call you. No one seems to know what to do with that god-awful set they've put behind me. Have you seen it? Apparently it cost the network quite a few gold doubloons, so they want to keep it and amortize it over the next hundred years."

I shook my head, following him into his dressing room. "Some things never change. I was just feeling a twinge of homesickness for this place, but you just reminded me how it felt working for the big bad network."

"Can you fix that thing?" He kicked the door closed, grabbed a foam ball from the floor, and shot it into a small basket mounted on the wall. "I feel like a huge ogre crouching in front of a kids' toy train set."

"So what's wrong with that? Take a look in the mirror, bub."

He growled, arms straight out like Frankenstein, grabbed my shoulders, and started pushing me back. "Don't sass me, Cassie."

"You seem to have mistaken me for someone on your payroll," I said, arms in the air as he pinned me against the stucco wall.

He giggled. "Ooh, that's right. Does that mean I have no power over you?" He ran his hands down the side of my body, then brought one hand up, catching me in the crotch and squeezing. "Oh, I'd say I still have some power here." He grabbed tight and massaged through the light cotton of my painter's pants.

Although I liked his proprietorship, the reminder of days when he used to reach out and grab me there and start something, I would not be deterred. "I'm not in the mood, TJ. I came here to talk."

"What, you didn't come here to come?" He moved his hand away and pressed his pelvis against me, his erection jabbing my stomach. "Feel that? Doesn't that suggest something a whole lot more fun than talking?"

"TJ, I . . ." The sentence ended in a sigh as I felt myself responding, wanting the sex with a very primitive craving.

"Come on, Cassie. You know you want it, and we're both unattached. Why the hell not?"

A convincing argument, but the facts spoke for themselves. I wasn't seeing anyone right now, sex with TJ was always fast, and he did know how to push my buttons to bring me to climax. We could squeeze in a quick one, some meaningful conversation, and I wouldn't even be late picking up Tyler from school.

"Fine." I pulled my black sweater over my head and tossed it aside. "But afterwards, we are going to talk, mister."

He was already growling into my chest, his nose burrowing between my breasts, his hands cupping my nipples like a man who'd been stuck on a desert island for years.

We both stripped down quickly and he lay back on the sofa, massaging himself until I found a condom in his desk. I slid it on, then straddled him. I had to be on top with TJ, had to control the speed and depth of the thrust, had to pilot this ride. He was lousy at missionary, too eager and frenetic, just like his stage personality, but at least he had the good sense to give up control in this one area, letting me slide him in, squeeze my muscles over him, stroking us both in a steady rhythm that made orgasm inevitable.

"I've missed you, Cassie. Missed this."

I tossed my head back, not wanting to admit that I didn't really miss him at all, didn't miss the long hours and crazy outbursts and supercharged volume of his life. Yes, I missed the sex, but I had discovered it wasn't too hard to find that, especially when the guy found out that all I wanted was a physical relationship. No involvement, just quick recreation so that I could go home and pour my heart into more important matters.

My heartbeat quickened, my nerves straining as I rode him to orgasm. TJ let out a holler, then let his fingertips slide down along my hips, outlining my shape.

"Aaaach!" He groaned like a contented bear as he scraped off the condom and tossed it behind the couch. "That was great, as usual."

I stretched like a cat, leaned down to pluck my panties off the floor, and slipped them on before I took a seat again beside his furry legs. Around other guys I felt self-conscious about the extra five pounds of baby weight on my hips, but with TJ, who was not in the best shape himself, it seemed okay. "Now, about your son. We really need to set some ground rules here, TJ, or you're going to break his little heart."

He turned over on his side and closed his eyes. "Has anyone ever mentioned your talent for killing a buzz?"

I adjusted my bra and glared down at him. "Not funny. Did you notice? I'm not laughing."

"The cheap laugh isn't everything. Sometimes I just strive to entertain." He rubbed his genitals, then glanced down. "Would you look at that? Mr. Happy may be coming back for an encore."

"Don't be a dick. I'm all done, thanks. Now on to more important matters."

"Now, Cass, just look at that." And suddenly we were both staring at his cock, which seemed to thicken by the minute. "You wouldn't want to make Mr. Happy sad, would you?"

"You can give Mr. Happy a hand any time you like." I leaned down to pick up my sweater, thinking that one day I would make a list of all the ridiculous things men named their penises. Actually, there were probably already countless blogs on that topic, so dear to the hearts of men.

"Don't try to dodge the subject," I went on. "You're not being fair here. You know, Tyler is getting old enough to have a real relationship with you. Old enough to—"

A knock on the door made TJ flinch, his hand freezing over his groin.

"TJ?" came a woman's voice. His writer's voice. Melissa the viper.

"Shit!" He swung his legs off the sofa and sat up.

"I thought she was on vacation this week," I said.

"Shit, shit, shit!" He dove for his pants, shoved one leg in, then hopped around as he shoved his boxers into a desk drawer.

I crossed my arms, watching his freak-out. This was the reaction of a man who had everything to hide. "And you said you weren't involved with anyone . . ." I didn't feel betrayed as much as annoyed that he would lie just to screw me. I mean, really, if he was seeing someone else, then screw her!

Calmly I slid into my boots, then faced the mirror to straighten the chain of my necklace as TJ hopped, zipped, and smoothed himself back into place behind me. "When are we going to talk about Tyler?" I asked.

"Just as soon as I convince Melissa that we weren't doing what we were doing," he snarled.

"Ooh." I raked my hair back and reached down to pick up the foam basketball. "You know, I think I'll take a rain check." TJ was just pulling on a sweatshirt when I opened the locked door, coming face-to-face with the pert, smooth face of Melissa Diamant, her rhinestone-studded designer glasses reflecting my own angry, red face. She'd risen to head writer and executive producer in the time since I'd left, and Bree and I blamed her for making the show's atmosphere too cutthroat for Bree to sign a new contract.

"Cassie?" Her hand flew to her face in a dramatic gesture. "Oh, sorry, sweetie. I didn't know you were here."

The hell you didn't.

"We were just discussing the Coit Tower as a phallic symbol," I said. "What a bold design for your new set. Has that subliminal seduction thing panned out in your ratings, or are people put off by the lack of subtlety?"

She blinked. "We wanted something new for sweeps week."

Ha! A non-answer, if ever there was one. I turned to TJ and launched the foam ball at him. "We'll talk later."

He caught the ball and squeezed it in his hand, having the good grace to look sheepish, for once.

As I walked toward the bus stop, I felt my throat choke with tears, and I wasn't exactly sure why. Maybe the sex wasn't worth the entanglement with TJ. Maybe it was disappointment that he wasn't taking the initiative to be a father to our son. Or maybe it was the realization that my cheerful, madcap home at *TJ's Night* no longer existed.

Another family dispersed like dust in the wind.

6

"Mice, Mom! They've got mice!" Tyler's eyes opened wide. His voice was breathless, his moves frantic with adrenaline as he hunkered down under the clothes rack and scrambled toward the scampering creature. Hardly surprising to find mice in this windowless room used for storage at Rossman's, but Tyler didn't understand that this was not a playground.

"No, wait!" I cried. "There might be some traps set. Tyler, be careful!" I hitched up my Mrs. Claus skirt and dove under the clothing rack after him. "Tyler, come back now, honey!" Heavy raincoats slapped at my face as I crawled after him.

"Aaaw! He got away," he groaned.

Ducking my head, I moved in the direction of his voice and crawled out from under the hanging clothes to a pair of shiny black boots. Not Tyler's cute little curled-toe elfin booties, but man-sized boots topped by red velvet pants.

I sat up and smoothed my hair back, expecting to find one of our Santas. But it was Mr. Buchman, dressed in a Santa suit.

"There's a little mouse in here, brown and gray. I saw him," Tyler was telling the corporate hatchet man. "I tried to catch him but he got away."

"Mmm. They're known to move rather quickly."

I stood up and dusted off my Mrs. Claus skirt. "Tyler, you can't just go chasing a mouse like that. Cornered animals tend to lash out. He could have bitten you. And maybe it was a rat."

"He was tiny, Mom." He cupped his little hands down to the size of a walnut. "He won't bite me."

"Besides, there might be mouse poison on the floor, or traps set."

"I think not," Mr. Buchman said, looking like a lean Santa with his hands on his narrow hips. "There was no mention of infestation in the last maintenance report. I'll get Mr. Chalmers on it immediately."

"Can I have it?" Tyler asked both of us. "Can I keep the mouse? Please, Mom."

"Honey, they have to trap it first. And it's not like the mice in the pet store. It's a wild mouse."

"A wild city mouse." Mr. Buchman squatted down so that he was face-to-face with Tyler. "A sarcastic, jaded mouse. It probably takes to the streets at dusk and spends its night gallivanting on the town."

I bit my lips to keep from cracking a smile. So Buchman actually had a sense of humor and a certain way with kids.

"I can help you trap it." Tyler spread his hands out to Buchman, making his pitch. "I can trap it in a safe way. Like . . . I'll put a piece of cheese under a box, and the box gets propped up by a stick. And when the mouse goes inside the box, I'll pull the stick out and the mouse will be trapped in the box."

Buchman scratched his chin thoughtfully. "A clever design. A humane trap."

"But you would have to wait here all night until the mouse got to the right spot," I said.

"Mom . . ." Tyler moaned. "I don't care. I can do it."

My son should have been born during *Little Rascals* times, in the days when kids built wheely carts out of old milk crates instead of sitting catatonic in front of a television to work the joystick of a computer game. He's so full of inventions, of ways to trap animals so that he can study and love them, of a million uses for the old tires abandoned in alleys or empty cardboard boxes, discarded wooden planks, or the endless Styrofoam packing peanuts that shed tiny electrostatic cling-ons over our carpet, clothes, and skin.

"Young man, I like the way you think," Buchman was saying. "Would it be possible to take a look at one or two of your designs for this mousetrap?" He swung around to me. "I imagine I can delay notifying maintenance until after we've tried a humane approach."

I winced slightly, imagining the reaction among the salesclerks when word got out that we were having an infestation.

"Now, Mum . . ." Mr. Buchman cocked an eyebrow. "You can't blame the boy for trying to build a better mousetrap."

"I can do it," Tyler vowed. "I'll start working on it right now."

"Excellent."

A group of clerks rolled a rack in through the door, and the three of us turned toward them with conspiratorial grins.

"Well, then . . ." Mr. Buchman straightened his red coat. "Santaland awaits, doesn't it?"

It was November 25, the day after Thanksgiving. Not only the busiest shopping day of the year, but also the opening of Rossman's Santaland. Definitely an odd time for the hatchet man from Chicago to be playing Santa.

"Mom, do you have any sticks?" Tyler dropped to the floor to look under the racks again—one last search for the mouse. "What about boxes?"

"We'll see." I pulled him up, put my hands on his shoulders, and guided him alongside Buchman toward the door. "I'm surprised to see you suited up, Mr. Buchman, especially on the biggest shopping day of the year. Is this part of the Rossman's challenge?"

"No, actually, it's more like triage. When Ms. Hayden informed me that we had two Santas down with the flu, I didn't see any alternative but to suit up, as you so aptly put it. I do practice what I preach, you know."

"Well, good luck deciphering the wishes of good boys and girls," I told him.

He smiled, gesturing for Tyler and me to go on the escalator ahead of him. "Ah, but the bad ones are much more challenging, are they not, Ms. Derringer?" This man was surprisingly fresh. He leaned closer to Tyler and asked, "And what do you want for Christmas this year, young man?"

Tyler turned back, grinned, and answered, "There's nothing like cash." Just like Sally Brown in my favorite video.

Tyler's answer and Buchman's horrified expression made me laugh out loud. "He's echoing Sally in the *Peanuts* show. You know, *A Charlie Brown Christmas?*"

"*Peanuts?*"

"You know . . ." I helped him out. Maybe they didn't have *Peanuts* in England. "Snoopy and Charlie Brown?"

"Ah . . . yes, the rap singers."

"No, they're not!" Tyler giggled as he leaped from the top of the escalator to the landing. "They're cartoon characters."

"Of course they are. Charlie Brown is the boy who owns Mickey Mouse, is he not?"

Tyler giggled again.

"I have to ask, Mr. Buchman. Are you married?"

"My grandmother would call that a cheeky question, but the answer is no. Not anymore."

Which meant that he had been married. Always better. Divorced men usually weren't so idealistic about relationships. "Any children?"

"Not that I know of." He coughed, then glancing up the escalator at Tyler, pursed his lips together. "Actually, that's not true. There are none, I'm certain of that." He coughed again. "Why do you ask?"

"It's just that you seem to know how to talk with kids. You seem to have experience."

"Yes, well, my sisters will be pleased to hear that all the forced exposure to their little buggers has amounted to something."

Tyler jumped off the escalator at the top and whirled toward us. "I know! I can use one of those cardboard things from toilet paper."

"Beg pardon?" Buchman squinted.

"The mousetrap, he's still trying to think of ways to build it."

"Ah. You need a dowel or a spindle." Buchman nodded. "So then, we must fetch you some toilet paper."

A family with grade-school-age kids turned and stared at us, Mr. and Mrs. Claus and an elf, and I realized how odd it must look, this North Pole family with Santa shouting something about toilet paper. I bit my lower lip to keep from smiling, keep from enjoying Mr. Buchman's sense of humor. If I didn't watch out, I'd actually have myself believing that he was a nice guy.

7

Over the next few days a festive atmosphere took over Santaland, with Mr. Buchman leading the way, counseling and cajoling children. He thought of ways to move the queue faster when the line grew long. He made arrangements so that each child would receive a free Rossman's balloon at the end of the line. He ignored overbearing parents but wasn't beyond acting silly to make their children feel comfortable. Two other Santas also saw children around the other side of the Christmas ice mountain, comforting older men, both with grandchildren of their own, but something about Santa Buchman kept drawing me back to his side of the mountain.

When a little girl brought a long wish list with toys cross-referenced with page numbers from the Neiman Marcus catalog, he squinted at the pages, pretending that the mention of the rival store hurt his eyes.

After she jumped off his lap, I took her aside to talk about the real meaning of Christmas. Not that I had a definitive answer, but I knew that Christmas wasn't about receiving twenty-eight doll sets and electronic robots, and I hated to see this little girl setting herself up for major disappointment.

"Jenny's a planner," her mother said. "You can see she's got strong sense of organization."

"That's a great skill, and I'm sure Santa appreciates the work you put into this," I said, staring intently at Jenny. "But can you try to picture Christmas morning? What one toy would you like to see under the tree? What toys will you play with, day after day?"

Jenny picked the two dolls at the top of her list. "But I do want them all," she said. "I really do."

"She knows what she wants," her mother said proudly.

Watching them go, I felt a twinge of guilt over the fact that I couldn't afford to get Tyler the two video games he wanted. Couldn't afford them but also didn't want to perpetuate an electronic Christmas that cost more than a hundred dollars for two small disks for a five-year-old. I worried that I was failing my son, that he'd be disappointed on Christmas morning. In years to come, would he look back on this Christmas and talk longingly of the gift that Santa forgot, the toy that didn't arrive? The real question was, what did a parent need to give her child for Christmas?

Buchman stepped down from his platform, escorting a boy down the stairs. "Can't save them all, though, it's a pity," he said in my ear.

I realized he was right, but there was one Christmas gift my son needed . . . something that he would remember and cherish in years to come, and if I was going to provide that, I needed to make some arrangements.

I decided to take Tyler out of school and take him right to TJ's studio—a forced meeting, but even TJ wouldn't be so coldhearted as to deny a little boy to his face. I wanted a commitment from TJ, a promise to spend one afternoon a week with his son, and a plan for them to do something special at Christmastime, a memory Tyler could hold on to forever.

That night, after we'd changed out of our costumes, I guided Tyler toward the escalators, putting an arm over his shoulders. "I have a surprise for tomorrow. Instead of school, we're going to go to your dad's studio. You've always liked that, right?"

"Sure," he said. "But the most important thing . . . Can we stop and check my mousetrap on the way out? I'm sure there must be something there."

So far he'd gone four days without a nibble on the dried-out cube of cheddar. "Okay," I said, mentally calculating that it wouldn't hurt to catch the next streetcar, since we could sleep a little later tomorrow.

On our way into the storeroom we ran into Buchman, who seemed to be on his way out. "Ah, Master Tyler, it appears your invention has made some progress."

Tyler's eyes popped wide. "I got him? Is he there?"

"Not quite yet." Buchman winced. "But he's made off with your cheese."

"He took the bait?"

"Come have a look," Buchman said, leading Tyler off to the corner, like two naturalists tracking elk through the plains.

As they hunkered over Tyler's trap and speculated over ways to secure the bait, pondered other types of bait, and tried to track which route the mouse had exited, I considered the dilemma I'd be in if they did catch this mouse. Small dogs were allowed in our building, but I could only imagine the reaction of my landlady to the adoption of a department-store mouse.

Then again, my son had constructed a trap out of cardboard, tape, and string—hardly a solid, mouse-proof trap, despite Tyler's labors to double-tape everything and surround it all with a circle of Elmer's glue. Although the trap was flimsy, I was proud of my son's efforts and ingenuity. This was something TJ needed to experience for himself, to marvel over the enthusiasm and craft of a five-year-old inventor. Once TJ got to know the little person Tyler was becoming, I knew he would fall in love with him, too.

The next day started lazily as thick fog rolled in and seeped onto neighborhood streets, turning the bright purple storefront of a Haight Street store into a milky pink and covering the signs for Cha Cha Cha and the Red Victorian Hotel that Tyler always tried to read through the fog as we passed. As we rode the street-car to the studio I rehearsed my formal speech for TJ, deter-mined to hit on all the important points as I pleaded Tyler's case.

In some ways I felt like I was in for the battle of my life, secur-ing a father for my son. But I knew how important it was; I re-membered how much I missed having a father. It still hit me at times. A few years ago when I attended a wedding with TJ, the band started playing "Daddy's Little Girl" and the bride rushed into her father's arms on the dance floor. I stood alone, watch-ing with a lump in my throat. So corny for everyone to watch as they swayed and talked into each other's ears, but it took me back to that empty feeling, the nights when I'd stretched out in bed and stared up at the ceiling and imagined my father a prince or at least a wealthy, kind man who would come and whisk me away from the crazy instability that orbited Agate.

I'd shared those fantasies a few times, telling Bree and Jaimie about the scenarios I'd made up of Dad flying us off to a ski re-sort in the Swiss Alps or a Caribbean island for an exciting vaca-tion. Jaimie was always sympathetic, Bree not so enthused.

"Fatherhood is overrated," she told me. "My father was around, always home from work at six, regular as a clock. But he's never taken me skiing or off to any islands. Honestly? I think he finds happiness in garden tools."

What Bree didn't understand was that I would have been happy to mow the lawn with my father, thrilled to nip the aphids from his roses. Sometimes it's not so much what you're doing as who you're doing it with.

When we arrived at the studio, it soon became apparent that this was not going to be an easy meeting.

"Where's Darlene?" I asked the security guard, a man I didn't recognize, though his nameplate said Kelly. Last name or first name? I wasn't sure.

He sat back in his chair. "Excuse me? If you'll tell me Darlene's last name, I'll look her up for you."

I parked Tyler on one of the chairs and bent over the security desk. "Darlene? She's usually here at the door. I used to work here and we're friends. Is she on vacation?"

His eyes hardened. "Apparently she's not here today."

The man was a wealth of information. "Oh, well." I pulled the book toward me and started signing in. "Maybe she went back to school. It was something she wanted to do."

"Hold on there." He pulled the book away from me, causing a jagged line of ink on the page. "Who are you here to see?"

"TJ Blizzard. We're old friends."

"Do you have an appointment with Mr. Blizzard?"

I glanced back at Tyler, relieved that he didn't seem to notice my rising annoyance over this man's attitude. "He'll see us. My name is Cassandra Derringer, and this is his son, Tyler. Call inside, if you want."

"You're definitely going to need approval from the producers," he said. "And before we get any further, I need to see your driver's license."

It seemed like the ultimate insult for my son to have to wait outside while a rent-a-cop checked his mother's ID, and all this to get an audience with his father . . .

Don't upset Tyler. He's only five.

I slid my license out of my wallet and snapped it on the desk.

"Go on and have a seat," the guard ordered.

I moved back toward Tyler but didn't interrupt him from his Game Boy.

Don't let him see you sweat. Just get through the crap.

Ten nervous minutes later, the assistant director came through the door, her face tight with stress. "Oh, it's you, honey." Concepcion shook her head at me, as if she'd been expecting a two-headed monster. "I didn't know what was what. What are you doing here?"

"Tyler is here to see his dad." He didn't look up from his game, but I put a soft hand on his shoulder. "This new security is ridiculous. Do we need badges or something?"

"Honey, there's no reason for you to go in. TJ isn't here, 'cause it's not a tape day. Nobody's here. We're rerunning a 'best of' show tonight."

My spirit sagged with the frustration of a wasted morning, a futile trip. Tyler had no trouble switching gears, heading back to school, but I was the one who needed a lift, a way to ease my disappointment. We decided to stop for lunch under the giant Christmas tree at Neiman Marcus.

While I'd been working on my Christmas windows I'd been careful to stay away from our competitors to ensure that my designs would be fresh and original, but now I thought it was safe to take Tyler to visit the giant tree in the atrium of Neiman Marcus. I vaguely remembered the furor when I was a teen over the demolition of an old turn-of-the-century store to open this one, but the huge glass-domed ceiling of the Rotunda Restaurant had been saved, and over the Christmases that followed it had become one of my favorite spots. Tyler and I lifted our chins and let our eyes rove up along the towering tree covered with enormous gold, blue, and red balls to the glass ceiling above.

"I see the big ship," he said without looking down. "And a gold sword. And I see some angels in the waves."

"Angels, really?" I let my eyes rove the exquisite gold and white glass framed by circles of white lights hung on the rotunda balconies.

"And those long curly papers that old-time men used to write on."

"Scrolls?"

"And look at the end. It's a head of a lion. Or a ghost."

"Ooh, I see that. Or a creepy man."

"Mom, when you were a little kid, did you always come here with your mom and look up at the ceiling over the tree?" he asked out of the blue, the way children let you know what they're thinking.

"No, honey. When I was little, my mom didn't celebrate Christmas."

"Does she like Christmas now?"

"I don't know." Agate had burned through so many phases, from latter-day hippiedom to holistic medicine to iron-body fitness to the practice of Wicca. Perhaps she'd spun from white witch to country minister in the years that we'd been apart.

"Maybe she does," he said. "Maybe she'd be proud of you for being Mrs. Claus."

I reached across the table and smoothed down a tuft of his hair. "And you for being an elf."

"Mom . . . Are you still sorry that you don't have a dad?"

I let my finger trace a holly pattern on the tablecloth as I thought about that one. "I don't think about it much anymore. I guess I've moved on."

He nodded. "I'm not sorry about my dad. I just need *you*." His coy smile stole my heart until he stuck a long french fry in his mouth.

"But your dad loves you," I said quickly. "I know he doesn't spend a lot of time with you, but he's going to get better. You'll see."

Tyler shrugged, his focus on the construction of a ravine in the ketchup heap with the help of french-fry bulldozers. He didn't seem worried about gaining the acceptance of his father, much to my relief. Better for him to concentrate on building a bridge of fries or a humane mousetrap.

For now, his mom could sweat the big stuff.

8

As luck would have it, after I dropped off Tyler and called Bree to vent, I kept getting her voice mail. Then when I arrived at Rossman's and stopped in Jaimie's office, I saw her job-share partner and realized it was Jaimie's day off. Not that I couldn't call her at home, but the woman had a three-month-old baby to take care of; did she really want to hear my frustrations with laundry, dishes, and cooing baby bearing down on her?

Really, if I wanted to get myself out of Neverland, it was time I grew up a little. Fortunately, the Mrs. Claus suit made me feel calm and dignified, a lot more grown-up than my usual painter's pants and cotton henleys.

Santaland was crowded that day, and I spent a good deal of my time walking through the line of children, giving out lollipops and making conversation to help them pass the time. One family was three generations of women—mother, daughter, and granddaughter—and as I talked with them I realized the grandmother was a dead ringer for Agate. I joked with her that she reminded me of my mother, and she countered that she simply couldn't be old enough to be the mother of Mrs. Claus.

Watching the older woman hustle her grandchild along, I

wondered if my mother was playing grandmother to anyone. Was she still living in the Bay area? Did she have any idea I had a son now?

I felt a twinge of curiosity, especially since Tyler had been asking about her lately. "I wish we had some family," he said sometimes when I was tucking him in at night.

"You know, you do have family. There's your dad, and his parents live in Pennsylvania. Would you like to meet them sometime?"

"I guess." Always a half-hearted response, without the same interest that he showed for Agate. He fantasized that Agate was much kinder than she'd been, and I didn't have the heart to correct him.

"You should have told me you were going to the studio. I need to stop by and get some paperwork signed by one of the producers," Bree said when we met for coffee the next morning. Jaimie was also there with Scout napping in his stroller, and though Bree and I argued about holding him she refused to let either of us disturb him while he was sleeping.

"How can a kid nap already at nine o'clock in the morning?" Bree asked, watching as Scout pressed his cheek into the fabric of the stroller.

"It's easy when he's up at five," Jaimie said.

"Up at five." Bree winced. "Ach! That's going to be my life if I get this job with *AM San Fran*. Which is why I need those references signed at the studio. In fact, I'm going to call over there right now." She flipped open her cell phone.

"Don't worry, I have to go back," I said. "TJ wasn't there. The show was on hiatus and they were showing an old segment."

"What?" Bree squinched one eye shut over her phone. "They're not on hiatus. I saw it last night, with the mayor doing a guest appearance."

I shook my head slowly. "You must be confused . . . It was probably an old one."

"No. He was talking about marrying gay couples in San Francisco. I'm sure . . ." She held up a finger to pause as her call connected. "Yes, this is Bree Noble. Well, hey, Milo, how's it going? Listen, are you guys on hiatus this week?" She nodded, wincing. "No. Oh, goody. I have something for you . . ."

My heart dropped heavily in my chest as the truth sank in. TJ had been there yesterday; the entire staff had been there, and they'd lied to me, they'd turned Tyler away.

That hurt. Most of all, I felt stung for him, five years old and turned away at his father's door.

Jaimie finished tucking a blanket around Scout's waist, then turned back and touched my arm. "Oh, Cassie, that's awful. What a despicable man."

I wrapped my hands around the paper coffee cup, trying to think of the best way out of this one. "They all lied. Well, at least Tyler doesn't know that. He'll never have to know."

"Of course not," Jaimie said. "But it sounds like TJ is really pushing you away. What are you going to do?"

I collapsed on the bench in her office and slapped my hands over my face. "I've really made a mess of things, haven't I? Tyler would have been so much better off if I'd stayed with TJ. Moving out of his house was the beginning of the end."

"Oh, come on!" Bree slapped her phone shut, her nostrils flared in preparation for a fight. "Do you actually think you could have tolerated that man one more day? Honestly, staying on as TJ's dutiful girlfriend would not have been a positive role model for your son."

"It wasn't always a bad relationship," I said.

"Don't sugarcoat the past, Cassie." I had always considered Bree to be the bolder of my two friends, but Jaimie could be relentless as a bulldog when she sank her teeth into an issue. "Moving out was the end of a long good-bye that probably started when Tyler was born. You noticed how TJ started pulling away from you when you had the baby."

"Well, sure," I said, "but a lot of men do that." And when it happened, I really didn't mind. The routine of our lives, the hours on the set in rehearsal and lighting and rewrites seemed old and staid in comparison to the days and nights of my baby, feeding him until he fell asleep in my arms, waking in the night to hear his sweet breath in the bassinet beside me. Scout let out a baby sigh, and I turned to Jaimie. "Haven't you noticed Matt pulling away since Scout was born?"

She frowned. "Truthfully? I can't say that I relate. Matt is all over this kid when he gets home from work."

I straightened the stack of sugar packets on the table. "It's frustrating. When is TJ going to figure out he has a son, ready and willing to love him?"

"Let's see . . . like . . . never?" Bree scowled at me. "Sorry for the tough love, honey, but TJ obviously is not the paternal type. He is what he is. And if you look back with a modicum of honesty, you'll remember hating him at times."

"When you were first on the show?" Jaimie prodded. "Remember how he treated you? How he was sleeping with you and a summer intern?"

"Remember when you wished he would die? When you tried to kill him on the Presidio?"

I laughed. "That sounds ridiculous."

"But there's a grain of truth in it," Bree said.

She was right.

One afternoon a bunch of the crew from the show went running on a hilly trail at the Presidio, and I went along hoping to be part of the crowd. But one of the writers got on me about the condition of my running shoes (dilapidated) and the cost of changing sets for our skits (a union issue). Of course, I expected TJ to defend me, but he jumped in, adding a few nasty slurs about my latest set design. By the time we approached the green rise of the hill, I hated all of them, TJ especially. I challenged him to a race, which he felt obliged to accept, and then I pulled ahead.

"Hey, you're fast," he called, loping up beside me.

"Mmm-hmm." My pulse beat steadily as my legs pounded, but it felt good to push on. As we passed other joggers, I wondered if TJ had ever had his heart checked. He was a little overweight. If I pushed really hard, maybe his heart would pop.

I pushed ahead until the muscles in my legs burned with pain.

"You're really fast, Carrie," he gasped from behind me.

"Cassie," I tossed over my shoulder as the Golden Gate Bridge rose before me. "Cassie . . ." I muttered as I sprinted over the rise, hoping to hear him drop behind me . . .

"Okay," I said, returning to the coffee shop. " I hated him at times."

"And this is the man you want to father your child?" Bree asked.

I shrugged. "That's a done deal."

Jaimie reached out and squeezed one of my hands. "What we're saying is, cut your losses now. You got Tyler out of him, a real blessing. Why don't you let it go at that?"

"Take the kid, take the money, and run," Bree added.

"But a child needs parents. Tyler needs his father."

Bree put her hands over her ears. "I totally don't buy that. And if parents are so important, where is your mother? If you really value family, why did you cut her off?"

Jaimie looked sheepish. "That's a little harsh, Bree."

"It is, you meany," I told Bree. "But there's some truth in it too."

Jaimie checked her watch. "I gotta go. Scout has an appointment with the pediatrician."

"I have to get to work." I stood over Scout and touched his smooth cheek. "But I'm glad we did this. It's always a pleasure to get chewed out over coffee."

Bree threw her arms wide for a hug. "Honey, we're hard on you because we love you."

"Great. I'd hate to hear what you'd say to me if you didn't like me."

9

That day Jaimie was picking Tyler up from school and keeping him until I finished work—a new arrangement we'd worked out so that he didn't have to spend quite so much time at the store at night. Not that he was ever a problem hanging around in Santaland, but it worried me that our schedule was keeping him away from a home environment for so long. Although he was well behaved, I had to remember, the kid was only five.

I was busy playing Mrs. Claus, trying to negotiate with twin boys, one of whom didn't want to see Santa, when Fred climbed onto the snow platform in Santaland. "I hate to get caught here," he said, looking over his shoulder. "If I don't watch it, Buchman'll turn me into an elf, but you need to know about this."

Immediately I thought of Tyler. "What's going on?"

"We had a short on the second floor. No fire, thank God, but two of the breakers popped. When I reset them, those snowflake lights in the bedding and lingerie departments stayed dark. Seem to be shorted out, and I'm wondering if they caused the circuits to pop."

"I wouldn't be surprised. Those things have to be at least fifteen years old," I said. I'd been reluctant to hang those old snowflake lights throughout the store, concerned that they weren't as energy efficient as new lights, but there wasn't enough money in the budget to replace them. "So now we have two departments with dark decorations?"

He nodded. "Don't know what you want to do. Your call."

"Actually, this is one problem that demands a higher authority," I said, heading toward Santa's platform.

Fred scratched his chin, confused. "Santa Claus?"

"No! Mr. Buchman."

As Fred and I went before Buchman's ornate Santa chair to deliver our news, I felt as if we were subjects granted an audience with the king.

"The snowflake lights?" Buchman tugged down his white beard. "I take it those are the lights strung throughout the store?"

"Yes. I was able to purchase new lights for the window displays, but we were stuck with these old snowflakes throughout the store."

"Sounds like a possible fire hazard. We must replace the lights that are out on the second floor immediately. As for the others, that decision can wait until tomorrow."

"We close in fifteen minutes." I looked at Fred. "Did you have plans for the evening?"

He sighed. "Not anymore. I'll go get the ladders."

As the shoppers began to dwindle, Fred and I quietly set up ladders in the back of the bedding department and began to remove lights. The snowflake lights had to be untangled from the garlands thick with Christmas balls and bells, then replaced with new strings of white lights from our Christmas shop before the garlands could be reinstalled in display areas.

Half an hour into the job, Fred and I were stringing garland piled on a sales counter when Mr. Buchman appeared, no longer in a Santa suit but wearing a shirt and loose tie, his arms folded as he watched the process.

"This is going to take a while," Fred said.

"Indeed." Buchman tapped his chin. "Tedious work. Do we not have garland with prestrung lights?"

"Rossman's doesn't carry it."

He nodded. "Well, we may be forced to dispatch an emissary to one of our competitors in order to obtain the decorations we need throughout the store. For tonight, though, let me lend a hand."

We showed him what to do, and Buchman began stripping the old lights out on a third set. As we worked, he questioned me about the cost of new lights and about the best places to purchase them. He asked Fred if he could snoop around in the morning and drum up operating costs for running the snowflake lights during the past few Christmas seasons.

"I would love to replace all the lights in the store," he explained, "however, we must present a brief cost analysis before we embark on the project."

"And you can sell the old snowflake lights on eBay," Fred said. "At least, you can sell the ones that still work."

"A shrewd plan," Buchman agreed. "Sure to offset costs. Another thing to investigate."

By the time the lights were replaced and rehung, the store was empty except for the night guards. Fred lowered the overhead lights for maximum effect, and the three of us gazed up into the warm halo glow that set off the sparkling purple, red, green, and blue of the ornaments. The merry elfin figures that surfed the garland and rode the jingle bells were silhouetted in the darkness, as if resting for the night.

"Lovely," Buchman sighed, and for a moment the air in the shoe department seemed magical, like the fluttering excitement and expectation of a Christmas morning.

Then, suddenly the mood fizzled as Fred went to the wall and brought up the lights. "See you tomorrow."

Inside the ladies' locker room I nearly fell on the bench, so tired. I tugged off my boots, undid the coat of my Mrs. Claus suit, and let my fingers smooth the white fur trim as I hung my head.

Bone tired. Mr. Buchman pushed hard. I felt my eyes closing when the air stirred.

"Ms. Derringer . . ."

I lifted my head.

"Based on our conversation I've worked up some costs on the matter of replacing the old snowflake lights, and it appears that your instincts were correct."

He stood before me, his hands clasped together, his eyes intent on me. I was slumped down so that the jacket fell open, exposing my black teddy and significant cleavage.

"Well, that's a relief." Reflexively, I straightened, which probably revealed even more.

Mr. Buchman didn't seem to notice. "Energy efficiency is a primary, long-term concern, and cost analysis indicates that . . ." His voice trailed off as his eyes trailed down my body, following the gentle rise and fall of my chest. "That we should buy a new set of bulbs. Smaller bulbs. Nothing too . . . too flashy."

He was losing his train of thought because of me, and I liked that feeling. I stood up and stepped toward him, taking his hands and slipping them inside my open coat. His eyes went wide, but he didn't stop me as I placed his hands over my breasts. "I was thinking small and very compact." I directed his fingertips around the nipple of one breast, which pressed tautly against the fabric. "Just about that size?"

"Yes, that would do quite nicely." His voice was barely a whisper now, his eyes simmering with heat.

His fingers worked skillfully, and I suspected that Mr. Buchman knew his way around a woman's body. I wanted him and I knew he wanted me. A bad idea, with this whole employee-boss thing going on, but there was no denying the dampness between my legs. As I reached out for his crotch, he turned away suddenly.

"Mr. Buchman?" Desire burned through me. I wanted to have sex with him now, worry about the fallout later.

"Ms. Derringer." He took a composing breath, then turned back to me. "I shall see you tomorrow."

"Oh, God, do you think he's gay?" Jaimie gasped when I told her the story of my rejection that night as I was picking up Tyler.

I'd had to twist the details a little to keep the identity of the rejecter anonymous. "Maybe you freaked him out."

"I'm sure he likes women," I said confidently. "This guy is straight. I think the freak-out was more over the boss-employee thing. Worried about fishing off the company pier."

"This is someone who works at Rossman's?" she probed. "Who?"

"I can't say. Really. You don't want to know."

"Did you tell him how discreet you can be? That you don't want to date him, you just want sex? That no one at work needs to know about it? Except me, of course."

"We didn't talk about it. I was undressing, he sampled the goods, then took off." I didn't mention the incredible letdown I'd felt when he turned away.

"So what are you going to do?" Jaime asked. "Will you be embarrassed to see him tomorrow?"

"I don't blush over sex," I said, fastening the Mrs. Claus coat.

"You . . . Oh, Cassie, you wouldn't! Not in the store . . . during the daytime."

"Calm down, Ms. Rossman. The store isn't open yet, and it's not a holy place."

"I can't believe this is happening on my day off!" she said. "Call me as soon as you . . . just call me."

Mr. Buchman's refusal had ruined my night's sleep, his face appearing as a giant visage washing through my dreams. I was determined to end that now, this morning, in his office as scheduled. It was still early, too early for the secretaries to be manning their desks in the corridor of the third-floor offices. I knocked on Buchman's door, then stepped inside the shadowed office and closed the door behind me.

He looked up from the light of the monitor, dropping his hands from the keyboard. "Ms. Derringer . . ."

"Mr. Buchman." My pulse beat faster than normal, and I pressed my back to the door, drawing composure from the coolness of the metal. "About last night . . ."

"Yes, we should talk. I . . . I want to say I'm sorry if I compromised—"

"Don't. You don't have to go there. I'm just sorry you left." I moved over to his side of the desk, hitched up my skirt, and sat up on the desk with my bare knees inches from his chest. "Here's what I'm interested in. A discreet relationship. No emotional attachment."

"Do you think we can really do that?" he asked, swinging his chair toward me.

"I know I can. You know I have a son, other demands on my time. I'm in no position to get involved."

He drew in a breath and ran his fingertips along the inside of my thighs, reaching in under my skirt. I sucked in my breath as he set my nerve endings on fire.

"But you're sure this is what you want?" he asked as his fingers explored, teasing.

I let my head fall back as I succumbed to the warm sensations between my legs. "That, Mr. Buchman, is exactly what I want."

10

"Have I got news for you." I squeezed into the vinyl seat, back to back with a stranger, which was the way everyone got seated in the House of Nan King, the best Chinese restaurant in San Francisco with the unfortunate ambiance of a crowded camp mess tent. I scooted my chair in, chest to the table. It had been a long time since I'd had big news to announce at lunch. The last time was probably when I was pregnant with Tyler, and that had met with mixed reactions (probably since my friends weren't crazy about the father and—oops!—we weren't married).

"It's about this new guy, isn't it?" Jaimie tucked her hair behind her ears. "Please, tell me something juicy. I've got a three-month-old and the only juicy I'm getting these days is wet diapers."

Bree put up her hands. "Stop right there. Exciting news is not guy stuff. I just read an article that said too many women seek validity through men. So let's talk about more noteworthy things, like this year's candidates for the Pulitzer. Or euthanasia in Sweden."

"Actually, part one is not about a man. I called Agate. Broke the silence."

Jaimie's eyes went wide. "You spoke to her?"

"I left a message, but I think it's her machine. She's got this new age music playing in the background, sort of like wind chimes."

"That sounds like Agate. If it's her, I'm sure she'll call you back."

I thought of the halting message I'd left her. "Agate? If this is you, it's me . . . Cassie . . . your daughter. If this is you, can you give me a call? I'm fine, and I have some news. I . . . should really tell you in person. So call me." I left my cell phone number. I was about to hang up, but didn't want to sound too impersonal. "Oh, and I'm not on TJ's show anymore, so don't call there," I rambled on. "But I have another job. I'm a designer. I did the windows at Rossman's Union Square. Have you seen them?" Suddenly I remembered the way Agate had shunned material possessions. "Maybe she'll call me."

"Good for you," Bree said. "You identified your fear and you called her on the phone."

"I guess." Bree needed to get a job so that she wouldn't spend so much time reading those self-help magazines.

"So what's part two?" Jaimie prodded.

I shot a look at Bree. "Close your ears if you're looking for edification. Part two is about a boy. Mr. Buchman, actually. We are now officially *lovahs.*"

"Mr. Buchman?" Jaimie shook her head so furiously her hair bobbed.

"Tell me, why would you want to sleep with a man you call mister?" Bree asked.

"Well, for starters, he does have a sense of humor. And Tyler relates to him. Actually, he seems okay with all kids. I've seen him in Santaland, surprisingly patient, and he just talks to them like they're smaller people."

"Brits are so weird." Jaimie shuddered. "Their cuisine is crap and they don't wear enough deodorant."

"Jaimie, that's incredibly politically incorrect of you. Besides, you've met Buchman. Does he have BO?"

But Jaimie was off on her rant. "All that 'check under the boot' and 'bloke' and 'did you fancy him?' Oh, I fancied him. Fancy this! Well, fancy that. Trust me, I spent a semester abroad, stuck in some godforsaken industrial town. I know."

"And their teeth are so bad." Bree thrust her lower jaw out in an underbite. "Did you check his teeth?"

"His teeth are fine."

"Seriously, did you look in the back? Check the molars? All black and sometimes the front teeth are worn away into spikes. I don't think socialized medicine covers dentistry."

"He's top-level management of a Fortune 500 company. The man's got good dental."

"Really, did you take a look?" Jaimie pressed. "You have to check the back teeth."

"I didn't give him an oral exam," I said.

Bree wiggled her eyebrows. "Not on the first date."

"We didn't really have a date, we just . . . had sex."

"Now you're cooking with gas." Jaimie patted my hand. "I'm so proud of you. If you can just keep it up—"

"Or keep him up—" Bree cut in, brandishing a mock Groucho cigar.

"—you, too, can join the fuck-buddy club. Ah, those were the days. You meet once a week—"

"—More. I can meet two, three times a week, just as long as it doesn't cut into my social life."

"And there's no membership fee and no dues," Jaimie said proudly.

"And God knows," Bree added, "we've all paid our dues."

I folded my arms. "You two should take that act on the road. And I don't care what you say. There's something oddly attractive about Mr. Buchman. I like him."

"No, no!" Bree pounded the table. "Not the *like* word! Pop a zit and loan me a tampon and we'll be back in junior high."

The two men sitting behind Bree swung their heads around to

glare at us. I suppose all our talk of tampons and zits didn't go too well with the kung pao chicken.

"You're right," I said, raising my brows at the offended diners. I lowered my voice. "Thanks for the reality check. It's a silly attraction, and I'm in no position to do much more than look under the boot, anyway. I've got a kid to raise, a job to do and . . . I would never do that to Tyler. He needs a solid mother and father in his life; my crap, and who I fancy, will always take a back burner."

"Not that I'm keeping score," Jaimie smoothed the dark hair over her left ear. "But are you saying that you're interested in pursuing a relationship with Mr. Samuel Buchman?"

"No, I am not. I'm tied up raising a son and pursuing his father. There'll be no relationships for me until Tyler is off to college. I figure thirteen, maybe fourteen years."

"I'll never understand that bizarro vow you've made to yourself," Jaimie said. "How does it go? Sex is okay, but no involvement?"

Bree shook her head. "That's just like a man . . . You're having sex like a man. Better watch it or soon you'll be eating dinner like a bachelor, leaning over the kitchen sink. You'll have no knives left in your kitchen because each one will go out in the garbage in a box of Entenmann's cake."

Jaimie gestured toward Bree with a theatrical flourish. "Ladies and gentlemen, the comedy stylings of Bree Noble."

The two gentlemen behind Bree turned back, eyeing us curiously just as Bree's phone started to jangle. I pressed my napkin to my face to hide a laugh while Bree bowed her head and reached for her cell. "Ba-dump-bump." She held her cell phone away from her face to squint at the text message. "Well, would you look at that. *AM San Francisco* wants to see me back tomorrow."

Jaimie lifted her chopsticks. "You got the job?"

"It's looking that way, and let me tell you, the best part of that gig is not the salary or the benefits but the adorable line producer, Franco Verti. Don't you love the way his name just rolls off the tongue? So good-looking, such an eye for wardrobe you'd bet he was gay, but my friend Zhanna swears that he likes the ladies. So . . ." She wiggled her eyebrows. "Let me call them back and set up my final interview with Franco Verti." She punched in Redial, then shot me a look. "Oh, and I've got to get over to TJ's studios to get someone to sign off on my references."

"I'll go with you," I said. "I am totally focused on getting through to TJ. Right now, my life is all about Christmas—making it wonderful for Tyler and giving him the best gift a boy could have."

"TJ?" Bree winced. "You see TJ as a gift? That's scary."

"You know, you defend TJ too much," Jaimie said. "Tyler's a smart kid; he'll see right through your pretensions that this is *Father Knows Best* land."

"I want him to love his father."

"You've got to let that happen with the real TJ, not some cuddly stuffed bear of an absentee parent. You can't make TJ something he's not."

"I'm not trying to," I insisted. "Look, a mother knows, right? You have certain instincts about what your child needs, and I know this is right for Tyler."

Jaimie used that moment to shove a shrimp roll into her mouth.

"If you say so, honey," Bree told me. "I'll set something up with the producer at TJ's, get us onto the set later this week."

"Perfect." I dug into the mandarin chicken with new resolve. If Bree could get us in this week, I just might get Tyler reunited with his father by Christmas.

11

That night I found myself working late, until the store closed, and Tyler was safely tucked at Jaimie's for the evening. I was straightening one of the decorative displays in Santaland as overhead lights began to go out.

"Is it that late?" I asked aloud as I twined the drooping branch of a snow white evergreen to its trunk.

"Very late, indeed." Mr. Buchman passed by with two sales associates who continued on toward the escalators. "Only Christmas mice are out and about. And speaking of Christmas, that's a very sad tree you have there. Are you putting it out of its misery? Death by icicle decoration?"

"A new Santaland was not in the budget," I said, a little nervous to have him watching me so intently. At last I managed to secure the branch. I fluffed up some of the needles, picked up a few fake flakes from the ground, and tossed them over the sad little tree. "There. Good as new."

"I suspect not." He drew in a breath. "However, nothing we can do about that until next year."

"Really? Do you think there will be more money in the decorating budget next year?"

"I'll recommend it. Of course, it would be based on whether the store turns around and starts making a profit again."

"Well, it helps that you found the money to replace those snowflake lights," I said, picking up a candy wrapper from the snow path. "A lot of the old decorations needed to be retired. But I hope that whoever takes the job next year holds on to some of Rossman's Christmas classics. Like this sleigh." We paused in front of the giant sleigh, which was truly the centerpiece of Santaland.

"Tell me you're joking? That sled . . ." He shook his head in dismay. "A giant replica of Santa's sled in a bed of snow. Doesn't it strike you as odd that we have to create an elaborate snow scene in San Francisco? I mean, it's not as if the natives can relate. When was the last time you saw a snow-covered Telegraph Hill?"

I hitched up my Mrs. Claus skirt and hoisted myself onto the sled display. "I have always liked this sled," I defended, moving a package so that I could sit on the emerald and purple striped velveteen seat. "When I was a little kid, my mother brought me here, and the first thing I'd look for was the sleigh. It worried me that it might not be here one year, that it might get lost or damaged and that would surely foil Santa's journey, because I knew in my heart of hearts that this was the sled that did it all." That was back in the years when Agate's second husband had us celebrating Christmas.

"It's a creaky white elephant, destined for the junkyard come January." He leaned in beside me. "I'm surprised it can even handle your weight without buckling."

"Are you kidding? This thing is solid." I smacked the seat beside me and found it surprisingly sturdy. "It can take you. Climb on up. We can take you on."

To my surprise he planted one foot on the floor and in one move swung himself into the seat beside me.

"See? What do you think of that?"

He took a deep breath, staring forward. "I think, Mrs. Claus, that your knickers are showing."

"They are?" I glanced down and sure enough, my hitched-up

skirt was way up over my fitted cotton boxers. "Oh. Sorry." I pushed the skirt over my knees and started to slide out, but his hands were on my waist, helping me down. Warm, solid hands. When I touched ground, he touched my skirt, gathering it in his fingers.

"Please don't be shy." The velvet whispered up over my knee, tickling my skin as he pulled it up my thigh. "This may make me sound like a fetishist, but how many blokes have the opportunity to examine what Mrs. Claus wears under her skirts?"

I held my breath, watching his face as he lifted my skirt and explored. "Ah, tonight she wears her Calvins, of course. White cotton boxers. How practical."

"They match the trim on my costume," I said weakly, feeling the dampness of the cotton between my legs. I had wanted the other morning not to be an anomaly, and now here, with his fingers stroking my thigh, my body was responding with frightening speed.

"I want you," I whispered. "But somehow, I don't think Santaland is an appropriate place."

He lowered his face to mine. "Where else should Mrs. Claus be defrocked?"

I stepped away from him. "I have a few ideas. Follow me." I tugged his hand, pulling toward the women's sportswear section.

"You know, we could go down to my office," he called after me. "Or perhaps you just want to go down."

"Come!" I motioned him ahead, and suddenly we were looping around circular racks, headed toward the dressing rooms in the corner.

I burst into a large corner booth, and he kicked the door closed behind us. We quickly tugged off our clothes and moved toward each other.

"Let's see, where were we?" he asked, reaching down to my inner thighs. "Right about *there*. Yes, that was it."

"Perfect," I whispered, loving the way he always eased into seduction, working slowly to the core of sensation. In this, he could have me. I might argue design and business and principle, but when it came to his plying fingers and breathtaking kisses, my body and his were in total agreement.

He glanced down at our half-stripped bodies. "These are rather restrictive, though, don't you think?" He pushed his fingers under the bottom cuffs of my boxers without much progress, then pressed his hand over the cotton crotch and nudged into the warm folds there. I closed my eyes and groaned over the stirring motion of his fingers. He was pushing me toward orgasm, but I wanted more of him, real flesh on flesh.

"That's fabulous," I breathed. "But I want more."

"Don't worry, we shall get there."

12

"And it was at that moment that the Christmas bear knew it was time. This was the year that Santa would choose him from the toy shelf, place him in the giant bundle of toys, and gently carry him down a chimney to wait under the tree until Christmas morning . . ."

From the corner of my eye I saw an elf signal that the line was moving, so I started wrapping up the story for the children sitting on cushions at my feet. I had started telling stories to pass the time while the children were waiting in line, and the device worked so well that we'd worked it into the daily routine, bringing groups of eight or ten kids over to sit beside the giant sleigh that had been part of this Rossman's decorations since it opened. The stories were not elaborate, just tales I'd made up as Christmas bedtime stories for Tyler, adapted and edited with his input.

I finished the story, then ushered the children from our cozy snow enclave beside the sleigh back to the path to Santa's house.

"Bye, Mrs. Claus." One boy waved, nearly sliding away as his mother yanked his hand.

"Mommy, can I have a Kwissmiss bayoh?" a three-year-old asked her mother.

"You have loads of stuffed animals," the mother said, her mouth a stern line. "I don't know why you would need one more."

"Bye! When you see Santa, be sure to tell him that his Christmas stew is almost ready!" I waved as the children and their parents disappeared through a trellis covered with glittering white branches. The storytelling was one of the highlights of my job as Mrs. Claus, and the low point had to be dealing with the moms, the ladies dressed in ivory whose cool composure on the cosmetics floor had little appeal when used to put a four-year-old into a deep freeze.

My first week as Mrs. Claus had been an eye-opener in the area of child care. Why did these women even bother having kids? They wanted the nanny to tote them through Santaland. They wanted to drop off their kids and pick them up at the end of the day. They wanted little Jeffrey to stop throwing a terrible-twos tantrum, little Suzie to stop crying and tell Santa what she wanted for Christmas.

Don't judge them, I told myself one night, when the first week of overtime was beginning to take its toll. *You've been there. You've lost your temper a time or two.*

"How's it going up there?" I called.

Tyler's head popped up from the floor of the sleigh. "I need more wheels. Did we bring more wheels?" he asked.

I told him I wasn't keeping track, and he explained the elaborate wheel system he planned for his Lego truck. Although Tyler's trap had not yet caged a mouse, Mr. Buchman had suggested that Tyler design a vehicle for the creature to ride in, like Ralph the Mouse or Stuart Little. The suggestion made me wince, but it was right up Tyler's alley, the only thing he'd been able to talk about for the past few days. School had closed for the holidays yesterday, which made today Tyler's first long day at Rossman's. Although Jaimie was going to take him for her days and evenings off, I was already feeling a little off pace, having missed my morning with Mr. Buchman.

Since our first fling I'd become a regular visitor to Buchman's office. Mornings with Buchman were my *Breakfast at Tiffany's*, my time to regenerate and let loose and pretend that great things were possible in my life. Actually, great things *were* possible astride Buchman, just not with the kid around.

Although I'd secretly started to enjoy his wry and self-deprecating comments, I kept reminding myself not to get attached. This was all temporary—my stint as Mrs. Claus, Buchman's presence here in San Francisco. These were aberrations to be enjoyed until they ended, just as the Christmas season would surely run its course and dwindle headlong into January gloom.

Fortunately, my involvement with Mr. Buchman helped solidify my other life goals: raising Tyler, building a family, and enlisting his father. So far Bree hadn't been able to get us into the studio yet, and TJ still wasn't answering my calls. With Christmas only two weeks away, it was time to let TJ know I was serious. Last night I had spent thirty minutes in phone consultation with a lawyer.

First, Nina Cho tried to talk me out of employing her. "You don't want to pay me to do something you can do yourself," she said in a slightly nasal voice that suggested she was no fun pulling all-nighters in law school. "It's always best for the couple to work things out among themselves."

I told her that we weren't really speaking. Then I told her that Tyler's father was TJ Blizzard, the Snowman, the Blitzer, the talk show host.

Suddenly, she was warming to me. "Maybe I can help you . . ."

That day while I was working in Santaland, Jaimie stopped by and I brought her up to speed on the legal services of Ms. Nina Cho. We talked quietly as I went through the line of kids, handing out lollipops. "She's going to contact TJ, who'll probably refer her to a lawyer, and we'll take it from there."

"Sounds like a reasonable plan," she said. "Are you prepared for your worst-case scenario? If TJ says he wants no part of raising Tyler?"

"Nina Cho can be very persuasive," I said, hoping she would

prove worth the retainer I'd paid. "But she did spell out the law, that TJ is not obliged to see Tyler at all, as long as he pays child support."

Jaimie shrugged. "I wouldn't expect too much from the Blitzer."

"This is such an important life issue. In the end, when TJ really understands what I'm asking for, I'm confident he'll reach out to Tyler."

"Mom!" Tyler ran up the side of the line holding something out toward me. He had been down in the storage room, checking his mousetrap with Buchman. "Look what the mouse likes . . ."

The other children turned to stare at us as Tyler placed three empty Tootsie Roll wrappers in my open palms. "He went for the bait. Mr. Buchman thought he'd like Tootsie Rolls. Only problem is, he got away again."

"The little stinker," Buchman said, putting his hands on Tyler's shoulders. "Next we're going to try peanut butter."

"Peanut-butter pretzels." Tyler's eyes grew wide. "Mouses can't resist peanut butter."

"Mice," I corrected him, handing back the icky wrappers.

"Who can resist peanut butter?" Jaimie said.

As the guys discussed new strategies for capture, I was once again relieved that they hadn't been successful. Mouse hunting was not among my favorite tasks, but I was glad Buchman was willing to indulge Tyler and encourage his ideas.

Jaimie and I had turned away from the boys to chat. We were discussing Scout's new sleep patterns when a woman in faded jeans, a short fake fur, and long, striking silver hair strolled up to us.

Not your typical Rossman's shopper, I thought, watching her from the corner of my eyes. I braced myself for some sort of Santaland complaint when she stepped into our space.

"Cassie?"

That square chin and demure nose were hauntingly familiar. "Oh," I gasped, surprised by her sparkle, by the easy way she sauntered up to me. The years had been kind to my mother. "Agate . . ." I leaned forward and she embraced me. After all these years, it was the oddest sight to see my mother walk into a department store and find me working the line in a Mrs. Claus suit. "I'm in shock."

"I got your message, honey. Philip and I were out of town, visiting his brother in Arizona, and you know me with answering machines. Well, I just about raised the roof when I heard your voice last night." She lifted a piece of hair from my shoulder and gently pushed it back. "How are you, Cassie?"

"Fine, I'm fine." I blinked, realizing my friend was standing beside me in awe. "Agate, do you remember Jaimie?"

"Merry Christmas, Agate," Jaimie said, pouring on the charm with that demure smile that got us out of trouble when we'd vandalized a neighbor's garden in fourth grade.

"Jaimie?" Agate looked from my best friend to me, her head ponging back and forth. "I didn't know you were still in the picture. Are you two . . . partners?"

Jaimie's eyebrows shot up and I let out a breath. "Actually, we're just good friends, Agate, but you score major points for open-mindedness. Jaimie is married, with a little baby boy at home."

"Congratulations!" Agate squeezed Jaimie's shoulder with a warm smile.

"I can't believe you're here," I said, thinking that the silver-haired woman before me was more Mrs. Claus than I would ever be. "Do you have a few minutes? I'll take my break in the café, and we can—"

"Mom," Tyler interrupted, "is it okay if I use my Legos as part of the mousetrap?"

Agate clapped her hands together, her mouth popping open in glee. "Is this little one yours? Oh, Cassie! He's a living doll."

Tyler's nose wrinkled as he forced a smile. "No, I'm not."

I kneeled beside Tyler. "Honey, I know you've heard me talk about my mother. This is Agate. Your grandmother."

Ever the diplomat, he opened his arms for a hug. Agate embraced him with passion, then leaned back to cup one smooth cheek. "Such a doll. Do you like frogs, Tyler? I've got lots of them near my cottage."

He nodded. "Sure. Am I supposed to call you Grandma?"

"Definitely not." She winced. "We'll need to come up with something else. Mimi or Nana or something more palatable."

I smiled. Still the image-conscious Agate.

As we headed off to the café I passed by Buchman, who lightly patted my back, a small, simple gesture. He'd always struck me as a man who bulldozed over things and insisted on taking control, but in truth, he seemed to know instinctively when to take a step back. A surprising trait for the imperious hatchet man from Chicago. I filed that one away for exploration at another time.

Once we were settled at a table with food, the tales and details couldn't pour forth quickly enough. Agate was living in the same cottage, still practicing Wicca, searching for the goddess within every spirit. Last year she'd hooked up with Stu, a social worker who specialized in counseling teens.

I brought her up to date on the past few years, the slow fizzle of my relationship with TJ and the continuing struggle to create a relationship between TJ and Tyler.

"Mom," Tyler interrupted when we started to discuss his father. "Can we not talk about this anymore?"

"I'm just filling in Agate, honey."

"Not that. Can you stop trying to get me a father? I don't need one. Really. Timber doesn't have a father and that's okay." Timber was one of his classmates.

Agate's astute eyes looked to me to resolve this one.

"We don't have to talk about it right now," I said.

He slid out of his seat and backed onto my lap. "All I need is you, Mom. I'm okay with that."

Such adult language from such a little one. I tightened my arms around him and rocked him back and forth. "You're tired, I know."

"No, I'm not."

"Tyler, have you made a list for Santa?" Agate asked, adeptly changing the subject. "What do you want for Christmas?"

"Game Boy stuff and alien racers." He pursed his lips, thinking. "Bionicles. And I want my mom to stop making me see my dad."

I swallowed hard, stung by his wish. He'd never stated it so baldly before.

"You know, Tyler . . ." Agate leaned closer to the table to confide. "That is the absolute opposite of what your mother used to wish."

"That's true," I admitted. "I would have given anything for a chance to meet my father." I studied my mother, wondering if she remembered that her refusal to reveal his identity was the reason for our long split.

Agate sighed, her shoulders dropping dramatically. "Your poor mother," she told Tyler, who was totally tuned in to her. "I couldn't let her meet her father, because I was afraid he would try to take her from me, and I couldn't bear to lose her."

And yet she did lose me . . . years later, over my father.

She clasped her hands in front of her and stared down at the table as if looking into a crystal ball. "He was far too mercurial, a Beat Generation poet, an existential giant who couldn't make a cup of coffee. Never had money for food or rent."

I was riveted to her words. "A poet. What was his name?"

"Quentin." Her fingers spread, then formed a loop against the table. "Quentin McAllistair was his name. I'm not sure if he's still alive, though I heard he had a heart attack a few years ago. He never knew about you, Cassie. So dramatic and swashbuckling, he would have stormed in and claimed you as his daughter without following through on responsibility. A thrilling man, yes. Exciting and reckless. But not father material. He would have destroyed you, honey, and I couldn't let that happen. It was my job to protect you."

Not father material.

How many times had I heard that about TJ?

Was I so inept, so ill raised that I didn't understand how that could harm Tyler, or were my instincts correct, that TJ could find his fathering abilities if he just tried hard enough?

I was quiet through the rest of the dinner, lost in myself.

Agate and Tyler didn't seem to mind, having found common ground in old tales of my misbehavior.

As I gathered Tyler to head back to Santaland, he went around the table to give Agate a hug, this time a genuine, soulful squeeze.

"I'm glad you came tonight," he said. "Now we can be a family."

A family. I didn't want to push it, but I did see the possibilities.

I could just imagine the days ahead. Cozy storytelling around the stone hearth in Agate's stone cottage. Tyler skipping through a field of wildflowers behind a white-gowned Agate who turns to take his hand and tells him she's so proud he'll be participating in his first skyclad ritual . . .

Hold on. Rewind to the part where I tell Agate that, much as I trust her love for Tyler, I don't want him coerced into practicing Wicca or veganism or anti-faux grois or whatever the cause, at least, not until he is of a more discerning age and ready to make his own informed decisions.

I took her hands in mine and her dark eyes snapped onto mine, as if trying to receive a telepathic message. "Thanks for coming, Agate."

"I'm glad you called. Tyler is a dream."

"Thanks. I'm not really sure how we do this," I said, feeling awkward.

"We meet again. Maybe a few times. You come to the cottage and I'll visit your place. Before you know it, you'll know my number by heart again."

I hadn't forgotten it over those six years, but I didn't want to admit that just yet.

"Don't worry, honey." She nodded at Tyler and pressed a palm to my cheek. "We'll take it slow."

13

I have always prided myself on being a mother who listens to her child, a mom who is in touch with his needs and worries.

Which would explain why I lay in bed that night after my reunion with Agate and needled myself over Tyler's wish to be saved from his father. I kept reminding myself that he was five, still a child who didn't understand the ramifications and consequences of a life without a father. I was the adult here; I knew better.

I flipped onto my other side, my ear folded uncomfortably against my pillow as I picked at the metaphysical wound. How did all of this look from Tyler's perspective? He was well-adjusted, got along well with friends at school. He was secure in his mom's love, saw other kids getting along fine without a dad, and he didn't know his father well.

From his size 8 sneakers, he didn't know what he would be missing by not having a father.

I rolled over on my back, the weight of molding this little life heavy on my mind. Tyler was too young to understand the sense of loss and emptiness caused by growing up without a father. The snide comments from kids in high school about whom my mother had slept with. That cold, abandoned feeling and the yearning to know why he wasn't there.

Besides, I'd read reports of the risks fatherless boys faced—a higher rate of youth suicide, of dropping out of high school. And boys who grew up in homes without fathers were twice as likely to end up in jail than kids from two-parent families. Those statistics seemed so cold and distant, silly to think of a five-year-old in those terms, but when he grew to be a man would I kick myself for not pushing him toward his father?

I had to press on. Bree had an appointment at TJ's studio in the morning, and I was going with her. If my legal shark hadn't managed to get a bite of TJ yet, maybe I could get through to him this time.

From his turret bedroom Tyler snored slightly, then his breathing calmed. "Good night, moon," I whispered as doleful moonlight slid in over the café blinds. "Good night."

"He's an aaaaaass! She's an aaaaass. They are all major ass-holes!" Bree's bright Midwestern twang carried so well through the bus that I thought I saw the driver turn and scowl from way up front. We were on a bus from the studio, trying to make some sense of the meeting with TJ and his "people," and Bree's reaction reassured me that I was not the screwball here in the TJ situation, even as it worried me that we might get kicked off the bus before we got to the downtown area. The woman sitting across from us seemed on the verge of complaining. One more "aaaass" was going to drive her over the edge. One look at her rinsed red hair and plaid tam-o'-shanter and I sensed that she'd been pretty close to the edge before we came aboard.

"How did we ever work in that looney bin?" Bree asked me.

"Work there? I lived with the guy." I couldn't shake my three-by-five monitor of TJ making inane comments about father-hood. "We must have been smoking some very potent stuff."

"And we weren't even smoking at that point. Grrr . . . If that Melissa told me about her fabulous alma mater one more time, I was going to pin her diamond ass to the freaking bulletin board."

I shot a look at the tam lady, who now seemed resigned to clicking her tongue as she watched passing buildings.

"Our lives were different back then." The conciliatory note in my voice surprised me. Maybe I had let go more than I thought. Certainly, after today's meeting with TJ, I'd learned something, hadn't I?

"TJ is not a nice person," Bree said firmly. "Think about that when you try to hook him up with Tyler. Do you really want him in that environment, with the 'me' focus? What kind of an example does it set when everyone is catering to this man, this cranky, shortsighted, morally depraved man?"

"You've got a point," I said, thinking back on the meeting in TJ's dressing room. TJ insisted on keeping his two head writers in the room, Melissa Diamant and a geekmeister named Jersh. I'd been flanked by Bree, who is quick with a comeback but was so caught up in putting down Melissa, the woman who'd replaced her on the show, that she didn't have much to contribute to the discussion of Tyler's future.

I had tried to ignore the two writers and proceed with a more personal discussion of Tyler, but TJ was clearly put off by the fact that I'd hired an attorney. He felt threatened, and his response was to toss off a barrage of one-liners.

"Have you lost your mind? Why would you pay a high-priced shark to come after my ass if you're going to show up here and chew it personally?

"I wish the kid well, but I was always honest about who I was, right? You didn't expect me to wake up one morning with the sudden desire to change diapers and push a stroller, did you?

"If you think the boy needs a father, go out and get him one. Someone qualified. You wouldn't hire a plumber to do an electrician's job, would you?"

TJ's face, on a three-by-five monitor, haunted me as I rode the bus from the studio to Union Square. Of course, I'd argued back with saintly patience and restraint, knowing that losing my temper would only alienate TJ that much more. I'd kept pulling him back to the topic that mattered—Tyler. And he'd kept rolling his eyes and claiming that he was not a bad person, that he was not father material, that he just wanted to be left alone.

After a very sour thirty minutes, I'd decided to retreat from the battle in hopes of winning the war. The personal approach was unsuccessful, but Nina had other tactics. I would back off and let her work her legal magic.

"Are you going to be okay, honey?" Bree asked as the bus neared my stop at Union Square.

"I just need to move on right now. Bury myself in some work so I don't have to think about being disappointed with TJ."

As we said good-bye, I realized that I'd misjudged TJ. He wasn't Charlie Brown . . . not at all.

At Rossman's I changed into my Mrs. Claus suit, wanting to lose myself in a pack of bawling children whose problems could be solved with a potty break and a lollipop. By the time I was in costume it was after two. Time to report in at Santaland, but I just couldn't, not yet. I had to see Buchman. I felt a strong physical urge to have him, to lose myself in a captivating session of mind-blowing sex with him. With all that was going wrong in my life, it seemed like the healthiest stress reducer.

His secretary told me he was finishing a call with Tokyo, that I could go into his office and wait. I stepped in and waved, surprised to see him wearing dark-framed reading glasses as he went over some paperwork with the caller. The glasses gave him extra sexual cachet, and as I locked the door behind me I felt as if I were about to seduce a college professor. Very naughty.

He was wrapping up the call, saying something about his job here. That he was wrapping it up here. Expected to be dispatched to Tokyo or maybe New York in the new year.

My heart seemed to stop beating for a second. Buchman, leaving?

As soon at he hung up, I pinned him down. "So you're leaving after the holidays?"

"That has always been the plan, much to the relief of the staff. Actually, if I may quote Imogene from shipping, 'thank God that windbag is outta here in January.'"

The idea of his departure, of Mr. Buchman not filling this office, filling my days as well as some nights, made me a little sick inside. Suddenly, sex play lost its appeal. "I knew about the plan," I said. "I guess I assumed it was off for the time being. I'm going to miss you. Our mornings together."

He removed his glasses and put them on top of his papers. "You'll miss our mornings? Ms. Derringer, I do believe you've been using me as an object of sexual desire."

"And that would bother you because . . . ?" I left it open so that he could fill in the blank, a feeble attempt at a joke.

Buchman turned away and rubbed his chin thoughtfully.

"I'm sorry," I said, feeling clumsy. "Most men are in it for the sex, aren't they? And you're right. That's where my head has been. I don't have time to be emotionally involved right now.

"I've got Tyler to take care of. And his father. I've been chasing after his father, trying to get him to act like a father."

"Yes, of course. But do you mean to say you've never been emotionally involved in our . . . *mornings* together?"

It was my time to turn away, and I had to move quickly so that he didn't see the tears filling my eyes. All along I had wanted it to be about sex—just a physical relationship—but now it was clear that I'd become attached to Buchman in other ways. As a friend to Tyler and as an escape. I enjoyed his company, his self-deprecating sense of humor, his way of moving on quickly from one subject to another.

"She turns away, lest he note her eyes rolling mockingly to the back of her head."

"No." I turned back to him, shaking my head. "That's not it. I've gotten more attached than I wanted. Really, it's meant a lot to me, our time together, and I—" I pressed my fingers to my eyes, trying to swipe away the tears.

"Oh, Ms. Derringer, come here, please." He rolled his desk chair back and swung me into his lap so that my head rested against his chest, just under his chin. "Shame on me for making you cry."

"It's not your fault."

"Please, just this once will you let me believe it is about me and not some other bloke who looks like Charlie Brown and appears on the televisions of half the world every night."

So he had been listening; he had been keeping tabs on the events in my life. I held my cheek against his chest, afraid that if I looked in his eyes I'd burst into hysterical sobs. Here at last I'd grown fond of a man, a person, and he was already on his way out of my life.

"It *is* about you," I whispered.

"Oh, you are a gorgeous creature but a terrible liar."

"Can I ask, what are the chances of you staying here in San Francisco?"

"Slim, Ms. Derringer. Chicago is already making noises about reeling me in."

"Will you make me one promise?" I asked. "Promise you'll spend Christmas with us? It would mean a lot to Tyler, and to me."

He fell silent.

"Did you have other plans?"

"Actually, I had investigated the hot turkey platter at Denny's; however, I shall have to forgo it for the boy. Christmas is truly about children, is it not?"

"Children and generous hearts."

"Yes, well, perhaps your ex will come through as a generous heart this holiday season. Christmas might be just the thing to melt his cold resolve and deliver him to his son's doorstep."

"That would be nice," I admitted. "But I've realized something about TJ. He is not like Charlie Brown, not the downtrodden underdog. The slumped shoulders and hands in his pockets, it's all an act. TJ lacks the social consciousness and pure heart of a Charlie Brown."

"So you're saying exactly what? That Tyler's father is a failed man because he does not resemble a comic-strip character? Hmm. I'm not sure I could ever meet your high standards."

"I'm saying that today, for the first time in years, I got a clear look at TJ Blizzard and I didn't like what I saw."

"Yes, I got that part. But back to the comic strip. If you were to peg me, could I rank among the Pigpens of the world? Or perhaps the canine Snoopy."

"Stop!" I pinged his arm.

"Woodstock? Odie?"

"Now you're in the wrong comic strip."

14

As we switched into high gear to serve all the children who needed Santa in the height of the season, I pushed Buchman's departure to the back of my mind, telling myself that it was all for the best. He'd been the perfect choice for a transitional relationship, and to be honest with myself, he'd been a fine role model for Tyler. Buchman fit into my life very well, but I'd always known he was a temporary fix. Come January, we would all move on with resolutions and renewed spirits.

I didn't hear a word from TJ until just before Christmas, and then the message came through his famous lawyer, a weasel of a man named Eric Cartwright. In that disarming way that so many lawyers have, he decided to pay me a visit one evening while I was working in Santaland.

"Do we have to do this here? Right now?" I gave the attorney a harsh look. "If you didn't notice, I've got a few dozen kids to coddle along to the North Pole, with just two days till Christmas."

He folded his arms, barely creasing the lines of his expensive suit. "Your lawyer stated that time was of the essence—your terms, not ours." I turned away, hating this weasel man who followed me as I escorted a little girl up the stairs. He nearly hit his head on the low doorway leading into one of Santa's visiting spaces—a cottage cute as a country dollhouse—but he kept talking. "And my client is concerned about his reputation. He's a public figure."

I turned back so quickly he stopped short of slamming into my chest. "His reputation? I'm Mrs. Claus. How about my reputation as the woman beside Santa, the baker of cookies and mender of the red suit each year at Christmas?"

I thought it was at least a little funny, but weasel face apparently didn't share my sense of humor. Across the snow path I saw Buchman peeking out of his Santa den, his blue eyes locked on me and the lawyer. On this particular night he was filling in for a sick Santa, and to my relief he quickly came around the path to join us.

"First, I want you to know our offer is nonnegotiable," the lawyer said, "and it's a one-time deal. You don't accept it tonight, the offer is withdrawn."

"Sir, everything is negotiable," Buchman interjected, having joined us, "and your terms sound somewhat illegal—a little shaky, shall we say? However, go on."

"The terms are very simple," he said. "You'll get your 17 percent of my client's income no matter what, possibly more. Beyond that, my client has two offers. A, he will sign away parental rights and give you sole custody. Or B, if you want my client to see the child, we've compiled this list of dates that he's available. Of course, with the demands on my client's schedule, he would need assurance that he'd have full visitation of the boy on these dates."

My heart beat merrily as he handed me the list. At last, I thought, a light in the darkness. TJ was coming through, revealing himself as the father I knew he could be. He wanted Tyler, for quite a few days of the year, from what I could see on the list before me. They included December 24, 25, 26. January 1, 2. February 14. The entire week of Tyler's Easter break . . .

A puff of air escaped my lips. "Is this a joke?"

The lawyer grinned. "Not at all."

"Christmas Eve?" Buchman was reading over my shoulder.

"And Christmas Day? Oh, and the day after that. And Valentine's Day. St. Patrick's, I believe, isn't that March 17? Why, I believe your client managed to mark off every holiday of the year, and then some."

The realization cut through me as I stood there staring at dates. This was half of the year—and all summer, those precious months when there's no school and we spend afternoons in the park or take trips down the coast.

TJ would take my son away from me for the sole purpose of hurting me, ruining holidays, heaping guilt and longing onto my heart, squeezing the sweetness and joy from my life. "Bastard."

"Easy, Mrs. Claus." Cartwright was smiling now, a weasely, thin-lipped grin. "You've got that reputation to uphold."

"Indeed, and it's certainly in jeopardy if she's seen around men like you," Buchman told him.

"So what's your decision?" Cartwright zipped his expensive leather portfolio. "Hate to rush you, but as I said, this offer is only good today."

"You want me to make a decision now?" I gaped at him. "I haven't talked to my lawyer. This is all a negotiation."

"Not for my client. I meant what I said: that's our final offer. Take it or leave it."

I looked from weasel lawyer down to the list of dates. Losing Tyler to TJ in this way would be devastating, probably for all three of us. This was not what I wanted. But I knew it wasn't what TJ wanted, either. He was bluffing, forcing my hand, putting himself in a position to look like the good guy when in fact he wanted me to refuse the offer and absolve him of all involvement and guilt.

I couldn't let him do that. I couldn't let him buffalo his way out of Tyler's life.

"Fine." I folded the paper into quarters and tucked it into the pocket of my Mrs. Claus suit. "Tell your client I accept his offer. He can have his son for holidays, weekends, vacations . . . whatever."

Cartwright paled.

"Cassandra." Buchman touched my arm. "Why don't you take a moment to think this through?"

"I've thought of nothing else for the past five years," I said, stoically staring down the lawyer. "My son needs his father, and I've promised myself I'd do everything in my power to make that happen. Do you want me to sign something, Mr. Cartwright?"

"I don't . . . Well, yes, you'll need to do that. In my office," he stammered, clearly taken aback. "Sometime next week, I suppose."

"After Christmas?" I pressed him. "So then, TJ won't be taking Tyler this Christmas? Or is that still on the table?"

"Oh, my client is taking the boy for Christmas, all right," Cartwright snapped.

I held up my hands in mock surrender, trying to ignore the sickening feeling in my stomach caused by this whole charade. "Fine. Just trying to get things straight. I'll have Tyler ready on Christmas Eve," I said, picturing my son dressed in a Little Lord Fauntleroy suit with a suitcase and his favorite teddy bear. Such a pathetic ruse TJ had cooked up . . .

"Christmas Eve, then." Cartwright tucked his portfolio under his arm and headed down the Christmas path, his Gucci shoes padding softly on the white carpet of fake snow.

"Oh, God." I hugged myself. "What did I just do?"

"I was wondering that myself," Buchman said. "What were you thinking? Surely, you don't intend to give up your son?"

Of course I didn't, but things had become so complicated. "I've got to call my lawyer," I said, thinking that I would never reach her at night. "Tomorrow. Why is it that the bad guys can afford lawyers who make house calls at night?" It was at that moment that a slight movement in the sleigh beyond Buchman's shoulder caught my eye. As my eyes focused, the sensation of horror blossomed.

Tyler. His glassy eyes shone at me from the crook of the sleigh. He pulled back, scared and near tears.

"Oh, honey . . ." My arms flew toward him and I realized he must have been there during my entire conversation with

Cartwright. What was he thinking? Did he hear everything? "Tyler . . ."

But he squirmed in the other direction, hopping off the back of the sleigh and disappearing behind white frosted bushes on the Christmas landscape.

"Let me go," Buchman said, backing away quickly. "You don't want to corner him at a time like this."

But I did want to go, I did want to run after Tyler and corner him and pull him into my arms and tell him that I would never give him up. Never.

15

When Buchman returned with a sheepish expression ten minutes later, I braced myself for the worst.

"I'm sorry, but he must have slipped ahead of me. I went directly to the storeroom where he keeps the mousetraps, but he's not there."

"I'm not surprised," I admitted. "His favorite bear, Lemon, is gone, and so are his Legos and his art kit. He's hiding. Or else he's trying to run away."

"He can't have gone far," Buchman said.

"What if he left the store?" I pressed a fist to my mouth and fought back the rising panic. Tyler was gone. Oh, God . . .

"Hold it together," Buchman said sternly. "We'll have security start a sweep through the store immediately. And perhaps we should alert the police. I will make those calls. You focus on Tyler. What he was wearing? We'll need a description."

My beautiful five-year-old with bright eyes and freckled nose. Green elf pants with a green and white striped jacket that he hates. Underneath he was wearing his HAIGHT STREET KIDS T-shirt. And curly-toed green elf shoes over his sneakers.

While Buchman made the calls I paced Santaland, wanting to

be in a dozen places at once: at the top of every escalator, in front of every door, at the sleigh where he'd been playing, inside every dressing room, and under every rack of clothes.

Tyler, where are you? Let us find you! I prayed as I crawled in the hatch that led to the dusty area under the Santa platform. When I lifted the white skirt of fake snow, enough light shot into the darkness for me to see that the scratched linoleum floor was empty.

Hope flooded through me when the security people appeared one by one, Tadashi and the other familiar faces.

"We've gone through this dozens of times," Tadashi told me. "We always find them. Always." Something was reassuring about the way they listened, their earpieces in place. A clerk would be stationed at all doors and the team would search the store, one quadrant at a time.

I wanted to be part of their search but the police were on their way. "We'll maintain radio contact," Tadashi said. "We'll let you know as soon as we find him."

They would find him. Of course, they would. It wasn't as if I'd lost him in an airport or foreign country. Rossman's was our second home.

And yet, it was in Union Square, a busy shopping district in a busy city.

Oh, please, God, whoever and whatever you are, please, bring him back to me.

I called Jaimie at home, and Bree, who was participating in the Sing-It-Yourself Messiah. They both promised to come if I needed them. Then I called Agate, whose calm voice made my throat grow thick with emotion. "I'm sure he'll turn up soon."

"He thinks I don't want him," I choked out. "He thinks I'm giving him to TJ." I paused to swallow back a sob. "I'm a terrible mother."

"Honey, we've all been there," she said. "Harried and overworked and barely grown up ourselves. No one person can do it all; as the saying goes, it takes a village. Let's brainstorm after the holidays and we'll figure out what I can do for Tyler. Use your friend Jaimie. And let Tyler lead you sometimes. He's old enough to know whose company he enjoys."

I thanked her, wiping my eyes as a police officer stepped off the escalator. It seemed like hours had passed already, but checking my watch, I saw that Tyler had been missing for less than half an hour. I told Agate good-bye, faced the young patrolman, and answered his questions quickly.

"Ma'am, do you think the boy's father might have picked him up? Taken him somewhere?"

"I . . . don't." I pressed my lips together, thinking that TJ wouldn't stoop so low, would he? To send his lawyer and follow right behind to scoop up Tyler? Besides, in Tyler's state of mind, I doubted he would go with TJ.

"Are you sure, ma'am? The fact is, when children are missing, most of the time they are with another family member. An ex. A relative."

I was nodding. "I don't think so, but we should check, right? I'll call his father."

Of course, TJ refused to take my call, even when I got through to the studio and explained the situation to Concepcion. Finally, I asked the police officer to handle the call, and within minutes he was speaking with TJ, ascertaining that TJ had no knowledge of his son's current whereabouts.

I was surprised when the cop handed me the phone. "He wants to talk to you."

Taking the phone, I felt my teeth clenching. "I don't have time for this."

"What the hell is going on there? Did you tell the cops I kidnapped him?"

I scoffed. "That's sweet. Always about you, isn't it?"

"Listen to me, Cassie. I haven't seen the kid, and I don't intend to see him. Ever. I don't care what you and Cartwright agreed on. I don't have the . . ." He sighed. "Why can't you accept that I don't have the right temperament to raise a kid?"

"Because you're a big boy and you can control your temperament. You have control over your own behavior, TJ. You alone."

As I talked I moved quickly, stopping to circle clothing racks and dig inside to make sure he wasn't hiding at the center. Impatient and anxious about Tyler, I was only half listening to TJ.

"You know I was never good with self-control. Listen, the show is leaving San Francisco. Not final yet, but talks are on to move us to Los Angeles. Bigger market, more affiliates."

"Los Angeles?" I was in the women's dressing room on the third floor, peeking under doors and clothing racks. "What are you talking about?" I said as I swung out of the dressing area and spotted Tadashi in the aisle.

"Anything?" I called, ignoring TJ's ramblings.

"Yes, yes! I was looking for you. Come!"

I don't remember hanging up or stowing the phone, but I will never forget Tadashi's warm smile as he told me, "We have found him. Everything's fine." I think Tadashi will also remember that moment, as I threw my arms around him and burst into tears.

"Oh, Mrs. Claus," he said, patting my back. "Please don't cry. Your elf will be home for Christmas."

16

Tyler had been discovered with Lemon Bear and a bucket of Legos in the bedding department. He was curled under one of the fake bed displays and admitted that he planned to hide until the lights went out, then crawl into the bed, which was just his size.

Buchman was already there, the two of them sitting side by side on the floor, leaning against the elf bed that featured cushy flannel sheets with square panels of cheerful reindeer faces. Tyler's face was red from crying, probably a good match for my own blotchy complexion. When he spotted me his face puckered, bringing on a new round of tears.

"I'm sorry, Mom."

I dropped beside him and pulled him into my arms to breathe in the smell of his skin and kiss his salty cheeks. "No, I'm sorry," I said in my most reassuring voice. "I'm so sorry you thought for a moment that I would ever, *ever* let you go. 'Cause that's never going to happen."

"I know," he said glumly. "Except to my dad."

"No, not to him, either." I leaned back and looked in his eyes. "I realized tonight that I've been wrong about you and TJ. Yes, he's your father but . . . Honestly, he lives a life that isn't the best place for a five-year-old boy right now. The best place for you, T, is right here with me."

He sucked in a breath of delight. "I love you, Mom." He flung himself into my arms and hugged me with such genuine drama that tears stung my eyes.

"I love you, too."

As we talked about what Tyler had heard and thought, what he had worried about so much that he felt it better to disappear, Buchman sat by quietly, reassuring us both with his presence. I wanted to kick myself when Tyler pointed out that he ran away because I kept giving him the impression that I was trying to foist him on someone else. He thought I wanted to be free of him. All along I had been trying to create a balanced, healthy life for my son, and what had happened? I'd screwed up big-time.

"One of these days I'll get this mother thing right," I told Jaimie later on the phone.

"Oh, yeah, sure you will. We'll be like, ninety and wearing diapers ourselves. But we'll figure it out eventually."

That night as I tucked the fleece blanket under Tyler's chin, I flopped down beside him and stared out over the café blinds, out at the jagged lines of rooftops and trees dotted by streetlights, and I thanked God that he was safe. I'd come so close to losing him, maybe not physically, but on the emotional plane, where that connection between mother and child needs to stretch and twist and bend in time. I sensed that it had been pulled to a fine thread when I'd pushed him toward TJ.

In a burst of emotion I squeezed him tight and kissed the side of his head. "I don't ever want to lose you," I whispered, not sure if he was still awake.

"You won't," he murmured. "Good night, moon."

By the time the doorbell rang on Christmas Eve, Tyler and I had worked together to create a new family blueprint that included Agate and did not include TJ in any way. I had worked through custody details with Nina Cho, asking for sole custody of Tyler, along with a reasonable financial arrangement to ensure his financial security and his education. We planned a quiet Christmas Eve watching our favorite boy learn the meaning of Christmas with his young friends' help—an enjoyable Charlie Brown for me once again, now that I'd pushed TJ out of that equation. Tomorrow, we would all gather at Bree's, where she was hosting a dinner for our new extended family, which this year would include Agate, Franco Verti, and Tadashi, finder of lost children.

Most everything had fallen into place.

And then there was Buchman.

Tyler buzzed Buchman in, then scampered around excitedly as our guest arrived with gifts. Tyler didn't know about Buchman's assignment, and I didn't have the heart to tell him and ruin his Christmas. "Can I open mine?" Tyler crowed.

"One present on Christmas Eve," I called from the kitchen area, where a veggie lasagna sat steaming on the counter. I didn't want to come out of the kitchen, didn't want to emerge and start the clock ticking on our first and only Christmas with Buchman. Although the heat rising from the oven had to be wilting my make-up.

I felt a hand on my shoulder. "Let's give your mum her gift first, shall we?"

Summoning all my composure, I turned to face Buchman, who stared down at his open, empty palms. "I do hope you like it. It was a bear to wrap."

Tyler laughed. "There's nothing there! No bears."

"I know this one," I said. "You're giving me the world's smallest flea circus."

"Actually, I'm more of a spendthrift than that. Ms. Derringer, I'm giving you the gift of myself. For three more months, at least. I convinced Rossman's that I could do wonders on this store in that time, liar that I am. We'll reevaluate April first. Which gives us time to see how . . . certain relationships might develop. Or not. Whatever you think."

Hope surged through me and I leaped into his arms. "I think it's fabulous."

"You just caused me to drop your gift," he teased, pushing my hair off my face with his long fingers. He lowered his voice, adding, "However, I refuse to be used exclusively as a sex object this time."

I reached down to pinch his butt.

"None of that, now. You must let me in this time."

I sucked in a breath. "You were already in."

"I don't understand that gift. Is it invisible?" Tyler asked us. "Is my gift going to be invisible, too?"

"Your gift is quite tangible." Buchman turned back to Tyler and squatted down to his eye level. "Your mum is going to have my head, but I believe every boy must have a pet." He reached into the shopping bag and lifted out a small cage. Inside, a small white and gray creature crouched in a ball under some wood chips.

"A mouse." Tyler's face brightened. "Wow, cool!"

"I believe we've found our Christmas mouse," Buchman said, handing the cage to TJ.

"He finally turned up!" Tyler pressed his face against the cage. "Did you come into my trap?"

"More or less." Buchman straightened to my level. "Or there may have been a pet store involved," he muttered.

"What?" Tyler asked, but he was quickly distracted by the movement of the critter. "Look at him tumblesault. Maybe he's a stunt mouse."

"Nothing like the stunts I shall be doing when your mother lets me have it for bringing you a pet for Christmas." He winced at me, mouthing, "Sorry!"

Backing away from the cage, I sat on the couch and watched the two of them examine the mouse. The image of Buchman and Tyler leaning over the cage together struck a chord deep inside me. Theirs was a special relationship, a bond forged not out of obligation but out of mutual interest. It reminded me of something Agate said, about letting Tyler choose his own leaders.

"What are you going to name him?" Buchman asked.

"How about Snoopy?" I suggested.

"Squeak." Buchman chirped at the mouse. "Scamp. Scamper. Squirt."

"Mistletoe," Tyler said, nodding. "It's a good name for a Christmas mouse."

I folded my arms. "Maybe the gift will teach you some responsibility, T. If not . . ." I pointed at Buchman. "I'll expect you to be over here cleaning out its cage."

"An activity at the top of my list, to be sure." He sat beside me on the couch. "Can't think of much that would amuse me more than flicking away at mouse doodles in your lovely turret."

His face was close to mine, close enough for me to feel the light stubble along his jaw and to see the dark flecks in his blue eyes. We were leaning toward a woozy kiss when I felt something wiggling against the back of my head.

"Eee!" I bounced away from the couch cushions and twisted toward Tyler. "Was that a mouse in my hair?"

He dangled the mouse gently. "A little Mistletoe."

"Yuck!" I shrieked. Buchman stifled a laugh at the sight of me swiping my hands over the back of my head. "Do not ever, *ever,* put that thing close to my head. Do you understand?"

"But Mom, I have to put Mistletoe over your head if—"

"It's quite all right, Tyler." Buchman cupped the mouse against Tyler's chest. "You hold on to Mistletoe. Don't want to let the Christmas mouse loose again, do we? Hold on tight, and I shall hold on to your mum." Buchman put his hands squarely on my shoulders and pulled me toward him.

Tyler cleared his throat. "Can I tell you something? It's a Christmas tradition to kiss under the—"

"Please, I think we can manage just fine," Buchman said, his blue eyes hinting at amusement as his lips met mine.

We would manage, all right. I could see myself arguing through the spring window design with Buchman and talking him into increasing the design budget so we could replace those horrible fake summer flowers gathering mold in the storeroom. I could see Agate teaching Tyler how to tend a garden, all of us gathering in her cottage for vegetable stew. I could see Tyler growing more and more secure in his family's love for him . . .

and building a better mousetrap. Jaimie and Matt and Scout, Bree and Franco or whomever she decided to spend her time with—they would all be a part of our new, redefined family. And Mistletoe? Well, maybe Tyler's kindergarten class could adopt him during the school year. On second thought, did I want to be known as the mom who gave all those five-year-olds a reason to kiss?

Absolutely.

Miracle on the Magnificent Mile

Meredith

Chicago, December 2005

1

"With all due respect, Uncle Leonard, there is no way in hell you'll catch me wearing that red Santa suit." When the words slipped out during a budget and planning meeting with the Rossman's board of directors, everyone in the room laughed, guffawed even, at the notion of Meredith Rossman, their future CEO, masquerading as Santa's sidekick. A joke. An amusing diversion. At least, that was what I'd thought when he'd brought up the topic of the vintage dress turning up in the flagship store's collection of holiday costumes.

That !@#$ red suit. I remembered my mother opening it two years ago right here in the Michigan Avenue store, running her hands over the velvet fabric, nearly embracing the jacket as if it were an old friend. At the time, she expected me to wear it, despite the fact that I was getting my MBA, on a total corporate track. Back then I'd fended Mom off. Now, wearing the suit was out of the question, as was celebrating Christmas.

Call me Scrooge, but it's very difficult to have a holly jolly merry little Christmas when you're fighting off a seasonal depression that cuts right to your soul. Believe me, I know. I lost my parents two years ago on Christmas Day, which is ironic in that it was probably their favorite day of the year.

Somehow, it now seems disrespectful to their distant spirits, as if the holiday they had loved most had betrayed them and every Bavarian hand-cut glass ornament, every caroling quartet, every fa-la-la mocked the two people who had built this empire, created my world and held it suspended in emotional and material riches that I considered unending.

But even in tragedy the Rossmans forged on. Dad's two brothers worked double time to pick up the slack, and I plowed on, trying to prepare and educate myself to lead the company. That's the downside about being part of the Rossman dynasty; you're supposed to carry on, assume the mantle of diplomacy and goodwill for Rossman's. If it's good for the store, it's good for you.

"If you want to use the suit, I'm sure we can hire an actress to play Mrs. Claus," I added. I was beginning to wonder over the fact that Western civilization's archetypical devil was always depicted in red. The color of blood and stop signs and Satan and eyes that have cried all night. Really, when Santa had the wife whip up a superhero costume, what was he thinking?

"Such a spoilsport, Meredith," Daniel said, throwing it all back on me. "That suit has been in our family since it was made."

Although I only blinked at him, my thought waves were saying, *And thanks, again, Daniel, for proving yourself to be the weenie cousin from hell. Your bountiful gestures of greed, jealousy, and avarice are not lost on me. I'm keeping* records!

Unfortunately, Daniel wasn't the only person touting the magic of the costume. At that point I was ready to crawl under a giant gumdrop in Santaland if I had to hear one more time how my grandmother had sewn it with her own hands one year when the stores were in trouble, how my mother had been the first to wear it, in this very Michigan Avenue store, and—glory, hallelujah—how everyone claims that suit has brought luck and profits to two Rossman's stores—Baltimore and San Francisco—in the past two years.

"The suit is a miracle worker," Uncle Lenny proclaimed to the board members.

"Having seen the sales figures," I chimed in, "I'd say we've definitely witnessed a miracle. However, since the suit can't give a testimonial, and we don't have Tinkerbell here to help us refine Rossman's magic pixie dust, how about if we discuss some of the empirical evidence? Can we examine some of the other changes and programs implemented in Baltimore and San Francisco?"

"I think Meredith just doesn't want to wear the suit," my jerk cousin said, baiting me.

Which brought more guffaws from the board.

Beneath the table my hands balled into fists. Ooh, that Daniel! It was probably wrong to hate a blood relative with such flaming intensity, but our rivalry had been going on since we were babies and our parents had compared their difficulty with child labor, the ounces of formula consumed, or our dexterity with Cheerios. We'd both spent high-school summers as interns at Rossman's, both attended Stanford University, both reported to work at Rossman's Chicago the day after graduation. "A healthy competition," my mother used to say, but since she and Dad died I'd sensed the balance of power tipping toward the other side. Which was the reason I'd kept my focus and finished my MBA at University of Chicago.

People seemed to think I should have taken time off when my parents died, should have taken a break. To do what, I don't know. But at the time, I knew that I needed activity, and I knew my parents wouldn't have wanted me to derail my career and indulge in grief. The inside players at the store knew that I was the person destined to run Rossman's; I possessed the skill, I had inherited the fortitude and stamina and insight, and I had taken the time to learn the business from the buyers to the loading docks to the shoppers motivated by coupon sales. Uncle PJ was now handling corporate matters and Uncle Lenny had always been good with operations, but I felt confident that I could oversee Rossman's the way my parents had quite successfully.

Daniel, on the other hand, spent more time on golf courses and tropical beaches. Most of his proposals were short-term fixes, some of them quite costly. Not that he was a bad person, my cousin was just not cut out for the demands of retail management. If only he could accept that . . .

Uncle PJ pushed his shiny round glasses up his nose and turned to Daniel. "All joking aside, what do you have to show us for next year's budget cuts?"

"I'm still working that out with our accountants," Daniel said.

Translation: *Oh, crap, Uncle PJ, you were serious about cutting costs?*

"And knowing how Rossman's always likes a blowout at Christmastime, I've been focusing on gearing up for the season," Daniel added.

"We do love our Christmas sales," his father agreed. "What have you been working on for this year?"

Daniel grinned. "Trying to get Meredith into that costume."

This time there weren't so many laughs. At last, the gag was fizzling.

"Meredith." Uncle PJ's chair swivelled toward me. "Do you have something for us?"

"Of course." I stood up and smoothly launched into a Power-Point demonstration of a reorganization of staff that would cut more than 10 percent of our operating budget. "Framing" or "spinning" had been a valuable lesson in grad school, which simply meant that you never use words with negative connotations. So firing personnel was called a "reorganization" and firing the lowest achievers was called an "employee incentive program," and making people work harder for the same pay was called "raising the bar." Although eyes often glaze when it comes to talk of budgets, the members of the board seemed quite perky when they heard me say "10 percent savings." Talk like that made corporate hearts go pitter-patter. Visions of rising revenues danced on the chart in their heads. Ka-ching!

"Very interesting proposal." Uncle PJ tapped his glasses against his chin. "You'll get us copies to review?"

"It's been e-mailed to everyone here," I said, restraining myself from doing a wild *nanny-nanny-foo-foo* dance in front of Daniel. "But this plan is just the foundation—phase one in a three-part initiative." I paused a moment to get a read on my audience.

Eyebrows were arched with interest. My two uncles beamed with pride. Daniel steamed quietly at the corner of the table.

Marcus Aldridge, the bald man beside Uncle Lenny, looked puffed up with pleasure, his eyes gleaming marbles in his dough-boy head. "More ideas for cutting costs?" he gasped, as if I were offering him a drink in the desert. "Do go on."

Heads nodded eagerly.

"To start with, we need to ax the budget for Christmas decorations." I was on a roll now, confidence flowing. "I know we're competing with the best stores in Chicago, but our customers are loyal. I have already taken the liberty of ordering our designer to stick with the decorations we used for the last few years. What's wrong with last year's window displays and floor decorations? Market testing indicates that our customers are quite loyal; they'll shop at Rossman's whether we've got dancing reindeer or tumbling snowmen in our windows."

The room felt quieter, tenser . . . or was that just my own insecurity?

I forged on. "And then there's Santaland, a significant budget drain at holiday time." I sighed dramatically, as if the cost pained me. "I'm afraid Santaland is a luxury of the past. And if we can separate our sentimental attachment to these things, we must consider phase three, scaling back our Toyland to a novelty gift department with prewrapped gift packages for high-end shoppers who need to be told what's appropriate for their newborn niece or five-year-old nephew whom they haven't seen since last Christmas."

"Ax Toyland?" The doughboy deflated. "But people love it."

"I think we're all still kids at heart," Uncle Lenny said with a nervous laugh. "I don't want to give up Toyland."

"But much of our toy inventory ends up damaged," I said. "And every year we're stuck with a fair amount of surplus after Christmas. And then there are the liability issues . . ."

"Did you see that air gun they had on display last year?" someone asked. "My nephew loved it."

"And two years ago, we were one of the few department stores that carried Fatso Catsos," Nella Greeley chimed in.

"They've got a driving simulator that's just like the real thing," my own uncle PJ reminisced. "It makes such a funny sound when you crash, I ditch the car just for the fun of it."

"God forbid some kid sticks a Lego up his nose and has to spend Christmas Day in the ER," I said, trying to regain their attention. "Do you realize Rossman's would be liable?"

"I have driven that simulator!" someone said, wagging a finger at my uncle. "I read somewhere that NASCAR drivers use it to—"

"It's just not cost effective," I said, trying to make eye contact with someone, anyone in the room.

But it was too late. They were lost in reminiscences of dolls and cars and robots that could burp and high-five. Corporate babes in Toyland.

Much later, I would look back at this meeting and try to figure out exactly where I went wrong, at what point I'd lost the board's support.

Uncle Lenny tried to be helpful. "What can I say? Every person on that board is a kid at heart."

"And?" I threw up my hands. "They don't want to increase store profits?"

"Don't take it personally, Mer-Mer." He smiled, every inch the indulgent uncle. "You just can't take away their toys."

2

When I ran into Uncle Lenny the next morning, he told me the board was hinky about my proposal. "I'm not saying it's been rejected," he told me in the elevator. "They're just feeling . . . hinky."

Hit with "hinky" before my first cup of coffee. I had a feeling this was not going to be a stellar day.

Later that morning, Len leaned into my office with more news. "PJ had a notion, and I jumped right on it. We're going to make you the manager of the toy department for the Christmas season. Isn't that wonderful? Get you down in the trenches, Meredith. We want you to learn A, why our Toyland is a necessity and B, what it's like to manage a department firsthand."

"Ahum," was my brilliant initial reaction. I knew that a good manager needed experience at every level, needed the skills to do any job in the organization. I also had a strong feeling my competition would not be dealing in toys. "You know I've got retail experience, Uncle Len. I grew up here."

"Of course, but there's nothing like the toy department at Christmastime."

"Actually, I'd rather stay off the sales floor at Christmastime." The carols and the decorations were a little hard to handle.

"Meredith? Please. If it's good for the store, it's good for you."

I turned away from my monitor and folded my arms over my blue cashmere sweater. "Out of curiosity, what department is Daniel going to work the trenches in?"

"Daniel? He's going to stay on his project with the accountants. We still need to find some measures to cut down our overhead."

"But I'm the one with financial training and skill," I protested. "I finished third in my class at University of—"

"Of course, of course, we know you can crunch the numbers, missy. That's why we need you to learn the toy biz. And that's why we want Daniel on the financials, let him learn the numbers." He pointed to the side of his head. "The gray matter is still working, Meredith. Give your uncle PJ and me a little credit, would ya?"

"I can give you unlimited credit with 5.9 percent APR on purchases, no payments due until March first." I smiled. "That was a joke."

"Always thinking numbers, that's why you're so good at what you do."

"Mama didn't raise a slouch," I said, then thought of Daniel. Did it ever concern Uncle Lenny that his own son was a greedy little slacker? Leonard Rossman didn't seem to be bothered by much, and to his credit, he didn't seem to resent me for outshining his son.

"Your mother would be proud of you, God rest her soul. And I'm sure you'll do just as well down in the toy department. Why don't you check in down there after lunch. I'll speak with the manager, Brian Dombrowski. He'll be glad to have you."

"I'll bet I'm just what he wants for Christmas . . . a management puppet to breathe down his neck and step on his toes and second-guess all his decisions."

"Such a sense of humor you have," Uncle Len said.

* * *

Funny as I was, Brian Dombrowski was not laughing when I appeared in his beloved toy department with my clipboard in hand and my giant budget-cutting scissors strapped to my back. Of course, the scissors were invisible, but Brian in his psychic wisdom seemed to be aware of them.

"You can't learn the toy business overnight," he told me as he built a pyramid of bright yellow and green boxes filled with dancing frog stuffed animals. "I don't understand, really. Why are you here again?"

"To cut costs, increase efficiency, troubleshoot. All that Management 101 stuff."

Another joke lost on Brian Dombrowski. "Do what you want. You've got carte blanche, of course. But do me a favor and don't micromanage my sales staff. They're well trained, know what they're doing."

I had to admire a manager who defended his staff. "Before I make a move, I'll check with you," I said. "And before I start, which way is Santaland?"

He pointed up. "It's still on the ninth floor across from the café. I know, they're officially part of our department, but they're miles away, managed by HR. Are you going to troubleshoot up there, too?"

Translation: *Would you get off my back and go pick on Santaland?*

And so began my reluctant tenure in the toy department. I spent the first three days observing, splitting my time between the toy section and Santaland, which didn't run quite as efficiently as the evergreen toy department. Despite my recommendations to reuse old decorations, these gumdrops and snow mountains were a little tired, the Styrofoam peppermints gone from white to pale yellow. Furthermore, our league of Santas had been cut down to three, which made lines longer, children crankier.

The fourth day I dedicated myself solely to the ninth floor, watching the lines form, watching the elves hop around and make merry, watching children wait, cry, shriek, run, crash into candy-cane arches, and generally make huge nuisances of themselves.

At the end of the fifth day, I submitted a report to Uncle Lenny.

"The key obstacle in the smooth running of Santaland is the children," I said as I stood before his desk. "Get rid of the kids, and you'll have a smooth operation."

"What? Ditch the kids?" he barked. "We can't do that. It's all about them."

I touched the top button of my black wool Louis Vuitton jacket. "I was afraid you'd say that. You'll find suggestions for queuing, entertainment, and product placement in the report. The location of Santaland should really be closer to the toy department, but since it's too late in the season to make a move that extensive, we need to place some sample toys in Santaland. Get kids playing with the toys while they're waiting. And we should consider point of purchase. Maybe this year the elves can ring up the parents' toy purchases at the end of the line while the kids are seeing Santa."

Uncle Len was reading and nodding and listening, all at the same time. Not bad for male multitasking.

"Yes, yes, yes! We can give parents the option of ringing up their items for pickup at another time, when little Janey or Jeffrey isn't with them!"

"Exactly." That was item seven on my report, but who was counting?

"This is a moneymaker. Innovative and perfect for the season. No one else on the Magnificent Mile provides this service, am I right or am I right?"

"You're right." I rubbed the button again. "So, I'll leave you to absorb that. I need to get back to some cost-cutting strategies I was modeling for the board."

"What? Wait." He stood up. "You can leave that work for now. I need you on this. Your plan needs to be implemented and super-vised."

I'd been afraid of that. "I'll bet the manager of Toyland could roll it out."

"Ooh." He frowned. "I wouldn't trust it."

"He's a manager. He's in charge. We hired him because he was qualified to manage." To be honest, I had never met Howard Reichert, probably because he stayed holed up in his office in HR, which, after spending a day or two in Santaland, is not a bad choice.

"Meredith, I need you to implement this plan. It's too valuable to waste with some half-assed execution."

Foolish me, thinking I could weasel out of this bogus assignment by giving Uncle Len a brilliant plan. "If it's execution you want—"

"Now, now, Meredith," he interrupted. "I'm sensing that you're not happy with this assignment, and I've got a little goody to pass on, a little incentive for you."

I was all ears.

"I'm sure you've heard the rattling in the wind, some changes in the air. There might be some movement on the board, and I personally would love to be the one to suggest you for the next available seat."

I wanted to break into a happy dance but I figured a nod was sufficient. When my parents' estate was settled I was given their shares in the corporation but no voting power, as control of the corporation was something that had to be decided by the board of directors. "It sounds like this is the change I've been waiting for," I said.

"I thought so. That's why I want you in toys, Meredith. You recognized that we took a loss on toys, yes, it's true. But now, instead of just recommending that we slash the department, this is your chance to get in there and turn it around. Make it turn a profit. Here's your challenge. Bring the toy sales up by 50 percent from last year, and I will see that you get a seat on the board."

Suddenly my palms felt clammy. There is something alarming about having your dreams laid bare before you in a quick financial statement. It all sounded so easy.

"Fifty percent, hum?" Quickly I ran the numbers in my head, calculating whether Uncle Len's proposal was feasible. "I think I can make that happen for Rossman's. Yes, I accept." I rubbed my damp palms together. "I might have to whomp a few fannies down in Santaland, but—"

"I've been meaning to talk to you about that," he interrupted. "You've got to stop intimidating the staff. I've gotten a few complaints. You're bossy and very forthright."

"Complaints! From whom?"

"There's some concern that you're scaring the customers, especially the children in Santaland. So I have to insist that you wear the costume. Be Mrs. Claus and no one will worry about why you're roaming around Santaland with a scowl on your face."

"I don't scowl," I said sternly, "and I don't want to be Mrs. Claus."

"Be Mrs. Claus," he answered, "and would it kill you to be a little nice for a change?"

"Nice! Dammit, I'm always nice!"

He folded his arms. "You always did have your mother's temper, God rest her soul." His face grew sad just before his eyes dropped down to the report. "I still miss them both, Mer-Mer. Especially at this time of year." He sighed heavily. "What can be done? We move on. We forbear. I'll finish reading your report, you go try on the Mrs. Claus suit. I had Grace put it in your office. Wear it in good health."

Uncle Len had a way of graciously shaping a conversation to his satisfaction and still coming out as the nice guy. He was pretending to read when I headed down the hall feeling a mixture of joy and peevishness. Six years of college and for what? To portray the doting female accessory to some frosty old legend?

A frosty legend who was going to get the next seat on Rossman's board of directors.

3

"It's the most wonderful time of the year," that eggnog-smooth voice boasted throughout the store. Ahead of me, two elves swayed in time to the music as they meandered down the lane of gingerbread figures, approaching the short line of kids waiting to see Santa. It was late, a slow night, thank God, probably the best time to make my virgin patrol as Mrs. Claus.

I buffed my nails on the white fur trim on the Mrs. Claus suit my grandmother had sewn by hand, probably sometime in the Paleolithic age, and tried to look tough, tried to look like I knew what I was doing here in this ridiculous costume.

Why *was* I here?

My heart started yammering in my chest, all this Christmas regalia looming over me, making me lose sight of my true goal.

Increase sales by fifty percent. Fifty percent. Fifty percent.

A little boy waiting in line pointed at me, and his mother stared right through me as if I were part of the gingerbread landscape.

I ducked behind a gumball palm tree and took a deep breath. Perhaps Uncle Len didn't realize how hard this would be for me, how this suit would dredge up memories, how I might lose my cool and wing a giant gumdrop at some annoying kid.

Just changing into the red suit had been a feat. Dealing with the contents of that silver foil box and unfolding this costume had required great courage and emotional control. I had closed my office door and waited in the silence as memories rushed in. That brisk Christmas morning when the three of us had leaned over the pastry board in the kitchen to make sticky buns. Gathering around the fire with spiced cider to exchange gifts, and then the leisurely afternoon curled up on the sofa, reading our new books. The exchange of books was a holiday tradition. Ever since the days when Santa left packages under the tree, one of them had always contained a book and one a Lanz of Salzburg nightgown for me, and every Christmas morning after we ate sticky buns I slipped on my new frilled flannel gown and cracked open my new book.

The Christmas engraved in my memory started as an ordinary Christmas two years ago. But after brunch my parents had cleaned up the kitchen, showered and packed, trying to make the seventy-mile trip to the Lake Geneva house by sundown. "We don't spend enough time there," my father had said as he carried a suitcase down the stairs. "Really, such a cozy lake home and we spend our lives here, working in the city. It's wasteful."

"We're spending an entire week there," my mother calmed him. "We'll take the time to enjoy the gifts we have." She turned to me with a smile. "That's my New Year's resolution. Are you going to join us, Mer-Mer?"

"I'll probably drive out tomorrow," I told her, well into *The Da Vinci Code* and not willing to stop reading until I finished the story.

When they left, I was engrossed in the story, worried about breaking the code to reveal a message on parchment. My mother had paused at the Christmas tree, admiring the Bavarian glass ornaments that had been in her family for years. She remarked on how they took her back to the Christmases of her childhood, as glass ornaments were the only frivolity her father indulged. I don't remember whether I acknowledged her comment, having heard this bit about my grandfather a hundred times before. And then they were out the door, driving down Erie Street, and I didn't even get up off the couch to kiss them good-bye.

After I got the phone call from the police, after I'd seen the SUV that had rolled over and split in half, after I'd weathered the funerals and the condolences and the awkwardly averted eyes and the stiff hugs of friends and relatives, it occurred to me that I could have been driving with my parents. And there were times, after the media got wind of the huge amount of money and power I was in line to inherit, it seemed that I *should* have been with them.

Survivor's guilt.

One tabloid claimed my father was drunk at the wheel, a raging alcoholic. Two local radio personalities joked that my mother had grabbed the wheel and made the car swerve when my father admitted to having an affair with a diva from a rival department store. Another account charged that my parents were too cheap to hire drivers. *Guilty!* I wanted to shout. Guilty, though I didn't realize that wealthy people were not allowed to drive their own vehicles in the state of Illinois.

Guilty . . . of not even getting off the couch to say good-bye. Of not really listening to my mother's final words to me. Guilty of falling into a safe, steady niche with my parents, never realizing that the shell of my life was in jeopardy of cracking and shattering into sand.

Furthermore, I was guilty of being a Rossman. I was the poor little rich girl, barely into her twenties and already an orphaned millionairess. My media-hungry high-school peers recalled that I had been "the senior class nerd" and "the mouse of Oak Park." Even worse, college classmates recalled me "coming and going quietly," like vanilla pudding at a grand dessert buffet. Reading between the lines, I got it: the inference that I was not worthy, that I didn't have the mettle to carry on the family business, that I was undeserving of the family fortunes, the extent of which I had not been aware of since my parents led a comfortable but frugal lifestyle.

That afternoon in my office when I opened the box, I tried to block out the disapproving noise of the media and listen for the tenor of my parents' voices, not so much their words, but the current that had flowed among us the day we'd last seen this costume.

My mother's delight at the rich, dark folds of velvet, the red reflecting pink on her skin as she reached into the box.

My father recalling how my mother had turned heads and won over customers, the first and only Mrs. Claus in Chicago retail history.

The hopeful voice of my mother asking me if I might want to be Mrs. Claus . . .

I had to cut off the memory before my flat refusal, followed by my mother's disappointment. That Christmas had started like so many others and had ended with a finality that marked it as the last Christmas I would celebrate. After the devastating chain of events that led to a single phone call on Christmas night, I couldn't look at the garland strung over the mantel, couldn't bear to go near the tree glistening with crystal decorations from my mother's childhood. I put an end to Christmas, had the cleaning staff hire a bunch of people, I don't even know who, to come in and pack everything up and take it away. Remove the evidence. Distance the pain.

I flopped the silver lid onto my desk, locked the door, and quickly shed my Louis Vuitton jacket for the red coat, trying not to recall the way my mother's fingers had glided over the fabric, the way she had held the jacket under her chin in joyful reminiscence. I stepped into the skirt, zipped it at the waist, and moaned. It hugged my body as if Grandma had tailored it for me. Just my luck, the suit fit.

4

That first night in the red suit I accomplished nothing beyond proving to myself that the suit would not make me shrivel into a puddle of mulled cider. The next morning I suited up and climbed onto the snowscape of Santaland, feeling once again like an astronaut marooned on a distant planet without an umbilical cord. I was glad that it was too early for the dancing elves and Santas to be hanging around.

What was I supposed to be doing here?

Oh, right, Mrs. Claus. Toy sales up.

As I was admittedly weak on maternal instinct, I decided to focus my thoughts on my overriding goal, a 50 percent hike in toy sales. My new sales strategy, the "toys in Santaland" program that would begin as soon as we had working cash registers at the end of the line. Actually, this might be a good time to consider placement of the machines for cashing out. One of the latest trends in retail was the disappearing sales desk, the end of that stationary, looming counter that reminded customers of imperious schoolteachers and long, boring lines. I ventured along the snow path, looking for a suitable location near the exit. Maybe that gumdrop garden would work? And another terminal could be hidden behind that large gingerbread man as long as the electricians could wire it up there. I was peeking under the snow blanket for electrical outlets when an elf approached.

"Very cool outfit. I always say, when you want to get noticed, you gotta wear red." She seemed to be barely twenty, with a short, solid body decked in a green spangled jacket, curl-toed shoes, green and white striped tights, and a flouncy white skirt. She wore it well, probably because the girl seemed more outlandish than the costume, with spiked black hair dipped in fluorescent green, glitter make-up covering her skin, and a nose ring the size of a teacup.

"I never wear red," I said flatly, not sure what that said about me beyond confirming my college peers' observation that I came and went quietly. Without nose ring.

"I'm on that. When Personnel was handing out costumes, I told them green or black, nothing else." She tilted her head toward one shoulder, a cute gesture for such a gothed-out girl. "I'm Gia, and I don't usually talk about clothes, but you looked a little lost and I don't know, I thought, let's see what she's about. And what are you about, anyway? Are you a new Santa? The Feminist Claus?"

I told her that I was supposed to be Mrs. Claus, that I didn't know what that meant. As we talked, I couldn't take my eyes off that walloping nose ring. It reminded me of a hula hoop I had as a kid. I told her I'd never seen an elf with a nose ring.

She squeezed one eye shut. "You got a problem with that?"

"It doesn't fit my image of elfin . . ." I paused. Back in business school they had discouraged leaving a button open on a shirt; shoes that revealed toe cleavage were out, and forget about jewelry and body piercings. The astute businesswoman was allowed one pair of small stud earrings. "Not to squash your style, but do you have anything more Christmasy?"

"My emerald stud!" She grabbed my arm and squeezed tight. "It's perfect. I'll wear it tomorrow."

Which would save me from going cross-eyed staring at the hula hoop. I liked Gia's attitude and told her that I was going to start a new toy campaign in Santaland. Did she want to be one of the elves on the toy team?

"I don't know." She crossed her arms, her black-painted nails tapping on her elbows. "What does the toy team do?"

"The front line works the crowd, in this case, the kids in line. We'll have samples of our most popular toys up here, and elves will demonstrate to kids and let them play with them while they're waiting in line. We'll let the kids familiarize themselves with the toys, let them choose what they want, give their parents a chance to observe all this. Then, while the child is finishing up with Santa, the parents have a chance to go to one of the small terminals we have at the Santaland exit and order the toy for pickup at another time."

Gia shook her head, her eyes curious. "Who are you, and where did you come from?"

"My name is Meredith. I come from the land of management."

I'd meant it as a joke, but Gia wasn't laughing. "Okay. How do we get started?"

I quickly learned that Gia knew the names of every elf, every Santa, every hottie in Personnel, every Backstreet Boy. Over the next few days Gia Moscarella became my right-hand elf, and her assistance was invaluable. She had the cachet to sell the program to her elfin friends, the courage to make decisions, and the nerve to ask plenty of questions.

Through Gia I met the three Santas who worked in the chambers of our gingerbread house. She got me in with the elves, ten of them on two different shifts, and during lulls in the work she shared her unique perspective on college, fashion, and life in Santaland.

"We just have the best staff," she said. "Well, maybe a few clunkers, but mostly good people. I mean, to have a Santa named Jesus . . . is that freaky, or what? I think Personnel hired him for kicks, but he's so perfect for the job."

Jesus Sanchez was a Mexican immigrant with twenty-seven

grandchildren, many of whom stopped in to visit Santa during my first week in Santaland. "They love their poppy," he always said. "They get a little riled, but they're good kids." Jesus seemed to think that every kid was good at heart, even when they were shrieking or trying to climb the snow mountain or spitting out green lollipops because they hated lime flavoring. Watching him draw out a shy child or reel in a wildcat, I sometimes wondered if he was destined for sainthood.

There was one married couple who'd been hired to play Santa and elf—Dmitri and Irina Litowinsky. According to Gia, they also worked as a team painting and plastering homes, and Dmitri was said to have the hands of an artist when it came to smoothing concave plaster walls. "He's doing some work for my aunt on the South Side," Gia said. "I'll let you know how it turns out." They seemed like a lovely couple but neither of them spoke much, which I assumed was due to a language barrier. However, the kids didn't seem to notice, as long as Santa was willing to listen to their long lists of motorized cars and doll accessories.

Right off the bat my favorite Santa was a silver-haired man named Nick, who seemed to be the counselor and heartbeat of Santaland with his low-key, calming demeanor, his ability to get people to open up and share their concerns, and his campaign for staff and customers to relax and give the magic of Christmas a chance to transform their lives.

"He is so full of crap," I muttered one day as Nick talked with two young parents who were concerned that they couldn't give their child everything.

"No, he's not!" Gia's hoarse voice was defensive. "Nick is cool. He's giving them good advice. Listen . . ."

"You won't be able to give your child everything he wants," Nick said. "But you can give him what he needs, and that's your love and protection."

Gia swooned. "Just makes you want to up and marry him, doesn't it?"

"Hardly." I winced. "Really, what does he know about raising kids?"

She shot a look at Nick, her brows wiggling. "And really, what do we know about Nick? Did you ever catch his last name?" I shook my head no. "That's because he doesn't give it. I pressed him once and he was all, 'It's Nick. Like Nicholas. You know, St. Nick'?"

I rolled my eyes.

"Exactly." Gia nodded. "I mean, everybody knows I grew up on a farm and ran away to the city right after high school. We've met Jesus's grandkids and we know you're the Rossman princess, but Nick? I find him highly suspect. Like, maybe he's just out of prison, or maybe he's one of those guys who's been relocated in the Witness Protection Program."

"You have a fertile imagination. First of all, he wouldn't have made it through our HR department if he has a criminal record. All of our Santas have to be fingerprinted, with background checks."

She was still nodding. "That may be so, but you can bet there are some skeletons in his closet. Some dark secret beating in the heart of Mr. Nick."

I glanced over at Nick. His dark brown eyes were intent on the couple, his arms folded over his red jacket, that shiny silver hair a striking contrast to his youthful face. "I'm sure you're right." Dark secrets didn't surprise me. But I realized that Gia, at the ripe age of twenty-two, probably didn't have any skeletons in her closet yet. Lucky girl.

"Nick is the bad boy we all think we want," Gia said.

"That's not how he strikes me. He seems so in control, so reassuring. I think he's the daddy we seek. The protector. The soothing voice that comforts us when we wake up after a nightmare . . ." It had been a while since I'd articulated some of the things I missed about my own father, and it didn't feel so bad. Somehow, in the context of this conversation, the shadows didn't loom so large.

"That is so sweet," Gia said, "but I don't think I ever dated the protector type. Is that who you go after?"

"Me?" I was about to tell her that I don't date when I managed to reach back to college days, to the few guys I'd tried to fall in love while attending Stanford. One of them was a forced match—

the son of a credit-card company mogul. The marriage would have looked great on paper, combining one of the country's largest retailers with a major financing company, but Keith and I were not well suited for each other. I knew that when he told me that no woman could "do him" like a professional. My other relationships were just barely that. My overall sense was that these guys didn't really want to know who I was but wanted to connect with me for sex or my family's cachet or both. My mother kept telling me that I just hadn't met the right person yet, but I was convinced that I had, many times, in the guy in my anthropology class or the TKE pledge in my biology study group or the engineering student who told me I was pretty. I think I could have been happy with them, but they didn't want me, at least not for anything long term.

"Or do you like bad boys, too?" Gia went on. "Did you give your parents hell back in high school? I can see you on the back of a motorcycle, Meredith. Smoking outside the bowling alley. Sneaking out to meet a guy after midnight."

She was describing a world I'd never experienced. Was I such a goody-goody, living in a bubble?

But instead of telling Gia that cigarette smoke made my eyes burn and motorcycles were too dangerous, I just nodded. "Sure. That's my dark side."

Nick said good-bye to the couple and crossed the path to join us. "I got a question for you two. What's with all the toys I see these kids carrying around?"

Gia giggled. "What, did you miss the memo, Nick? We're pumping up toy sales."

"Actually, I've been trying to ignore the crass, commercial sales pitch."

"Really?" I put my hands on my hips. "Well, you can look the other way, but the sales promo is producing results. Toy sales are up 35 percent from last year at this time, with most of that increase happening right here at the checkout behind Santaland." And that didn't count today's sales. I was edging close to my 50 percent goal, my deal with Uncle Len, and I was ready to taste success.

"Whoa, Mrs. Claus." Nick's arms unfolded and he studied my face, as if seeing me for the first time. He pointed two fingertips to my eyes, then his, as if waving in a new line of vision. "We need to talk, you and I."

Gia touched my arm and leaned close to whisper, "Santa Claus is coming to town . . ." Raising her voice, she announced, "I think they need me at the gumdrop checkout."

Nick watched her walk away, then stepped in, as if trying to establish closer contact. I didn't mind. Goofy me, something came over me when he was around, just a nice feeling, though I knew it couldn't go anywhere. Not to be a snob, but really, any guy playing "Christmas-hire Santa" was really not going to be up to Rossman standards. Any kind of relationship beyond a business friendship was out of the question.

"When you work in the Christmas industry, you can't let yourself lose sight of what it's really about."

"The *Christmas* industry?" I shook my head. "We work in a retail establishment. Material goods sold in exchange for money."

"But at this time of year everyone's focus changes a little, don't you think?" His hands gestured, as if he were drawing a gentle landscape in the air. "People want to take a moment out of their lives to think back—whether they're thinking of that star that appeared over the manger or something from their own childhood, a Christmas morning or a long-awaited homecoming to the family table. This is a time for reflection and sharing."

"No," I protested, not wanting to go there at all. Nick was cute and persuasive, but I wasn't going to buy what he was selling. "This is our busiest time of year. In a bad year the Christmas profits can compensate for three-quarter-year losses."

His eyes were locked on mine as his shoulders went slack. "I see that we're speaking different languages. I guess what I'm trying to say is, what the hell is this toy program? The air guns and dolls and handheld computer games? I don't know, I'm just disappointed with Rossman's. That's all."

"Disappointed?" I scowled. "Hello? We're just trying to sell toys. We work for a department store."

He looked down at his black boots. "True. That part is true."

"Santa?" one of the elves called. "You have a visitor."

He pointed a thumb toward his gingerbread cottage. "I gotta get back. But let's talk about this again, okay?"

"Sure," I answered, hormones talking. There was something very appealing about Nick, the cloud of warm sincerity that surrounded him, those dark eyes that alluded to secrets. I liked being around him even as I realized that he and I had diametrically opposed life philosophies.

To think, he was "disappointed" about selling toys . . .

Maybe Gia was right. Maybe he had escaped from another life, a hippie commune . . . or a distant planet.

5

December fifth, and toy sales were up 47 percent since last year. The rising trend in sales figures indicated that we were on a roll, but I was working on other ways to bring the profits above 50 percent before the end of the week. The next board meeting was scheduled for December 21, and I wanted to make sure Uncle Len would have something to boast about when he nominated me.

At the moment I was perched behind a life-size gingerbread man, my stopwatch resting on his shoulder as I watched the line for Santaland go by, timing it, watching for snags in the flow. We couldn't have these kids getting hung up at any stage of our operation. Queuing was an important aspect in any service operation, and since an efficient queue produced customer satisfaction, I was on top of this line. I didn't pound away on an MBA at University of Chicago for nothing.

"Santa Lady?" Some little girl stepped out of line and stood before me, hands on hips, as if she were ready to rumble.

I stared past her and counted louder, figuring she'd go away. At the moment I focused on Gia and another elf named Kevin as they peddled toys at just about the right speed, taking a minute or so to assess each kid's age, skill, and interest level before matching them up with the toy of their desires.

"Santa Lady! I am talking to you, Mrs. Santa. Why are you egg-noring me?"

Without losing count, I shot a look at the smiley-faced girl who had squirted out of the line. Two front teeth missing, pale white skin, and cheeks so chubby she could have been smuggling walnuts.

"Listen, chipmunk, you'd better get back in line," I told her. "You'll lose your spot."

"I don't care about my spot. I got questions before I go in there. Last week I saw a Santa at Nordstrom and I know there's Santas all over, ringing bells and getting money."

"Santa's helpers," I said, repeating the Santaland corporate philosophy. "They all work for the big guy who lives at the North Pole."

Her eyes were slivers of doubt. "Then how come their suits aren't the same?"

I didn't have time for this. "I don't know . . . Santa encourages diversity, I guess. Why are you asking me all this?"

"Because you're Mrs. Claus. Aren't you married to the real Santa?"

At that moment I was struck by the fragility of our belief system—that parents would pass this elaborate Santa mythology on to their children while evidence to the contrary is all around them. Any alert kid, like this toothless little girl before me, would figure things out.

"Or that's why you egg-nored me . . ." She tucked her chin under a fist, eyeing me skeptically. "Maybe you're not the real Mrs. Claus."

"I am," I lied, "I am married to the real Santa." Not so much a lie; I was married to Rossman's, the nationwide Santa of the Christmas season, the biggest source for America's Christmas gifts and . . . Oh, hell it *was* a lie, but a harmless one.

Not quite sold, she stared at my shoes, my belt, my face. "Can you tell Santa something for me?"

"You can tell him yourself, if you get back in line."

"Not the fake Santa. You're supposed to tell the real one." Her lips twisted, as if she were tasting pickled beets. "You don't really know him."

Looking down at her sour little face, I tried to think of the best way to present the mythology of department-store Santas.

"Never mind." Quickly, she turned away and darted down the path, toward the exit.

"Wait," I called lamely. I wanted to chase her and make sure her Rossman's experience wasn't diminished by all this North Pole confusion, but Uncle Len had warned me to be nice and I didn't think it would look too good for Mrs. Claus to be lunging after a kid and tackling her on the fake snowhills of Santaland.

Especially with toy sales up 47 percent and climbing.

Instead, I retired behind the gingerbread man. Squeezing myself into his shadow, I went over the data I'd collected on my clipboard, wondering if I should write this up for the next board meeting. I was checking my calculations when two elves passed by and paused.

"I have go to sit or my toes are going to be permanently curled in these elf booties," one of them said.

She plotzed by the gingerbread girl a few feet away and pulled her feet up under her. From the back, I recognized Portia and Kevin, who sat beside her, his back so erect that the stripes of his elf shirt seemed to unfurl for miles.

I was about to suggest that they move on, that this was my gingerbread territory, but I didn't want to sound like a total bitch. Again, me trying to appease Uncle Len with the "niceness" request.

"That feels so good, just getting off my feet," Portia said.

"Yeah, well, don't get too used to it. The Rossman princess is on patrol, ready to bust our asses."

Apparently Kevin had missed the memo about being nice.

"Ugh . . ." She moaned. "And if you think she's bad, wait till they make it official about her cousin getting onto the board. Everyone knows they're the two biggest rivals in Chicago."

What? What?! Did she say 'cousin'? I wanted to jump out and shake her for more information.

Not necessary, as Kevin seemed to have all the details, too.

"Old PJ Rossman is retiring. Again. He just came back to get the store over the bumps when Evelyn and Karl died. But now, sounds like PJ is out, Daniel is in. Our new chairman of the board."

What?!

Bad enough that he was calling everyone in my family by their first names; he had all this inside information. How could that have happened?

I looked to the movement at the front of the line, and there he was, cousin Daniel, shaking hands with all the elves as if he were running for North Pole mayor.

Oh, no. That was it. First time in Santaland, Daniel had come out of his office for only one reason: to spread the rumors about his promotion.

I sprang from my position, startling the elves beside me.

"Consider your asses busted," I said, "in the nicest way. And Portia, find yourself a pair of elf shoes that fit. Didn't anyone warn you that you're on your feet all day in retail?"

Before they had a chance to pull together a response, I was marching toward the exit. I pulled my body along, trying to ignore the slow-motion feeling of being sucked back into Daniel's vortex. I refused to give him the satisfaction of smirking in my face. No, if his story was true, he could do all his smirking at the meeting.

Right now I had another cage to rattle.

The ride down to the fifth floor was blurred by a giant red pulse of anger. I do remember pushing past the secretary, finding Uncle Len in his usual position, reading glasses on, fingers zigzagging over printouts.

"Tell me there is no truth to the rumors about Daniel."

"You know, I told your uncle PJ this would be a problem."

"A problem? It's a catastrophe! So it's true?"

"All his doing, Mer-Mer. PJ put things in motion without consulting me, and you know it's all got to be approved by the board, but once PJ sets his mind to something there's no talking him out of it."

I grasped at the air in frustration. "How did this happen?"

He took off his glasses and leaned back with a sigh. "I'm sorry, Meredith."

I couldn't let him weasel out of this. "Sorry will get you nowhere right now, Uncle Len. What about our deal? I'm going to bring in 50 percent more profits in the toy department."

"A deal is a deal, but really, I'm just one recommendation, and I don't have to tell you that your uncle PJ doesn't believe in women at the helm. Remember how he and your mother used to go at it time and again?"

"But Daniel is not a leader. He won't take Rossman's forward. You know that, Uncle Len. I know he's your son and you love him, but you know he's all wrong for this."

He sighed. "Yes, yes, I know. At least, my head knows. My heart . . . My heart says he's my son and I must support him." He shrugged. "What can I do?"

"Support his interest in ice fishing or origami. Support him in something that's not going to come toppling down on him—just as the Rossman empire will if he tries to manage it."

"I do believe you're right. Daniel was PJ's pick."

"PJ is leaving. His reign is ending, thank God, and I am the person most qualified to fill his position. I need to know that I have your support when the final vote is counted."

"Meredith . . . Mer-Mer . . ." He rubbed the bald nub at the crown of his head. "You make this quite difficult, but yes, I am confident that you are right for Rossman's. If life were fair and just, you would be the next CEO."

"I am going to make that happen." I went to the door, then called back, "Even if I have to kill your son in the process."

"Not funny! I'm not laughing," he called after me.

"I'm not joking," I answered just before I closed the door to his office.

6

Although I marched out of Uncle Len's office pretending to have a sense of direction, I floundered once I reached the elevator. Despite my plot to cut off Daniel and land chief executive officer for myself, I wasn't sure where this setback left me. I punched Nine and returned to Santaland.

As I wandered up the gingerbread path, which at this late hour was nearly empty, all the pent-up emotion of the last few weeks began to rise inside me, a churning wave of disappointment. This whole situation with Daniel was incredibly unfair, and although I'd been competing with him all my life, I used to have my parents on my side, someone in my court.

But not anymore. I was in this alone.

The flood of Christmas memories, the degradation of being forced to play Mrs. Claus, the disappointment of losing the coveted position to my jerk cousin—all these things washed over me like an overwhelming wave of negative emotions.

I found my clipboard in the fake snow behind the gingerbread man. When I leaned down to pick it up, a tear slid from my eye and landed on the skirt of the Mrs. Claus suit. As my vision blurred with tears, I rubbed at the spot and thought of my grandmother creating this costume, choosing the fabric, neatly running the edges through her old Singer.

My childhood memories of Nana were vague, but her reputation as a pioneer and businesswoman was huge. What would she think of the recent events in the store she'd worked so long and hard to set on solid ground? How would she react to a man getting the top spot because he was a man with the Rossman genes?

She wouldn't stand for it; I knew she wouldn't. And neither would my parents.

I'd failed them. I pressed the clipboard to my face and sobbed.

"Meredith?"

I didn't want to lift the clipboard and acknowledge anyone. "Go away."

"Come here," the voice said as large hands clamped firmly over my shoulders.

I felt myself ushered along the path and through the doorway into one of the cozy gingerbread houses. "Come here. You'll be okay," he said as he pulled me onto his lap in the big Santa chair. Lowering the clipboard, I was face-to-face with Nick.

"I'm sorry . . ." I sobbed, sure that my face was stretched like a rubbery frog.

"You just cry it out there, honey. It's okay to cry, and you're in a safe space. No one will bother you."

It was a relief to hear him say that, a comfort to be held in his arms, against his warm chest, the crook of his neck smelling of lemony soap. My clipboard dropped to the floor but I let it go. Like it mattered. Nick closed his arms around my shoulders and rocked me gently. How long had it been since someone had held me, touched me so gently, as if I were a kid? Squeezing my eyes shut, I allowed myself one more moment of blubbering. Time to let the bad stuff drain out while this glow of energy and comfort surrounded me like a yoga aura.

When I finally took a deep, quivering breath and opened my eyes, I realized I didn't want to move yet. This spot felt solid, as if I'd hit bedrock and needed to hold this exact location for future rebuilding.

"Do you feel better?" he asked.

"Actually, I do." I would probably regret the tears later, but at the moment the anguish had drained, giving way to relief. I lifted my head, but he pulled me back against his chest.

"Don't have to rush off anywhere. Sometimes you just need to take a moment for yourself, a minute to regroup."

I sighed, surprised at the soft texture of his velvet Santa suit against my cheek. "Okay, then. You'll have to tell me when my minute is up."

"Ah, that's what I like to hear. Good for you. A lot of other people wouldn't be able to cut themselves the slack to take a moment. Do you want to tell me what that was about?"

"Not really."

"That's okay, too. I spend all day listening, I don't mind talking for a while. Want me to tell you what I want for Christmas?"

"Sure."

"Well, world peace used to be at the top of my list, but then this kid came in with an incredibly cool remote-control robot that you can train to vacuum floors and pick up your laundry."

"Robo-Housebot?"

"That's the one. I'm totally sold on that."

I drew in a smooth, deep breath, realizing it was time to go. Shifting away from his chest, I perched on his knees a second and let our eyes meet again. "Thanks," I said, surprised at how hard it was to extract myself from him.

"Hey, your time isn't up yet. Don't you want to hear the rest of my list?"

"I'd better go."

"And give up a chance to tell Santa all your problems?"

I smiled. "I'm Mrs. Claus. I have no problems."

"Wrong! We've all got something simmering under the surface . . . a few skeletons in the closet. How do you think I got this silver hair?"

"How *did* such a young man get gray hair?" I asked to change the subject.

"Silver. It's silver, and that is a story I can only tell over drinks in the noisy privacy of a tavern. A bunch of us are heading out tonight after closing, hitting the Berghoff. Want to join us?"

I smoothed my skirt down, thinking of Rossman's management policy. No fraternization with employees after hours. "I'm not allowed to."

"Not allowed?" He scowled. "That's a dumb rule."

"You're right," I said, thinking of Uncle Len and Uncle PJ and Daniel up in the boardroom, their heads huddled together as they rubbed their hands and laughed maniacally. "It is dumb. What time?"

"We'll walk over together after work. Meet outside the employee locker rooms."

I thought about Uncle Lenny running into me with the group of Santas and elves, actually witnessing me, Meredith Rossman, displaying un-Rossman-like behavior.

I could just imagine the look on his face. But really, what would he do, fire me?

The Berghoff is said to be the most venerable of downtown taverns, and when you walk into the main room with its dark paneling, old-fashioned globe chandelier lighting, checkered tile floors, and faux stained-glass panels, you can see why locals keep coming back here. I had eaten here with my parents a few times when we caught a burger after working at the Magnificent Mile store. Tonight, the walls were draped in low-slung garlands that added a little festiveness without changing the character of the tavern. Something about the dark, antique room made me feel safe and blessedly anonymous as I leaned over the bar and lifted a pint glass of beer. I didn't talk much but Gia didn't seem to notice, especially with the staccato chatter of our friends struggling to be heard over the music and the other patrons.

Somehow the conversation kept getting back to Nick, who had insisted that I sit beside him. Secretly I hoped that meant he liked me, but more likely he was worried about me after witnessing that sudden crying jag and wanted to keep an eye on me.

"This gig must be pretty different from spending Christmastime in Africa," Gerard told Nick. A tall, stocky elf, Gerard had devoured a plate of onion rings in the time it took me to find the hook for my purse under the bar. "Bet they don't have department-store Santas. Do they even have department stores?"

"There are large stores in Africa," Nick said. "Just not in the part I was living in, on the western coast. It's a huge continent, Gerard. Diverse landscapes and cultures."

"So did you play Santa there?" Jesus asked.

"You keep forgetting, I am Santa," Nick teased them.

Gia turned to me and whispered. "What did I tell you? Psycho, but probably a harmless one. Just a little delusional."

"I think it's a joke," I whispered.

She shook her head as Nick added, "Actually, most of my work there involved teaching the local people how to purify water for drinking."

"Mmm-hmm." Gia tapped a black-lacquered finger against her chin. "Purifying water? Next he'll tell us he was walking on it."

"What's your last name again?" someone asked Nick.

"I'm sorry, but if I divulge that information, I'd have to have my reindeer bump you off."

Some of us laughed, others persisted at learning his last name, but Nick wouldn't give it up. "I'm just Nicholas from the Midwest," he said. "Just a regular guy."

"Oh, you mean you're not from the North Pole?" Gia asked.

"Are you kidding? It's way too cold up there. Year-round."

Someone mentioned that Australia was currently having its summer, and Nick mentioned his love for Alice Springs, a town landlocked in the center of the continent. He pointed out that December was actually the hottest month of the year there, and that he'd once rescued some hikers in Ayers Rock on Christmas Day when they were caught in the sun without water or wet flannels to cool down their wrists.

"Did you rescue them on your sleigh?" Gia prodded him.

"Actually, I believe it was a Range Rover." I swear, there was a twinkle in his eye. "You can imagine how the tracks of the sleigh get buried in the desert sand. But enough about me. What are you guys doing for Christmas? How are you planning to celebrate our first day off in weeks?"

I felt a strange alienation, as if I were watching all this from a nearby deserted island, too far away to swim home. There was no Christmas left for me, and I didn't relish hearing about how families held pie competitions, or how they let the children play out live Nativity scenes, or how Dmitri and Irina were spending Christmas afternoon serving a turkey dinner for the less fortunate.

Now that was noble. It made me feel guilty for not doing something for others, but on that day I didn't have the spirit or the love to share. I could not give my Christmas away, as I had lost it, irretrievably, two years ago.

When Kevin asked Nick where he was headed for Christmas, Nick responded with the North Pole, of course.

"Oh, come on, Nick," Gia prodded. "Why don't you drop the secrecy and let us know what you're really about?"

"I am about Christmas," he said. "Santa brings toys to good girls and boys. Remember that one, Gia?"

She took a drink of her beer, stewing, as Nick added that she'd better behave if she wanted those earrings for Christmas.

Someone asked Nick if he used a bicycle to deliver toys in Holland, and he told the story of St. Nicholas helping out a poor family with three daughters. Since they had no money to pay dowries for the girls, they would be forced to live in servitude. To help them avoid this, St. Nicholas threw three bags of gold to be used for dowry money in the window one night, and they landed in wooden shoes. Thus began the Dutch tradition of leaving shoes out for St. Nick to fill with goodies, which became stockings on the hearth in America.

"I don't know," Mindy said, "sounds like Hanukkah gelt to me."

Nick spread his arms wide. "Of course. And that would make me Hanukkah Harry!"

I grinned, feeling so comfortable being next to Nick, as if his positive glow were showering a few sparks on me.

As the others laughed, Gia squeezed my arm. "He is so crazy!" she gasped.

"I know," I said. Nick was crazy, and I loved it.

7

Although Nick's "Santa complex" that night at the tavern charged up our spirits and kept us laughing, I still wanted some answers. Maybe he was really just Nicholas from the Midwest, but if that was true, what had compelled him to travel all over the world? And who had footed the bills for this aimless wandering? I mean, it's not like Santa impersonation was a marketable skill sought in the global job market.

Gia's theory kept niggling at the back of my mind, worrying me. Was it possible that Nick kept moving to avoid criminal prosecution . . . or Mob violence?

Part of me didn't want to believe that our personnel division would have committed a blunder so litigious as to let us hire a criminal. The other part of me just didn't want Nick to be a bad guy. Both parts of me knew it was time to find out the real truth (as opposed to Nick's excuses).

There was only one thing to do: raid the personnel files.

I suspected this bit of espionage was in violation of company policy and maybe even a few laws, but I couldn't help myself. I had to know.

Jennifer, the HR clerk, was all smiles until I admitted that I didn't know his last name. That brought on a few questions, some of which put me on the defensive.

"It's just that he interviewed so well," she said, scrolling through a list on her computer. "You're not thinking of firing him, are you?"

That depends on what prison he escaped from.

"That would be a shame," Jennifer went on.

"It's not in the plans at this time," I said quickly. *Just hand over the records, Mugsy!*

Instead of files, Personnel now stored employee information in their database, of course. As Jennifer printed it out for me I was glad I'd decided to go through official channels instead of skulking around for Nick's nonexistent file after hours. I could imagine myself tripping through this office in the dark feeling around for files—an adventure worthy of a few bruised shins and a dozen paper cuts.

"Let me know if you need me to intervene," Jennifer said as she handed me the printout. "I'd be happy to meet with him."

I bet you would, I thought, digging my nails into one palm to stop myself from being so territorial. I'd sat on his lap once. So had half of the kids in Chicago. It hardly meant commitment.

As soon as I stole away from Jennifer's cubicle, I was reading.

Nicholas Smith. Date of birth: November 3, 1970. So he was older than I was, almost ten years older. And he was single. Yippee.

After that, all interesting data ended. I wanted to double back and yell at Jennifer that she'd left all the good stuff out.

Nick had supplied three local references, one of whom had been called. She admitted that she was his aunt, but pledged that he was always a good boy, a scout and all. His social security number didn't set off any red flags in the computer, and he had been fingerprinted and cleared of any criminal record, thank God. Under previous employment, he'd listed "Santa Claus"— har-har—at department stores in New York City and in Dallas, Texas.

* * *

"Did you call the stores he used to work in?" Gia said when I ran the information by her in Santaland. "Because I'll bet you'll find out that they burned down in mysterious fires."

"You have got to put a leash on that imagination of yours," I said, panicked at the thought that she could be right. "But I'm going to do some of my own investigating before I go too crazy."

"Like what?"

"Check out his place. There's a local address listed."

"Breaking and entering?" Gia grabbed my arm. "Have you lost your mind?"

"I'm just going to walk by, check out the neighborhood, *maybe* see if he's home."

Her dark eyes stared blankly at me, as if I were sneaking off with her last tube of eyeliner. "Oh, you bad girl. You're falling for him, aren't you?"

"Me?" A squeaky denial is a worthless one.

"Just be careful tonight. Take your cell phone and call me if you need to be rescued."

"I won't," I insisted. "But it looks like the elves in the back need to be rescued for dinner. Why don't you take one checkout, I'll take the other until their reinforcements get back?"

Sometimes I found checkout very satisfying—the mere passing of a wand over bar codes to create revenues. Modern-day magic.

As I finished checking out items for a woman who seemed to hunker down under one of those strap-on baby bundles, an older woman in a suit approached and handed me her card. She introduced herself as Grace, from the Department of Social Services, Chicago. She was working on collecting toys to fulfill lists submitted by children in foster care. "What I really want to ask you is, would Rossman's be willing to make some Christmas wishes come true this year?"

"Oh, Grace." I felt my chest tighten at the answer I had to give. "This is a bad time." I still needed to bring the toy revenues up, now more than ever, and if I wanted Uncle PJ to take me seriously at all, I couldn't cave and just give away the profits because I was a soft heart. "I'm sorry."

She reached out and gave my hand a squeeze. "I understand," she said. "Believe me, I've heard it all around town, but we have to try. Just for the kids, you know?"

I nodded, feeling a lump form in my throat.

As Grace walked away I asked myself what my nana would have done. Would my mother have turned this woman down because toy profits had slipped last year? What would my father have said?

Then, clear as a bell, his favorite expression came to me.

"It's only money. We'll make more!" He'd said it time and again.

Sliding Grace's card into the pocket of my Mrs. Claus suit, I realized that this was not the Rossman's way. We were a family and a store that supported our community. And yet, I tucked that card away and returned to work.

Hating myself.

8

Nick's address was on the South Side of Chicago, an area I was somewhat familiar with from attending the University of Chicago. This neighborhood had gone through dramatic changes, from the influx of money in preparation for the 1893 World's Fair to the deterioration caused by industrial pollution and the encroachment of poorer neighborhoods some thirty years later. In the 1950s the university had led an effort to take back the neighborhood, a campaign that had proved to be successful as they preserved many classic Prairie School homes and some beautiful green parks.

However, looking up at the tired shingled building Nick called home, I wondered how this block had evaded restoration. Most likely these buildings were divided into rental units leased by students, the type I'd seen in class—the hang-out guys who lived on the quadrangle and lingered in coffee shops and bookstores and required no more than a mattress to crash on at night.

I pressed into the hedges as a couple passed by, both in watch caps and puffy coats. Now that I was here, I wasn't so sure what to do. Talk with his neighbors? Sit in the car and stake him out?

Somehow, standing out here in the cold was not the answer. I decided to head back to my car to think about it. Halfway down the block, I saw him coming. Or no, maybe it wasn't him. Hard to tell under that scarf and a fleece-lined cap . . . I played it cool, walking as casually as I could against the wind, but he stopped right in front of me, his breath coming out in a puff as he just stared at me from behind a brown grocery bag.

"Mrs. Claus, are you stalking me?"

"Oh, that is you," I said, trying to distract him.

"And I saw you hovering in front of my place. Wassup?"

"I used to attend the university," I told him, pulling my gloved hands into my coat for warmth. "I was just visiting the old neighborhood."

"Oh, sure. And this block is in all the architectural guides. Note the blatant disregard for any architectural style. The charming use of asbestos shingles. The subdued landscaping reminiscent of a desert spa."

"Okay, I came looking for you."

"Ah, at last a confession." He smiled, then cut up the driveway to his apartment. "Okay. Since you were honest, you can come in." I was three steps behind him. "Unless you want to stand out here and turn into a Popsicle."

"I'm coming," I said, curious to see how he lived.

Nick's place was on the second floor, but at least he had a private entrance in the back of the old house. Inside, it wasn't as bad as a lot of student places. The floors had been stripped to the old wood, and a printed oriental rug warmed up the sitting area. A laptop was set up on the coffee table, the screen saver flashing Santa's sleigh as reindeer pulled it over moonlit rooftops. He turned the computer off, then started unloading groceries on the kitchen counter.

"If I'd known you were coming I'd have gotten two hoagies. Do you like eggplant parmesan?"

"Sure, but I don't want to take your dinner."

"You're not. I always get a foot-long, and I'll give you half, but the salad is mine."

As I wandered around the apartment, rubbing my hands together to thaw, I paused in front of a desk with books flopped open and assorted papers, printouts, notes, ads, and old newspapers. A mess, but with its unique sense of organization, not unlike the resources for a student term paper. There was an ancient phone, a heavy, square unit with a cord. "Where'd you get this dinosaur?" I asked, hoisting it.

"It came with the rental, and I find it useful since I'm not a fan of cell phones. Our whole nation is now talking via satellite. We are in jeopardy of losing the face-to-face meeting, the way we lost storytelling as an oral tradition."

I was back at the desk, trying to read some of the papers without making any obvious moves like picking something up. One printout's headline was *St. Nicholas Center*. Another paper read: *Christmas Trees, Xmas, Candy Canes, Poinsettias . . .*

"Did you find what you're looking for?" he asked.

"Where's your Christmas tree?" I asked, cued by the printout. "Your crackling fire? All those little elves who help you make toys?"

"Got 'em stashed in the basement. You know, you're making me nervous. Do me a favor, sit down."

Glancing back at the coffee table, I saw he had set two plates out along with red wine in juice glasses.

He patted the back of the couch, the only seating in the room. "Take your coat off and tell me why you really came by to snoop on me. Here, I'll take your coat." I handed it to him and he flung it over his shoulder, glancing back to watch it land over the television. "I always wanted to do that."

I couldn't help but grin at his irreverence as I sat on one end of the couch and pulled a plate onto my lap. "Are you taking a class at the university?" I asked casually.

He sat beside me on the couch and dug into his salad. "Nah, I'm too old for that. I've moved on to the school of life. But the rent here was right, and the place came furnished. And I'm not going to let you distract me until you answer my question. Why are you here?"

I pulled a piece of warm crust from the end of the roll and popped it in my mouth, stalling for time as I chewed. "I don't really know. I'm very good at what I do, but I guess I'd make a lousy undercover operative. I wanted to confirm that you live here, somehow confirm your identity. You know, your employee file is rather thin, Nick. According to those records, your past job experience adds up to four months of work. I've got to protect Rossman's, and honestly, I want to know the truth about you."

"That burning curiosity." He took a deep bite, then shook his head as he chewed. "I noticed that with the elf kids, too. As soon as people find out there's something you don't want to talk about, that's all they want to hear."

"It's human nature. Understandable." The red wine warmed me right down to my toes. I took a second sip for courage.

"Sure, but why am I fair game? I don't see people asking you to expose the skeletons in your closets, Mrs. Claus."

I dropped the sandwich back onto the plate. "No. Probably because my problems are so public."

"Sorry. I wasn't taking a shot at you; I'm just annoyed that people won't leave me alone. Really, I'm an hourly employee, a Christmas hire. In less than three weeks Rossman's will be telling me bye-bye."

"So we should leave you alone?"

"Please."

"I agree with you in principle," I said. "But I . . . I can't leave you alone."

He put his plate down on the coffee table and turned to me. "Now we're getting somewhere."

"I don't mean . . . I mean . . ."

"You've taken a personal interest in me," he said.

"Yes, that's true."

"Nothing to be embarrassed about, Mrs. C." He took the plate from my hands and moved closer.

"I meant for business purposes," I stammered.

"No, you didn't."

I sighed, unable to look up at him. "You're right, I didn't. It is personal, Nick, but this is not something I do. Certainly not well . . ."

"You're here, aren't you?" He lifted my right hand to his face, kissed the palm, then pressed it to his cheek.

"Just barely," I said hoarsely. I let my fingers sink into his hair, round the back of his head, thrilled and alarmed that he was able to read my mind.

"You're doing fine," he said, leaning close to nibble my earlobe. He pressed against me and suddenly I was leaning back on the couch and our bodies were touching in very important places as I fell into Nick's kiss.

The next morning I awoke to rumbling walls. Not an earthquake, but a bass guitar. I rolled over in bed, realizing I was naked under the comforter of Nick's bed, his warm, furred legs beside me. I scooched against him and wrapped one leg over his, content in the moment.

"That's Oscar," he mumbled, putting a hand on my butt and squeezing tenderly. "Downstairs tenant. Bass guitarist. Not bad when he performs at the appropriate time. Which is not now."

"Mmm." I let my hand run along the bare skin of his back, massaging between his shoulder blades. I didn't care that the bass guitarist had woken us up. It felt so good to touch another human being, so soulfully beautiful to connect, that I dreaded having to leave Nick's bed. "For the first time in a long time, I wish I could take the day off from work."

"You probably could," he said. "You're the boss. But I can't. No excuses for the Santas for hire. Miss a day and big bad management will fire our asses."

I smiled. "I'd put in a good word for you, but I really have to go in."

"Oh, come on. What's so important that you have to go in?"

"Let's see . . . The board meeting is December twenty-first, and God knows what else my jerk cousin Daniel might have up his sleeve. I'm sure you heard about how he'd trying to usurp the CEO position from me. And I've got to stay on the toy sales. I made a deal with my uncle. If I get toy sales up 50 percent over last year, he's going to support my appointment to CEO."

Nick opened his eyes at me. "That's a mouthful." He closed

his eyes again and took a deep breath. "I read about some of Rossman's corporate maneuvers this week in the *Tribune*. Your cousin sounds like a real piece of work. Is he any good?"

"My unbiased opinion? He'll run the chain into the ground if they let him."

"So why is he wasting everyone's time?"

"Ego, I guess. And quest for power and money."

"And what motivates you?" He opened his eyes again. "What makes Meredith tick?"

"There's some ego involved, along with family pride and a sense that I think I'm really good at what I do."

"I believe that. But I don't understand this toy campaign. It flies in the face of what Rossman's used to represent in Christmases past. The tradition of charity at Christmas. Raising the store's profile with parents through giving, not pilfering profits."

"Okay, now you're sounding less like Santa, more like Robin Hood."

He moved his hand to the base of my spine and rubbed gently. "I'm just thinking big picture. Rossman's at Christmas, the way it used to be when the store was lit up like a Christmas tree and each kid used to receive a little plastic whistle or a toy balloon for free. It was a true celebration of the Christmas season."

I sighed. "And what does that mean? What does Christmas mean to you?"

"A time of charity. The magic of Christmas comes from people stretching beyond their daily lives, doing good deeds for others, even when that requires some personal sacrifice."

"Well, retail and magic don't mix," I responded quickly, though I hated sounding that way. "Bah humbug. I sound grouchy, I know."

"Really. Lose the Scrooge, and I'll give you one of my famous back rubs."

Lose the Scrooge . . . It was easier said than done, but definitely worth a back rub.

9

Before I left Nick's place that morning, he made us coffee and threw in a comment about me coming back another night. Although he seemed casual about it, in my mind that comment was suspended in the air with puffy hearts and flowers circling it, with a choir singing Handel's "Hallelujah!" in the background.

Nick wanted to see me again.

He liked me.

And I felt as if I'd stepped into the sunlight for the first time in years.

Great sex is a very good thing, but when you couple that with emotional connection, the results are a giddy satisfaction that lifts the soul. I felt like a better person after being with Nick, as if his goodness had rubbed off on me a little. Silly, I know, but I sang in the shower that morning and nearly caused a wreck on the way to work because I stopped to let another car go in front of me.

Of course, there was still an inaccessible part of Nick, the secret part that he withheld, but I was confident that eventually he would trust me enough to share that, too.

That morning when I got to Rossman's, I went directly to my

office, which seemed to be gathering dust while I spent my time down in Santaland hawking toys. I sat at the computer and ran some numbers to get a sense of how toy sales impacted our total monthly sales figures.

The numbers didn't surprise me. I formatted the results into color graphs and started copies printing as I fished into the pocket of the Mrs. Claus suit and found Grace's card. Her voice mail picked up, so I left a message asking her to call me.

As I sat back in my leather chair, it occurred to me that I generally didn't make such sweeping decisions without consulting Uncle Len. I put my hand on the desk phone, then paused.

Not this time.

Instead, I clicked on the Internet connection and went surfing for local children's charities. Maybe I wasn't CEO of Rossman's, but I was still manager of this store, still a Rossman, and it was about time I flexed a little corporate muscle and pulled this store back in line with my nana's dreams.

That day Grace returned to the store and we toured the toy department, trying to estimate the inventory and type of toys that would best serve the kids in Chicago's foster-care program. The cost of funding the entire program was significant, but I knew that Rossman's maintained a fund for charitable donations. I told Brian, the manager of toys, to go ahead and help Grace get everything she needed.

Over the next two days, Gia and I sorted through various charitable programs that served children. We decided to coordinate efforts with Joy of Toys, a program that sent volunteers into schools in the city's low-income neighborhoods. In less than twenty-four hours we were able to begin sending out batches of toys from wish lists, delivered by a Santa and three elves from our Santaland.

Nick and I brainstormed over a program that would help employees direct Rossman's money to charities of their choice. "I read somewhere that it's not enough to just give the money," I told him one night as we drank wine from juice glasses under the fluffy comforter of his bed. "It's in the doing. The act of doing something positive for someone else provides positive feelings, even health benefits for the person performing the good deed."

"Yes, I've seen those studies." He sat up and rested his chin on my knees. "So you want to guide each employee to perform a good deed?"

"But I can't force them, and I don't want them to feel like Rossman's is reaching into their pockets."

"Good point. Maybe we can bring a social agency into the store. Through a church or nursing home. You want some kind of wish list. Have the person in need write down something they could use, like pots and pans, or a set of sheets, or a warm sweater."

"An organized list. But each employee has a chance to go through it and choose something to shop for at Rossman's. We could give each employee a twenty-dollar credit. Maybe they can even help deliver it to the person if they have the time?"

"Now you're talking. I've seen that done with Christmas trees. Each ornament on the tree is a card that gives the recipient's first name, age, and wish."

"That would work." I put my wine on the crate that served as a nightstand and turned toward him. "We can use the tree in the atrium. We'll call it a wish tree this year, and the ornaments on the first floor will contain wishes." I scraped my hair back, then flung it in the air. "Oh, Nick, I love this idea!"

"Merry Meredith, your hair is flying!" He tossed the comforter back, separated my knees and made a dive for me, growling. "I love it when you get all benevolent!"

I laughed, then quickly squeezed my eyes shut as our bodies came together.

We worked so well together, Nick and I. Whether under the covers or planning charitable programs or just cajoling children in Santaland, we were a great match. Granted, my experience with relationships was limited, but Nick was the first guy I could speak to with a feeling of balance and equality, the first guy who ever talked to me through sex and listened to my breathless answers. So many firsts. After a week of sneaking into his bed nearly every night, I realized that this was probably the first man I had ever loved. I desperately wanted him to be the first and last, but those mysteries remained, like a bubble rising between us. Nick still eluded my questions about his past, his former occupations and family, though sometimes small glimpses of his childhood crept in, especially when he was around the kids. Stories of sledding in the winter and swimming in lakes on hot summer days. One story reminded me of my own summers on the lake, about how he and his friends had swum out to a floating dock and found a snake lingering in the deep water under it. Everyone was afraid to swim back to shore, and the group of boys lingered on the raft for an hour until Nick decided that the snake had to be a stick if it hadn't moved during that time. He dove down after it and popped up to the surface a hero, stick in hand. The boys had returned to shore, sunburned but charged up with a great story.

"Was that a true story?" I asked him later, as we drove from the school back to Rossman's. "The one about the snake in the lake? Or is it part of the grand Nicholas mythology?"

"There's no mythology," he said. "I don't lie about my life."

"Really? Isn't that the whole pretext of the Witness Protection Program—to live a lie?"

He scoffed. "I'm not living under an assumed identity. You know that. I'm Nicholas Smith, and I'll fill in the blank spots soon after Christmas. I'll answer all your questions some time in the new year. How about that?"

"Why don't you tell me now, and I swear I won't tell a soul. Don't you trust me?"

"It's not about trust," he said. "It's complicated. I promise you, I'll tell all in January, if you'll just give me till then."

"I am not a patient person," I admitted. Though January was just weeks away now. Considering the depth of my feelings for this man, what was wrong with giving him some space? Give the guy a few weeks. I could do that. "It's torture, but I can wait," I told him. After all, I'd been in a waiting pattern all my life.

*   *   *

The new programs brought a noticeable lift to spirits in Santaland. The wish tree was so enticing that customers wanted to participate, and we were able to open the program to many of Chicago's social-service agencies. The elves returned from school deliveries with stories of children who had touched their hearts, and Jesus asked me if there was a way to schedule more class visits before Christmas Eve. "The kids appreciate us so much," he said. "I wish my grandchildren could be there to see this interaction. I feel honored to be a part of it."

Chicago newspapers wrote us up as "the store that makes Christmas wishes come true" and touted, "Roll out the Holly— Rossman's Claus Is Coming to Town!" *AM Chicago* sent a reporter to one of our Joy of Toys visits in an elementary-school classroom, and one of the networks sent a local news team to our Santaland to get the inside story the following morning.

As luck would have it, just as we were closing up that night, two strings of lights burned out in the Santaland entrance.

"It's a wonder they lasted this long," the designer told me as I reached up to the top of the ladder to feed her the new lights. "These babies burn constantly, and they're three years old."

I thought of my hasty budget cuts at the beginning of the season. Next year, I would allot money for new lights.

The string Felicia now hung on the trellis held tiny icicle clear lights shaped in figures. They were difficult to see until Felicia plugged them in, and at once dozens of tiny toys were illuminated in the silvery branches of the trellis.

"Hey, what's happening?" Nick poked his head out of the gingerbread house and joined us. "That's nice."

"They're beautiful, Felicia." I moved along the trellis to take in the many shapes—spinning tops, balls and bats, dolls, trains, trucks, and cars.

"Cute, aren't they?" Felicia squinted up. "I think they work for Santaland."

"They remind me of the ornaments on our Christmas tree at home," I said quietly. "They were in the family for years. Austrian crystal. Clear glass shaped into boats and trucks and dolls."

Felicia folded the ladder up and hoisted it in one arm. "I'm glad you like them. Let me know if any other decorations go astray when the TV crew gets here."

As she headed off, Nick came up behind me and put his arms around me. "Mrs. Claus, I do believe you've had a secret life, too."

"I don't think so," I said quietly as I stared up at the magnificent lights. No, for me the only secret was that I really had no life at all. The secret was, my life had just begun.

Nick was delighted with the way Rossman's had turned into a store with true Christmas spirit. "Do you feel the magic?" he asked everyone around him as he strolled through Santaland. "Can you feel it?" he said, looking right at me.

"Always," I said, reminding myself that he was talking about Christmas magic. And actually, I had to admit that I was feeling something. Scary after these last years to have a Christmas connection once again, but I realized that if my actions made a happy memory for one boy or girl, that was all I needed.

The only downside of the Christmas of giving was Uncle Leonard's dark disapproval. "Newspapers and TV shows . . . Bah . . ." He waved a hand. "Who needs them? We're not publicity hounds, here."

"Weren't my parents in the press all the time?" I reminded him. "They were America's favorite couple."

"The media are fickle. They'll love you today, lynch you tomorrow."

"I'm okay with it, as long as they're sharing the love," I teased him, but he refused to be cajoled. He didn't like the giveaways, didn't want our employees to visit schools in high-crime neighborhoods, didn't think it wise to ally our high-end reputation with certain parts of town, and most of all, he didn't like the idea of "tossing away" Rossman's money.

"Giving away toys at Christmas?" He raked his hands through his hair. "Meredith, it's crazy nutty. Doesn't make sense at all. This is the one time of year when customers want to buy toys, and you give them away?"

"Uncle Len, what we're doing is very important," I told him.

"We're reaching out to people, helping the community. And what's good for Chicago is good for Rossman's."

He shook his head. "I'm sorry, darling, but I don't get it, and I hate to say it, but I know this will bring you down, Meredith. You realize I can no longer support your election to the board?"

Although I wasn't surprised, it still hurt to hear him say it. "Of course," I told him. "I understand."

Once again, it would be the poor little heiress battling the big bad board. But this time, I was ready to take them on. This time, I had Santa on my side.

10

"Here's a question for you, Mrs. Claus," Nick said one cold December night as we scraped the last creamed macaronis from a pot in his kitchen. "Here I live in a rented, barely furnished dump, but we spend every night at my place." He wiped a smudge of cheese from his mouth and straightened his sweatshirt. "What's the deal? Aren't you going to invite me over someday? I clean up nicely."

I turned away and dropped the pot into the sink. "My house isn't as comfortable as this place," I said, thinking of the living room on Astor Street with its cathedral ceiling, the oak center-hall staircase, the checkerboard wood pattern of the lacquered library floor. "It was my parents' place." Full of ghosts and memories. I was still afraid to use the good china, still reluctant to track mud on the patterned wool runner. "I live in two rooms, the bedroom and the den. Sometimes I feel like I'm just visiting, home from college for the weekend and they're away at the lake house."

There, I'd said the words, though it seemed so ungrateful. "I must sound spoiled. It's a beautiful house, really, and you've probably read that I've got pots of money. I could redecorate

like that." I snapped my fingers. "But I can't. I haven't quite figured that one out yet."

"There's no rush." He pulled me against him, surrounding
me with his arms. "You've got time, and you're welcome to stay
here, always."

I breathed in the fabric-softener scent of his sweatshirt, grateful to have found this man. Of course, I didn't want to think
about how my parents would have reacted to my involvement
with a "Christmas hire"; that was a bit of snobbery I'd put behind
me. This conscientious, hardworking man was far more lovable
than any of the society kids I'd been pushed to date.

"Guess I won't be getting invited to a sleepover anytime soon,"
he teased. "Which is probably good, since I don't own a pair of
pajamas. Haven't had one since my aunt got me that pair with a
Batman cape."

"Better watch it or you'll reveal your secret identity. And to
think, all this time I might have been sleeping with Bruce Wayne."

The last full weekend before Christmas brought crowds and
camera crews that had most of the Santaland staff working overtime. By Monday morning I felt as if someone had bonked my
head with one of those giant cartoon hammers. Turning over in
bed, I pressed against Nick, sucking up enough warmth to make
the cold dash to the shower.

"Don't go," he said. "Stay in bed and go in later with me."

"Can't." I sighed, nuzzling my face against his chest. "The
board meeting is Wednesday. I've got to prepare."

"You've been preparing for that sucker all your life," he
teased. "If they don't choose you, they're blithering fools."

"I gotta go."

As I drove to work a few flakes began to fall. I turned on the
wipers, gripped the steering wheel, and tried to stave off the
tremble that threatened to rock my body. My fear of driving in
snow conditions wasn't quite irrational, but it was highly imprac-
tical living in Chicago. I made plans to hire a driver that evening.
Ever since my parents' accident Uncle Len had wanted me to

use his service, but it seemed so extravagant to have a driver in a black limo take me everywhere.

I spent the morning in my office, printing presentations that would be covered and bound for Wednesday's meeting. I grabbed a quick lunch in the store café, then changed into my Mrs. Claus suit.

The accumulating snow had slowed some of our customers, but Santaland was crowded with preschoolers in shiny vinyl boots and puffy coats who dropped mittens and twisted hats as they waited in line. As I moved along the path, talking with the children, I wondered why the line was moving so slowly. When I made it to the front, it was apparent that something had broken down. Gia was sitting cross-legged, leading some kids in a game of rock, paper, scissors, and Kevin nodded as Jennifer from Personnel pointed at a clipboard.

"Finally." Gia beamed a smile up at me. "Some sanity has arrived."

"There you are. We just called up to your office but you were gone." Jennifer grabbed the clipboard from Kevin and thrust it at me. "Here's a list of some possible replacements. If you want to choose two or three, I'll call them in immediately."

"Replacements for what?" I asked, fighting back the feeling of dread.

"For Mr. Smith. He called this morning, said he couldn't be here during this next week."

"Mr. Smith?" I wasn't tracking, but then Jennifer wasn't winning any communications awards.

She lowered her voice, so the kids wouldn't hear. "One of your S-A-N-T-A-S."

"Nick?" The dread twisted into a sharp pain. "What happened?"

"He was a great Santa," Kevin offered.

"I know, I know," Jennifer said sadly. "It's a shame, but we'll do our best to fill his shoes, and quickly."

I tried to fight the panic that moved through me, toxic as poison. Where was Nick? What had happened? What could have possibly changed since this morning when I leaned over his bed to kiss him good-bye?

The snow . . . Could he have been injured? But he was going to take the el to work . . .

One of the other elves signaled, and Gia jumped up and led two kids from her group in to see Santa. "This is slowing us down already, and it'll only get worse," Gia said, moving closer to the rest of us. "Can we put someone like Kevin here into Nick's place? Then hire an elf?"

Kevin's face burned red. "Thanks, Gia."

"That's a great idea," Jennifer said. "Should we go with that?"

"Yes," I said quickly, unable to look at the names on the clipboard. "Go on, Kevin. Get someone to help you find his costume, and Jennifer will take it from there."

I rushed up to my office to call Nick's apartment, but there was no answer. And he didn't have a cell phone.

I paced behind my desk, wondering what could have happened, trying to ignore the sense that this was trouble. Something was wrong. Otherwise, he would be here, down in Santaland, listening to children and making them smile.

There was a knock on the door, and Gia poked her head in. "Mind if I come in? Wow, these digs are not very impressive. You'd think they'd do better for the store manager."

"The Rossmans don't go for frills. We pass the savings on to the customer," I said without looking up from my cell phone.

"And you look awful." She stepped closer, cocking her head to stare at me. "What happened? Where's Nick?"

I crossed my arms, hugging myself. "I don't know."

"Did you two have a fight?"

"No, nothing like that. I left him sleeping at his place this morning and now . . ." I shook my head. "He's disappeared."

Gia nodded sympathetically. "What an asshole."

"Looking back, I'm thinking I'm the asshole."

"It's not your fault. Granted, we knew there was something mysterious about him. But really, to just disappear when he could be a man and break up to your face."

"Do you think that's it? He doesn't want to see me again?"

She winced. "I don't know, Meredith. That, or he got called in by his parole officer. Or his wife threatened suicide if he doesn't come home."

I moaned, sinking into the leather chair.

"What are you going to do?"

"I want to go over to his apartment right now, see if he's okay, but since he's not answering the phone, I doubt he's there."

"So what are you going to do?"

I rested my elbows on my desk, sinking into the lowest of lows. "I don't know. I'm a Rossman. I guess I just go on."

"I would have a good cry," Gia said. "You know, sometimes being a Rossman must really suck."

"It does. It definitely does."

By the time I left work that night it had stopped snowing. As the driver headed south I could see that most of the side streets had been plowed, sometimes leaving a wall of snow over parked cars. People were out, bundled in hats and mittens and boots, digging out their cars, stomping ice chunks, scraping snow from their sidewalks.

As the driver turned onto Nick's street, I took out my cell phone, thinking that I'd call Nick one more time, just in case he was inside the apartment. I flipped it open to make the call, then noticed that the volume had been turned down and that I had a message.

A message from early this afternoon.

"This is the address, Ms. Rossman," the driver said, turning toward me.

I grabbed my purse and moved toward the door. "Can you wait for me here, please? I don't know if he's home."

The driveway and walk were not shoveled, covered with a pristine sheet of white. My boots sank into a foot of frozen fluff, the Italian leather too thin to provide much protection. I should've invested in some Rossman's vinyl snow boots.

The porch light shone yellow over Nick's entrance. I headed

that way, pressing my cell phone to my ear to listen to the message.

It was him.

"Meredith, honey, I'm so sorry to have to tell you this in a phone message . . ."

My boots scraped up the steps, marking the virgin snow.

"There's something I need to do. Something I have to take care of, and it's going to take a few days."

I slid my key in the lock and popped the door open to the dark, still kitchen. The only light was a pale glow from the digital clock on the stove, the only noise the hum of the old refrigerator. I stamped the snow from my boots just inside the door and pressed inside. I had to know if Nick had taken his things . . . if he would really be coming back.

"It came up suddenly and . . . You gotta know I hate to cut out on you like this. I made the commitment to Rossman's, and I know it's a busy time there. I feel bad about flaking on that, but this part is sort of beyond my control."

His laptop was gone. The mound of papers that covered the desk was removed.

The bathroom counter was bare.

I felt sick. Had I been duped? Was I the deluded one?

"I'll be back, Meredith. I'll be back for Christmas. And then I'll be able to tell you everything."

"Oh, sure." My breath formed puffs in the blue darkness as I cast about his bedroom, looking for something, anything that might show he was coming back.

The closet held an empty suitcase and boxes. The top dresser drawer was empty, but the others held jeans, socks, and sweatshirts . . . his beloved sweatshirts.

I took out his favorite, the red one with Nick's Bicycle Shop printed on the front. He wouldn't leave this behind. He was coming back. He'd promised.

The sudden blast of bass guitar riffs startled me. Oscar. A swell of warmth in this very empty apartment.

I tucked the shirt under my arm and headed back to the car. Hadn't I promised that I'd wait for Nick?

I didn't like the way he'd handled this, and I was going to give him hell about it when he came back. But for now, I would wait. I would wear Nick's sweatshirt to bed and hope that he'd be back to reclaim it. Oscar played me out as I locked the door and sank down the snowy steps.

11

"I don't want to tell you this . . ." Gia began.

"But you will," I said without looking away from the computer monitor. I was trying to weed through my e-mail before this morning's presentation to the board, and I knew it would be better to forget Nick and focus on the meeting right now, but I couldn't help myself. "Go on, lay it on me."

"Well, I talked with Jennifer in Personnel, and she says Nick left a message for his final check to be forwarded. To some address in Pennsylvania."

"Pennsylvania? But he said he grew up in the Midwest. Where in Pennsylvania?"

"Jenny-pie wouldn't give me the address, of course, but I'm sure she'll roll over for you."

Pennsylvania. The only things that came to mind were Dutch pretzels, Amish people riding in buggies, and William Penn, the colonial. And once I'd flown over Pittsburgh and the pilot had pointed out where the three rivers met.

I pressed my fingers to my temples. "I can't be thinking about Dutch pretzels when I'm presenting to the board."

"I love those giant pretzels, the hot ones, with lots of salt." Gia perched on the edge of my desk. "They're so yummy."

I shot her a look. "This isn't about pretzels. Do you have something else to tell me?"

She bit her lower lip, her gold loop earrings jangling as she nodded. The earrings were a bit much for an elf, but at least she'd stuck with the emerald nose stud. "There was this report about an escaped prisoner on TV. And it got me thinking. I went on-line and did some research, and it turns out this guy escaped from prison in Pennsylvania, right around the time Nick and I were hired. Like a week before. You can check it out on-line. The name of the prison is—"

"Don't you need to get back to Santaland?" I interrupted.

"Yeah, but . . . Are you saying you don't want to hear this stuff?"

"I can't think about it, Gia. It may sound naïve, but I promised Nick that I'd wait for him, wait for his explanation of everything, and that's what I'm going to do."

"Oh." She straightened. "Oh. I get it. You fell in love with him."

"You need to get back to work," I told her, logging off my e-mail. "And so do I. I'm next to present to the board."

"You look like hell," she said. "Nothing personal."

"Aren't you supposed to tell me to give 'em hell?"

Over the years I had developed an ability to switch to autopilot in business matters; I was able to tamp my emotions down and keep them suppressed while I operated at full tilt, presenting a program, thinking on my feet, juggling numbers in my head.

Autopilot helped as I presented my Christmas charity campaign. I made it through the presentation with a modicum of enthusiasm. Even without Nick, my support of our charity programs would not waver. The wish tree had transformed the spirit in our store, and our support of foster children and children from families with financial difficulties took the power of Rossman's far beyond anything I'd ever imagined.

When I'd finished the presentation and fielded a few questions, Uncle PJ lowered the boom.

"My problem with all of this is the element of social services, which is not germane to the business of retail," he said, his face emotionless behind the globes of his eyeglasses.

A few other members joined in, sharing his concerns about cost, reputation, and focus of our corporate mission.

"Really, Meredith, if you want to save lives, join the Peace Corps." That from Marcus Aldridge, who seemed to live in Uncle PJ's back pocket.

"I'm quite familiar with the business of retail," I said. "Ultimately, much of our business comes in because of our reputation for giving. But this issue is about more than dollars and cents. It's about Rossman's place in the Chicago community . . . in the world community."

Uncle PJ frowned. Clearly I was losing him. "Honestly, Meredith, your parents were much more frugal. I'm not sure that they would have approved the sort of spending you've already authorized here. Really, darling, you've gone overboard here."

Uncle PJ loved to call me "darling" in that derogatory way.

"Did you even once stop to think what your parents would have said about all this?"

"Actually, PJ, I did."

Everyone seemed to suck in their breath at my quick reply. Nobody snapped back at PJ Rossman, not even politely.

"My mother was a very pragmatic person. She did not approve of many of the excesses in American society. However, she would not have been able to tolerate the thought of a child going without a single toy at Christmas. If Rossman's didn't fund the toys for those foster children, my mother would have taken the money out of our own family budget and paid it gladly."

PJ's eyes were unreadable beyond the watery reflection of his wide glasses, so I turned to Uncle Len. "You know that's true."

"Yes, yes, that's how she was." There was a slight catch in his voice. "Evelyn would have stopped at nothing to make sure the right thing was done."

"She had a big heart," Uncle PJ charged. "Not like your father."

"Actually, I believe my father was the real softy in the relationship. I remember when I was going off to college. I was accepted at Stanford, but at the last minute I found out that I didn't get the scholarship I'd applied for. It was an essay competition, and my work wasn't the best. I worried about how much money this would require of my parents. A huge expense. My mother agreed that it was a pricey institution, but my father just laughed and told me he couldn't be prouder. He was proud that I got in. As for the expense, he said, 'It's only money; we'll make more.'"

A few of the members laughed.

"I remember him saying that," Nella Greeley said.

"That was Karl," Uncle Leonard said. "I used to ask him if he was going to print it in his basement."

"Yes, well . . ." When Uncle PJ spoke, the room went dead. "I must say, you've certainly presented a substantial body of material to make your case. I suppose your father was right." His glasses flashed as he turned to me. "It was worth the tuition."

I blinked, realizing that he was complimenting me, probably for the first time ever.

"Yes, that was an excellent presentation," Nella agreed.

"Leonard will let you know the results of our votes after we finish up," someone else added.

The door was opened and I was suddenly thanking them, gathering up my portfolio, and exiting to the hall, where Gia was pacing, the bells on her curly-toed shoes jangling. "Finally, you're done!"

"Did you come to cheer me on?" I asked.

"Oh my God, no! I wanted to come in and get you, but the secretary wouldn't let me." She scowled at Helen, who didn't seem to notice.

I held my portfolio to my chest. "What's wrong?"

"It's Nick. He's out on Michigan Avenue, acting like an asshole."

Just as she said the word, my two uncles spilled out of the conference room, followed by a few of the board members.

"He's got a sleigh and horses and he's pretending to be Santa, telling everyone he's waiting for Mrs. Claus."

I laughed out loud. "You're not serious, are you?"

Gia's head bobbed wildly as she grabbed my arm and tugged me down the hall. "You've got to come before he does something totally crazy and gets arrested. Or the police shut the street down." We were already jogging down the hall toward the elevators. "And who are all those creepy old men following us?"

"That's our Rossman's board of directors." I tapped the elevator button again, looking back to see my uncles winging around the corner, stampeding toward us like a herd of buffalo. Somehow, I didn't want them breathing down my neck when I saw Nick. "These elevators are so slow. Escalators!"

She followed me to the escalators, and we hopped and clunked our way down to the eighth floor, then the seventh.

"Oh my God, you are worse than my personal trainer," she called after me.

I lunged ahead, eager to see him, to shake him, to smack him for disappearing like that. "I can't believe he came back."

"Yeah, you called that one," Gia said. "Let's hope he's not hauled off to jail before we get down there."

As if skiing a downhill slalom, I looped around customers and cut sharp turns at the bottom of each moving staircase. When we descended to the first floor, I spotted a crowd gathered around the main entrance. It had to be Nick.

Cutting through the crowd was probably not the most ladylike maneuver of my life, but I managed to make my way outside, where an impressive sleigh rested on the snow, its red velvet upholstery and shiny looped steel runners more deserving of a museum than a snowy city street. The lunchtime crowd surrounded the sleigh and horses: moms telling their kids to stay back, businessmen munching hot dogs from wrappers and speculating how anyone could get a sleigh onto Michigan Avenue, old ladies charmed by the timely arrival of Santa's sleigh. All these people and more spilled out onto the traffic lanes of Michigan Avenue, but no Nick in sight.

"Where are you?" I pushed past two men in trench coats and climbed aboard the sleigh. "Nick?"

"That's her!" he shouted from somewhere in the crowd. "That's my Mrs. Claus."

Suddenly he was climbing up beside me . . . Nick in his red velvet suit trimmed in white fur, that silly Santa cap that only Nick could wear with finesse. I reached around him, hugging him, making sure he was real . . . and the crowd applauded and whistled.

So many emotions rippled through me: joy, relief, anger. I pulled out of his arms. "Don't ever disappear like that again. Where the hell were you?"

"Would you believe the North Pole?" he answered, causing the crowd to roar with delight.

I folded my arms, shivering in the cold. "It's all very funny, until someone disappears from your life."

The onlookers oohed over that. Clearly, this was not the sort of conversation that lent itself to an audience. I motioned toward the store. "Can we go inside and talk?"

"Wait. We can have a private talk, but let me take you on a sleigh ride." He reached down to the seat, snapped open a thick fleece-lined blanket, and draped it over my shoulders. "Now, you just need to sit quietly while I figure this out." He lifted the leather reins, trying to sort them out, his confusion not instilling much confidence.

I leaned against the velvet bench and gazed over the bobbing heads of the horses. "Don't you need a license to drive this thing?"

A cop stepped onto the side runner. "I was gonna ask you that."

"I can do it!" Gia emerged from the crowd. "I grew up on a farm, and I used to drive a hansom cab in the summer. You two just sit down, leave the driving to me."

She sat in the front perch, the coolest punk elf in Chicago, gave a shout, and the horses started pawing at the snow, dragging us ahead.

The crowd began to applaud as we pulled out, and a few familiar faces emerged at the edge of the group—my uncles and the members of the board. Uncle PJ was shaking his head in staunch disapproval, not a fan of public displays. But Uncle Len smiled and gave me a thumbs-up as we passed. Good old Uncle Len, not a bad guy, just saddled with a useless son.

And just like that we were gliding down Michigan Avenue, skyscrapers looming over us in the snowscape. The wind blew my hair back and ruffled the edges of the blanket, but I was warm enough to enjoy the ride.

"Where to?" Gia asked. When he gave the Astor Street address of my parents' house, I groaned.

"Don't be a spoilsport," he said, handing Gia a blanket. "There's something there I want to show you . . . my Christmas gift to you."

"As if this sleigh isn't enough," I said sarcastically.

"Don't go bratty on me, now. This is beautiful, isn't it? Snow in time for Christmas, and another thing: a horse-drawn sleigh is not an easy thing to find in downtown Chicago this time of year."

"It is pretty wonderful," I admitted, waving to a bunch of cross-country skiers headed into the park. "And it will be perfect, once we have that conversation. The details, man."

He nestled beside me. "You're still mad? I don't blame you, but I really couldn't help it. I got a call just after you left Monday morning. There was a cancellation Tuesday, which gave me a chance to present a paper I've been working on for a hundred years. I'm trying to get tenure at Penn, which is a godlike thing in this day and age, so I had to jump on a plane to Philly pronto and present my research findings all day yesterday."

"Philly . . ." I said aloud, for Gia's benefit. "That would be Philadelphia, Pennsylvania."

Gia turned around and mouthed, "Sorry!"

"Home of the cheesesteak sub."

Some of it made sense—the mound of papers, the laptop, the place near campus. I'd thought he might be a student but somehow never thought he could be a professor.

I squinted at him. "And why was this all such a big secret? The first top-secret sabbatical I ever heard of."

"The Santa gig was part of my research. Did I mention that I'm a sociologist? No, I don't think I did. But I needed to remain anonymous or else the research would have been compromised. I've been researching the belief of magic in cultures for so long, I couldn't blow it right at the end of my study. I've been working on this baby a hundred years! But I said that, right? I'm telling you more than you want to know."

"No, I do want to know. I want to know everything. The truth this time."

"It's not as if I'm a pathological liar," he said, and Gia turned back to cock an eyebrow. "What? I'm not! I tried to stick to the truth. Mostly I committed lies of omission. Which is almost not a real lie."

I smiled, watching him try to talk his way out of the situation. I was relieved that he was back and that he was not an ax murderer and that he hadn't run away from me. In the two days he was gone, I'd gone over all the wonderful things that Nick had brought to my life: the way he'd jump-started my life with feeling and emotion, the way he'd helped me and so many others embrace the true meaning of Christmas, and his joy for small things, small moments.

He'd helped set my life back on track. While he was gone I'd forced myself to take a deep look inside and ask some tough questions. The answer had been that I would go on. Even if Nick didn't return, I would continue to live with feeling. I would celebrate Christmas and find joy in small moments, because Nick had led me to find the real Meredith, and for that I would be eternally grateful.

But right now the real Meredith was thrilled that Nick had returned, and hopeful that we could see our way to spending next Christmas together . . . and the next . . . and the next . . .

"Here we are," Gia announced, pulling up in front of my house.

Nick was the first to hop down, helping the two of us to the ground.

"Come in with us," I said, slinging an arm around Gia's shoulder. "Will the horses be okay?"

She slung her blanket over her shoulders like a serape. "Who would steal horses from the North Side?"

As we approached the front door, Nick put his hands on my shoulders. "You have to close your eyes." From there, it was dark until he guided me five steps up, eight steps through the vestibule . . . and then I lost track.

"Okay," he said, "now you can look."

I opened my eyes to a tall evergreen tree in the same spot we'd always placed it beside the stairs. It was lit with gold lights and dotted with sparkling crystal ornaments, so like the ornaments we'd had in our family.

"Wow," Gia gushed. "Cool tree."

"Oh my gosh . . ." I stepped closer. A train. A doll. A spinning top. "Those look like the ornaments we used to have . . . the ones my mother loved . . ."

"They are," he said.

I squinted into the gold light. "But they can't be. I got rid of them two years ago. The cleaning staff couldn't even track them down."

"Take a close look; those are the Rossman's ornaments."

My throat was suddenly tight with emotion. "How did you do this?"

"I told you, my studies focus on the belief in magic. You gotta believe, Meredith. That's how miracles happen."

He put an arm around me and I linked arms with Gia so that we three stood together at the base of the tree, a line of energy gazing up at many lifetimes of glimmering ornaments, many generations of Christmases past that hovered in the gold light, protecting, cheering.

I saw my mother on a ladder, rearranging ornaments near the top.

My father dusted an ornament shaped like a ballerina with a fine sable brush.

My nana dipped an ornate crystal sailing ship into a cup of

pungent ammonia for cleaning and lifted it out with a satisfied smile.

And there I was dancing under the tree, my Lanz flannel nightgown hiked up to my knees, dancing to the Christmas carols playing on the old stereo system, dancing and dreaming of the kindness of Santa in his charmed northern home where elves lovingly crafted toys under a blanket of snow and Mrs. Claus waited patiently for her husband's return each year. I danced for Santa and the elves and Mrs. Claus and the reindeer.

One day, my daughter would dance barefoot under these ornaments, too. I held fast to my friends, wishing her sweet dreams and loving spirits.

EPILOGUE

New York City, December 2006

"This will only take a second," Olivia Todd told her husband as the elevator doors opened on the seventh floor of Rossman's Department Store at Astor Place.

"I don't mind." He linked his fingers through hers and looked ahead. "You've dragged me all over town, checking out sites and buildings with me. I think I can manage a few minutes in Santaland."

"I read somewhere that they've got a Mrs. Claus here this year." She leaned her head toward him, her red curls swaying. "I don't know, it sort of made me feel all sentimental. I just wanted to check it out, since we're here."

It was Olivia's first trip back to New York since she'd left the Rockettes, and she enjoyed showing Woody the familiar sights while playing tourist in other ways. When she lived uptown she didn't have a chance to visit this Rossman's or explore the Soho area. Now they were staying at the Soho Grand, walking to the Village, dining in Tribeca. She and Woody had gone skating under the multicolored lights of the Rockefeller Center tree.

They had bought roasted chestnuts from a street vendor, had sipped vodkas at the majestic, always Christmasy bar in the Firebird, and yesterday, for the first time ever, she had sat in the audience of the Christmas show at Radio City and experienced genuine joy, amusement, and holiday spirit—without a trace of envy toward the dancers on stage.

No jealousy. She actually didn't want to be on that stage, absorbed in the daily grind of three shows a day, then off on tour, living out of a suitcase, five cities in seven days for weeks at a time.

Not that she'd given up dancing. Olivia had opened a dance studio in Canton, in the building Woody had renovated. She gave lessons to little girls and more advanced dancers with career aspirations. And she danced. Through Woody's contacts, she had collaborated with the mayor's office to establish a program called Baltimore in the Wings that brought dancers, actors, and musicians to perform in public schools and conduct workshops with the students. She was working with other dancers to form an independent troupe to showcase local talent and original choreography. And to show that she could rise above it all, she had even played the Sugar Plum Fairy in a small production of *The Nutcracker* last year.

A group of teenaged tourists blocked the entrance, but Olivia excused herself and moved past them, and suddenly there was the sign with the painted red "Santaland" decked with a garland lined with fat bells. "Oh my gosh!" A hand flew to her mouth as she and Woody passed under the candy-cane arches, heading toward a gingerbread house tiled with swirled mints and gumdrops. Off to the side, children were being led to a motorized train—the North Pole Express—its green and red seats just big enough to fit most children under twelve.

Olivia misted over at the nostalgic sight.

The Christmas she spent as Mrs. Claus was a turning point in her life, the first time she'd ever seized control of her life, steered it in a new direction, and held on tight.

And what a ride.

"Seeing all this . . ." She turned to Woody. "I sort of miss being

Mrs. Claus." Not that she could go back; Olivia knew there was no re-creating past lives, no reliving specific eras in a life, at least not with the same passion and energy.

"Yeah?" Woody smiled. "You want a Mrs. Claus do-over?"

She laughed. "I'm saving my do-overs for the things that matter. Like softball." She leaned over the rail to search for Mrs. Claus. "And dance steps. And seventh-grade sweeties who fall away because you're such a dummy-head."

"Oh, hon, that's so sweet." Woody squeezed her hand.

She squeezed back, eyeing a group of elves helping children off the train. "I don't see her. Where is Mrs. Claus?"

Woody shook his head. "I don't think she's here. You know how so many department stores are scaling down."

"But that would be awful." Olivia gripped the rail, trying to peer through the one-way window into Santa's house. "What a shame. Did they bump off Mrs. Claus?"

"Do you have your list?" Cassie called after Tyler, who was moving through the gumdrop kingdom toward Santa.

Tyler held up the booklet, a list of inventions he'd sketched in pencil: ingenious Christmas toys like hover disks that would help him to fly over traffic on Madison Avenue to make it to school on time or shoes with scrub brushes on the bottom to help shampoo the streets of New York as people walked along. He'd made the list for Santa, confident that the elves could handle the construction of these mechanical devices.

"I hope he's not disappointed on Christmas morning when he doesn't see his inventions under the tree," Cassie had told Buchman one night.

"Hmm . . . Could be a problem," he agreed. "Perhaps we should find Tyler an inventor's kit? A chemistry set? Something to stoke the imagination?"

Cassie had pursued the idea, considering it a far better investment than another video game. It was uncanny how Buchman seemed to understand Tyler's needs, how he sensed when the boy needed to get out and run or simply needed quiet time to sketch or model clay.

He understands both of us, Cassie thought as she watched Buchman and Tyler move into the Santaland crowd.

Hands on the boy's shoulders, Buchman guided him along the path, chattering on about something that seemed to amuse Tyler. It was not a scene Cassie had imagined all the times she'd envisioned her son's future; she had always pictured Tyler with his biological father. She'd been so stuck on that, imagining TJ on the beach helping to launch a kite, or in the park picking Tyler up from a tumble on his inline skates. Now those scenarios seemed so unlikely, so unlike TJ, at least, and over the past year her vision had expanded, allowing Tyler to gravitate toward Buchman and the inventions and model constructions that fascinated them.

Turning back toward the entrance, Cassie checked her watch. Where was Mrs. Claus?

When Buchman had taken this assignment at the New York Rossman's, Cassie had been pleased that Tyler would have a chance to live in New York for a while, experience another city. She'd been surprised that Agate had wanted to make a move, too, especially one so far, but Agate's relationship with Philip had been fizzling and she wanted to make a clean break and, most of all, no one could bear to disconnect after they'd finally arrived at a sense of family.

In the blink of an eye, it had come together like one of Tyler's precise sketches.

With Rossman's paying the rent, Cassie had a blast searching for an apartment, finally settling on a two-bedroom in the east sixties, walking distance to the Central Park Zoo. Agate had found a Chelsea sublet through her network of Wiccan friends, and so she was just a subway ride away. The chief designer of the New York store was impressed by Cassie's work, and so Rossman's was all in the family with Buchman working in the management offices and Cassie contributing to the window designs.

When they were casting Mrs. Claus, Cassie had been skeptical about Agate's involvement with the store. "You haven't held a full-time job for years. You don't respond well to pressure. And you tend to buck authority." She had begged her mother to let the job go, but Agate, persistent as a bulldog, had clamped on to it and pushed ahead.

"Merry Christmas!" a familiar voice gushed warmth. "Oh, don't you look swell, all dressed up to see Santa! And merry Christmas to you!"

Turning toward the arched candy canes at the entrance, Cassie saw her mother moving along the line of children, exchanging greetings as if she were the mayor of the North Pole. In a way, she was.

"I was getting worried about you," Cassie said quietly.

"You made a picture for Santa? Wonderful!" Agate told a child. "Don't forget to give it to him." She straightened, her face relaxed in a smile that seemed out of place in the frenzied pace of Manhattan. "Sorry, Cassie, but the bus took forever. That crosstown traffic. Am I late?"

"Just by five minutes or so." Cassie lowered her voice so that the children around them wouldn't hear. "But you do realize you've got an eight-hour shift ahead? You'll be on your feet quite a while."

Agate's dark eyes gleamed with a warm light as she nodded. "I've been looking forward to it. You said this job changed your life, and I've been in a rut for at least the last hundred years. Well, I'm ready to shake things up a little."

"Good luck, Mrs. Claus." Cassie gestured toward the line of children and Agate hustled toward them, greeting them with laughter and cheer.

That's the difference between us, Cassie thought. Agate met change head-on, while it was Cassie's nature to fight it all the way. Until Buchman. Now she was learning to choose her battles.

"Merry Christmas, little ones!" Agate welcomed a new group of children with open arms. "May all your Christmases be bright!"

And to think that before this job came along, her mother didn't even believe in Christmas . . .

Incognito.

It was one of the things that made Meredith Rossman so comfortable in New York City. You might walk past Ben Stiller on the street or hear Jessica Simpson talking at the table beside yours at lunch, but no one made a big deal. No one cared that the woman who'd just bought vitamins and a pregnancy testing kit was heiress to the Rossman's department store dynasty, the "poor little rich girl" who'd found love at last with an eccentric sociologist.

Tipping back the brim of her hat, Meredith glanced at the tall "Santa's Village" sign that seemed to beckon as soon as she stepped off the escalator. Nice placement. And it was surrounded by tiny white glimmering lights which seemed to be . . . yes, they were the white miniature toys she'd adored last Christmas in the Chicago store.

Beside the entrance to Santa's Village was a tall Christmas tree decorated with gold foil and paper ornaments—the wish tree. She picked through the ornaments and pulled off a toy request for a six-month-old boy whose parents were disabled. Shopping for this little one would brighten her afternoon.

As she circled Santa's Village she thought of the wish tree in Chicago, of her own goals and wishes last year at this time. She'd thought CEO of Rossman's was the ultimate prize. What was that expression? Watch what you wish for?

In the end the position had gone to the best candidate. Uncle Leonard had supervised operations his entire life, and the board thought he was ready to oversee "the big picture." Meredith agreed, and she was pleased that the board recognized Daniel's weaknesses as a leader. He'd been given a place in assistant management at the Magnificent Mile store, and Meredith hoped that the position would help Daniel learn the real nuts and bolts of retail or help him realize that he needed to steer his career in another direction.

For all her achievements and hard work Meredith was offered a seat on the board—a sweet reward—but she'd turned it down. Although she wanted to stay with Rossman's, she knew it was time to take a break from Chicago, the city of her parents' dreams. Time to move on. And since Nick needed to return to U of Penn at the end of his sabbatical, Philadelphia was the most likely choice. Meredith had packed her bags and headed to

Philly as the new director of East Coast operations, which gave her Boston, New York, Baltimore, D.C., Philly, Baltimore, and West Palm. "Let Daniel have the Chicago store," Nick had joked, "you've got the whole East Coast."

Meredith let the shopping bags slide down her arm as she stood to the side of the candy-cane lane entrance to Santa's Village and silently timed the queue. Today was her first visit to the New York store. Taking a tip from Nick, she'd begun visiting the East Coast stores under the radar. *Keep a low profile; observe. Better not to let the employees know they're being checked until it's absolutely necessary.*

She surveyed the elves, who merrily moved through the line, engaging children and taking them for a ride on the miniature train. The costume design looked familiar and she wondered . . . Wasn't the Mrs. Claus costume sent to this store at the start of the season? Where was it?

One of the Santas stepped out of his gingerbread home and waved to the crowd. He was a thin, Hispanic man, but Meredith saw Nick there, her Nick with his real silver hair and his spark of enthusiasm as he spun one of his hundreds of Christmas tales.

Funny, but when she'd seen him at Penn he seemed equally at ease in a lecture hall, walking the aisles, jumping down from behind the podium to reach out to students.

Meredith couldn't imagine his wild reaction if the test in her bag proved positive. She hadn't mentioned anything yet, wanted to be sure first, because it was something they both wanted so much—a family of their own.

Her family life had stopped abruptly when her parents died, but now Meredith was ready to go on, ready to squeeze every ounce of satisfaction from each day, ready to bring a new life into the world.

She placed her packages on the floor and suddenly a lovely woman with long silver hair and sparkling gray eyes stood before her, smiling. Dressed in the rich, red velvet Mrs. Claus costume, this woman seemed to embody the legendary Lady Santa in a magical way.

"Hello." Meredith smiled, startled.

"Merry Christmas, Mom," the woman said. "Are you waiting on a little one?"

Meredith pressed one palm against her tummy, sensing that it all was about to come true. "Yes. Yes, I am."

"It won't take too long," Mrs. Claus said, reaching across the candy-cane rail to squeeze her arm. "And I'm sure you'll find it's worth the wait."

Meredith nodded, her throat thick with emotion as the woman moved on down the line and bent down to lend an ear to a small girl.

Yes, Meredith thought, *the new Mrs. Claus is perfect.*

"Oh, look!" A thin woman with long, red curls squeezed into the rail next to Meredith. "They do have a Mrs. Claus, and she looks so real." Olivia pressed her lips together to stave off the tears—happy tears—but tears that would worry Woody nonetheless. The year she'd played Mrs. Claus was a pivotal time in her life, and sometimes, thinking back, she realized she was so close to dancing her life away on a chorus line in a strange city. "I loved that suit," she said hoarsely.

"No, you didn't," Woody said. "You wanted to be a Rockette that year, but you broke your ankle."

She shook her head. "You're only remembering part of it, hon. Okay, maybe I didn't love the idea of the job at first, but I grew to like it. I'm telling you, there's something lucky about that suit."

Cassie couldn't believe she was hearing this. Another Mrs. Claus, right here at Rossman's?

She tucked a strand of hair behind one ear and stepped up to the redhead. "Hey, sorry to cut in, but I caught part of your conversation. Did you really play Mrs. Claus?"

The redhead nodded, her curls bobbing. "At the Baltimore Rossman's."

"I was Mrs. Claus in San Francisco, two years ago."

The redhead squealed, and suddenly they were hugging like old college roommates. After the woman introduced herself and her husband Woody, Cassie added, "And to make things even weirder, that's my mother out there this year."

Olivia sighed. "She's perfect for the role. Probably better than I was. I don't have kids, so I was fumbling all around, scaring the stuffing out of some of them until I figured it out."

"Ah, but you figured it out," Cassie said. "That's the power of the suit."

"Do you think it's lucky?" Olivia asked her as Woody waved an emphatic "No!" behind her.

"I think the Mrs. Claus role helped me find the magic of Christmas," Cassie said thoughtfully. "And it helped me see what really mattered in my life. My son." She took a deep breath, thinking of the ways Tyler had grown in the light of Buchman's subtle influence. "Luck sounds so fickle, but love, that's solid, a tangible. And where there's love, there's magic."

Listening in, Meredith caught the dialogue about the magic of Christmas. That was one to save for Nick at dinner tonight. She still argued about the existence of magic in the world, but at this time of year, with the tree lit in their library, Meredith knew she wasn't making a convincing argument. In the golden glow of their Christmas tree Meredith heard the rising voices of ghosts from the past and children from the future, and most remarkably, it all blended into the harmonies of her favorite Christmas carol.